THE KÖLN EPISODE

Philip Konomos

Copyright @ 2020 by Philip Konomos

All rights reserved.

ISBN 9798650962731

Cover art by Heather Knowles

For Karamella

Acknowledgements

My thanks to Dennis Brunning, who help me get this project off the ground, to Stuart Glogoff for his support and advice, and to Heather Knowles for editing and artwork.

PREFACE

Raymond DeBaets lit another cigarette, his thin frame and even thinner hair seeming oblivious to the cold. He exhaled a mixture of smoke and frost that swirled around tired green eyes. His younger brother Eddie, more massive and darker complexed, with a full head of brown hair stood next to him drinking the last of a pint of the local beer. Raymond looked up into the cloudless sky that had shown so much promise earlier that night. A mission that he had hoped would be their salvation had turned sour and possibly could mean their death sentences. Raymond was afraid, terrified, the kind of fear that takes over the body and mind. He had tasted that fear before when he and his brother served in Léopoldville. The Congo... he could remember the faces, the haunted faces of the Congolese; always the enemy, ever the hunted. Now, as the two stood on the station platform at the Köln Bahnhof, they were the ones chased. In the distance stood the city's majestic cathedral silhouetted against the clear night's sky. It had been built to house the remains of the Three Kings. A beacon to offer hope and strength to the believers. Right now, Raymond's prayer was that the Wehrmacht corporal would return their forged papers and let them board the night train to Brussels.

The brothers worked as machinists in their father's shop in Brussels. They hated the job, and they hated him for making them stay. On a frigid January day, while he was barking out orders to Eddie, the father's heart gave out. The two decided to join the army rather than carry on the drudgery of the family business. Their dreams of adventure were crushed when they arrived in the Congo. Belgium's colony of exploitation for rubber, copper, and later uranium. Their only rewards were the heat, malaria, and patrols to deal with insurgents. By the time they returned to Belgium in early 1940, the landscape of Europe had changed. The Nazis had disposed of Poland, and Europe was at war. The government declared their neutrality and hid behind the Koningshooikt-Wavre Line, the impregnable defense that would stop the Germans. On the 10th of May 1940, the Panzers came out of the Adrienne forest, and in 18 days, it was over. For the Belgians, there would only be a long dark winter.

The Corporal standing between the Brothers and the train scrutinized their papers. He scowled as if smelling shit that he didn't feel like cleaning up. He took his time reading, occasionally glancing at the two. Raymond tried not to look the guard in the eyes, and prayed that Eddie would not provoke him. The tickets were for arrival at Gare du Nord. The train had only a brief stop in Liege. Raymond's nerves were on edge, but he knew that he had to keep the situation under control and keep a tight rein on his brother, whose explosive personality, was especially evident when he drank.

....

Raymond was the older, smarter of the two. It was to him that the British first made contact. When Belgium fell, the lucky troops were able to escape with the British at Dunkirk; the unlucky ones, like the brothers DeBaets, were prisoners of war. Most of the captured soldiers went to camps in Germany, but those with critical skills such as machinists were pressed into serving the German war effort. The brothers were sent to Köln to work at one of the many synthetic fuel depots that ringed the city. In the spring of 1941, the British flew a massive raid again the Kölnische Gummifaden Fabrik tire and tube factory, reducing it to a cinder. Afterwards, the Germans took great care to conceal their factories. Of the many forays the Royal Air Force mounted, very few bombs hit their intended targets. They were more successful at killing civilians.

The Royal Air Force's Bomber Command attacks on the plants were frustrated by the weather, their own strategy of high-altitude night bombing, and of course the Luftwaffe. The RAF's attempt to drop a commando unit to act as pathfinders for an attack ended in disaster. Their mission was relayed to the Germans, and the men captured.

It was a lowly flying officer at High Wycombe who came up with the idea to use Belgian workers as saboteurs. Inquiries were made to the government in exile in London, and through the Resistance, they came up with Raymond and Eddie De-Baets. The local Resistance leader was not enthusiastic about the brothers for the mission. He argued that they had no real qualifications or experience. The British were willing to take a gamble on them because they had worked at the factory, and were unknown; less apt to caused suspicion.

In late November, the British parachuted one of their agents into Germany to make his way to Köln and contact the brothers. Major Hugh Griffin had served as an intelligence officer in the embassy in Paris, before being assigned to Special Operations Executive. Through his years in Paris, he had acquired, a Frenchman's prejudice toward the Belgians that made him reluctant to take on the mission. He wanted only to protect his career, and he was the right choice for his masters. He spoke both fluent French and German, and looked more Aryan than most German-born, sporting blond hair, a ruddy complexion, and a girth that divulged his love of beer. It was easy to imagine him in lederhosen.

The brothers had been alerted that someone from the Resistance would be contacting them, and it would be a mistake not to cooperate. They knew the Belgian Underground was riddled with informants, and worried they would be betrayed and captured. But it was Eddie who convinced his brother this might be an opportunity for them.

They met the Major in the tiny room they rented not far from the factory. Its twin beds, a small table next to an even smaller window, and cold-water sink left little space for entertaining. The trash was full of empty wine bottles, and the ashtrays overflowed. The dirty light blue walls were made even more depressing by the naked overhead bulb, which gave off the only light in the room.

The three of them huddled around the small kitchen table. There were no introductions nor pleasantries. Griffin started it off.

"There is an important mission that we need your help with. It will be low risk. You smuggle a device into the factory where you work, plant it on one of the fuel tanks, and then get out." The Major slapped his hands together as if it would be that easy.

Neither brother said a word. They found the Hun to be a tolerable employer, while it was the British that had abandoned the Belgians at Dunkirk and left them to the Stukas and prison camps. If not for their profession, the brothers would be wasting away in some forced labor camp. In dealing with the British, they couldn't forget General Pownall's assertion that, "We don't care a bugger what happens to the Belgians."

They had weighed their choice: refuse the mission, or go along with an English plan. Knowing the way the British worked to say no would mark them as traitors and most certainly earn them both a bullet in the head from their countrymen. On the other hand, if captured, the Germans were known to make life incredibly unpleasant for their prisoners.

The brothers waited a second before making it clear to

the Major that their interests were not patriotic. Whatever the deal was to be, it had to include money and freedom. The demand did not faze the Major. Griffin pulled out a pack of American Chesterfields and lit one while he studied the two brothers. Blowing the white smoke into their faces, he replied, "How much money, and escape to where?"

"250 Pounds Sterling," answered Raymond, "each," with Eddie adding, "And escape to Britain."

The Major put out his half-smoked cigarette and took another out of his pack, the brothers noting that he didn't offer them one. He let the room fill with silence as he thought the demands over, the two becoming anxious. Their shadows played on the wall in the dim light. Of course he would pay them the pittance they wanted. He was prepared to pay more but would not offer these petty criminals anything beyond what they asked. Lighting his cigarette, then flicking a piece of tobacco off his tongue, he said nonchalantly, "Half now, and when you complete the job, we'll pay you the other half in London." He seemed to be merely hiring laborers.

A look of triumph crossed their faces. "What is it you want from us?" Raymond asked.

Griffin laid out the plan for Operation Pathfinder, so simple that he believed even these two could follow. The brothers will receive an incendiary device with a timer. They need to smuggle the bomb inside the factory where they work, place it on one of the fuel depots, set the timer, and leave. It must explode at midnight on December 6. An hour later, 100 Lancasters will commence their bombing runs, guided by the fires that will result from the explosion the brothers set off.

"The Germans expect something from the outside, but their security on the inside is lax. Can you do this?" asked the Major.

Raymond ran his hand through his hair. "There is still a matter of searches before entering, and guards, and of course we will need to come up with an excuse to leave the building and set the bomb."

"Can you smuggle the bomb into the factory, set the timer, and escape without drawing attention?"

The Brothers looked at each other, but again it was Raymond who spoke. "It will be difficult, but not impossible. We will need money for bribes."

"Money that doesn't come out of our share," Eddie quickly interjected. "What is important to us is how will you get us out of the country?"

"As you said, difficult but not impossible. Evacuation by air is dangerous but even more so from Germany. You must find your way back to Belgium. December 6 is St. Nicholas Day, people will be traveling to spend the holiday with their families. We will supply you with identity cards and travel documents. Your cover story is you are embarking on a 2-week holiday leave. Once in Brussels, the Underground will hide you and bring you to the extraction point."

"And the explosives? Where do we collect them?" asked Eddie, "And we will need a pistol."

Griffin ignored the demand. "In the next few days, you will be contacted. Follow your directions to the letter."

"By who?"

"They will identify themselves by asking you for a light for their cigarette. You reply: I gave up smoking when my mother died. They will counter with: I should have when my Grandmother died." Eddie went to write down the sequence but was quickly admonished by Griffin, "Write nothing down, you fool! Remember the tiniest mistake could mean your deaths."

"Just remember who's the one putting us in great danger." Eddie angrily shouted back. Raymond placed his hand on his brother's arm to calm him down.

"Dangerous?" asked Griffin, pushing away from the table. "Of course it is dangerous. Do you think I'm going to pay you for dicking around?" He unbuttoned his coat and took out his wallet, giving view to the Browning automatic he had tucked in his belt. He counted out 250 pounds sterling in large bills and placed it on the table. "Half now, half when the job is complete."

After the Major left, the two stood at the table, looking at the bills. They had never seen so much money at one time in their lives.

....

Raymond DeBaets wondered how many more times the corporal would go through his papers; did he detect a flaw in the forged documents? It was cold on the train platform, but he patiently answered each question, praying his brother would do the same. Finally, a guard from inside called him to come and help interrogate a family that had missing documents. Without saying a word, the Corporal handed the brothers back their papers and walked away. They quickly boarded the train, squeezing by people with luggage looking for seats. They arrived at their small compartment and open the door, their relief turning to surprise when they realized their traveling companions were four nuns.

CHAPTER 1

Valentin de Vos was awakened by the blaring bell of the alarm clock at 7:30 AM. He laid there, wishing for another few minutes of sleep. Reluctantly throwing off the covers and rolling out of the small bed that barely contained his body, the wooden floor felt cold beneath his feet as he fumbled in the dark for the light switch. The lamp gave off a dull yellow glow, and as his eyes adjusted, he could see himself in the mirror on the opposite wall. A hand across his stubble told him he needed a shave before today's meeting. Looking at his wavy brown hair, he disliked the specks of gray that multiplied with each passing day. At 38, Valentin was still in good shape physically, even though he carried a little more weight than he would like for his 180 centimeters height.

Switching off the light, Valentin raised the slat blinds, the divider between himself and the world, and peer into a dark street. Throwing open the window, be breathed in the cold air, filling his lungs and then exhaling as he did every morning. Though unsure if it had any health benefits, he was confident that it cleared his mind and prepared him mentally for the coming day. He had enough by the fourth inhale, the cold burning his lungs. He shut the window and lowered the blind. The sun would rise around 9:00 AM in Brussels, until then he would need to keep the blackout curtains drawn.

As he walked down the long narrow hallway to the bathroom, the walls covered with pictures of family and long-ago holidays, he passed the closed door of the room where his wife chose to sleep alone. He paused, momentarily, to listen for any signs of her presence. Was she there deep in sleep? Or was her large bed, which they once shared, empty again? Elise had a lover, and it was barely a secret.

Valentin no longer cared whether his wife Elise was behind the door or not. Only if she had spent the night with her German lover was he interested. If she had, she would surely be gushing with gossip and information later today. News that he would be able to use. Of course, Elise never came out and said she was spending the night with Herr General; it was always a visit to her sister's house across town. And her sudden knowledge of military affairs? Just little bits of information she heard at the coffee shops. Elise spouted what she had learned to irritate her husband, never realizing how important the information was. Two weeks before, she had mentioned that the General couldn't make an appointment because he would be meeting a troop train. Valentin passed along the report to the Underground, who, in turn, welcomed the troops to Belgium by blowing up their train.

The sink, bathtub, and commode were all crammed into the tiny bathroom, Valentin leaned into the mirror, working lather into his shaving brush, and thought about the early days with Elise. She was a Belgian beauty, and they could hardly keep their hands off of each other.

They met during his studies at Catholic University of Leuven, where he was learning to paint. She told him he looked like a movie star and she held equally romantic notions of being an adventurer and a world traveler herself. After the university, they leisurely traveled through *la belle* France, still scarred from the battles of the Great War. A slow boat took them down the Rhone to the Mediterranean...from the south of France a train through northern Italy—Lake Cuomo, Milan, Venice...from Trieste, the night train down the Adriatic coast to Brindisi... and finally, a steamer to Corfu. Corfu, its harbor city and landscape waiting for them.

They were a typical Belgian couple who momentarily got away from their little country. During the day, he would paint, and she would read. Then a bottle of wine celebrated the sunset. Nights were for making love. They existed on a small inheritance from Elise's family; none of Valentin's work ever sold. At the end of three years, they had exhausted the money and decided to return to Brussels to start a gallery. With a loan from Elise's parents, they bought a former butcher shop, with an apartment above not far from the Place Royal. They married. He transformed the old meat market into a showcase and continued to paint. She decorated the apartment, and together they set out to create a salon society at their new gallery.

Valentin still liked to think of those early days and nights with Elise. He wanted to think about what their life would have been had they not returned to Brussels. For in Brussels, the former butcher shop had become his prison. As time passed, he had to acknowledge that while technically adept, he did not possess the soul of an artist; his work lacked originality. The loan quickly ran out, and with artworks in supply but not demand, Valentin needed to find another way to pay the bills. They existed mostly from hand to mouth. He was able to eke out an existence restoring paintings and touching up photographs. Barely getting by was not the lifestyle Elise had imagined for herself. As life became a daily grind, he spent his time taking any job that paid. She drifted away after a while; neither of them seemed to care.

Valentin sat at the kitchen table and savored the coffee he had made. Who could have guessed it would be so precious? In the first few months of occupation, the German troops and administrators had been perfect gentlemen. The King, under house arrest in his Brussels Palace, and the Government-in-Exile in London, both acknowledged how organized and efficient the Germans were. Unlike 1914 when they had pillaged and raped, undisciplined and out of control.

But by winter 1941, a new war, unfavorable to the occupiers, had begun. While the Germans handled Belgium with restraint, they launched a fierce aerial attack on Great Britain. Throughout the summer and fall of 1940, Göring sent thousands of his Junker bombers and Messerschmitt fighters to pummel the Brits into surrender. It failed and in a very public way. Just as the Germans did not succeed in destroying allied forces at Dunkirk, they could not use their state-of-the-art war machines to destroy the English. The fight to take back Europe began in the form of Royal Air Force bombings of German shipping and select targets in Holland, Belgium, and even Germany.

As the war intensified, the Germans in Belgium got mean, vindictive, and practical. They took Belgians into the Fatherland as forced labor. Crops and livestock became the property of the Reich. Motorized transportation was almost non-existent; regular people got around on horses and bicycles.

Since the arrival of the Germans coffee, and all the other items one had come to depend on had disappeared. Most Belgians were making a substitute from chicory, but in Valentin's kitchen, there was real coffee along with sugar, butter, fresh vegetables, and even a bottle of scotch. Elise would tell him she was able to secure ration coupons and shopped the black market, but he knew it was all made possible by her German lover. He would not dwell on that, though; his mind was racing with more pressing matters.

As a citizen of an occupied country, Valentin initially behaved as many Belgians did: while not liking the situation, he stoically accepted it. He lived with the shortages, feeling the bone-chilling cold that would not lessen through this first winter of the war. The Germans commandeered all heating oil for even the most basic furnaces. Then Elise found her General, and life started to change in ways that were embarrassing to Valentin. But for many others, life started to become frightening.

Within the arts community, many of his friends, mostly Jews, Socialists, or Communists, were arrested or disappeared. The turning point came on a cold, dreary day in November 1940. His friend Benjamin Steinem, a local jazz musician and a Jew, was arrested. His wife, Rachel, was inconsolable, and unable to find out any information, went to the police station to demand his release. No one knew what was said or done, but the next morning Rachel was found in an alley in a working-class section of town. The trains ran through by the minute after exiting the Gare du Nord, as Rachel lay with a bullet through the back of her head. Benjamin was never heard of again. It was that day that Valentin decided he had to do something more than just publish Underground papers on his old printing press.

He made discreet inquiries, and before long, a member of the Belgian National Movement, one of the many resistance cells, contacted him. At first, they asked him to do simple tasks, such as courier messages, or record troop train movements through the rail yards. It was when the city police arrested a resistance leader that Valentin's real talent surfaced.

Betrayed by an informant for the local police, Dominque St. Vincent found himself in the police headquarters near the justice palace courts on Avenue Louise. In happier times the Avenue had seen crowds of people on weekends frequenting its many restaurants and theatres. Now the only business of this blighted neighborhood was Justice Courts and Gestapo Headquarters. The police would have to hand St. Vincent over to the Gestapo. Were they unpatriotic-collaborators? Not even the Resistance believed this yet; in fact, useful information came out of police headquarters. The word was, there was time to intervene in St. Vincent's fate.

The MBN put Gie Desmit in charge of pulling St. Vincent's escape. It had to happen quickly, before the Gestapo transfer their man to Headquarters.

Desmit was a typically black-humored Belgian. When his cell's members met to hatch the plan, he laughingly almost dismissed Valentin's proposal. "Gutsy, you think we can waltz right in and pinch the poor son of a bitch right from under their big Kraut noses?"

Undeterred, Valentin convinced them, especially Desmit, that he could produce the documents, forge the signatures, and create all papers needed to get St Vincent out of police headquarters and then out of the country. Suddenly the old printing press gave him the means to liberate a compatriot. On it, he produced what Gie described as "Masterpieces!"

But more than his artistry with the forged documents, it was his execution of the plan that moved him from an errand boy to an asset. Valentin had painstakingly created a disguise, lightening his hair and adding a thin mustache, black rim glasses, heavy coat, and hat. He arrived at the police prefect office, shouting orders and threatening like a perfect Gestapo officer. No one dared look him in the eyes. He was in and out within minutes, and had St. Vincent on his way to the Spanish border by nightfall. In this singularly daring act, Valentin found himself, creatively and morally. His fight against the Germans began in those moments. Life as artist, collector, husband, lover became his past.

Valentin finished his coffee, bundled up, and maneuvered his way down the narrow stairs that led to his shop. Today he would leave the shop's opening to his young employee Clarette; he was on his way to meet Gie Desmit. He stepped out on the street for a brisk ten-minute walk to the Café Laffite. There were only people and bicycles on the road.

All fuel having been taken by the Germans, there were rarely any private vehicles on the street. Occasionally a tram would roll by, its interior crammed with passengers. If an automobile or truck was on the road, it was safe to assume it was military or worse, Gestapo.

Valentin walked through the glass entrance doors of the Laffite, a café in a neighborhood just off the Gare du Nord. It was a favorite of Desmit's. The Germans tended not to frequent it, and delicacies were always available. Of course, the prices were black market, and only the most well-heeled of Belgians were customers. Gie was already seated at a table near the rear, past the long bar. He liked to sit next to the double doors to the kitchen. With his back toward the wall, he had a direct view of the entrance and could make a quick dash through the kitchen and out to the alley if need be. Gie's appearance commanded respect, his sharp features and broken nose making him look more like a middleweight boxer than the furniture maker that he is.

For four generations, the Desmits had produced handmade furniture for the world. Gie's pieces graced the mansions of England's royalty, Parisian politicians, and a few Hollywood movie stars in faraway California. Desmit's grandfather crafted Kaiser Wilhelm's favorite writing desk, the one he sat at to sign the orders to begin the Great War in 1914. Valentin had met Gie years before when he was looking to have custom frames made for a client who had too much money and too little taste--except, of course, for the sumptuous Desmit's frames.

The invasion, the occupation, the humiliation, the hardship, the cruelty, all worked to turn Gie Desmit into a genuine spy, patriot, and member of the Belgian National Movement, and eventually a cell leader. Working in small separated groups, he planned rail and communication disruptions, sabotage, and assassinations of the enemy and their collaborators. With his own money, and millions of Belgian francs and gold provided by British Intelligence, he placed spies everywhere in the provisional government. He took great pleasure in knowing that within police headquarters and the military high command, he had many loyal people. It was axiomatic that he trusted no one, for he knew all too well that the country was full of traitors and informers. "I shoot them in the face when I catch them," he often told his subordinates, "they don't deserve to be shot in the back of the head." Even the Germans knew about the faceless Belgians who ended up in canal and ditches, or thrown over wrought iron bars of the King's Palace.

Valentin stood before the Café's coal burning stove for a few seconds to shake the morning cold. Once he could feel the tips of his fingers again, he joined Desmit at his table. They chatted about the weather as the owner waited on them, arranging Bleu du Gand, bread rolls, and glasses of beer champagne, Gie's morning favorite. Belgians love their beer; Valentin preferred cognac, but had to settle for an inferior brandy. Gie methodically prepared his Montecristo cigar and lit it; Valentin chose not to smoke one of the few Gauloises he had in his jacket.

They waited for the owner to disappear into the kitchen before the briefing began. Desmit informed Valentin that a mission was forming just inside Germany near Köln. He needed papers from his master forger, documents for two brothers. The required information was inside the newspaper he would leave on the table when he left. Even with his close friend Valentin, he told him no more than he needed to know. Gie took a long draw from his cigar and said, "I need them by tomorrow, the day after at the latest." Valentin nodded his understanding. He knew that it was hopeless to argue about the tight deadline; he would work through the night and keep his mouth shut.

They sat in silence, tasting the cheese and sipping beer. A stylishly-dressed elderly couple entered and took a table by the stove. "Regulars," Gie whispered. "They come every morning for a shot of jenever to start their day." They watched in amusement as the owner brought two frozen shot glasses of the clear liquor. The couple toasted each other, downed the drink, and trundled off. Gie and Valentin's eyes met, both wondering if either of them would live long enough to see old age.

Valentin was still smiling when Gie whispered, "I am concerned about that damn paper you are publishing. We were lucky the last time, but we cannot depend on luck again."

Le Citoyen Libre! (The Free Citizen) was an Underground newspaper, highly verboten and a passion for Valentin. He gathered information from the BBC, his colleagues, the Resistance, gossiping customers, and of course, Elise. He or his colleague Michel Verhoeven would write the articles, then print and distribute the newspaper. It wasn't as large as the other Underground publications, *Het Vrije Woord* or *La Voix des Belges*. Much of their information was fascinating to the readers and an irritant to the occupation authorities. Six weeks before, Gie had alerted Valentin that the police had learned the location of the studio and would be raiding it that night. Valentin closed down and move the machinery just in time.

Now, after laying low for a few weeks, he was at it again-this time in spectacular fashion. They stole a small airplane and flew over Brussels, sending thousands of copies into the night sky. Unfortunately, many of the papers were unreadable, as a light rain fell in the early morning and caused the ink to run. But the Germans were not as concerned with the paper as they were that an airplane could find its way around Brussels airspace without a response from the Luftwaffe. There were reprimands from Berlin. The most junior flying officer was demoted and sent to Russia to fly supplies to Stalingrad. Most troubling for Desmit was that an intensive search for the people involved had begun.

"There are many who feel that the paper is high risk but with low returns." Valentin knew better than to ask who the many were, just as he knew that they did not know who was publishing the paper or who he was. It was the way Gie operated; the less people knew, the less they could betray. "People need to know we are resisting, but the authorities are sweating everyone they suspect and passing money out to every informer. The Krauts fear words as much as bullets and bombs, it seems."

Valentin knew that Gie was not overly enthusiastic about what he perceived as the dangers of printing a clandestine newspaper. He hoped to reassure him. "We are working on another edition but it won't be ready for a couple of weeks. It will not interfere with the task at hand."

Gie nodded his head and raised his hand for the bill. "We have reason to be careful. Your friend Denis Van Damme is dead, found in an alley, a bullet through his head."

Valentin could not hide his shock and sadness as Desmit told him of his friend's death. It was Van Damme who had saved him when the Gestapo was closing in on his printing operation. Here was another member of their small band, betrayed and killed. Gie showed no emotions in telling what had happened. Too many of his soldiers had been murdered in the last year, and he would tell everyone the only sure thing is more will die. Paying the bill, Gie leaned close to Valentin. "Remember, I need those papers soon."

CHAPTER 2

Alain Legrand sat comfortably in a first-class compartment on the train out of Brussels, headed toward Köln for a 7:30 PM arrival, which was now going to be over three hours late. He had enjoyed the brief layover in the Belgian capital; more French was spoken there in the southwest quarter of Brussels. Like most Frenchmen, Legrand found it humorous and odd; this country divided into its languages. If you needed help in Belgium, you always had to guess at the response. Finding a French-speaking Belgian wasn't a problem. It was dialect.

Legrand also counted among his customers a more esteemed, challenging, and admittedly dangerous clientele. Men like Goering, Goebbels, Himmler—they owned homes and apartments throughout Germany and the occupied territories. No matter how much he groveled to them, no matter how exquisite his gifts, they cheated him. He felt odd and absurd, raising his hand and shouting "Heil Hitler." What did they want, he asked himself. He didn't know!

He knew some thought him a collaborator. But that is not how he saw himself; he was a wine merchant to the right customers. LeGrand claimed, in his heart, he was a patriot, spiritually and morally in sync with a new Europe. Did he not pass along information to the French and Belgian Resistance groups? In return, they would insult him, saying he provided no hard intelligence, only gossip.

At this moment, as Herr Legrand was chugging towards Köln, his mind was not on wine or the General's staff he catered to, but the young woman pushing the refreshment cart from car to car. He traveled this line often and was smitten by her. He anticipated the knock at the compartment door. Her head would pop in, those blue eyes against a pale face, to ask "Refreshments monsieur?"

When there were others in the compartment, he would let them order first so he could admire her. She always wore the same outfit, a long blue jumper over a white blouse, a thick blue sweater, and flat shoes. The uniform obscured her figure, but Legrand imagined a slender body, small breasts, and a firm rear end. He guessed that she was 21 and liked that her short black hair made her appear boyish. He allowed his imagination to run wild, dreaming of making love to her.

His spirits lifted as she entered the compartment, but she seemed preoccupied today. She ignored his banter about how well she looked and only gave a shrug when he inquired about business this night. They both knew that if she didn't make her money in the first-class cars, there would be no breaking even. Next was the coach cars, where they always brought their food. With the war on, fewer and fewer people were allowed to travel, let alone first class. Even with rationing, he knew there would be a good offering on her cart as both Wehrmacht officers and Nazi Party officials always insisted on the best. Today's offering included beers from Germany: Columbia or Baron Boch; cured ham on French rolls; Edam cheese from the Netherlands; and chocolates. He took his time before settling on the meat. From his satchel, he produced his wine, proudly showing her the bottle. "A good local red, not even a label, something to keep me company until we reach Köln." He was preparing to open the bottle. "Of course, you are welcome to drink this wine with me," he mumbled timidly. "Can you remain for a moment?"

"Monsieur, who would do my job?" she said with a tired smile.

Legrand was perplexed. Usually, these young women responded sweetly and flirted more. Her reply was always non. Polite but firm. His one major accomplishment after many trips was learning her name, Febe Janssen, from one of the porters. But that was the most he was able to find out about this young Belgian woman. Instead of being put off, it only gave him more determination to bed her.

Monsieur Alain Legrand might not have been so determined to have a tumble with the young lady had he known that she belonged to the Resistance. Heart, mind, and soul. Her assignment was to collect information from those who traveled the line, reporting back to her cell leader in Brussels.

To her, Legrand was a collaborator, and that made him a marked man, the walking dead, who could very soon meet an unpleasant end. Maybe it would be from an unknown assassin, or possibly from Febe herself. Under her sweater, tucked in a belt behind the small of her back, she carried an FM Model 1910 pistol, 7.65 caliber shells in a six-shot clip, with a sound suppressor. She had already fired it once in anger and would love to make Herr Legrand her second victim.

....

By December of 1940, most passengers on the Brussels-Köln route were members of the Wehrmacht, employees of the German government, or businessmen who plied their trade with the Reich. The passage was a telegraph wire of useful intelligence, particularly amongst the troops that rode in third class, who would bring their schnapps and had eyes for any woman in a dress. Desmit needed someone reliable to be his eyes and ears. He had received reports about Febe's ability to converse comfortably in Flemish, French, German, and English, and most importantly, he heard that she was smart. He recruited her knowing that most members of the cell would not work with a woman, and was pleasantly surprised how quickly she learned her trade. She became adept at casually getting information from drunken soldiers or encouraging officers to show their importance by boasting about themselves. She learned much about how many men they commanded, where they posted. The Allies' catchphrase "Loose lips sink ships" was a given around liquor. After every pass of her cart, she would scribble down what she had learned, using the code she created.

The faceless men in London had been pushing Desmit to challenge the Germans and carry out acts of sabotage. In the fall of 1941, Desmit put together their first principal mission. Febe had collected information that a troop train would be arriving the following week. Their plan was to dynamite tracks at a rail junction on the route to Germany, inside the Belgian border. In one stroke, they would kill Germans, destroy equipment, and cause havoc, that would take weeks to clean up. Desmit had a plan and the people but needed help with the execution. The British had their Secret Intelligence Service parachute an army explosive expert into the dense forests southeast of Brussels. British SIS, always cynical and forward-looking, spent the years before the war plotting how to get agents into Belgium in clever ways. Just about every clearing had been mapped and rated for risk of clandestine drops. Contact with the Underground had been undertaken and safehouses secured.

Febe was to be part of the team, but as with smaller missions, her job would be again a lookout. Before she was to leave and meet up with the team, Febe traded words with Desmit about her role. She stood at a beer and frites stand on Quay 6 at the Gare du Midi. Desmit leaned against the tin bar, some Chimay Blue in a glass foaming as he took a sip. He eyed his frites and listened as Febe made her case.

"I know the countryside, yet I do not lead. I speak four languages, but I do not speak, I can set an explosive device, but am told to be a lookout. I share the risks but not respect."

Desmit smiled. He knew he'd have to count her in more; she itched for involvement, excitement, danger. She was smart and could think quickly on her feet, so there would be change. Just not now. The men would never accept her as an equal, let alone as their leader. He asked her to be patient.

She blew smoke from her last Belga in his face, then turned and walked away. He winced; he loved those cigarettes too, but they were in short supply now, having been banned by the Germans as being too patriotic.

The night of the mission, the sky was heavy in cloud cover, with no moon, no shadows. Perfect. Only a damp coldness pierced the air and chilled the bone. The British commando chose to set the charges on a curve that had a gentle incline dropping off to a ravine. The men worked fast to dig a hole around the tracks to hide the explosives. Twenty meters up from them, Febe took her position atop an abandoned water tower. Climbing up an attached wooden ladder, she feared the whole valley would hear her as each rung gave a sickening groan. From her vantage point, Febe made out two figures approaching the target site, one carrying a military flashlight, the other an automatic weapon. They were sweeping the line for saboteurs.

Febe moved quickly to warn the others of the danger by signaling three short blinks from her flashlight. The Germans passed under the tower heading steadily toward her men. There was not much time to camouflage their digging, but they did the best they could in a few seconds before moving to the top of the ravine. The sentries slowly approached, shining the flashlight along the tracks and then out to the sides. Not far from the group, they stopped. One lit up a cigarette and then lit his partner's with his own. It was camaraderie-a break in the lonely cold night of a job whose essence was boredom.

Febe overheard one talking jovially about his leave in Munich and the splendid beer he had during Oktoberfest. Febe hoped they had more to gab about and then would move on.

The commando signaled the others to lay low; all thought the Germans would pass without incident. Suddenly, something caught one of the soldier's eyes. Febe could hear one call to the other: "Hans, put the light down there!"

It was the British officer who realized first that they had run out of options. He quickly rose, and from a few meters away he let loose two bursts from his Sten gun. The silencer made a coughing sound as both Germans fell to the ground. It all happened so quickly that the Belgians stood there, shocked. "Let's get these two in the brush, set our charges, and get out of here," the officer quickly commanded. They all knew that in the morning, there would be retribution when the authorities discovered the soldiers, but there was nothing they could do now.

Febe saw the two men collapse on the rails, and she also could see what the others could not: a third soldier coming up behind them. By the time she had circled to where the group was, he had the drop on them. He stood there, his Mauser raised, shouting orders. Her group was standing with hands raised, shocked. The German appeared shaken too, and not sure what to do next. He kept screaming at the men to get to the ground, face down, but no one did. Febe feared that he might open fire out of fright. Perhaps it was too dark for them to comprehend the German's motions, or they didn't understand the language. In any case, Febe carefully approached the German from behind. The thought passed through her that there could be many more coming and that death could be waiting for her this night. But no one else was coming; she could tell by the shrill in his voice that he was as scared as she was. His shouting allowed Febe to come up behind him and place her pistol under his right ear. "Make a move, and I'll kill you," she whispered in German.

He dropped his gun, and when he turned, she could tell that he was no more than eighteen, his face still marked by pimples. He pleaded not to be shot, tears running down his face. He was a raw recruit, not one of the shock troops that marched into Belgium and then France. The veterans were now on the Russian Front. He was a child, poorly trained, and assigned to garrison duty in a place where he could not get into much trouble. One of the Resistance operatives slapped him hard enough to knock him off his feet. Everyone then turned to the British officer, their eyes asking what to do now.

"What do you think?" came the dry reply. "Do it now and do it quickly."

None of the men had ever killed before, at least not close enough where they could feel the target breathing. As the officer resumed placing the explosives, the three argued over who would finish this business. None of them wanted to do it. Febe, disgusted said that she would handle this. She put the gun to the soldier's head and walked him out beyond the track. He stumbled as she pressed him along, all the while pleading with her not to shoot him. When they got to the spot where they had laid the other dead Germans, she thought he might bolt. Instead, he started crying. She motioned for him to get on his knees. He slumped down as if resolved to the fate of the dead soldiers piled in front of him. Before he could utter another word, she put a bullet through his brain. She had neither second thoughts nor feelings; all she could think of was the enemy. This simple thought guided her.

After planting the explosives, the officer dismissed the men but kept Febe with him to wait for the train, which would be arriving soon. They ran the wire under the gravel on the rail bed out into the bushes that lined the tracks. Febe could hear the giant locomotive before it came into sight. The Brit gave her the honor of manning the plunger.

A successful mission—a train derailed, many Fritzes dead, the Boche beaten for the moment. Over the next month, there were repercussions, and many a good man and woman were taken in by the Gestapo and never seen again. Innocent folks ended up in Breendonk, the ancient fortress north of Brussels toward Antwerp. Febe would never let herself think of how many Belgians paid for those dead Germans on the troop train that night.

Though Desmit had problems at first in accepting Febe as an equal partner, he soon found that she was someone he could depend on to handle any job, whether blowing up a train or seducing a collaborator who thought he was visiting her for an evening of enjoyment. He particularly enjoyed busting in on an unsuspecting traitor who had expected a night of sexual pleasure and taking him for his last walk.

....

Glancing out the window, Febe knew that the train would soon be approaching Köln. Once in the terminal, she could set her mind to the task at hand. At the bottom of her cart were almost 2 kilos of British-issued explosives in an Incendiary bomb. She needed to move the device from the train and deliver it to the two brothers who worked for the Germans as laborers.

Gie Desmit was never happy with this mission, believing the brothers were untested and undisciplined, but it was a British show, and they were in charge. Febe was to instruct them on how to use the bomb. Unknown to them, she would also shadow the two on their return to Brussels. But Desmit's orders were specific in the event they should balk at the last minute. "They are not what I would call committed members of the MBN. Their only incentive is money. If they give you any trouble, shoot the two of them and come home." And more cryptic, "Maybe, shoot them anyway."

CHAPTER 3

The Brussels-Köln Express slowed down steadily as it approached its destination. Febe glanced out the first-class window as she handed a Luftwaffe officer change for his last beer before their arrival. The majestic cathedral spire stood out against the city's soot-coated buildings and a leaden sky. She never liked Köln. Febe's first memories were of a city that had the red banners of the Nazi party displayed everywhere and gangs of thugs policing the streets looking to take care of the communists, homosexuals, and of course, Jews. She would never forget the German boys who moved through the city in their Hitler Youth outfits. Their brown uniforms, and red swastika armbands. In the years that intervened, she never changed her first impression. The banners multiplied, and those German boys were now facing the Russian winter.

The click and clack of the train slowly bouncing over the rail ties like a clock winding down meant the Köln station was near, and that she had but a few minutes before arrival. She moved car to car toward the baggage carriage, where she bolted the door and quickly went to work. Taking the unsold food out of the cart, she lifted the false bottom exposing her valuable cargo. She carefully lifted the incendiary bomb out of its hiding place, a gift from the British Intelligence Service. At less than two kilos and well under a meter, it fit snuggly into her travel handbag. Next to it, she placed the timer device and connectors.

The ten-car Brussels-Köln Express announced itself with a blast from its steam engine horn, as it lumbered across the Hohenzollern Bridge into Bahnhof station. The 30-year old engine, known as the Belgian State Railways Type 10, chugged away, happy to still be running. The Germans... unhappy with the state of steam locomotives in their territories... had decided to build a new fleet and would soon replace this relic. As the train stuttered to a halt, she could hear rain falling against the platform's metal awnings. Febe worried that if the weather continued like this, RAF would cancel the raid. The English expected a few good flying days after this storm had passed, and they needed to strike when the opportunity presented itself. Regardless, like so much in her life, it was out of her hands.

    The old locomotive had hardly pulled to a stop when carriage doors opened, and she glimpsed the terminal's official clock, the universal timepiece found in all European train stations. It was 11 PM, late as usual. Febe smiled, knowing that in Paris where the train started, the French were indifferent to not being on schedule; but to the Germans it was a source of irritation. A swarm of porters approached and started removing baggage and mail, and assisting departing passengers. Joining them was the portly catering supervisor for the line, Herr Littmann, despite the rationing, never seemed to miss a meal. He stood in front of Febe, a ledger in hand for an accounting of all sales. Herr Littmann, who was an able and agile businessman, loved to talk to Febe. He took pleasure when she had a rewarding financial trip and was quick with a suggestion and encouragement when the purse was empty. His favorite topic was his wife's cooking, and he was always inviting her for a home-cooked meal. She accepted once and spent the evening with the Littmann family, eating pork and sauerkraut and listening to his five young children sing church hymns. She had trouble reconciling his precious family with the monsters that tortured her country. Febe politely informed Herr Littmann that it had been a long trip, and she was off to sleep. She paid her account and cart rental fee and bade him give her love to his beautiful family.

So far, Febe's job made her an asset for her handlers. Police and Wehrmacht troops took her as a familiar face in both Brussels and Köln. She would take no offense when a young soldier or laborer in transit would flirt with her; public life had not returned to pre-war freedom of romance and flirtation. For unlike Legrand, these young men were too shy to ask her out for a drink. There was always the possibility of an overzealous guard, one who would insist on seeing her papers and examine the contents of her bag. She blended with the arrival passengers making their way to the exits, scrutinized by a variety of official personnel. To the casual observer, it appeared that there were more police, soldiers, and Gestapo than there were travelers. From the back of the train, she viewed the Wehrmacht officers debarking from the first-class cars while the ordinary soldiers left from the coach. She moved quickly to avoid Monsieur Legrand. No problem there; Legrand exited first class, quite a distance down the platform, met by some German businessmen. Where there is wine, you have customers, Febe thought—even in this God-forsaken country.

Upon entering the grand terminal, she bumped into a soldier who she knew from her many visits. He teased her that she worked too hard and should come with him and his friends for a beer and a bratwurst once he was off duty. Looking up at the clock and giving him the sweetest smile she could muster, she whispered to him that it had been a long trip and maybe another time. "I am so tired I can barely carry my bag," she told him. Her heart skipped a beat when he lifted the bag off her shoulder and offered to carry it to the exit. Remaining composed, she walked with him, recounting the trip and telling him about this old lecher on the train who was always trying to compromise her. Though her heart was in her throat the whole time, it did offer her free passage through the terminal and out to the street.

At the main exit, she was happy to get her bag back, mumbling something about books when he asked why it was so heavy. A kiss on the cheek to get his mind off her handbag, and she was away. Home for the night would be the Hotel Rhineland, the preferred lodging for most of the railroad staff. The owner gave the train crew a low rate, and, on most days, there was hot water in the shower down the hall. The cathedral sat eerily on her right, dark and foreboding. She knew that the RAF would use its majestic spires as a reckoning point for bomb runs. The idea of the cathedral being hit by a bomb would have made the people of Köln nervous had they cared about it surviving intact through this stupid war. Life had become hard in Germany, and the concern was for their survival and not a cultural treasure.

The Hotel Rhineland was not far from the station in Köln's Old Town. It was built in the late 1800s. As the city turned toward a new industrial era of advances in technology, including warfare it enjoyed a profitable existence serving as an inexpensive tourist hotel for pilgrims from all nations. As workers and architects put the finishing touches on the Great Cathedral, the Germans also embarked with other countries into a new century of expansion, which meant war. As the Great War started to go badly for the Kaiser's empire, so did the fortunes of the hotel. The depression that followed nearly closed down the place, and would have had it not been for the rise of the Nazis. The economy started to improve, people began to travel, and the family owners believed in Herr Hitler. No one seemed to mind when Czechoslovakia and Poland fell, and after the battle of France, the owners gave thought to expansion. Their thinking slowly changed with the invasion of Russia, then war with the United States. Suddenly there were shortages of everything, and plans were put on hold as the thousand-year Reich was fighting for its life. To the fourth-generation owner, it was the Kaiser and stupidity all over again.

Febe made her way through the alleyways that made up the Old City and entered the small lobby of the hotel, shaking the rain from her umbrella. She walked past what was once the hotel bar, now only a storage space since most of the guests could hardly afford to pay for their room, let alone a drink, to the reception area. Before she could speak, the grey-haired man behind the desk told her she was lucky. There was only one room available on the fourth floor. Jacob who had been at the hotel for many years and was always happy to see Febe, held the key in his hand. She smiled and assured him that would be fine.

The lift had stopped working a few months before, and there were no parts from any German vendor for an elevator built in the 1800s. Still she preferred the upper level. With the lift out of order, the stairs sounded like they would give way with every step, but she welcomed this natural alarm system of squeaks and groans as weight met old wood. She paid for the room and surrendered her passport before receiving the key. She signed a visitor's card, which undoubtedly would be reviewed the next day by the Gestapo. She also paid for the use of the shower: an extravagance, she knew; but in Brussels these days, hot water was hard to come by. There usually was an extra charge for the shower towels, but Jacob always included them for free. Febe thought it was because he always seemed to find his way upstairs when she was to shower. She was sure that a half-naked woman with a towel around her was preferable to the overweight men who frequented the hotel.

Febe carefully climbed the stairs; it was a slow journey up to the fourth floor. She used the skeleton key for the room; at least it worked. She had changed her accommodations twice in the past because of broken locks. Room 412 was like all the single rooms that she had stayed in at the Hotel Rhineland. A little over three meters wide and four meters deep, it felt more like a prison cell than a hotel room. She enjoyed telling friends that the beds were slim, with nonexistent mattresses and pillows stuffed with rocks. Against the wall was a small dresser with a washbasin and pitcher on top; two hooks were attached to the door to hang clothes. Febe checked the radiator and smiled to herself when she felt some heat. Things were looking up! She quickly stripped off her clothes and hung them on the hooks to be ready for the return trip home. She wrapped the towel around her, slipping her pistol into the hand towel, and then headed down the hall to wash. This late at night, she knew that she wouldn't run into anyone and that the shower would be available. As she entered the bathroom, she could hear the night manager lumbering his way to the fourth floor.

The room consisted of a large bathtub, but because it was too expensive to fill with water, it had been unused since the war started. One washed with a hand-held hose attached to the spigot. The hot water felt good on Febe's body as she quickly lathered and washed off. The shower price included 5 minutes of hot water, but rarely did you receive the full 5 minutes. Febe remembered one of her first showers, rinsing off with frigid water. She dried off, wrapped the towel around her, and returned to her room, passing the old hotelier from downstairs. He had picked this hour to change a light bulb. She smiled, he nodded, and she disappeared into her room.

Febe was tired, and tomorrow was an important day. There would be a meeting in the morning with the two brothers to deliver the device. She dropped into her bed, automatic under her pillow, and readily drifted off to sleep.

CHAPTER 4

Frau Schröder rarely acted as an alarm clock for her guests, especially foreign male laborers. But the DeBaets brothers had told her that they wanted to attend 7:00 AM mass. They would be leaving for home on a 2-week holiday and wanted to give thanks for their good fortune of having work, and pray for a safe journey. She believed they were fallen Catholics or, worse, atheists. She knew they'd lived some years in the Congo and who knows what occult beliefs and behaviors they might hold. Of course, she would get them up to attend mass. The brothers heard the pounding on the door, and Eddie's first thought was the Gestapo was on the other side. But when they heard Frau Schröder's shrill voice, they hollered back that they were up. They grudgingly got out of bed. After a 12-hour shift that ended at 11:00 PM, and then a few drinks at the little bar down the road from the factory, it seemed they had barely laid their heads on the pillow before the pounding started.

Neither of them was what could be called a good Catholic, and neither could recall the last time he'd attended mass. The MBN had arranged a rendezvous at the Great Cathedral. The message was delivered by a nondescript middle-aged Belgian who showed up at their room. There was a tense moment when he gave the code, and neither brother could remember the response. It took them three different tries before Raymond replied: "I gave up smoking when my mother died." The man gave his name as Monsieur Zoets. Wearing a heavy overcoat and with a fedora pulled down to his brows, he eyed the room and then the brothers before delivering the message. A pharmacist by training, he lived in Köln and spoke German well. His instructions were simple: attend 7:00 AM mass. At the church, if it were safe, they would be contacted and given the bomb and instructions for its use. If there was no contact, then they had been followed and should continue with their day.

Eddie splashed frigid water on his face, feeling terrible. He couldn't decide whether he was hungover or still drunk. "Why the bloody hell does it have to be so damn early? Why all this secretive shit? Couldn't they just drop off the damn thing here last night and be done with it?"

"Get dressed, and let's get this over with," an irritated Raymond replied.

It was dark when the brothers set out for the Cathedral. Raymond looked up to see a clear sky with no cloud cover, and he knew it would be getting colder. He also knew that a clear sky would bring the bombers tonight. He turned his collar up and lit a cigarette, sharing it with Eddie while they waited for the bus. When the bus did arrive, it was crowded; they barely squeezed in. Neither spoke as they endured the endless stops to the train station. To Raymond, it appeared that no one ever stepped off the bus. Stop after stop he would look at his watch as more people kept crowding in. He knew they would be late, and what would that mean? There was an undertone that he detected not only with the British major who contacted them but also with his fellow countrymen. There was no appreciation for the danger he and Eddie would be in nor for the service they were about to perform.

From her vantage point high on the south tower, Febe saw the bus arrive at the Köln Hauptbahnhof, nearly 15 minutes late. She saw the brothers quickly leg it to the Cathedral, hurrying past the stonemasons who worked year-round. She paid close attention for any kind of surveillance; no one was following. The boys appeared to be alone, but she would stay longer scanning the square until she was positive they had not picked up a shadow. She had risen early and walked to the church, her satchel slung over her shoulder. Once she arrived, a member of the German resistance showed her to the tower.

Today's mass was in one of the smaller chapels as the magnificent Cathedral itself would dwarf the few dozen mostly pensioners and widows who came to pray at this morning. The service had already started, the brothers, trying to be inconspicuous quietly took a pew towards the back and waited. To Eddie, the service seemed to drone on forever. He hadn't attended mass since shipping off to the Congo. In the hell that was Léopoldville, he would tell Raymond that God had forsaken them. His betrayal was confirmed with the German invasion and Belgium's surrender. "If there is a God, then why weren't we evacuated to England?" he would often ask, "instead of being slaves to the Boche."

While Eddie was impatient, Raymond felt time slipping away. He was concerned that no one had tried to contact them. Did their handler leave when they didn't show at seven? Was he arrested? As much as he preferred not to be involved in the mission, his desire to be out of harm's way and safely in England was greater. For weeks he had been telling himself, *just a little lethal mischief, some explosive slipped into the factory, and then—freedom.* He nervously looked around for anyone who looked subversive, someone with a killing purpose. No one seemed interested in the DeBaets. They were just two guys who came in from the cold. The service now was finishing, both chose not to take communion, and Eddie was delighted there was no sermon this day. The priest knelt before an exquisite alter backlit by winter's light settling through the stained glass, said a prayer, and then dismissed the congregation.

The two were uncertain what to do next when an old lady stopped at their pew to kneel and genuflect. As she stood to leave, she whispered, "The south tower." Eddie shrugged at his brother as if asking him, *what kind of Sunday school is this*? They crossed over to the south tower, where a stonemason was mixing mortar and getting ready to lay more brick. With his head, he motioned for them to enter the tower, and then lifted his eyes to the top. The brothers climbed the 533 steps to the top, passing the bell chamber, home to the Dickke Pitter, or Fat Peter.

At 100 meters up, the Cathedral's south tower offered a view to the Siebengebirge mountains. While not a perfect day, they knew that it would be good flying weather for the Royal Air Force soon. Looking out across the city, they never heard the person walk up behind them. Waving her cigarette, she asked, "May I have a light?"

They immediately turned to see a woman in a blue jumper, a satchel slung across her shoulder. They stood speechless, both forgetting to give the reply. They could see her hand move inside her jacket. Both seemed taken by the woman: Raymond, because he was expecting a man; and Eddie because he admired her slender body and soft face. Raymond seemed to surprise himself, blurting out the passphrase. She responded, giving each a good look before withdrawing an empty hand from her coat pocket. "You two were late this morning."

"The bus was late," exclaimed Raymond, as if to ward off criticism.

"What does it matter anyway?" Eddie snarled. "We had to sit through that whole fucking service before you contacted us."

"We had to be sure there was no one following you," Febe said, zeroing in on Eddie, "and as long as you are taking our money, you'll sit there until there are warts on your worthless ass." Looking at Raymond, "There must be no 'late buses' tonight, or any kind of slip-up. The raid is a go, and the device must be detonated precisely at midnight."

Raymond could sense that Eddie was about to respond and spoke first. "Everything will go according to plan, don't worry."

Febe looked at Raymond. "Where will you place the bomb?" she asked.

"There is a cluster of large fuel tanks to the north of the factory; I go out there often to repair the valves and recalibrate gauges."

Febe reached into her satchel and pulled out a black metal cylinder a little more than half a meter long, 15 centimeters in diameter, with magnets at either end. "Listen carefully," she said. "When you reach the tank, attach this to the side," holding up the device, "then connect the timer," which she displayed. "Connect these wires, turn the timer one full turn, and then get out of there."

"How long do we have?" asked Raymond.

"You will have one hour, and you must time it so by midnight there will be a roaring fire. The bombers will be overhead by then."

"We had requested cigarettes to help us with bribes."

Febe reached into her satchel and pulled out a carton of American Old Golds, Eddie reached for them, but she pulled them back and handed the box to Raymond. "Just remember we went through hell securing these."

Raymond held up a pack he pulled from the carton. "This is how we will get the bomb into the plant."

"When you leave the factory, go directly to the train station, do not return to your apartment. Here are your papers and tickets. The train should be full of travelers, mostly Germans. Take your seats and stay put until it reaches Brussels. Keep your mouths shut, nurse a couple of beers. When you arrive, walk out to the main concourse. Someone will meet you and take you to a safe house. My recommendation is not to screw up the passphrase again. Do you have any questions?" Febe asked, instinctively looking away into Köln's skyline.

Eddie put his hand on Febe's shoulder and turned her toward him, now eye to eye, he rubbed index finger and thumb together—the universal sign for money.

"You will receive the last half when you complete the mission," Febe said, quietly, sullen as if this were the least of her problems. Stepping closer to Eddie, she snarled, "If you ever put your hands on me again, you'll need your brother to help you put your guts back in your stomach."

Raymond forced his way between them, giving Eddie the pack to sling over his shoulder. He put the wires and timer in his coat pocket and pushed his brother toward the stairs. Febe's impression of them was the same as Desmit's; she had very little faith that they would even show up at work tonight, let alone plant the bomb. She looked out at the plaza, watching as they crossed over to the station and merged into the crowd.

CHAPTER 5

Valentin de Vos boarded Tram 3 at the North Station, clutching a small sack, his satchel hanging off his shoulder. It was rush hour, and he looked like any person leaving work on their way home. The station was busy with train departures to Antwerp and city workers jumping on trams bound for a hundred different places in Brussels, the occupied city. The winter's sun was swiftly going away. He was happy there was no snow as the two cars made their way through the Vilvoorde section of Brussels. Life had been tough in this working-class neighborhood even before the Germans invaded, so when the goose-stepping troops and the red swastika appeared, adversity just changed gears. They had already endured winters without heat and barely enough food to feed their families. Most worked in the coal plants or for the trade unions. The trade union workers had a distinctive mark next to their names on the Nazi rolls. Hitler had taken care of the unions in Germany and would show them the same honored place here.

Valentin found one of the last seats on the tram, but soon gave it up to a pregnant woman. He now stood in the back with other men who gave up seats. For a brief moment, the pregnant young woman distracted Valentin; what life would the unborn child have in an occupied Belgium, or worse, a Third Reich? Would any of them be around when the child was born? Could the Nazis be stopped? The British and Russians were experiencing defeat after defeat, and where were the Americans? A year after declaring war, they still had not engaged. The tram stopped suddenly, and the passengers swayed forward as one, a movement abrupt enough to snap Valentin out of his trance and back into the reality of the moment.

Valentin was taking the tram into Vilvoorde to meet with Michel Verhoeven, his publishing partner for the Underground newspaper *Resistance Verzetan!* The current Nazi administration hated this broadsheet and wanted to put it out of business, and its publishers out of existence. He clutched a small sack of food for his friend, and in his satchel, a story for the next issue. When the war first started, Valentin was like most Belgians-- uncertain about what to do, accept, or resist. When he entered the fight, he was like most, passively resisting, listening to the BBC; then he came upon the idea for the paper, or as Michel preferred to call it, "The Sheet." Of course, Gie Desmit disliked the idea, not because of what they wrote, but because it increased the odds of him being betrayed and captured. For Gie, the pen was not mightier than the sword. "A bullet between the eyes, that's all they understand," he would preach.

Valentin thought about shutting down the paper, but he loved being a boil on the ass of the occupation forces. Their most recent issue caught the attention of the city dwellers and the ire of the current administration. Anyone found reading the paper, let alone distributing, would have some lonesome nights in the basement of 453 Avenue Louise, Gestapo headquarters. The authorities put extra effort into finding the culprits after the stolen airplane incident, and in due course, they found the printing press. Had it not been for Gie's network, the secret police might have also found Valentin there that night.

Since then, Valentin and Verhoeven had taken a break from the newspaper business. They spent most of the time looking for a new place to print the paper and had found it in Vilvoorde. The brother-in-law of one of the members of the

Belgian National Movement had space in the basement of his tailor shop. He was barely making ends meet, and he couldn't remember the last time someone came in to order a suit. No, the order of the day was patching, sewing holes, making an old suit last even longer. The proprietor was willing to brave the wrath of the occupiers for the small stipend that the MBN gave him for housing the printing setup. Michel was able to find an old press from one of the many legitimate newspapers that had stopped publishing by decree of the occupiers. He had a hell of a time to disassemble it, move it, and then assemble it again. He hoped that moving again wouldn't be necessary for some time, but knew that depended more on the German than him.

Printing an Underground newspaper was dangerous; circulating one, even more so, but Valentin wanted to give the people hope. He wanted the people to know about acts of defiance; to show the people of the city, the people of Belgium, and the people of Europe that the Nazi war machine was not invincible. He was on his way to meet Michel to give him the story that he wrote detailing the German army's precarious position in the east. Through contacts and purloined papers acquired from informers, he felt they were ready to tell a different story than the propaganda that came from Berlin.

He stayed on the tram as it passed his stop. Taking no chances, he exited at the next stop. The many shops allowed for casual visits and a chance to check if there was a tail. Convinced there was no one following, he disappeared into an ally and then cut through Hessenpark, giving a nod to the statue of King Albert before continuing on Koepoortstraat. The trip had been nearly an hour, with Valentin starting and stopping, carefully observing his surroundings, and feeling confident that no one had followed him. He passed the tailor shop and entered the store next door, where a man laboring over a pair of aged working boots did not even look up. Valentin moved through the store and out the back into the alley. He hastened to the delivery entrance of the tailor shop, entered, and locked the door behind him. To his right was a doorway to the basement. He struck a match, as the light switch had long ago stopped working, and descended the narrow staircase keeping one hand on the wall and carefully placing his feet so as not to lose his balance on the steep decline. He concentrated so much on his footing that he ignored the match until it burnt his fingers. Swearing he struck another.

At the bottom of the stairs, there was another door to pass through. It led into a room with a dim light burning; it was impossible to make out anything. Suddenly a bright light exploded in the space, surprising and blinding at the same time. Focusing, he could see Michel sitting on a chair, a switch to the floodlights in one hand, a Walther in the other. Michel Verhoeven was around 45 but looked 55. His hair was entirely gray and he had a nose that his friends referred to as significant, but he called Roman. There were heavy wrinkles around his eyes, and because of an injury to his leg, sitting still for long was painful. He was a large, powerful man who could take care of himself, and despite his ailments, Valentin never once heard him complain. He could be gruff, but also had a charming way with the women. Pre-war Michel had been a longshoreman in Antwerp, his job of loading and unloading cargo ships vital to the nation's security. Everyone believed that he would stay out of the fighting. To his surprise, he was called up during the general mobilization of 1939 and found himself posted to Fort Eben-Emael between Liège and Maastricht, on the Belgian-Dutch border. On 10 May, Wehrmacht glider-borne troops attacked the fort and made short work of it. One of the charges used to penetrate the bunkers shattered Michel's leg. He convalesced in a military hospital for months, and then was judged worthless by the Germans and discharged. With the country bankrupt and occupation forces in charge, there were no benefits that accompanied a disabled veteran who needed a cane to walk.

Michel eventually found a home with the Resistance and was used as a messenger before meeting Valentin in the winter of 1941. Valentin let him live for a time in the cellar of the gallery, and they would spend many evenings drinking cheap wine and talking rebellion. He would look down to his useless leg and would tell Valentin that there was a score to settle. When Valentin suggested they publish a newspaper. Michel liked the idea and quickly learned the subtleties of setting type and working the printing press. It was Michel who came up with the plan to drop the newspapers from a plane and found one of his old army mates to pilot it.

Valentin looked around the small basement, the printing press in one corner, boxes of typeface and paper in another. Across the room was Michel's living space, a small cot, a chair, and a hot plate on a small table. The room smelt of printing ink and solvent. Valentin always warned Michel that it was dangerous to breathe the basement air. His answer was to light a cigarette and say that it smelled better than the Germans. Michel laid the Walther on the bench. "What do you have for me, my friend?"

Valentin set down the sack he been carrying on the small table. "There is some stew made by the old widow that cooks for Monsieur Desmit," and like a magician pulling a bottle of wine out of the inside of his jacket, "and this."

Michel cleared off the table, sending newsprint and papers to the floor. From the cupboard behind him, he pulled out two glasses. "I am thankful for what you bring. It appears that the tailor's wife only knows how to make soup without any meat or vegetables."

Valentin sipped a little wine as he watched Michel savor the piece of meat from the stew. "I have almost forgotten what meat tastes like."

"I am surprised you can taste at all after breathing these fumes." Michel picked up a cigarette and lit it, smiling as he took a long drink of wine. "What do you have for the sheet?"

"The master race is not doing too well with those Russian hordes. It appears that General Paulus and the 6th Army are sacrificial lambs for the honor of the Reich."

Michel picked up the manuscript and started to read. When he came to the part about the army's losses and the Luftwaffe's inability to supply the troops adequately, he laid the paper on the table. "This is all true?"

"It is."

"Do you think people will believe us?"

"It will at least give them pause for hope, and certainly stir up the Germans."

"I agree with that, and they will surely pull out a few tongues to find out who gave us the information."

"And of course, they will want to know where we print the paper," added Valentin. Looking around, he tried to take inventory of what the publication needed to continue. But between the dim light and the clutter, it was impossible. "How are we set for supplies?"

"We have enough paper, thank god, the Germans have made it almost impossible to find. But we do need more ink. I have asked our friends on the black market to purchase some for us; unfortunately, the price keeps going up. I have arranged to meet them tomorrow, they want half upfront, and then half on delivery."

"I can have the money for you tomorrow."

"No need for you to travel back here. I can meet you closer to the city center."

"Very well, let us meet tomorrow at the Café Roa. It is a local bar not far from Parc du Cinquantenaire. Walk through the park around noon. I will be sitting by the Tripe Arch. I'll make sure you are alone. If so, I'll follow you to the café."

Michel nodded.

"Don't take a table, order at the bar. After a while, I will go to the toilet, their water tank is on the wall, and I'll leave the money behind the tank. After you retrieve the money slip out the back door and I'll cover your escape. Our backup will be the bookstore on Rue Archimede."

"Agreed." Michel lifted himself out of his chair to see Valentin out and to bolt the door. Valentin tried to talk him out of climbing the stairs, knowing every moment must be painful. But Michel wouldn't hear of it. "Tomorrow, my friend."

CHAPTER 6

Eddie DeBaets drew the smoke deep into his lungs and held it there before exhaling, sending white rings into the darkness. It tasted horrible, the result of rolling his cigarettes from rationed tobacco and butts that he had found. He wanted one of the Old Golds from the carton they were carrying, but as his brother told him, they were no longer his, and the recipient would not be interested in sharing. He marveled at how easily their handlers procured the cigarettes, even while protesting that it would be impossible. The British were desperate for this mission to succeed. Now the thought that they had settled for too little money entered the younger brother's mind.

Eddie and Raymond made their way to the service gate on the south side of the building. The workers in Lagerhalle Köln #3, if not German, were mainly French or Belgians who had long ago given up the fight. They labored through twelve-hour shifts and were paid less than their German counterparts. But most were relieved the war was over for them.

At most of the aviation fuel and machine plants in Germany and Poland, Luftwaffe police provided security. They were trained to distrust everyone and everything, especially foreign laborers. There was concern about everything, especially the workforce sabotaging equipment. Security was always tight; people searched and items examined.

Raymond knew that they would need help in smuggling the device into the plant. Even the laziest of the guards would find the bomb after a simple search. But one thing he'd learned quickly in Nazi Germany was everything had a price, especially friendship. There was a sergeant, Uwe Busch, a man who liked to tell people his nickname was the Bull, but all his men referred to him as Fat Uwe. He was known to look the other way for workers who wanted to walk out the gates with tools from the plant so they could work side jobs and collect extra cash. Of course, there was a price to pay.

Raymond had negotiated with him before when Eddie was too drunk to come to work. The bosses at the plant had little sympathy for illness, let alone a hangover, and Eddie had a reputation for missing work. He had been given reprimands in the past and warned that one more time and he would be dealt with severely. "Severely" usually meant a one-way ticket to a concentration camp. Fat Uwe gladly accepted a week's pay from the brothers to keep Eddie off the report. Now Raymond told him that they had to return some tools they had taken some time ago, as they were now needed, and he was the logical suspect in their disappearance.

"Oh, you and your brother are both dumb," Uwe bellowed. "Never steal your tools, steal someone else's." Then he let out a hearty laugh, his ample stomach shaking. "But, letting you in the service gate is a lot more dangerous for me than reporting you present."

"I know, and I am willing to show my appreciation." The sergeant's right eyebrow twitched as Raymond waved the carton of American cigarettes in front of Fat Uwe's face. "This for merely looking the other way." He could see the wheels turning in Busch's mind as he calculated how much he could profit from the contraband. "You could sell them individually and make a mint. You wouldn't even need to deal with the black market; just at the plant, you can make a small fortune."

The sergeant smiled and told the brothers to return to

the gate before 11:00 AM shift started.

Raymond and Eddie approached the service gate on the south side of the factory. A ten-foot gate, with rolled barbed wire at the top, blocked the entrance. A white brick guard house was on one side and a machine gun surrounded by sandbags on the other. The sentries followed their movement as they approached. A corporal came out of the guard station, curtly told them they needed to enter through the front gate and started back to his post.

"We have business with Sergeant Busch," Raymond announced with all the authority he could muster.

The guard turned around, looking irritated that his morning coffee was being interrupted by these two. "What business?"

"It is between the Sergeant and us."

Another of Fat Uwe's little business dealings, the sentry thought to himself. We do his bidding, and he gets the money. It would be nice to trip that fat bastard up. "Follow me," he said as he walked back to the guardhouse. He had no idea what these two men wanted, but if it involved Busch, it was no good. He was sure they were carrying money or contraband in the handbag and decided to find out. Entering the small shack, he ordered them to show their papers and place all their belonging on the table.

The brothers were in a panic; they wanted to run, but it was too late. If the corporal discovered the explosive device, all of the American cigarettes in the world wouldn't keep them from the gallows. A gruff voice from behind saved their lives. "I will handle this matter, Corporal," Turing they saw Sergeant Busch's bulky 140 kilos and 180 centimeters frame. He wasn't wearing his helmet, and sweat from his bald dome dripped down the side of his face. His mouth was lopsided as he spoke. "I will handle this. Dismissed." The two glared at each other before the disappointed sentry walked out and closed the door behind him.

Busch looked out the window before pulling down the shade and turning to the brothers. "You brought the cigarettes?" Raymond pulled the carton out his sack and handed it to the sergeant. Busch inspected his bribe, opening the carton and counting the packs before opening one and lighting up. A smile crossed his face as he drew the smoke into his lungs, savoring the taste of American-grown tobacco. He took several drags before turning to the brothers. "Follow me," was his only command. They followed him out, and with a wave of his hand, the gate opened. Busch escorted them to the main building where they would change into their work jumpers. "I will check you in, now go to work. Oh, and you can forget that we have ever done business."

Lagerhalle Köln, an impressive expanse of brick buildings and petroleum storage tanks, lay close to the Rhine in the southern industrial section of the Reich's great city of the west. The plant was first used as a regional storage depot, utilizing barge tankers on the river. The Rhine served Germany well as barge after barge traveled north and south on Europe's lifeline. But with the war raging, any fuel that wasn't being sent directly to the eastern front was being stored in the plant's massive tanks.

Since Raymond and Eddie had experience repairing machinery, they were used all over the plant. But their greatest talent lay in their ability to fabricate a part no longer available in Germany because of war. The reality was that the military prioritized all spare mechanical parts for weapons and aircraft production. The brothers preferred these projects most, as they challenged them and broke the monotony of working in this strange and violent country. Another one of Raymond's duties was to check the gauges on all the storage tanks and repair or replace them. A faulty gauge in a Polish plant had sent the whole place and all its workers up in flames.

The day dragged on for the DeBaets brothers, and with each passing hour, their anxiety grew. Early evening as they were sharing a coffee and a cigarette, Eddie suggested they not go through with it. "Why get ourselves killed for these assholes? Plus, we should have asked for more money. Let's tell them we planted the bomb, and it didn't go off"

But Raymond reminded him that they had accepted money, and the Resistance probably had spies here in the factory observing them. "If we don't go through with the mission, the British will track us down for stealing the money, or the Belgians will put a bullet in our heads for being cowards. We have no choice but to go through with it." Raymond passed the cigarettes to Eddie, whispering, "Let me handle this. Just keep your mouth shut and listen to me. By tomorrow we will have our money and be on our way to England and safety."

Eddie looked forward to a shot of English gin and wondered what the women in Britain would be like in bed as he took the last drag on the cigarette and then flicked it to the floor. Raymond had given much thought to when and how to plant of the bomb. He planned to use the possibility of a faulty gauge as his excuse to leave the building. But the timing was everything. If he approached the foreman too early, he might send another man out, but if it were too late, they would save it for someone on the next shift. At 9:30 PM, he caught Eddie's eye, and with a twitch of his head, alerted his brother the time had come. He took a second to control his breathing and then approached the shift foreman's office.

The door was open. Sticking his head in the office he spoke to the man sitting at the desk. "Herr Winkler, a leak has been detected on tank six, and upstairs wants me to investigate."

Nils Winkler, the shift foreman, looked up from his desk, "No one told me about a leak," he said, taking the poorly rolled cigarette hanging from his lip and crushing it in an oversized astray that was overflowing. "It is already a shit night, and now this," Winkler muttered, dumping the ashtray in his trash can. Raymond stood there as Winkler searched across the desk for his tobacco pouch and then took forever to roll a cigarette. No one was sure where he got his tobacco, though the consensus was that it was mixed with horse shit as it had a most disagreeable odor. "Who gave this order? And how do they know?"

"Krause from upstairs just told me." Raymond was turning and motioning in the direction of the administrative offices on the second floor. "Someone doing guard duty reported it."

Winkler fussed, "Goddamnit, they are supposed to send down a work order."

Raymond smiled to himself. Winkler was acting true to form. "Listen, it is cold out there, and it could take me a while. I am happy to stay put."

Raymond knew that Winkler would send him. No one wanted to be responsible for wasting the Reich's fuel; men were shot for less—or worse, transferred to Russia. The foreman fiddled with his left ear, a nervous tell that he'd do anything to get by this problem. He had been sent out before without a work order, and fuel was a precious commodity.

"Go, get out of here, but be back before the shift ends, and make sure you take a guard. I don't want you shot while wandering around in the dark." These words came out fatherly. Raymond winced. No Belgian needed to hear this from a Kraut.

"I'll also take Eddie with me."

"This isn't a fucking two-man job," Winkler shouted, as Raymond dodged the specks of tobacco flying from his mouth. Herr Winkler always had something in those jowls, and nothing could turn a tiny projectile into a weapon like the German language.

"If I go out there and need a part, Eddie can come and fetch it. You know the guard won't lift a finger to help. It will be less than an hour with Eddie."

"Just be done before the shift ends," Winkler said, turning back to the tall pile of orders on his desk. Raymond knew his mind was elsewhere, his body tired, never at rest, listening and waiting for those bombers or any other development that might keep him late or kill him.

Raymond gave him a nod and was about to exit the office when he saw smoke coming from the trash can. "Herr Winkler, I believe your trash is on fire."

He could hear Winkler yelling "Holy Fuck" as the trash can turned into a roaring fire. A group of men rushed into the office in response to the foreman's summons. Raymond moved over to the workbench to collect the bomb, which he put at the bottom of his tool kit and with a quick nod motioned his brother to fall into step with him.

They walked over to the guard post and informed Sergeant Busch that they were ordered to check on a gauge and would need an escort. "Where is your work order?" Busch demanded.

"There isn't one," replied Raymond, hoping his voice wouldn't crack from the fear
he felt.

"No work order, no work."

"You'll have to take that up with Herr Winkler, Sergeant."

"We'll see about this. You think after a carton of cigarettes, we're best friends?" Busch picked up the phone on the wall and asked for Winker. Raymond was unsure if it was the shit day the foreman was experiencing, or the fire in the trash can, or the thought of losing over a hundred thousand liters of the Führer's fuel, but Herr Winkler made short work of Fat Uwe's complaint.

The sergeant looked over his men huddled near the coal-burning stove. Off to the side, their machine pistols were scattered against an empty wall. Raymond kept track, as best he could, of the number of active arms the security force owned. Busch settled on assigning a newly-arrived recruit, Gunnar, a tall pimply kid of 17. Busch figured none of the older men would obey an order to stand guard in the cold. Gunnar scowled when commanded to guard the Belgians to the tank area. He'd been reading a comic book. He was a slow reader, moving his lips to pronounce each word.

Considering the rain and clouds they had the last few days, the brothers were surprised to see a clear sky and the moon bright as they walked out to the storage tanks. Eddie, always talkative, tried vainly to interest Gunnar in a little banter. Gunnar ignored his broken German.

As they walked toward the fuel tanks, their path illuminated by the moonlight, Raymond rehearsed the plan he had hatched for planting the incendiary device. He'd calculated where the explosion might make the most damage and where the factory firefighters would have the most trouble putting it out. He had chosen storage tank #6, right in the middle of the group of 12 huge tanks that held millions of liters of refined fuel. Number six stood far from the perimeter chain link fence topped with coiled rolls of razor wire. The Luftwaffe guards patrolled inside and outside the wall. They grouped like the hands of a precise Swiss watch, making their rounds every half hour. Lately, they had upped the number of patrols by two.

Tower 6 was given less attention by the guards owing to its proximity to the center of things. As they approached the tanks in the dark, the giant cylinders looked sinister and foreboding. The brothers and their escort made a turn and headed into the midst of the tanks to look for number six. Off the path and in the center of the giant steel forest, they plunged into pure darkness that had all three fumbling for army-issued lamps. Raymond reminded them of the blackout policy, and told them that he would only light his to check the gauge and then turn it off.

Standing in front of the giant tank, the three of them shivered as a brisk wind whipped around its base. The clear night also brought cold weather, and the long walk out had chilled them to the bone. The main readouts were higher up on a platform; steps would take Raymond part of the way, then he would have to climb a metal ladder to get to the calibration unit.

The walk out was enough for Gunnar. It was bitterly cold, and he didn't fancy the idea of being out there for an hour. Producing his flashlight, he shined it on the side of the tank. "I don't see no leaks."

Raymond shouted down, "Hey Dusseldorfer, if you want to help, keep a steady hand and aim the light on the ledge."

"It seems all right to me," grunted Gunnar, stamping his feet on the ground to keep warm.

"Well, by all means, let's go back and tell them you have cleared it for use," Raymond shouted as he continued up the stairs.

Gunnar ignored the sarcasm and turned his back. Raymond gave his brother a nod to get the guard's attention. Eddie pulled out the pack of tobacco and called to Gunnar to asking if he wanted a smoke. Gunnar leaned his Mauser rifle against the staircase and shinned his flashlight on Eddie while he rolled two perfect cigarettes. Eddie offered Gunnar a light from his box of matches. They huddled together, trying to get some shelter from the wind.

As if on cue, Raymond yelled at both of them: "Goddammit, what are you doing? We've got gas leaking into the goddamn Reich, and you're ready to torch the place." Eddie and Gunnar looked like two naughty teens. "If you are going to smoke, move away from here."

The next few minutes were critical. Gunnar might not be the brightest Hitler youth from Dusseldorf, and he might be frozen; all indications were he was distracted; yet his German inclination to distrust foreigners might be enough for him to figure out Raymond and Eddie were up to no good. Eddie handed Gunnar another cigarette and leaned over to light it for him, close enough to smell onions on his breath.

"These taste like shit. Where did you get your tobacco from, Herr Winkler?"

"Well, my friend, if you have any Turkish cigarettes in your pocket, pull them out."

Raymond was struggling with the timer. He had easily attached the device to the side of the tank behind conduit that ran from the gauges but there was trouble connecting the bomb. He had gotten grease on his hand, which was now on the end connectors, making contact difficult. He tried a half a dozen times to force the wires into their base, but grease had gotten into the crevice and made a connection impossible. Raymond pulled out his pen knife to clean the contacts.

Eddie sensed something was wrong; it shouldn't have

taken this long to attach a bomb with magnets, connect the detonation device, turn the timer and get out of there. Yet now the cigarettes were nearly smoked, and Raymond remained upstairs. Eddie got nervous, putting out a half-smoked cigarette and starting on another. He tried to keep his attention on the guard, but his glances were upward where his brother fiddled with the bomb. Gunnar sensed Eddie's fidgeting and caught his furtive glance.

"What's is wrong, Liebling? Do you hear bombers or something? Or you just Mama for your brother? What's taking so long?" Gunnar picked up his rifle and started toward where Raymond was working to hurry him along.

"I say we stay here, or there'll be work for us!"

Gunnar stopped, nodded, and took a long drag from his cigarette. Eddie hoped whatever it was Raymond was doing, he would finish quickly.

Raymond removed the bomb from the tank's side and started re-cleaning the connectors. Using his pen knife and a piece of cloth, he eventually was able to remove residual grease from the connectors. Even in the cold, sweat was starting to roll off his brow. Damn, he could have used Eddie's help. He needed another pair of skilled and steady hands as he fumbled with the bomb and timer.

Gunnar took a last drag off the cigarette and flicked the butt away into the darkness. He looked at Eddie and motioned with his head to start back to find Raymond. Eddie, who had been nursing his cigarette, begged for another minute to finish. Gunnar had no interest in spending any more time in the cold than he had to. He unslung his rifle and barked out, "Let's go."

Raymond had finally attached the timing device to the bomb. All connectors fit snug, and he was about to reattach the explosives to the side of the tank when he heard Eddie and Gunnar approaching. His brother's voice was carrying far into the still night. Raymond meant to ease the device back on the side of the tank, but between the grease, cold, and moisture from sweat on his hands, it slipped out of his grasp, and the magnets drew it to the metal with a definite clank of metal meeting metal. The explosive was at an angle, not completely hidden behind the pipes, the tip with the timer exposed. Raymond struggled to straighten it as Eddie and Gunnar came into sight.

"What the hell was that?" Gunnar demanded as he came around the giant holding tank. He shined his flashlight towards Raymond.

"I'm trying to convince an unwilling valve to see it my way," Raymond chuckled, quickly collecting his tools, intent on moving his minder as far away as possible. But Gunner was curious.

Gunnar put his light on the valve and shaking his head he exclaimed, "It doesn't look like you did anything."

"I did enough to get us out of this damn cold," Raymond shot back. Climbing down, he and Eddie picked up the tool kit and started toward the path. Gunnar took one last look at the valve, shrugged his shoulders, and was about to join the brothers when something reflected off of the flash light beam. He walked closer to get a better look as the brothers froze.

"What's that?" Gunnar was pointing to the exposed part of the bomb. He climbed halfway up the metal ladder, shining his light and straining to look at the timing device. Confused he said, "This looks like a watch, why would...," He would never know the answer; Eddie yanked him off the ladder, and as he hit the ground used a large pipe wrench to split his skull.

Raymond was stunned. "What else was there to do?"

shot Eddie. "Anyway, they'll all be dead in a couple of hours."

"He was young, he was stupid, and we could have told him anything. He just wanted out of the cold. Now we are in it, how do we explain why he isn't coming back?"

I'll take care of the body, you think of how to explain." Eddie grabbed the dead German under the arms and dragged him to the small pumping station 10 meters away. He crammed the body under the pipes and hurried back to Raymond. "All hell will break loose before they find him."

The brothers returned to the main work area to find a relieved Winkler waiting for them. They had completed the repair, and now he wouldn't have to explain to his superiors the loss of their precious fuel. As they walked away, Winkler called to them. Turning, they saw he was holding up a piece of paper, a work order, shrugging his shoulders as if asking, "so where is it?" Raymond simply shrugged back, lifted his wrist, and pointed to his watch before yelling back, "I'll get it for you first thing tomorrow."

Raymond hurriedly cleaned up his work area aware minutes were ticking away, as Busch came looking for Gunnar. "He was right behind us, probably enjoying a cigarette or a taste of liquor from one of the sentries." The sergeant looked irritated and went off to find his young recruit. Raymond found Eddie in the lavatory cleaning up. "Let's get out of here now." Within minutes, they changed into their traveling clothes and were on their way to the station and freedom.

CHAPTER 7

Manfred Hergenreder and Luther Ulmen shared emptying the last drop of schnapps they kept in a canteen; it kept them warm and almost content as they patrolled the kilometers of barbed wire that ringed Lagerhalle Köln. Being two of the youngest guards, they pulled sentry duty most nights. It was monotonous, making these rounds, bundled in their standard issue greatcoats and fortified by the (contraband) schnapps. After paying for the liquor, there was little left over for fun or alternatives to army food.

Manfred stood sixteen centimeters taller than Luther. Born in Kiel, in Germany's northern state of Schleswig-Holstein, he was used to winter's cold dampness in the industrial Rhineland. Luther hailed from Freiburg in Breisgau. In the tradition of German division despite the Reich's unification theme—Deutschland uber Alles—this Mutt and Jeff security team, when drunk, often could not understand each other's German.

They took a break in the shadows of Tank 7, away from any prying eyes, but they could still see the fence. They smoked and tried to coax more schnapps out of the canteen. Luther liked to take this time to refine his plan on getting out of the army. The cold affected his asthma and he hoped to obtain a medical release. All that was needed was a sympathetic doctor. Then he could return home and apply at a university.

No one in Manfred's family had ever gone to university, and no one in the foreseeable future would. Manfred's thoughts were more about staying put in Köln and praying the conflict on the Eastern front would be over soon.

"I'll apply for medical release. You know all too well how I can't breathe this damn air and not get sick—I'm coughing all of the time now."

As usual, Manfred replied, "For the hundredth time, dummkopf, you give them that sissy excuse and you'll be sent you to the Russian front. Who cares about your lungs? Do you think there is no one coughing in Stalingrad? And fuck going to school," he added. Manfred quit school early, and he hadn't even thought of attending a university. He was smart enough to heed his own words.

They stood there, not quite looking at each other, smoking their cigarettes down to stubs. Luther broke their silence. "I wonder where that prick Gunnar is? We've done most of the fence, and he's *poof*—gone like a fart in the wind."

Manfred laughed. They both laughed. Fat Uwe would have Gunnar's balls one way or the other. Both thought the young kid was sleeping somewhere warm. The two believed Gunnar lacked the courage to disappear. They remembered the case of Corporal Schmidt, who decided to take an afternoon off without permission. He broke detail early one day and, after a few hours of drinking confiscated brandy, took a staff car into Köln to service a comrade-in-arm's wife. "I wonder if Schmidt is enjoying Russian soup. Hell, they shipped him off fast—probably got to Stalingrad and discovered the drip Frau Kotter gave him. Dick falls off right before *bang*—a bullet in the brain from some Ivan sharpshooter." They both chuckled

But it was a nervous laugh; they need only look up to the heavens and see the bright clear sky. They knew that it not only brought the cold but most likely the RAF. They tried to keep themselves focused on checking the plant's perimeter and looking for Gunnar, but what they feared most was the rolling sound of engines. Luther often would tell Manfred no imagination was needed to know what would happen to them if they were caught out in a bombing raid.

By the time they reached the middle tanks, Manfred had to relieve himself. Unfortunately, taking a piss along the fence was strictly verboten. The commanding officer had walked the fence line months before in warmer weather and had complained it smelled like a pig farmer's outhouse out there. He decreed that no longer could the guards or workers relieve themselves so freely. They must use the proper facilities. During the day, everyone followed the rule, but at night with only blackout lights, no one paid much attention. So it was this night for Manfred, at least.

As he walked away, he could hear Luther calling, "You sure you want to expose little Manfred to this cold?" He quickly disappeared from the lights and behind the petrol tank. For Manfred, urinating, in the cold always presented a challenge. First, there were bulky gloves to remove, then his greatcoat, and finally fumbling with the buttons of his trousers. More than once, the pee went running down his leg before he could accomplish his task. He winced when his cold fingers touched the sensitive skin. He made quick work of his business and was heading back when he kicked something with his foot. He pulled out his flashlight and illuminated the dark ground. He had stumbled over--- a rifle, a Mauser K98, just like the one slung over his own shoulder and was that blood on the ground? He passed the flashlight to his left hand and with his right, swept the rifle to the ready, chambering the cartridge and yelling in a panic for Luther to come.

Luther arrived in seconds, finding Manfred scanning the area; he nodded at him to look at something on the ground. He flashed his light on the rifle. There was a simple shake of the head from Manfred. "There's blood here," he said.

Luther was astonished. "Blood?" he said as he unslung his rifle.

Manfred scanned the area with his flashlight and found a rust-brown trail. They followed it until it stopped at the pumping station, a few meters away. There was something cramped underneath, a body.

"It's Gunnar," Manfred whispered, as they probed with the flashlight.

"I'm not touching him! Luther informed Manfred, but as his companion grabbed a leg, he reluctantly took the other. They pulled the body out for closer identification and could see a crushed skull. Blood was oozing from the wound, already soaking the length of the soldier's tunic.

Manfred ran to one of the call boxes that was situated on each of the giant tanks and called for help. Luther had covered Gunnar with his greatcoat, and now was freezing. Manfred could see no point in the act. "He's already dead; he doesn't care if anyone sees him now. Now your coat is ruined, and you'll freeze your ass off waiting for the police." All true, but Luther felt that he had done the right thing. The first to arrive was Sergeant Busch and a handful of guards. Manfred led them to where Gunnar lay; the Sergeant carefully lifted the coat and stared at the brutality of the wound. He gently placed the coat back over the body. Fat Uwe treated Gunnar better in death than he ever had in life. At least Luther thought so. Luther looked at Manfred, who stared straight ahead at the corpse. Both men were getting nervous at the slow pace of the sergeant.

Busch shook his head and wondered if this was now going to reflect on him. He sent a runner back to report the death and to seek help. "Christ," he thought, "now I'll have to deal with the Gestapo and the commandant." Every officer and noncommissioned officer worried about how superiors understood war's accidents, these twists and turns. The troop trains to the East weighed heavily on everyone's minds. They all moved away from the corpse as if his lifelessness could be contagious. They smoked and wondered what could have happened. He had gone out with a crew to check on a leak and ended dead.

It didn't take long before a vehicle approached, small slits of light in the blackout. An Opel Olympia Cabrio stopped in front of the men and killed the lights. No military markings, just drab and bureaucratic, painted black and showing its age with worn tires and sooted windshields. The soldiers knew only trouble would step out of that car.

Two men emerged from the darkness of the interior. Neither was wearing military uniform, but uniforms all the same. They matched in their dark suits, leather trench coats, and black fedoras. One had a scar from under his right eye to where his mouth started. Captain Krintz had just returned from spending two years in Poland rounding up Jews. The other, with striking good looks and clearly in command, was Major Kaufmann, a protégé of the late Reinhard Heydrich. They didn't bother to identify themselves, which said it all.

"Who's in charge here"? The man with the scar softly asked.

Hesitantly Fat Uwe stepped forward. "I am Sergeant Busch at your service."

Kaufmann bean his flashlight in the Sergeant's face. "Tell us then, what are the facts, and how do we know them?"

Busch turned to his men, trying to defer to Luther and Manfred. Krintz cut him off.

"The Major asked you, Sergeant, not them."

Despite the cold, the Busch was sweating profusely. *Holy Christ,* he thought, *a fucking Gestapo major.* The two agents looked at each other. They were too accustomed to the quality of home security, its contempt for procedures.

"Why was he out here?" Kaufmann asked.

The sergeant explained the leak report, the detail he dispatched, all the information he knew.

"And the two men who were out here with him, where are they now?"

Fat Uwe looked at him blankly.

By now, more soldiers from the security forces had arrived. Their leader, a young Luftwaffe officer, swaggered up to the two men in black suits.

"I am Leutnant Haser, and this now a Luftwaffe investigation."

"I think not" grunted Krintz as he flashed his warrant disc. "Major Kaufmann is in charge."

The officer immediately snapped to attention. Kaufmann turned to him.

"Take some men and go to the apartment of the workers who were out here. If they are not there, call this number," he said, handing them a card. "Tell them that on Major Kaufmann's orders, you are reporting them fugitives." Kaufmann grinned at Krintz. It was now getting fun.

Haser saluted and took his squad off to arrest the brothers DeBaets. Kaufmann turned to Bosch and asked to see the body. They followed him to the pumping station, where Kaufmann pulled the coat off the corpse and tossed it aside. He examined the body like a true homicide detective. He deduced the man was struck from behind, and with real force.

He looked down, saw the blood trail, and followed it back to the giant petrol tank. In front of it was a large pool of dried blood. "This is the spot where someone struck him," he told his partner. "See, he was dragged from here, probably by the arms, with the boots digging in and causing this trail." He ran his light along the ground to press his point. "But why? Did the repairmen know the private?"

"No," the Sergeant replied.

"How was he chosen?"

"He was the youngest man in the guard room, and I saw no reason to send a veteran out in this cold."

"Sergeant have your men check the fence, look for breaches."

Busch wasted no time. He turned on his heels, shouting at his men, wanting to get as far away as possible; but before he could make his escape, Kaufmann called to him. "Sergeant, your men can handle the search. Please fetch the paperwork on these laborers. Who ordered this repair? And who selected these men?"

Fat Uwe weakly stammered, "There was no paperwork, they…"

Kaufmann cut him off before he could finish, staring him down, the major returned to examining the storage tank. The sergeant, noticing that his men wanted to be as far away from him as possible, could feel the cold Russian winter at his back.

"You say they were out here checking on a reported gauge leak on holding tank six?"

"Yes, sir."

"And you have no idea who ordered it? Nor did you require a work order?"

"I asked for a work order but was ordered by Nils Winkler, the plant foreman, to proceed without..."

Again, he was interrupted by the major "The head of security takes orders from a plant foreman? I would recommend you go find this person, and both of you wait for me in his office."

Sergeant Busch took off for the main building hoping that Herr Winkler had not already left. Kaufmann continued investigating the area. He shined his light on the gauge, saw nothing strange. In better times, they'd get forensics out here to thoroughly comb the crime scene. The war's chaos and destruction had put an end to that. He'd trust his intuition. His gut said no evidence of a leak and no proof that the workers replaced the gauge. He strolled around the tank, poking his flashlight here and there.

"Have the men spread out and see if they can find anything," he said to Krintz. He turned his attention from the ground to the tank, slowly moving his light across the pipes, and then, "There!" he pointed. Sticking out behind the return pipes was the head of the device. "Bomb!" he shouted. The guards instinctively pulled back. Krintz moved forward toward his partner. Kaufmann lifted his head toward the device, giving Krintz the silent order to investigate. He approached the pipes, pulled himself onto the platform, and put his light directly on the explosive.

"It is a British-made incendiary device with a timer and detonation cap. Crude but effective."

"Can it be disarmed?"

Krintz bent over and pulled the connections out with one hand. With the other, he pulled the device away from the tank. Climbing down he handed it to Kaufmann. "Amateurs."

"Amateurs or not, they are saboteurs. Bold ones, the worst kind."

Kaufmann and Krintz headed back to their car to deal with the plant foreman and the sergeant. At that moment, someone snapped a photo of the dead man. The flash from the bulb momentarily illuminated the scene. In the white light, faces revealed, no one was smiling.

....

Leutnant Haser's squad approached the DeBaets' rooming house, unsure of the reception they would receive. Before they left the factory property, the plant foreman was still in his office and had a secretary type out the names and address, and attach photographs of the two brothers. Handing Haser the thin dossier on the brothers, he gave a warning. "I knew they were up to no good. They are a nasty couple of thugs, and they won't go quietly."

The plant's military guards were not police; they had never made an arrest. Haser convinced himself that a quiet, simple approach was best. He made his men chamber a cartridge and take their weapons off safety. "Stay alert." The two young guards with him said nothing, faces ashen with fear. He sent one of them around to the back of the house with orders to shoot whoever comes out the back door.

Haser stood at the street entrance of the apartment house, with the prospect that death could await him on the other side of the door at the forefront of his mind. He tried the knob; locked, he cursed to himself. From inside the house, the landlady, Frau Schröder, could hear movement outside and went to investigate. Opening the door, she came face to face with the Oberleutnant. Before she could say a word, he put a finger to his mouth to motion her to be quiet. In a low whisper, he asked which room the DeBaets occupied.

"Why, what have they done?" she gasped, stepping back.

"The room number, Frau?" Haser whispered.

"Up the stairs, room six." Haser pushed her to the side and started to move inside the house.

"They're not here," she yelled at him. "They went back to Brussels for the St. Nicholas holiday."

Haser turned to breathe a sigh of relief; this was no longer his business. He pulled Kaufmann's card from his pocket and asked to use her phone. In the distance he could hear air raid sirens going off.

CHAPTER 8

Major Kaufmann sat at his desk in his small, spartan office of the EL-DE building, Gestapo headquarters in the middle of Köln. He was anxiously awaiting news of the saboteurs. Next to his office was an interrogation area; he rose and looked through the one-way window that opened up to the room. He expected them to be apprehended quickly, and was already making plans for their questioning. He pictured them in the room, already broken, bound, heads bowed.

Kaufmann knew the detail sent to the apartment wouldn't turn up bodies, but intelligence was much better than dead bodies. Germans were patriotic and in terror of the Gestapo. As it turned out, the woman who ran the boarding house swiftly gave destination, time, and state of mind. Also, a guard at the railroad station had mentioned they seemed anxious to leave the city that evening. Kaufmann frowned—*wouldn't you be?*

Kaufmann reviewed tonight's intelligence reports: As he predicted, Raymond and Eddie boarded the last train out before the air raid. Oh yes, the air raid. Kaufmann believed the act of sabotage and the attack were connected. The city could hear the roar of the engines, hundreds of Avro Lancaster bombers swooping in over the cathedral and then making the turn in the direction of the storage tanks. Anti-aircraft bursts were lighting up the sky, Luftwaffe night fighters moving in and out of the formations.

Fortunately, there was no fire to guide the bombers

tonight. Once again, the RAF killed more civilians than destroyed military assets. Kaufmann thought to himself, *I'm sure fat Göring will get them back tomorrow night.*

There was a knock at the door, and Captain Krintz entered, handing his boss the latest update. The major scanned it. "So the two are fleeing back to Mudder."

Krintz replied, "Yes, the train is the daily Köln-Brussels —it has a long stop in Liege."

"No other stops?"

"No other stops. We have alerted Liege, and they will be waiting for them."

"Do you think they will jump the train?"

"No. I'm sure they heard the planes overhead and probably believe their mission was a success."

"I hope you are right." Kaufmann quickly read through the report-informative; but the only thing he wanted to hear was that the two saboteurs were in custody. "What about the British bill tonight?"

"Seven Lancasters downed and parachutes sighted."

"Excellent news! Once we have live crew members they will help to put all the pieces of the puzzle together." No visitor to Gestapo interrogation room 5 stuck to name, rank, and serial number for long. There is no Geneva Convention in hell.

"We were lucky tonight," offered Krintz. "The bombs fell well short of the storage tanks. Who knows what could have happened if the guards hadn't stumbled upon the body. Priceless petrol lost, and the plant destroyed."

"Idiots. How many times have we told these plant managers that the foreign workers are not to be trusted? And that damn sergeant was the worst. What was his name?"

"Busch."

Kaufmann scribbled some notes. In the morning, he wanted the sergeant shipped to the Eastern Front, and the plant supervisor shot. "I want to speak to the commandant in Liege personally. I know him from our time in Poland, and I can assure you the only thing that will get him out of bed in the middle of the night, other than collecting Jews, is collaring saboteurs. Ask the operator to put the call through." He made a mental note to impress upon the Liege commandant that unlike in Poland, he wanted the two fugitives returned to Köln and not to have them reported: Shot while escaping.

....

Eddie and Raymond sat comfortably in their compartment. To their surprise, they shared accommodations with a group of Belgian Sisters of Mercy, traveling from a mission in Köln home for the holidays. What hesitation they may have had about a compartment full of nuns quickly faded away. The good sisters were clearly in the holiday mode, producing a basket of cheeses, sausages, and what appeared to be an endless supply of delicious beer. "We brew it at the nunnery," the Mother Superior proudly stated. They ate, drank (more than ate), and sang along with the sisters, relieved that their part of the mission was over.

Raymond sipped his beer, making it last, while Eddie downed three bottles in a row. Raymond worried about this, a drunk brother and fugitive. Eddie had forgotten the fix they were in; the money sat foremost in his brain. Raymond knew better. What they started wasn't over until they touched English soil. As he drank and thought about the next hours, Raymond couldn't get the sight of the young soldier's crushed skull out of his mind. It weighed heavily on his conscience. It hadn't been part of the plan. All they were supposed to do was plant the bomb and escape in the resulting confusion. Raymond felt helpless. Things like this—his life—never worked out, didn't go by the numbers. He and his brother were saboteurs, killers, far from home in the Third Reich. And now like a couple of dumb Belgians, they were drinking too much beer.

Febe had watched the two brothers arrive at the station and board the train. She feared that there might be an incident at boarding, but after the usual patdown, they passed right through. Now they were in their compartment, hopefully behaving themselves with the nuns, Febe had played that one well; the Sisters regularly traveled the Köln-Brussels line. She watched as the boys took seats by the nuns and then prayed that they would not get drunk. The two would need all their wits when they arrived in Brussels. She had already made one pass through the train with her cart; the train was fuller than usual with the holiday travelers. *How strange she thought, even in war, holidays go forward.*

The trip to Liege was taking longer than expected. The train was already some two hours off schedule. They stopped on a spur to let a military train haul by at full speed. She did not doubt that, like most troop trains, its final destination was Russia. Intelligence drives military success, and Febe's handlers in the Resistance taught her to observe all. She wanted to get a good look at the passing train. She had taken her cart back to the catering car for them to restock, then found her way to an open space above the coupling and lit a cigarette. In the darkness, she worked hard to identify the cargo that sped by her: flat car after flat car carrying tanks covered in grey canvas, their large cannons sticking out from under the camouflage. She couldn't make out what was in the boxcars that followed, but was sure it was equipment and not people. She remembered one moonlit night as the freight cars passed, hearing the sounds of people crying out, begging for help, over the clacking of the train wheels. She prayed she would never hear that again.

It was not too long before they were on the move again. Febe made one last trip through the train and returned to the baggage car. Hoping to have a few minutes of rest, she laid her head on a mailbag and drifted off to sleep, but was soon awaken by the train slowing. They had entered Liege and were approaching Guillemins railway station. Late, as usual; it would put them into Brussels in the early morning. With a little bit of luck, she and the brothers would blend in with the crowd as they left the station. Hopefully, they would not raise the curiosity of any patrols.

As they approached the grand old station, Febe maneuvered to look out the small windows mounted on each of the double cargo doors, the aging terminal in front of her. The last time it had been worked on was in 1905 for the World's Fair. She was startled by what she saw. The platform was full of armed troops, too many to be on sentry duty. What put fear in her heart was the fact they were all focused on the train. There was nothing about this scene that she liked. Instinctually she knew they had come for the brothers.

She calculated there was only a matter of minutes before all hell broke loose. She made her way to the brother's compartment, passing a few people who were still awake at this late hour, but fortunately looking out the windows and not noticing her movements. She quietly slid open the door to the compartment and entered. Raymond was awake and would have said something had she not placed her finger to her lips, pleading for silence. She whispered in his ear to collect Eddie and come to the baggage car-now! Raymond nodded his understanding. He wasted no time in waking his brother and forcibly pushing him from the compartment while making it clear this was not the time for questions. Making their way to the baggage car, Raymond could see figures through the steam that was being produced by the engines. There were German soldiers, and even worse, men in long trench coats. He and Eddie were moving as fast as they could without running. They burst into the baggage car expecting only Febe, but found themselves face to face with the conductor. He had come to see what was happening and to secure the compartment. To everyone's surprise, he pulled a pistol from his waistband and aimed it at the two brothers. Febe pushed him off balance. Eddie grabbed him from behind, wrapped his arms around his throat, and with a violent motion broke the conductor's neck. He held him for a moment, making sure he was dead before letting him slide to the floor.

"He only would have caused us problems," was Eddie's reply to the other two.

"Police are everywhere; we have to make them think you have left the train," Febe warned them. She pointed at the cargo door opposite the platform and told Eddie to open it just enough to pass through. She had already surveyed the car and believed their best plan would be for the brothers to hide behind the luggage racks. She had Raymond pull out large bags stacked in the corner. "The two of you need to hide behind those bags, and I will try to convince them you killed the conductor and escaped." They both looked at her skeptically. "It is the only move we have. If they fall for it, we will sneak you off in Brussels. Quickly! There is no time to argue."

And indeed they'd run out of time. The train had stopped, doors opened; they could hear the heavy boots pounding in car aisles, the yelling at passengers. The soldiers were demanding papers and asking about two men traveling on the train. Without a second thought, Febe directed Raymond to slap her across the face, hard enough to make it look like she put up a struggle. Raymond's slap was light, pointless; Eddie stepped up and gave her a stiletto jab with his left fist below her right eye. Febe staggered a second, then crashed to the floor. Raymond pulled Eddie back to the hiding place where they quickly dragged a few suitcases and mail sacks in on them. Febe was in a fog. Her right eye felt like it would explode, and she felt something running down her cheek; when she touched it, she realized it was blood. Seconds later, two SS men came through the carriage door, armed with machine guns and right behind them, a Gestapo officer. Febe lay next to the dead conductor. She lifted her head and pointed to the door.

"They have escaped. Surround the building," the officer shouted. Stepping over the corpse and Febe, he made his way to the platform, still barking orders.

Febe was trying to clear her head when another SS officer appeared. He had no concern about her injury, let alone about the dead conductor lying on the floor.

"Tell me what happened!" was all she heard. It was said in a low voice, but with complete contempt for her.

In slow German, as if not able to speak the language well, she explained that two men burst in on her and the conductor. One of them punched her, and that is all she remembered. Disgusted at her lack of cooperation, he checked the conductor, surveyed the area, and then joined the men searching around the train. Soon a railroad official arrived, and only then did someone inquire if she was alright, or do anything about the dead body lying on the floor.

All in all, it worked for Febe. Two hours passed before the agents released the train to continue to Brussels. For the brothers hiding in the baggage racks, it seemed like years. Febe feared they would bring the dogs in the car, but there were so many Germans and officials in the small space, they all believed the baggage car secured. The consensus was the fugitives were on the run, and they didn't want to waste any time closing down the city. One of the conductors wanted to take Febe off the train to have her injury examined. She was insistent that she was alright and could proceed to Brussels. "It is the holiday, and I want to spend it with my family," she begged him.

Febe thought it a sign of the times that the passengers quickly settled back into their routine and once again were drifting off to catch a little sleep before arriving in Brussels. There was a dead conductor, escaped saboteurs, Germans with guns everywhere--yet as the train got up steam and pulled out of Liege Station, life again became normal. A new conductor arrived, and he stayed with Febe for a short time. Soon he headed back to check on the passengers and to collect tickets from those who might have boarded in Liege.

Now, with so much going wrong, Febe had to keep improvising. The next move: getting Raymond and Eddie off the train in Brussels. The idea of just walking off and meeting their contact was out of the question... or was it? She had misdirected the pursuers in Liege; could she do the same in Brussels? Looking around the car, she noticed a pile of grey dust jackets that workers used when loading and unloading the baggage. If the brothers could pass themselves off as baggage handlers, then maybe there could be a chance. She pushed away a trunk to free them from their hiding place.

"We've got to jump before this thing gets going any faster," offered Eddie.

Febe took control of the situation. "No, there's a better way." Raymond and Eddie listened as she explained, "After we pull into the station, one of the local managers will board and total my take. While he's tallying the receipts, put on these porter jackets and start moving the baggage down to the platform porters. The porters are usually rushed and shouldn't notice anything more than the luggage. If questioned, tell them you've transferred from Köln. Don't worry. We will be out of here before anyone can check your story. Once inside the station, make your way to the toilets, take off the dust jacket and move to the east entrance. Our contacts will pick you up there. And for god's sake, come out separately! Don't look conspicuous."

Raymond and Eddie lay cramped behind luggage for the rest of the trip. Febe ventured out a couple of times and saw that most of the passengers were fast asleep. She made her last round a few minutes before the arrival in Brussels. She was doing a brisk business in tea and the ersatz coffee. The winter's sunrise broke through one side of the train, a reddish-orange angular light which prompted some passengers to pull down window shades. Their faces seem to say; *another day of occupation, but we're back home.*

She returned to the baggage compartment, passing the conductor, who advised her they would be in the station soon. In the baggage car, she took count of her inventory and prepared her paperwork for the catering manager. She could feel the train slowing and forced herself to look out the window, fearing what might be out there. It was a relief to see only a few guards, and business going forward as usual. Good, the search for the two had not spread to Brussels. They would be pulling up next to the Berlin-bound train with much activity going on. Even more diversion. She moved to the racks and started pulling the bags out. She helped the brothers into their dust coats and gave them last-minute admonishments.

The train finally came to a halt, and at Febe's direction, Raymond threw the cargo doors open. As directed, they moved the baggage to the edge of the car to allow the other porters to take it directly off. The catering manager jumped on board and was every bit as efficient as Herr Liftmann in Köln. The brothers enlisted the use of one of the carts with steel-banded wheels that stood on the platform. They piled the luggage on it, and carefully moved into the station. It was as if they had been porters all their life. Within minutes, Febe was able to follow them into the station. The guards seemed preoccupied. The holiday season and crowds made them long for home and gentler times. No harassing the travelers this day, no sudden searches.

It was good to be back in Brussels. At the East entrance, Febe could see her contact, Valentin de Vos. The brothers were outside, like two workers stealing a smoke before returning to work. Febe followed de Vos as he exited. Raymond and Eddie, after disposing of their dust jackets, followed her. She was always nervous around de Vos; the rumors were his wife was a collaborator. But whenever she worked with him, he showed courage and leadership that were lacking in most of the men of the Resistance.

They stuck to the side streets until they reached the Rue Duquesnoy gallery. They entered through the back and moved to the basement. Valentin looked at Febe, her right eye bloodshot and an ugly purple bruise on her cheek. "Are you all right? What happened? Did the Germans do this to you?" He touched the side of her face with a tenderness that startled her.

Febe waived off his inquiry. He then turned toward the brothers and, with controlled anger, asked; "Could you two have fucked this up any more than you did?"

From the two, there was only silence; Febe looked at him, unaware of what he meant. "They not only didn't set the device, but they also killed a guard. The bombing raid was a bust, the Germans have stepped up security in Köln, and before long, they will surely trace this all to Brussels."

It was Eddie who tried to put up a defense. "He stumbled upon the bomb. It was either him or us."

Raymond quickly interjected, "We placed the bomb."

"Not very well; it was found! The British are livid; they say they couldn't have made this any easier for you."

"How do they know that it wasn't their device that was faulty?"

"What do we do now?" asked Febe

"We need to move them to a safe house. There is a small farm north of the city. The owners are MBN; these two can stay there until we work the arrangements out with the British. The Boche won't take kindly to trying to blow up one of their plants and killing one of their guards. We also received word that a conductor on the train was killed. We can expect a clampdown on us. We will all have to curtail actions. Unfortunately, this means you will need to handle them a little longer."

"I'm not scheduled for another trip until next week," Febe offered.

Valentin nodded. "Let's hope it doesn't take that long." Taking Febe by the arm, he walked her out of earshot of the brothers. "The longer we hide these two, the higher the danger. Arrangements have been made to move them out to the country. There is a produce truck that makes the trip daily and is a common sight on the road between the north farms and Brussels. The driver bribes the guards by giving them fresh fruits and vegetables. They long ago gave up tearing the truck apart to look for anyone."

There was a rap on the back door. Valentin pushed it open to find Pieter Moens, the truck driver who would take them away. When Eddie saw the truck only sat two, he hesitated and wanted to know where he would sit. He received a short reply from Pieter, "In the back under the boxes, you fool!" He jumped up on the truck bed to arrange the crates. "Come, you lay next to the cab and behind the boxes."

Eddie was about to protest, but Raymond pushed him up. The two lay down as Pieter positioned the crates.

Valentin helped Febe up to the cab. "We will contact you soon," he said, as she strained to hear his voice over the howling truck engine. As he walked away, she thought of the way he touched her face.

Valentin waited as the truck exited the alley and then headed up to his studio to meet with his benefactor, who also happened to be his wife's lover.

CHAPTER 9

Much was on Valentin's mind as he made his way from the alley to the back of his shop. He thought about the DeBaets brothers. How long could they hide them before word got out and reached the Germans? And word would leak out, that much he knew. It terrified Valentin how many betrayed agents there had been in the last six months. Between collaborators, fear, and money, the Germans had been effective in identifying their enemies and silencing them. He had no doubt that they would one day come for him. Whether hiding the two hapless saboteurs would tip his luck, who could know?

The British also worried him. They were angry, on the ground in Belgium and those in London. They weren't wrong; his men had messed up the mission. The Brits relished success and would not tolerate failure.

"There is always the possibility of failure," Gie Desmit like to tell his agents; "matter of fact, the chances of failure are far greater than the chances of success." Desmit never openly shared the British view with his men; what would be the upside? But, Valentin often heard him say that at heart, the British took honor seriously. They divided the world into the enemy and allies. All fought hard at Dunkirk.

No, Valentin's real worry had to be the Germans. They had lost men at the hands of a Belgian attack, and the Gestapo saw this as an insult. They conquered; they did not retreat. There was always extra money for informers, or the families of suspects found themselves threatened. A weak link would be found and exploited. German security was complex and well-established in Belgium. They practically ran into each other before the hostilities, establishing networks at the highest levels of the kingdom's government and military. Some of the older agents had worked for Belgium in the First World War. Some even had stayed, marrying Belgian girls.

Then there was Febe. Valentin racked his brain—how much—how much did they know about this young woman? He found himself drawn to her. He admired the way she carried herself. She was fearless and decisive, but she was also smart and beautiful, and that excited him. She was everything that Elise was not.

The back entrance to the shop was a heavy wooden door that took two hands and a shove to open. No matter how many times he shaved the door or oiled the hinges, the damn thing still stuck. His workroom was large, occupying most of the store's space. Paintings under restoration sat on easels, all at different stages of completion. Valentin enjoyed working on three or four at once. It broke the boredom if he moved from one to another. Restoring was a long and tedious task to get it right, to get it perfect.

Since the Germans had come to town, the work was steady. The Nazis were spending as much time stealing private artwork as they were occupying the country. It seemed they all had the same idea: clean up their booty for a journey back to Germany. It was an open secret in Brussels that the Nazis were stealing from private collections, mostly those of the Belgian Jewish community.

Valentin did his best to catalog and keep track of where the stolen art was going and which person perpetrated the theft. At times he was able to rescue a painting and find a safe place to keep it away from the Third Reich. But these were rare and far between. He could only pray that someday, the thieves would be held accountable.

From the large work area, Valentin passed through curtains into a small reception area. He liked to sit in this room. Two giant windows, though almost clouded with winter's grime, let in plenty of light. He remembered the early days, how the morning sun played on Elise's hair; she glowed like an angel. But those days were long gone, replaced now by war.

Clarette, his young assistant, sat behind the counter. Since business was good, Valentin needed help, and with his wife's time taken up with her romantic adventures, he had to hire someone. His neighbor's daughter Clarette found school difficult and her family needed money. In her teens, she was a hard worker who would put in extra hours if it meant additional francs. Clarette also understood the importance of not noticing any of the non-art activities that went on in the shop. With blue eyes and blond hair that fell to her shoulders in large curls, she was a favorite of the German officers who visited the gallery. They would long for someone as sweet and warm as her to pass the long Belgian nights. She had grown particularly adept at deflecting their advances; unlike Elise de Vos, she understood the term collaborator. She still dressed like a schoolgirl in a checkered jumper and usually spoke in giggles, which Valentin tried to correct; but on the whole, she was more than competent.

Elise was sure that Clarette was his mistress. Valentin suspected that she had convinced herself of that to ease her conscience, or what remained of it; to justify carrying on with her German general. Clarette was sixteen, with teenage fantasies and dreams. She was young enough to believe that someday the Germans would leave, and her life would go on as before. Her real desire was the delivery boy, Alphonse, who brought Elise's black-market goods and gifts from her lover. Alphonse, too, was smitten with Clarette, and never forgot to bring her chocolate. Valentin was honored and respected as her boss, but never thought of as a potential lover. Clarette sensed, too, Valentin had other interests; those from which she needed to stay far away.

Today Valentin expected Generalleutnant Gottfried Beck. Beck came into possession of a painting exhibited in the Royal Museum. Nicolae Grigorescu's *A Flower Among Flowers, Miss Millet*, which he had asked Valentin to replicate. Beck told Valentin when he first brought the treasure in, wrapped in simple brown paper: "Herr de Vos, this painting reminds me of your beautiful wife," pushing his fat finger into Valentin's chest.

"Yes, a likeness, no doubt," Valentin mumbled in German flecked with Flemish. Occasionally Herr General would show off his French, and that was alright with Valentin. He doubted Beck knew much Flemish, although it wasn't a difficult language for a German.

Every morning, two soldiers collected the painting from the museum and brought it to the studio. Valentin set the canvas on an easel next to his copy, carefully checking each brushstroke. He experimented with the oils to make sure the color and hue of the original matched the imitation. Valentin knew once he completed his replica, the original would find its way to Germany, and the soldiers would take the fake back to the museum. The General was just doing what others, especially Goering, were doing—the systematic looting of occupied countries' art. But, he was trying to be more discreet than Fat Göring, who took openly took.

The General met Elise at an opening of Germanic Art in Brussels, an exhibit by Herr Goebbels' culturists that reinforced the Aryan aesthetic way and strength of the new order. Ignored by most Belgian artists, it found an audience with those eager for German acceptance. Elise attended with a friend who thought an evening of art, caviar, and champagne was better than another night going to bed hungry because of the occupier's strict rationing. They paid little heed to the truth that the gallery owner needed to fill the room with attractive women for Wehrmacht officers and high occupation government officials.

The romance and seduction were neither romantic nor subtle. Elise had tired of a life of not enough food, or lingerie, or make-up. She knew that in 1942 Brussels, the Germans were the only ones who could provide those goods and more. In her mind, this was not about collaboration, but survival. Valentin and Elise often fought. One night, a bit drunk, she cursed him for his inability to care for his wife. "To hell with you and those phony friends of yours who look to make trouble and starve. I want to be warm and content."

For the General, Elise in her late 30's was still attractive. Her body, perhaps not as thin as it once was, was still a far cry from Frau Beck, the General's wife, the plump mother of four, grandmother of six. At first, he wanted this mistress only for sex, but he came to enjoy her soft skin and her willingness to listen to him complain about his unfair treatment at the hands of the German High Command. While he stopped short of parading her in public, no one in the city didn't know she was the General's Belgian frau.

Elise helped to break up the boredom and bitterness the General felt. Beck was a distant relative of Field Marshal Beck, former chief of the German General Staff. Gottfried Beck had a meteoric rise through the ranks, but when his uncle fell out of favor with the Führer in 1938, he became something of a non-person within the army. He saw limited action in Poland, none in the battle of France, and now was assigned to garrison duty in Brussels. It infuriated him that junior officers who saw action were dining in Paris while he languished in the low countries. The High Command made a point to give him an administrative post and not field command of any of the troops.

Beck took comfort with expensive wines, sumptuous food, and high-priced prostitutes. Once a dashing cavalry officer, tall, thin, and with a regal bearing, his indulgences and failures had turned him into a caricature. He looked older than his 56 years, and walked stooped over, with a growing belly, his mustache and hair a dirty grey.
As the General's star continued to fall, his stream of women dried up. He believed that it was a stroke of good luck that he found Elise, so willing. In return, he showered her with all the gifts she craved. At first, Valentin was outraged when she returned home after her little trysts with the General. She loved to flaunt the gossip that Beck carelessly confided in her. After too much wine, the General would babble, sometimes to show his power or to vent his anger against his superiors. It mattered not, because over morning coffee Elise would drop tidbits about the movement of troops, supply trains, enemies of the state.

General Beck's entourage pulled up to the shop precisely at 11:30 AM; two soldiers on motorcycles preceded the General's large touring car. In addition to his driver, Major Herbert Kohler, Beck's adjutant accompanied him. The driver always offered Valentin comic relief in his routine of parking the car, jumping out and running to open the passenger side, then quickly running past the General to open the entrance to the shop. Nether the General nor the Major felt obliged, or maybe knew how, to open a door on their own.

Beck's large body lumbered into the shop, his officer's greatcoat draped over his shoulders, his large hands enclosed in leather gloves, his shoes buffed to a mirror finish. Clarette rushed to take his coat, hat, and gloves, her small body disappearing in his stack of clothes. The General found a wall mirror to straighten his tunic and run his hand through his hair. Valentin smiled because that touch of vanity meant that Elise would be making an appearance soon. Beck greeted Valentin warmly, taking his hand in both of his and with a voice strong enough to drift to the apartment above, "Herr de Vos, how are you this dreadfully cold morning? And your wife, she is well?"

"I'm sure she will be down before long to see the General," Valentin replied. "I know how she looks forward to these visits."

The General smiled, a man in charge. "How is the painting progressing? Come, you must show it to me." They descended to the studio to view the half-completed work. "It is beautiful," exclaimed Beck, "but progress is so slow."

Valentin thought the longer he could keep the painting with him, the longer he would have to think of a plan. This was another picture to keep from the thieves. He was painting two copies, one to go into the museum and one for the General. He was almost finished with the first forgery and then would make the switch, keeping the original safe until sanity returned to Belgium.

"It is difficult to find the correct pigments for the colors," replied Valentin. "See how subtle these colors are?" he said, pointing to the original. "I'm afraid it is a slow process."

"Whatever you need, my dear de Vos, let me know. If I am not available, Major Kohler will be pleased to help."

Throughout the visit, Major Kohler looked upon the scene with his expressionless face betraying nothing; he was by nature a suspicious man. While Valentin thought the General somewhat of a buffoon, Kohler was another matter. Curious, suspicious of everything, and ruthless, Valentin kept his guard up with the Major. He preferred to maneuver the general rather than Kohler.

"Where do you obtain such colors?"

Valentin carefully explained, "They need to be created

by hand, sir, and the pigments needed are found only in a few places."

"Here in Brussels? Paris?"

Valentin continued, "I must mix the colors myself as Grigorescu did. Unfortunately, the pigments we need are only available in the bazaars in Tangiers." A nice touch, he thought; official travel documents across the Reich could come in handy.

"Tangiers?"

A skeptical Kohler interjected, "Surely Grigorescu did not venture to Africa for his color?"

"He may have purchased them from the merchants in Antwerp or Amsterdam. But those days have long passed."

The General rolled the thought around in his mind. "Do you think they have them in Morocco?"

"I do, Herr General."

"Perhaps, General," Kohler again interrupted, "one of our couriers could shop for the supplies rather than Herr de Vos making the long journey."

"Don't be ridiculous, Kohler--a courier, left to pick the colors? No, that wouldn't do at all."

Kohler bowed his head and moved away, although Valentin knew that he was not buying any of this. The General, his hands resting on top of his stomach, nodded approvingly, "Yes, Morocco." He liked the idea of getting rid of de Vos for a while. "And how long would such a trip take?"

"Two weeks, maybe three."

Ah yes, two weeks travel for him, the General thought, and two weeks in the country for Frau de Vos and me. Before the conversation could proceed any further, Elise made her entrance, looking a little too radiant for the time of day in a tight dress that displayed her cleavage, but unfortunately also highlighted her growing backside. The one thing that Valentin and Kohler could agree upon was the transparency of the charade. The routine was always the same: the General acting surprised to see Elise, then taking her outstretched hand and kissing it, and then turning to Valentin to say what a lucky man he was to have a wife so beautiful. "The General flatters me," she would say with a blush; and then the same invitation, "Please, you must come up for a drink."

Oh yes, thought Valentin, *liquor, coffee, and sweets you provide.*

"Frau de Vos, I don't want to be an imposition," Beck lamely protested.

The group followed Elise up the stars to the parlor. The small talk was labored, with the General barely negotiating the tight staircase. The men took seats in the drawing room, its large windows letting in the gray of the day. Elise had laid out sweets and was in the kitchen brewing coffee.

"Herr de Vos," the General began, "how much longer after you get the colors will it take to complete the painting?"

"You asked for a perfect copy. For that you cannot rush."

"Yes, yes, I know, but how long?"

"Six weeks, maybe a month."

"If you can have it for me by the first of February, I will double the commission." Looking sheepishly towards the kitchen, the General leaned in to Valentin and whispered, "I am going back to Germany for my wife's birthday, and I would like to give it to her as a present."

Elise brought in a pot of coffee and glasses for cognac.

"This is excellent coffee, Frau de Vos," exclaimed Major Kohler after taking a sip, "Where did you possibly purchase it." Of course, the Major knew she hadn't purchased it, that it was part of the loot she received weekly from his boss. But he always took enjoyment at seeing both Elise and Beck fidget uncomfortably. Even Valentin found satisfaction in the quiz. The only one that wasn't amused was Beck. It reinforced his belief that he needed to replace this reptile he did not trust.

But Elise would not be detoured by Kohler, "Smart shopping, Major," and turning to the General, "How is your masterpiece proceeding General?"

"Slow, my dear, but your husband is very talented, and it looks beautiful, just like the original."

"I must go to the studio and see it soon."

"Nonsense! de Vos, go down and fetch it, I would like to show it to your wife." Beck had been giving orders for so long, he knew how to do nothing else, and casually expected everyone to be his subordinate. But Valentin knew the routine all too well. He nodded, smiled, and announced that he would be back soon.

No sooner had he left, than the General and Elise wandered over by the window to discuss their next rendezvous. In lowered voices they decided on a time and place. The closeness of her body, the warmth of her breath, made the General wish he didn't have responsibilities for the afternoon. "Kohler," he yelled, "bring the car around. I will be down shortly."

Like Valentin, Kohler nodded, smiled, and left the room. He passed Valentin on his way down and made no acknowledgment. The Major always depended on his intuition, which told him that there was more to de Vos than just painting. If it were up to him, the art dealer would be his guest in an interrogation cell. But with Beck as his guardian angel, Kohler needed evidence to arrest de Vos. Better yet, he needed to rid the army and himself of General Gottfried Beck. Kohler was sickened that a coward, thief, and adulterer could hold a position of authority, but he believed the day would come when the General made the mistake that would cost him his life. He just needed to find a way to hurry it along.

CHAPTER 10

Eddie DeBaets was already tiring of life on the run. First the cramped ride in the baggage compartment of the train and now this vegetable truck. But what angered him the most was the reality that other people were running his life. He was angry to be blamed for the failure of the mission and the deaths that followed. Hell, if Raymond had planted the bomb correctly, it would never have been found, and the guard would be alive. The conductor? What was he to do? Did Raymond, or the woman, actually think he would have let them just walk away? To hell with them all, they should have taken the money and disappeared.

Every bump in the road tossed Eddie up and then back down hard to the bed of the truck. He whispered into his brother's ear, "This jerk has found every pothole in Belgium to drive over." His body ached, and the smell of rotten fruit mixed with petrol from the truck only made him more miserable. He wanted to stretch his legs and to grab a pint and a puff or two of real tobacco.

Raymond could tell his brother was agitated but believed that he was bothered more by the discomfort than the danger. He closed his eyes and felt every bump that lifted him slightly, and when it slammed him back down, he wished he had done the same to the British major who came to see them. Maybe they had been too greedy. Maybe helping out hadn't been a good idea. Life wasn't so bad being employed by the Germans. There was work, an occasional beer, a place to sleep; so what if they had to put up with Boche shit? He knew they had been lucky to escape from the train and worried how much longer that luck would hold.

The compartment under the boxes, while out of view, wouldn't stand up to a thorough search. Surely any guard at a checkpoint would easily flush them out of this hiding spot. Once in the hands of the Gestapo, he had no illusions about what their fate would be. The rumors of what happened when the angels of death came knocking on your door were well known. Once in the hands of the Gestapo, you could only expect long hours of torture, torture even after you had told them all they wanted to know, pain so bad that you craved death, and yes, death would follow. These thoughts were in his mind as the truck approached the first inspection station. Their bodies tightened. Not a sound, not even a breath was coming from either brother. They waited for the end, no weapon to defend themselves, just cowering at the bottom of a fruit truck.

But capture was not to be. After two years of occupation, the troops had grown bored and lazy. The sentry waved the vehicle to the side of the narrow road. The truck was a common sight on this route, and the sentries enjoyed the fresh vegetables they received. As an extra enticement, Gie Desmit always made sure the driver had French cigarettes to give away. Usually, it was no more than just a cursory search. So it was today, with the added attraction of flirting with the fraulein seated next to the driver. The guards watched as Febe collected a box of vegetables for them. The young men, far from home, dreamed of what pleasure they could take with her. Febe, from her experience on the train, knew what would delight the sentries. A smile, then getting close enough that they could smell her perfume. There would be a few pleasantries exchanged, a breathless "merci" from her, and then they were off. But she knew that once the search for the fugitives expanded to Brussels, the casualness would stop, and Gestapo agents would oversee the inspections.

The safe house was near the village of Vlezenbeek, southwest of Brussels. To keep up appearances, they stopped at farms along the way to pick up produce. These detours meant the trip progressed slowly. The delays made the journey one of many hours, and for the brothers, much anxiety. At one of the stops, Eddie had yelled from his hiding place that he had to pee and to let him out. Pieter yelled back to shut up, or they would all be caught and hanged. "Piss in your pants you bloody fool, and if you yell again, I'll shoot you myself" Neither Febe nor the brothers doubted that he would do just that. Their driver did not like the two men, nor care for a woman to be involved in this sort of activity. Febe found out how gruff he could be while trying to start up a conversation. He made it clear that he wanted nothing to do with her or the cargo in back.

They arrived at the farmhouse late in the afternoon. Darkness had settled in, the kind you got when the clouds were low and black, a fine mist coming down. Trees and brush obscured the house from the road. It was difficult to see. An old iron gate protected the entrance with a rusted link chain secured by a new lock that went through the bar and an eyelet bolt. Pieter found the key hidden at the top of the post. He retrieved it, dealt with the lock, and drove through. A narrow road of quarried stone set in short grass brought them to a traditional country home. Next to the house was a large barn. The double doors slid open, and a short, stocky man in his 70s waved to them to drive directly inside. Pieter pulled in, switched off the engine, and shouted to the farmer, "Maurice, let's make fast work of this."

He wanted to be rid of his charges and back on the road, hopefully pulling into Brussels and unloading before it got too late. He and Maurice immediately set about removing the boxes and sacks off the compartment the brothers were hiding in. As the two were uncovered, the stench of machine oil, sweat, rotten fruit, petrol, and urine came billowing out. The smell was enough to make Maurice's head jerk back. Slowly the two climbed out. Raymond thanked his host and shook his hand. Eddie gave only a glare before jumping off the truck and lighting a cigarette. The old farmer scolded him to be careful, lots of loose hay lying around. "You'll need to smoke outside," he said, "and only during the day." The brothers stretched their tired limbs while Febe tried to keep a distance from the odor.

Quickly Maurice helped Pieter reload the truck, adding his goods for the market, and reopened the barn doors and guided the vehicle out. The mist was now turning to heavy rain. Maurice walked over the driver's side, as Pieter lowered his window, and called out for him to be careful on the trip back.

There was a nod from Pieter, and then a final admonishment, "Be wary of those two boys, my friend, they are bad news." Maurice acknowledged his warning with a wave and then turned back toward the barn, the rain soaking into his wool coat.

Maurice Staelens and his wife Dora had sheltered people since the beginning of the occupation. Like everything with the Underground, they never knew from one moment to another their next assignment. It was occasional and always at the last moment. Their only child, Suzette, had married Oren, a Jewish professor at Louvain University. Within weeks of the May 1940 defeat, he lost his job and was banned from teaching and publishing altogether. Finding simple work to support him and his family became impossible. Rumors of what was happening to Jews in Poland and Czechoslovakia convinced Oren to escape Belgium. With the help of friends, they devised an escape plan. At considerable expense and danger, they chose to journey overland to Portugal and then on to England. From England, they moved on to Canada to live in French-speaking Montreal. When the Staelens were lucky, they received mail from the New World. The letters were always the same: *Please come to Canada.* But no matter how much they missed their daughter, the idea to leave this farm would never enter into their minds. For them, it was better to defeat the Germans and have Suzette return to them.

Maurice entered the barn and looked at the three beaten souls in front of him. "Mademoiselle will stay in the house with my wife and me. You two," looking at the brothers, "unfortunately, will have to stay out here. We have blankets, and the hay doesn't make a bad bed, we will make you as comfortable as possible. My wife is preparing dinner." He looked the two up and down and proceeded, "I will ask her to heat water so you can bathe." They both got the idea this was more of an order than a request.

He led them through the dark side yard, rain pelting them, to the kitchen door. They entered a large stone room with a table in the middle and a stove and massive fireplace in the corner. Madam Staelens had already hung two large pots of water over the open fire. The smell of freshly-baked bread overpowered the three travelers.

Madame Staelens remarkably resembled Monsieur Staelens. Both were short and stocky, with ruddy complexions, their greying hair cropped close to the head. She nodded to the three, her only sign of greeting. Their dog that had been curled up by the stove leaped into action, first growling at the group and then moving over to Febe for a pat. He conspicuously wanted nothing to do with the two brothers.

Maurice motioned to the brothers to grab the pots of water and led them off to the bath, while Madame Staelens entertained Febe with a cup of tea. "I'm sorry, dear, but I only have this horrible black tea." Febe's eyes were not on the drink, but the freshly sliced bread that was about to be put on the table. She couldn't remember when she last ate; certainly not today or even the previous evening. The dog, believing there might be crumbs falling, moved closer to the table only to be met with a stern call of his name from Madame Staelens. "Flea, get back to your bed," which he immediately returned to by the stove.

"Your dog listens well."

"Oh, we have had him for years; my husband found him out in the woods, wandering around covered in mud. We thought that he was a giant wood rat until we washed him and realized we had a puppy and not a rodent. He is very protective, but he likes you."

Febe sipped at the strong black tea and tried not to eat the bread in one bite. Madame Staelens returned to the large pot on the stove. "Whatever you are cooking smells wonderful," Febe called out.

"Stew, with vegetables and a little meat, but it will fill you up."

There was a long silence as Madame Staelens went about her work. "It is very kind that you let us stay, Madame," Febe called out at last.

"Not at all, we try to be helpful." Madam Staelens replied as she filled a pitcher with wine from a small barrel in the corner of the room. "English airman, wanted members of the Resistance, Jews fleeing. They stay for a while, and then we have no knowledge of where they go or what ever happened to them. That is the hard part."

Maurice reentered the room holding the brothers' clothes at arm's length. "We need to find them something to wear," he announced.

"In the attic there's some clothing that Oren left behind,

It will probably be big on them but better than too small."

Maurice nodded and made for the attic. Madame Staelens returned to her cooking. Febe looked out at the torrential rain beating against the window. In the other room, Raymond and Eddie whispered to each other.

"Everyone treats us like shit," said Eddie. "What will become of us if the British double-cross us?"

"They wouldn't do that," Raymond protested.

"They think we fucked up," Eddie shot back. "Hell, they might even do the Germans a favor and shoot us themselves. We should make a run for it."

"To where, Eddie? Every Kraut has our description and probably our picture."

"Maybe we can make a deal with them."

"You mean right after they shoot us for killing two Germans?"

"We know stuff."

"Not enough to save ourselves, and if they didn't kill us, the MBN would." They fell silent sitting in the darkness, naked, waiting for Maurice to bring them something to wear, and perhaps some hope.

CHAPTER 11

Valentin gave thought to his talk with Pieter as he walked this rainy morning to meet with Gie Desmit. Last night he had made his way back to Brussels before curfew, passing on to Desmit that Febe and the brothers had arrived at the farm and were waiting for orders. "Those boys," Pieter had said, "they are no good." The sooner they are out of the country, the better for everyone." He didn't need Pieter to tell him about the DeBaets; everyone's life was in danger. The German dragnet expanded daily, and it was only a matter of time before they came looking in Brussels.

He entered the Café Drie and shook the wintry rain off his overcoat. The dim light outside mirrored the equally poorly lit interior of the Café. It took a moment for his eyes to adjust. He forced a smile as the maître d' greeted him with a handshake. Valentin announced, that "Monsieur Desmit will be joining me today." There was a nod of acknowledgment before being seated in the back at Gie's favorite table. On this cold and wet morning, the Café Drie was a warm place to be.

Wehrmacht and SS officers often frequented the Café, so it never lacked for heat or any of the other necessities that most businesses under the occupation did without. The aroma of freshly baked pastries and coffee floated through the air. Valentin preferred to meet elsewhere, but Gie took a strange enjoyment planning an operation a few tables away from the German officer corps. Three brothers owned and operated the Café Drie; it had been a fixture in Brussels for years. Their father, a Dutchman, purchased it in the 1920s and named it Drie to celebrate his three sons. After the father died, they made improvements, changed the menu to attract a more affluent crowd, and started counting their money. Since the occupation, the business couldn't have been better. They were astute at cozying up to their new masters, staging stag dinners for the officers, catering events, and entertaining people that most Belgians avoided. Someday, the Germans would be gone, and there would be a reckoning for these three brothers. But today Valentin was only concerned about the DeBaets waiting for a plane to England. And the café-well, it served Gie's odd, ironic, stratagems.

The maître d' was Brother Louis. He was always impeccably dressed, white laundered and starched long sleeve shirt, three-piece black chalk striped suit carefully pressed. He considered himself a lady's man with his slicked-back black hair and a pencil-thin mustache. He returned Valentin's handshake with one that was weak and indifferent; unlike the slaps on the back he offered his new German friends. Valentin had particular contempt for Louis since he knew from the Resistance that he and his mistress were frequent guests of General Beck and his mistress, the lovely Elise. Rumors circulated that drinking often led to the exchange of partners.

It was too early for much of a crowd at the café. The pricey coffee and Reich customers were too costly for the average citizen, which contributed to a select clientele who minded their own business most of the time. Ultimately in Brussels, no one knew who was a friend, or an informer, or a patriot. The Germans were smart enough to understand that every man had a price for collaboration, whether it was voluntary or not. They thought nothing of offering money or sex, and they almost always got their way. The winter was too cold and life too hard for people not to succumb to the enticements. When the soft touch didn't work, there were threats of torture or family members disappearing.

Valentin settled into his seat and waited. Gie Desmit always requested this table. de Vos thought it too close to the kitchen, with noise from the servers making it difficult to hear the conversation. Of course, that is precisely the reason Gie preferred it.

"If you can't hear me, how are the Germans going to?" was his reasoning.

Gie also liked this table because it offered a full view of the dining room, no surprises. "When they come for me, I want to make sure I can take a few of them with me" was his constant reminder to everyone that he would not go willingly, and anyone with him would undoubtedly die. Valentin knew that Gie preferred to believe there were always options. Shots, confusion, an escape out the kitchen. Live or die; in any case, there would be no heroes.

Valentin reached into his pocket for his cigarettes, pulling out one of his cherished Gauloises. He was just about to light it when the waiter approached the table; he had the tired look of a man who worked double shifts. His freshly starched white shirt was in contrast to the dark circles that highlighted sad eyes. He gave a slight upward nod of the head, indicating that he was ready to take the order.

What to order? This was the part that Valentin liked best, as he knew that Gie would pay. The waiter hardly looked at him as he ordered a pot of their best Brazilian coffee, rolls, and a glass of beer-champagne. The waiter gave a twitch of his head as his acknowledgment, then dipped into his pocket, pulling out a lighter and igniting Valentin's cigarette before setting off for the kitchen.

As Valentin waited for his coffee, two German officers came in, chatting together and oblivious to Café customers. He could see their staff car double-parked and idling outside

THE KÖLN EPISODE

the front door. The wait for Gie seemed intolerable: no newspaper to hide behind, and a room full of Nazis, but the suffering was short-lived. Gie casually strolled in, dressed impeccably in a three-piece brown tweed suit. He received a warm handshake from Louis (much more cordial and enthusiastic than one given Valentin), who relieved him of his topcoat and umbrella. As he passed the officers' table, there was a brief stop, a chat, some laughter, and then having spotted Valentin, a friendly parting and on to his booth.

"That damn Colonel had me build him a bed and has yet to pay, he keeps telling me he is awaiting funds from home, bastard!" he exclaimed, all the while keeping a smile on his face. Valentin had already swapped seats with Desmit as he knew that he never took a chair with his back to the action. He watched as Gie did a quick survey of the layout before setting down.

There was small talk between them as their order was delivered. The server, familiar with these men, instinctively placed the Champagne in front of Gie, who then withdrew the traditional morning cigar from his breast pocket. Slowly he rolled it in his hand. Pulling a clipper from his vest pocket, he cut the end, then struck a match and invited the flame to ignite the cigar. A sip of the Champagne, a drag of the cigar--these were pleasures that Gie enjoyed, and, he was not interested in talking until they had taken their desired effect. Valentin savored the coffee, only made better by his second Gauloises. The traffic in the Café began to pick up, and activity around the kitchen made conversations challenging to hear.

After a few minutes, Gie asked his first question. "What news from the countryside? I heard a farmer was outstanding in his field."

Valentin ignored Gie's humor, an ironic comment on a city man's wry disinterest in the rural life, cynically coupled with reality—the Germans had taken most of the crops and animals for the Reich. Valentin leaned into Gie, almost whispering into his ear, that he had contacted Pieter the previous evening. Without missing a beat, Gie laughed out loud and shouted: "You don't say, tell me more about the scoundrel!"

Gie then sat quietly, listening to the update while watching his smoke rings rise through the air. He waited as a couple of businessmen were seated at the next table and then leaned over to Valentin. "You know the British don't want them back. They say our boys voided the agreement. The mission was a disaster because of their incompetence, and the situation in Belgium is worse for their agents. The Gestapo is arresting everyone."

"The Brits can't renege," was all Valentin could utter before Gie cut him off.

"Oh, believe me, this kind of talk from them doesn't surprise me. The English believe every mission must be a success; they have no idea how lucky we are to accomplish anything." He paused a moment to select the right words to express himself. "I told them if they ever hope to recruit another agent from Belgium, they need to make good on getting the DeBaets out of the country. They weren't happy, but they've got a Hawthorne warming up."

Gie sketched out the plan for escape. The RAF would do an air extraction the day after tomorrow. In the early hours a plane would land if weather permitted. It would be Valentin's responsibility to move the DeBaets to an open field a few kilometers from the Staelens' farm. They had used the site just two weeks before to grab two Brit airmen. Same pilot, same crew; they knew the area and the risks.

Desmit always impressed Valentin, the way he did the job. Everything was in order and motion. Gie already decided to have Pieter's truck go back on his route, and two members of the Resistance enlisted to help. The two would accompany Valentin and assist with the handoff. "Get them on the plane and then get the hell back," commanded Gie.

"And the woman?"

Gie finished off the last of his champagne, turning the glass upside down. Rubbing his chin, and with a smile he leaned into Valentin, "Ah, the lovely Febe, bring her back, of course." Pushing away from the table, he fetched a wad of francs from his pocket, leaving more than enough to cover the bill. He started to go, then stopped. "There's ice in that woman's blood, Valentin. I need her that way. Don't try to thaw her."

The idea of thawing Febe had long been on his mind. He watched while Gie made his way out, waving to Louis and then the German officers as he exited. Valentin had no intention of leaving until he had finished off the last of the coffee.

CHAPTER 12

The alley was bathed more with shadow than light. The sky had waited until nightfall to unleash a savage rain that was now flowing freely down the old stone pathway, taking with it trash, animal feces, and all the other unimaginable garbage one finds near a port. How easy life would be, thought Major Kohler, if a pure rain would rid him of the trash he encountered daily. The water pelted him, pushed by an invisible force. He pressed himself against a doorway, hoping to keep from getting drenched. The door gave a little; the lock, old and rusted, still held. The water paid no attention to his umbrella or raincoat but made its way to his suit and socks, the sogginess now feeling like stone weights.

Despite his misery, he kept his eyes fixed on the end of the alley, a Walther firmly against his thigh. He hated this section of town around the Brussels-Willebroek canal, the city's link with the Scheldt river, and ultimately the sea. To the north were the big train yards, and in between, warehouses where once imported goods were stored. Now all the buildings were taken over by the army. It was a rundown area with its drunks and whores, its longshoremen who frequent the few bars ready to cut your throat. Kohler knew that it made no difference to them if you were the town fool or a Wehrmacht officer. If there were something for the taking, it would surely disappear. He often thought if the Gestapo wanted to do something useful, they should clean out this area. But it was more fun for them to chase Jews.

Tonight, there was much to be learned as he leaned inside the doorway. In his jacket was an envelope with hundreds of francs. Francs to be given to his informer, that one person who would sell his soul for a few pieces of gold. But he needed this Judas. You could torture a man all day long, and the information he gave you might only confirm what you already knew or believed. But an informer always gave you something you did not know. They smile and act like they are doing you a great favor when in actuality, they don't want the money to stop. These were tough times, and having an influential friend never hurt. But the man Kohler was waiting for was no friend of his. Kohler despised him. He hated him for making him wait in a dark alley on this godforsaken night for information; he despised him because he only told parts of the story, never the whole story. But his informer, like all informers, was scared of being found out. So, a meeting away from the eyes that could report back to the Underground. Kohler believed that his informer played both sides of the fence, and when he wasn't selling the Major information, his secrets found their way to the different Resistance groups.

Kohler played this game but knew that informers were found out in the end. How often did his patrols find a man alone in a ditch with a bullet in the face? No, if the Underground didn't shoot this fool, then the Major would one day: *right after I rip his guts out.* Tonight, the promise was the location where they are printing Verzetan, the Underground newspaper. If correct, by tomorrow night he will have shut it down and arrested the propagandists. The Major was willing to take this gamble and, with any luck, would soon say adieu to the Low Countries. Yes, shutting down the printing press would be Kohler's ticket out of this abysmal posting in Belgium. Paris, yes...even in cold and rainy winter, Paris shone brightly in Kohler's ambitions.

So, he waited in the dark and the rain. As a gust of wind turned his umbrella inside out, he silently cursed that his canary should come soon or else. For the information he hoped to receive tonight, he was willing to put up with these inconveniences. He cursed again as he adjusted the collar of his worn coat and pulled his battered hat more snuggly to his head. He leaned harder against the doorway but found no relief from the elements. He could only look down with hopelessness as his shoes filled with water.

A noise at the entrance of the alley caught Kohler's attention. Through the rain and low light, he could make out a solitary person clinging close to the building. A clownish figure fighting with his umbrella, which had given up all life. It was turned inside out and ripped by the ferocity of the storm. The man cast the umbrella aside and went running after his hat, which had flown off his head. Running might not be the word as he moved like the overweight middle-aged man he was, slowly, and struggled to pick up his fedora that had found a home in a puddle of water. Kohler watched in amusement as the fool moved back against the building, putting his back flat against it. Like a reptile, he clung to the wall, sidestepping the length of the alley. When he reached midway, he stopped and looked into the blackness where Kohler was waiting. The moment of truth: if this is to be a trap, this is when it will be sprung. The Major released the safety off his gun and emerged from the doorway. A faint slice of light struck him, and he became visible. It seemed an eternity to him, but his guest spotted him and moved in his direction. Kohler stepped back quickly into the shadows.

The man approached, breathing heavily and wiping his glasses with a wet handkerchief in a futile attempt to clear them. He put them back, but they were covered with water immediately.

The Major addressed him coldly, "Could you not find a more sinister location for a meeting?

The man answered, "This city is a sieve of informers. We both have our reasons for being discreet. That much we have in common."

Kohler looked at this man with death in his eyes as he said, "We have nothing in common."

"As you say, Herr Major."

"As I say, Herr Legrand."

Kohler had done business with this Frenchman before. A wine merchant who cozied up to the German officer corps and the Underground. Playing each against themselves, feeding one expensive wine, and the other information. Tonight he had offered information that would be enough to get the Major noticed. Something that he, not General Beck, would receive recognition for. How often had he discovered a downed airman or a hiding Jew, and Beck would take the credit and rewards? No, not this time.

"The information you have for me better be worth a wait in the rain," warned the Major as both crowded into the doorway to find a little relief from the deluge. The conspirator's words could not be heard over the racket of the storm, both men speaking loudly to make themselves audible.

"Herr Major, before we proceed, I believe the information I have is worth your inconvenience. I also believe it worth more than we originally spoke about."

Kohler tightened his grip on the automatic.

"I must amend the agreement and ask for double now."

Kohler slipped his finger through the trigger guard and let it rest on the trigger.

"We had a deal, Legrand."

Even in the low light, Legrand was able to catch a glimpse of the Walther. Trying to get saliva into his mouth, he blurted out, "I know, but I can give you something more important than just the newspaper."

What could be more than the newspaper? Of all the illegal papers printed, this one would not go away, and its information seemed to be straight from the German files. No, what could be more important than the newspaper? Kohler put the pistol in his coat pocket and grabbed Legrand by the tie, pulling him within inches of his face. Close enough to smell the sour breath of old wine and cigarettes. "Do not fuck with me, little man, or I will kill you here with my own hands and let the dogs feast on you."

"Herr Major, please" – Kohler could see, even with the cold and rain, that Legrand was sweating.

"What is it you have that can be more important than where they print their trash?"

"I can tell you where the saboteurs are hiding."

"The saboteurs?" he replied, not understanding Legrand's answer

Legrand yelled into Kohler's ear, "The two brothers that tried to blow up the plant in Köln and killed the sentry and the conductor."

Kohler's mind exploded with anticipation, and he looked at Legrand in disbelief. *Could this be happening? The opportunity to put an end to the newspaper and to capture the spies?* But he caught himself quickly. "How did you come by this information?"

"Major, I cannot give you my source, but I can assure you it is what I say it is. Have I ever been wrong? Did I not lead you to the British pilot? Or the Jew Steinberg and his family trying to flee? Haven't I always been right? Have you not always been successful with my information?"

Pilots and escaping Jews were not novelties anymore; more and more citizens were betraying their neighbors for a few pieces of gold. Only Luftwaffe intelligence cared about the airman, and fanatical Nazis worried about the Jews. No, he would not find his way back to Paris—or perhaps merely Berlin--bringing in wounded airmen and scared Jews. But the whereabouts of the newspaper had eluded the best of them since they occupied Belgium, and no one in the high command believed the saboteurs were anywhere near Brussels. To take them both in one evening would indeed be a prize.

Kohler looked at Legrand for a long minute and finally answered, "Agreed."

Legrand began to tell Kohler about the Tailor shop in Vilvoorde. To the Major's frustration, it was too wet to write anything down. He didn't dare take his black notebook out of his jacket pocket for fear that it would become soaked and lose all the secrets he kept there. Kohler surveyed the area, nothing but padlocked doors. The entrance behind him showed promise. He pushed Legrand aside and gave it a shove. It moved a little. He gave a kick and then another; finally, the door tore away from the lock. He felt for the light switch, but nothing came on when he turned it. They stepped into a dark room with Kohler immediately pulling his lighter out and striking it. Little was visible. The Major made out a workman's bench with a lamp on top of it. He found another switch, flicked it and a very dim light appeared.

"Close that damn door now!" he screamed at Legrand. The pudgy Frenchman did as ordered.

They had entered in some sort of workroom, windowless, cold and stuffy. Empty crates cluttered the area; a crowbar lay on the floor. The containers had Wehrmacht markings, the same as the ones used for shipping field rations. Kohler suspected these never made it to the military but instead found their way to the black market. As his eyes adjusted to the low light, he could see that dust and cobwebs were the room's only décor. Two doors led out of the room. He assumed that one went to the front and the other to a warehouse. The Major turned to the greasy workbench littered with trash, and using the back of his hand, swept all to the floor. He looked around for something to write on and spotted an old calendar hanging on the wall. It was from 1939; a faded tulip adorned the month of May. Walking to the wall to remove it, he could feel his feet slide from the water inside his shoes. The room was chilly, and now out of the rain, he realized how wet and cold he was. He ripped the calendar off the wall and laid it on the table.

Looking across at Legrand, he ordered him to proceed. Drawing a map on the back of the calendar, Legrand gave him directions to a tailor shop that housed the printing press. Most importantly, he gave a name: Michel Verhoeven. "The operation is set up in the basement of the shop. My sources tell me Verhoeven is down there by himself most of the time," Legrand added.

"And his accomplice?"

"That information I was not able to obtain, Herr Major."

Kohler pulled a pack of Gitanes out of his jacket. Carefully picking a cigarette out and then lighting it with a silver lighter, he gave Legrand a long hard stare. It was the boss he wanted, not the hired help. However, the printer and the press would be an excellent start. He would extract the name of the mastermind from whoever was captured, and save himself a few Francs from dealing with this slime again. "And the saboteurs?"

Legrand reached into his inside jacket pocket.

Kohler looked up in alarm. His hand dipped into the pocket that held the Walther, "Slowly!" he barked.

"Monsieur," replied Legrand, "slowly is the only way I know how to move." He cautiously removed a folded sheet of paper. "They are in a village a few kilometers from Vlezenbeek. I have no address, but I was able to obtain this map. They are staying at the farm of a man named Maurice Staelens."

Kohler wrote the farmer's name down and then studied the map. The location was familiar to him. It was from this area that the restaurants in Brussels received much of their produce. Less than three weeks ago, he had conducted a sweep of the villages and found nothing out of the ordinary. But now he knew precisely where to look.

"How long have they been there?"

The fat Belgian paused, then slowly gave up, "A day or two, at most."

Kohler pressed, "And how long will they stay?"

Legrand felt more confident. "That I do not know, but it is the usual procedure not to leave anyone in one place for long."

Kohler nodded his head, collected the maps, and put them in his coat pocket. He put out his cigarette and was about to turn off the lamp when Legrand cleared his throat.

"The payment, Herr Major."

Kohler pulled a heavy brown envelope out of his jacket and laid it on the table; he then produced his wallet and counted out more francs. "Herr Legrand, I do not need to tell you the consequences if this information is not as you told me." With that, he switched the lamp off and opened the alley door, allowing Legrand to leave first. He watched as the fat man waddled down the alley, before stepping out himself and disappearing into the night.

CHAPTER 13

Michel Verhoeven stood with his hands on his hips, surveying his little basement kingdom. *What a mess, he thought, what a fucking mess!* Yesterday, after a long day of setting up press type, and before he could he eat or rest, the rains came. The storm was so violent that the water made its way to the basement and overtook the meager sump pump. For hours Michel used the tailor's hand pump to flush the water out into the alley. It felt to him that for every liter of water that went out, two more came rushing down the stairs. At his weakest, he almost gave up and thought about abandoning the basement. More bad weather was coming, but he knew he couldn't quit. After all the pain, suffering, and deaths to get the word to the people, he couldn't let the elements do him in. He cursed the lowland winter weather and the Nazis and continued. Eventually, the rain let up, and by 5:30 in the morning, he was able to pump the last of the water out. It took him another 3 hours to clean up the place; he was dead exhausted.

Michel climbed the stairs and made his way to the alley to have a smoke. The clouds were breaking up, and a dull sun even tried to show through the stone-grey sky. It was cold, frigid, and the wet clothes he wore chilled him to the bone. He was startled when Frans, the tailor, put his hand on his shoulder. He spun around, instinctively reaching for the pistol tucked in his belt.

"You look horrible," Frans told him in a flat voice.

"I feel worse than I look," Michel shot back.

"Listen, I took a look downstairs. It will take hours for your place to air out," Frans said, giving a casual wave in the direction of the basement. "It's not a good idea having you just lingering around. My apartment is across the street. Wash up, put on some clean clothes, have a little food, and the world will look much better to you."

Michel was too tired to think, but he knew that he needed to bathe before seeing Valentin, and some food wouldn't hurt. Nodding his approval, he collected a change of clothes and followed Frans. They hurried across the street as fast as Michel's lame leg would allow. They moved past the chestnut vendor roasting his goods, the aroma reminding Michel just how hungry he was, and entered a building lobby that had seen better days. The walls were bare, with visible outlines of where pictures once hung, the nails still there. A worn couch sat to the right, one cushion gone. The standing ashtrays on each side were overflowing with cigarette butts. To the left was a thick oak counter that the owner of the building, a Madame Nelissen, once stood behind, dispensing mail, reminding tenants that their rent was due, and generally involving herself in everyone else's business. That all changed when France declared war on Germany. Her husband, a Jew from Portugal, came to Belgium after the Great War and made money in buying old buildings and turning them into tenements. He decided it was time to return home to Lisbon. He saw what the German war machine did to Poland and had no doubt that Belgium, in spite of its neutrality, would suffer the same fate as the last war. During the phony war, when neither France nor England wanted to fight Germany, he liquidated his holdings and left just days ahead of the Panzers. The current owner cared little about human suffering and more about the rent.

They climbed three flights of stairs to the tailor's apartment, the cold making Michel's leg hurt more than usual as he took each step. Frans's wife, Alice, was still in her nightgown when they came through the door. Surprised, she pulled her robe tight around her and smoothed her hair with her hand. A pleasant-looking woman in her mid-forties, with red hair and very pale skin, Michel had seen her occasionally at the shop and appreciated the way she would flaunt her small waist and big breasts.

Alice's parents were Dutch, and she had a hard accent to her French. She was not unhappy to see Michel; she appreciated any diversion to her dreary life, and she had always had a sweet eye for him. Often when she was alone looking after the shop, she wanted to make her way to the basement and see what was going on. But Frans forbade her to visit Michel. "Never go down there," he had told her, "the less you know, the better."

"Michel has had a hard time of it with the storm," Frans explained, "and I told him that he could clean up here."

She motioned for him to have a seat at the table. "It looks like you spent the whole night in the rain." Her smile was the first pleasant thing he had seen in days. "I hope Frans didn't promise you a hot bath?" They had not known hot water in the building for at least a year. When they were lucky, the gas would work, and they would warm enough water to bathe. "Fortunately for you, Monsieur, the gas is on today. A somewhat warm bath, but a bath all the same."

"Please, Madame, don't go to any trouble on my account."

"Nonsense." Alice moved to the sink and filled a large pot with water, then placed it on the stove, using a stick match to light the burner. "It will take a while for the water to warm. Would you like some coffee?" she asked softly.

Michel, not wanting to be a bother, thought of refusing,

but she already had the coffee pot on the last available burner.

"Listen, my friend," Frans bellowed, "Have some coffee and rest a while. It must be damp and depressing in that basement. What would we do if our only tenant came down with pneumonia? I'll be back for lunch, Alice."

Michel couldn't figure Frans' politics. Was he a true believer in the Resistance, or did he simply enjoy the extra money he received from the Underground for the use of his basement? He knew it concerned Frans to have the printing press on the premises; he always looked uncomfortable when Michel was in the building and would encourage him to get out as much as possible. At first, Michel was suspicious of Frans and didn't trust him, but then he realized that the tailor was under the illusion that if the Germans came and they didn't find him there, there would be no repercussions.

Frans had chosen not to give thought to the persuasive powers of the Gestapo. He knew, just as Michel did, that nothing was a secret in Brussels for long and that their time would come. For Michel the Germans weren't that smart, so it troubled him to learn of the betrayal of his comrades for a bag of coins by friends or neighbors. He considered himself lucky to escape the last time and was determined to stay ahead of the Gestapo. Plans were already in motion to move the operation after the next paper was published

Michel sat at the table and sipped the pale brown water that passed as coffee. Alice had moved into the bedroom, leaving him to smoke and relax. He took a drag of his cigarette, and it had no taste; the smoke burned the back of his throat. Michel rubbed his tired face. Exhausted, with bones aching, he quickly fell asleep sitting in the chair.

It could not have been more than a few minutes later when Alice came into the room and nudged him awake. "The water is warm, Monsieur," she announced, feeling guilty for waking a man who was in such need of sleep. "Can you help me with the pot?"

Michel took the towels that Alice handed him and wrapped them around the pot's handles, then followed her into the bathroom. It was a small room with the tub occupying most of the space. The floor had seen better days. In its black and white art deco design, many of the tiles were broken. On the back wall, there was a small window that looked out to an air shaft. Alice had filled the tub a quarter of the way with cold water and now had him pour the hot water. "I'll warm up some more water."

He lowered himself into the lukewarm water and used a bar of lye soap and a scrubbing brush to take away the night's filth. The water felt good after the frigid night. He lay there covered with soap and daydreaming, his head hanging over the back of the bathtub. What he wouldn't give to spend 5 minutes in a steaming bath, to let the hot water run until he could no longer stand it. The door to the bathroom opened, and Alice brought in a new pot of warm water. She poured the water over him and washed the soap away. Clearing the soap from his eyes, Michel noticed that her bathrobe had given way to a loose nightgown. She sat on the edge of the tub, lit a cigarette, and as she leaned over to put it in his mouth, he could see her hard brown nipples. Slowly she traced the scars he had on his chest with her index finger, following a line down his stomach and into the water.

....

Just a few blocks away two grey staff cars were racing through the streets of Brussels on their way to Vilvoorde. In two years of occupation, a vehicle with armed soldiers inside was not an uncommon sight. Unfortunately, everyone who lived in the city knew that nothing good would come for some poor unsuspecting person on the other end of their visit.

Everyone knew what became of those visits: torture, concentration camps, death. Most people would look away and say a prayer. It was always the same prayer: please, God, don't let them be taken alive.

But alive is just how Major Kohler planned to take the occupants of the tailor shop. He hoped to be upon them before anyone in the neighborhood could sound the alarm. Kohler's goal was to bring them back to the barracks and persuade them one by one to give up all their secrets. He knew their routine: first a show of defiance, a refusal to talk, maybe even spitting in his face. All for nothing, for after hours of sitting in a bathtub of ice water, then being strung up and beaten, and finally getting electrodes to the testicles, they always broke. Kohler knew that once they started talking, they wouldn't stop, for fear the torture would begin again. He expected to make short work of the printing press before moving on to the countryside and the saboteurs. Nervously he loaded and unloaded the clip to his service Luger.

....

Michel turned and looked at Alice one last time. She lay spread out on the bed, a cigarette in her hand, her hair disheveled, naked and unashamed. She seemed exhausted when she whispered to him in almost despair, "I'll see you again?"

He wanted to say no, that once was enough. He didn't want to worry about the Germans and now a crazy husband. Instead, he smiled and nodded. It had been so long since he had been with a woman, so long since he had felt that sort of warmth.

Michel moved down the darkened stairway and past the lobby, emerging to a blast of cold air. The chill made his eyes water. He was happy to be clean. The crispness of a new shirt against a clean body and the scent of Alice still in his nostrils gave him energy as he moved across the street and back to the tailor shop. Frans was with a customer when he entered--Madame Troye, whose husband was a conductor on the trolleys. She was shaking her head and trying to get Frans to explain how with all the rationing and shortages, her husband could still put on weight. Michel smiled when Frans suggested that it wasn't the food but probably the beer that everyone in Brussels had taken to brewing. He assured her that there was still room to let the coat and pants out just a little bit to accommodate the extra kilos.

Michel waited for Madame Troye to leave before telling Frans that he would be gone the rest of the afternoon. He felt obliged to thank him for the use of the apartment but felt like a scoundrel, knowing that it probably wasn't meant to include use of the wife. He continued to the basement to collect his case before going off to receive the money from Valentin.

In the apartment, Alice sat at the window looking on to the street. She thought about Michel, and the excitement of making love to him in the same bed she shared with her husband. She sat there dreaming about her next rendezvous with him when she saw two gray military vehicles approaching at high speed. One turned toward the alley as the other pulled up in front of the tailor shop and stopped suddenly. Six Germans soldiers exited and with their weapons drawn approached the shop.

Michel looked at his watch; he still had a few hours before he was to meet with Valentin. It would take that long to arrive at the park. There would be no direct route for him. One never knew if someone was following. The trip to town would include changing buses and disappearing into crowds. He looked forward to publishing the latest edition of the paper. There was also a new development to tell Valentin. Yesterday evening Michel had received word that a group of students who were unhappy with the disruption of their education by the Nazis had volunteered to distribute the newspapers to factories in the area. *Better than dropping them from an airplane*, he chuckled to himself.

Michel took a last look around the basement. The large room was still damp and smelled musky from the flooding. He accepted that there was not much he could do about the situation. A couple more days and he would be looking for a new place to work. He looked over at the printing press, sighing at the thought of moving it once again. He headed upstairs, grabbing his battered attaché case, a reminder of better days when the leather was fresh and the locks still worked.

Michel went to ask Frans to lock the back door after he left. He felt it more comfortable exiting through the alley than the front. In the main room, Frans' back was to the entrance and he could not see the German staff car that pulled up, driving over the curb. Michel hesitated for a second; soldiers were exiting the vehicle, weapons drawn.

"Frans, out the back door, now!" he yelled.

The command confused Frans. As the first German approached the front door, Michel pulled his Ceska Zbrojovka and fired, shattering the glass and killing the intruder. A hail of automatic gunfire erupted from outside. "Out the back quickly," he yelled again while jamming another clip into his automatic. The attackers now took positions behind the cars and poured fire into the room.

Frans moved to the back of the shop, but the Germans were already in the alley trying to break down the door. The firing stopped. Major Kohler called to them that there was no way out of the shop. "Surrender and you will not die."

Michel knew what waited for him if he gave himself up. They would extract the names of everyone he had worked with before they let him die. There was nothing left to do but to carry out his escape plan. Crawling, he made his way to the back of the shop. "Keep down and don't try to be brave," he yelled to the tailor before descending the stairs and locking the door that led to his studio. Frans hugged the ground and had no intention of being brave.

Major Kohler and his men cautiously entered the building, moving from the front salon, to the sewing room, and then the back-storage area. In the rear, they found Frans like some ostrich hiding his head in the floor. Kohler lifted him by the collar and pointed the Luger at his head. "Where is he? Tell me now!" The tailor had never been so scared in his life; nodded towards the heavy iron door. "Get the torch," Kohler ordered, "we'll cut the hinges."

Michel could hear soldiers moving from room to room. Frans cried that he was unarmed and that he had been forced by the Underground to cooperate. There was a call for the acetylene touch. He knew that they would make quick work of the door. He had gone over many times in his mind the exit plan, and now he went into action. He pried open the 20-liter barrel of paint thinner used for cleaning the printing press. From under his bed he took out the two grenades that he had kept for this very day.

....

Alice looked on in shock at the chaos unfolding in the street. After the staff car arrived, she watched as someone from inside the shop shot one of the soldiers; then the barrage of gunfire from the Germans in the street. No one could have survived that. The shooting stopped, and she watched as the soldiers entered the shop and then came out with Frans. They held a gun to his head, and he was crying like a baby when they placed him in the staff car. A man who she took to be in charge stood on the sidewalk smoking a cigarette. A few minutes later, another truck arrived, and welder and his equipment entered the building.

She looked on as shop keepers shuttered their stores, and residents tried to steal a peek from behind closed curtains, too scared to venture out. The chestnut vender had moved away. She grabbed her suitcase and packed what few essentials she needed, working hard to overcome the fear she felt. Then there was more activity outside. The troops were readying their weapons, and then stormed into the building. A minute later there was a massive explosion. She watched as injured men staggered out of the tailor shop, some helping wounded comrades. Even from her vantage point, she could see the anger on the officer's face. He slapped his leg in disgust, then got in the car that was holding Frans and drove off. Alice knew that Michel was gone, and Frans would soon be spilling his guts. She picked up her suitcase and hurried out the back of the building.

CHAPTER 14

Valentin arrived at the Parc du Cinquantenaire a few minutes before the agreed time. Only a few people were strolling the grounds, a surprise considering the rain clouds had moved on. A mother pushed a carriage, the child asleep; an elderly man slowly shuffled along, cane in hand. Otherwise, the park was empty, the days of picnics and family outings, gone; children running with kites, a bottle of wine shared with friends also gone.

Valentin took a bench that gave him a view of the Triple Arch. On beautiful spring days, he and Elise use to walk hand in hand for hours through the park, imagining the future. It was in this park that they decided to travel to Greece. He smiled when he thought how Elise's eyes used to roll when he talked about how King Leopold II created the park to celebrate the 50th anniversary of Belgian independence. Now huddled against the cold, he could only think of how that independence and his life with Elise had evaporated. The low winter sun was a respite from yesterday's rain, but it gave him no warmth.

He checked his watch, hoping that Michel might arrive early. After they concluded their business, there was still the drive to the safe house. He knew that meeting Michel was cutting it close, but publishing the paper as soon as possible was essential. It was the only outlet most residents had to read the truth. He could hear Gie yelling, "The mission is the DeBaets, not your damn paper!" Valentin believed the paper helped the cause as much as all the clandestine operations. Unfortunately, publishing was now too dangerous. The Germans were putting effort into finding all the Underground presses. He and Michel had decided that after this edition of the paper, they would take a break. They needed to move out of the tailor's basement, and finding a suitable place would take time.

Valentin read the book he had brought with him, a collection of poetry by Karel Van De Woestijne. Every a few pages, his eyes would glance up to scan for Michel. He tried not to look anxious, but as each minute passed, he worried that something might have gone wrong. He waited the agreed time--30 minutes--and not seeing Michel stood up, stretched, and slowly put his gloves back on while taking time to look around. He slipped the book in his coat pocket and moved toward the traffic circle at Schuman Boulevard. From there, it was a short walk to a bookstore on the Rue Archimede, which was their alternative rendezvous. Valentin stopped in front of the shop but did not go in. He peered through the glass window at the new books on display. What was once a wall of international writers now offered only German authors and mostly Nazi favorites. If there, Michel would be standing by the biographies, wearing a hat to signal that it was safe to enter. But there was no Michel, and a jolt of alarm ran through Valentin. It was not like his friend to miss both contact points; something was wrong. Had Michel been captured? Was this a trap? Valentin turned and started walking down a side street, fearing arrest at any second. Was he being followed? No one appeared, and the road was empty.

He walked a block, then crossed the street and headed to where there was a collection of shops. Passing the stores, he continued around the building to an alley. Valentin knew that If Michel had fallen into the Gestapo hands, they would soon be looking for him. He checked his watch and saw that he was late for the lift to the country. He would get word to Gie to have someone check on the tailor shop and report back.

Valentin hopped a tram heading north, then after two stops switched to one bound for the city center. At the station, he blended in with the travelers, a crowd of humanity, busy getting somewhere. The men's lavatory was the next stop, and then slipping out the luggage holding area door. By now, he was sure that no one was following him. He took a bus to the square where farmers had created a word-of-mouth market. The Germans had issued a restriction on food, particularly what you can sell, mainly so they could be the benefactors of fresh vegetables and fruits. Belgians preferred selling to their own—besides, it paid more. The markets would spring up at different spots in the city and then dissolve into thin air.

The market was nearly empty by the time he arrived. Most of the vendors had sold all their goods and left. It was after 4:00 PM; already, fading light and darkness was fast approaching. Valentin spotted Pieter Moens' truck at the end of one of the buildings.

"You're late," Pieter spit out, then looking up and down at Valentin, he added, "You supposed to be my helper, but you dressed like you're going to church."

"There was no time for me to change," Valentin started to explain but was cut short.

"I don't care, and I can assure you the German won't care when they stand you up against a wall and put a bullet into your stupid fucking brain."

Pieter went to the back of his truck and opened up a box, pulled out an old pair of overalls, and threw them at Valentin. They were dirty and smelled, but Valentin said nothing.

"We need to be out of the city before the curfew, now get

moving!"

Valentin stepped behind the truck and changed into the overalls. Pieter appeared with two young men. "These two belong to you."

My god, Valentin thought, *these are the men Desmit sent to help*? They introduced themselves as Max, a baby faced, chubby boy with curly blond hair; and Sebastian, taller and thinner, with short dark hair. They both claimed to be twenty, but Valentin had his doubts.

Pieter asked, "Do you two know what you are getting yourselves into?"

"Don't worry about us, old man." Max shot back.

Pieter stared at Max, choosing his words carefully. "When we come to the checkpoint, act dumb, that shouldn't be too hard for the two of you. Don't try to be creative. Give simple answers." Turning to Valentin, "I have no fears that the Germans will believe those two are farmers. It is you that worries me. You don't look like you've done a hard day's work in your life."

Valentin rode in the front with Pieter while the boys sat in the truck bed. The inspection station came up sooner than he expected, and it took longer than usual to pass through. Pieter explained to the corporal, a familiar face from his numerous trips, that they were traveling out to the country to collect their goods and returning the next day to deliver them to the markets. Yes, he had more workers than usual but needed them because his back was ailing. The sentry Febe had flirted with inquired where she was. Pieter told him that he hoped to bring her back during tomorrow's run. "Much better company than these stiffs, if you know what I mean," he winked at the guard.

The sentry was lifting the barricade to pass the truck

through when an officer emerged from the command center. He shouted not to raise the barrier and walked over to the vehicle. With a snap of his fingers, he demanded papers. He ordered his men again to search the truck, and this time look under the chassis. He ignored the private who told him that he had already checked their papers. He carefully looked at each document, calling out their name and when they acknowledged, looking at them from head to toe.

Finally, he addressed Pieter. "Herr Moens, you seem to pass through here often."

"I try to make a living, Captain," Pieter replied. "Collecting vegetables from the farmers and bringing them to the Reich markets is my livelihood."

"Tell me, what vegetables do you deliver in the winter?"

"Sir, you are not a farmer, no?"

The Captain straightened up and glared at Pieter. The soldiers nervously unslung their weapons, unsure what to do next. Even more disturbing to Valentin was Max and Sebastian also looking scared. He prayed they wouldn't do anything stupid, like run.

"Broccoli, cabbage, endives, carrots, cauliflower, and of course, our famous sprouts, all winter vegetables," Pieter replied, smiling.

The Captain had had enough; no glory arresting this sorry crew. He threw their unfolded papers back to Pieter. "Move!" was all he said.

The boys jumped into the truck while Pieter walked around to the driver's side, showing no sign that this encounter worried him. There would be two more checkpoints before they reached Vlezenbeek. As they move deeper into the country, there was increased activity on the road. German

Kubelwagens with automatic weapons mounted on them, motorcycles with sidecars, and roving patrols. There was uneasiness between Pieter and Valentin as they could see that security had increased.

"They have set up one more security stop today than there was yesterday," warned Pieter.

"Do you think they know something?"

There was a *who knows?* shrug from Pieter as they headed toward the countryside. But the increased security bothered him. The truck was too conspicuous to be in the area with a group of strangers. Plans had to change. Turning to Valentin, he broke the bad news. "It is too dangerous for me to drive to the landing site. The truck will draw too much interest. You and your group will need to travel cross country. It is not more than a three-kilometer walk from the farm."

"In the open country?"

"Stay off the roads and you'll be alright. The boys know the area and will be able to find the way in the dark. I will come through in the morning and pick you and the girl up."

Valentin reluctantly nodded. He didn't like the idea that those two boys in the back could be the difference between the mission's success or failure. It was almost 8:00 PM when they made Vlezenbeek. When Valentin still had dreams of being a painter, he would come out to this country, Pajottenland, part of Flemish Brabant province. It was mostly farmland, and he would paint along the river Dender. Many a day would end with him at a local pub finishing off a pint of Lambic beer, a draft that was brewed in the town.

Within 30 minutes, they arrived at the Staelens farmhouse. Pieter drove directly into the barn, and Maurice had the door closed and secured before the truck stopped. Raymond, Eddie, and Febe were all waiting. When Valentin exited the cab, Febe was relieved that he was with them. He wanted to touch her face, puts his arms around her, but stopped himself.

Max and Sebastian climbed out of the back of the truck.

"Who are these two?" demanded Raymond.

"They have come to help, plus they know the area," Valentin said.

"They're schoolboys," Eddie moaned, "and why the hell did they get to sit in the back when we had to lie in that coffin for hours?"

"That's what happens when you fuck up your mission, asshole," shot back Max.

Valentin moved between them. "There is no time for this. We must be at the landing site before midnight, and the situation has changed."

All eyes were now on Valentin. He detailed the sizeable German presence they saw on the road. A groan came from the group when he announced they would have to travel on foot. Pieter went to the truck and opened the auxiliary gas tank on its right side. From its opening he pulled out four torches and passed them to Max. Next came two Sten machine guns, which he tossed to Sebastian along with extra clips. "Something new from our Limey friends." His last bag contained two Browning 9 mm pistols which he gave to Valentin and Febe.

"And where are our guns?" demanded Eddie.

"You'll not need one in England," Pieter snapped. "Now, gather around."

He laid out a map of the area and circled the landing site. "No more than three kilometers away. It is an open field with a gently sloping hill. You will set up the torches on the four corners so the plane can spot the landing area. The pilot will land long enough to make the pickup and then depart immediately. If, for any reason, you sense danger do not light the torches. He will return tomorrow night at the same time. Understood?"

Everyone nodded their understanding. Pieter handed the map over to Valentin. "The boys will return to their homes and stay until they are needed again. Sebastian's uncle's farm is less than a kilometer south of the landing site." Pointing to it on the map, then turned to Sebastian. "The cellar in your barn, where we kept the downed pilot a few months back. That's where I want you to hide the weapons. Make sure you cover the opening with hay. I don't want anyone getting nosey."

Looking at Valentin, he instructed, "There is a road to the left of the field. Once you complete the mission, follow it west for a couple of Kilometers. There you will find a stone bridge over a stream; I'll pick you up there at 6:30 AM. If you are not there, I will come the next morning again. May God be with you." With that, he closed the fuel tank and then climbed into the cab. He nodded to Maurice, who doused the light and swung open the door to the barn. They all watched the truck disappear into the blackness.

"OK, Let's move out," snapped Valentin.

CHAPTER 15

Ida Claes was awake in her bed, facing away from her husband, Walter. It was 10:30 at night, but the family had already been asleep since 8:00. The day started early on the farm, with cows to milk, pigs to feed, fields to tend; plus cooking, sewing, and washing. With her husband and five children, it was never-ending.

Tonight, like many nights, she stared into the bedroom darkness and wondered if it would be seven days a week for the rest of her life. The line between survival and the abyss was fragile, but somehow, they managed. They sold to the Germans at the mandated low prices, they sold on the black market at ridiculously high prices, and they produced enough for themselves. She knew that she should be thankful to be away from the city and the dreaded Boche, but after two years of occupation, it was all wearing on her. What was to become of her and the children? The other day she had taken down the giant mirror in the hallway, because walking past it betrayed her. A glance and she saw she was not the young woman she remembered, but someone much older-looking than her 35 years.

She lay in bed with her demons and Walter's snoring. Usually, a nudge to the ribs was enough to shut him up for a while. But then, did she hear footsteps? And voices? Was her mind playing tricks? She sat up in bed, a hand on Walter to wake him, when she heard a crashing sound downstairs.

Major Kohler and his men had arrived at the Claes farm

a short time before. They parked their vehicles down the road and sneaked on foot toward the house. He could see that it was dark inside, and the Major was unsure if the occupants were asleep or maybe they had already departed. He moved cautiously nearer the house, dividing his men into three groups. There was only one order for the men: "Take them alive."

The first group entered the barn, flashlights scanning the area, slowly moving up a ladder to the loft. They found no one. The second team smashed down the back door of the house, entering through the kitchen. The third group came in through the front door, using a battering ram. Had any of them checked, neither door was locked.

The soldiers charged up the staircase. At the top landing, they encountered a night shirted Walter who attempted to ask what was happening. His question was cut short by a rifle butt to the stomach. The men moved through the bedrooms, dragging a screaming Ida and her crying children out and deposited them all in the living room. Kohler had expected a gunfight and was relieved when told the house was secure. His mood turned sour when he saw before him not the saboteurs, but two adults and five children. The woman was doing her best to quiet the weeping amongst her boys and girls.

Kohler walked over to Walter, who was on his knees with a soldier's rifle muzzle firmly against his spine. "The saboteurs, where are they?"

"I don't know any saboteurs, sir," Walter spoke, his voice cracking from fear.

"We know they are here," Kohler screamed, "tell me now, or you will regret your treachery!"

It was Ida who now spoke up. "We don't know what you are talking about; there are only us here, search, look. Do you think I would endanger my children?"

Kohler, unimpressed with her denial, walked over to Ida and slapped her hard enough to knock her off her feet. With one hand he pulled her up by her hair; with the other, he drew his Luger and put it next to her head. Looking at Walter, the Major spit out, "I will not ask again! Tell me, or I will shoot her now."

Walter pleaded with him, "There is no one here except us. What can I do to convince you? On my children's lives, we are alone!"

"What have we found here?" Kohler asked the sergeant who searched the barn.

"Nothing, Major."

Kohler wondered if the wine merchant gave him the wrong information. He looked back down at Walter, "Are you not Maurice Staelens?

"No, I am Walter Claes."

"Your papers," he demanded, holstering his weapon.

"They are upstairs."

"Kriel," he yelled to his sergeant, "take him upstairs and collect his documents."

Kohler looked at his watch; it was getting late. In front of him were five whimpering children and a woman who undoubtedly wanted to scratch his eyes out. Walter returned with his papers, and after reviewing them twice, the Major turned to Sergeant Kriel. "You bloody fool, we are at the wrong farm! Fetch the map, you idiot."

Kohler sent Ida and the children upstairs and then spread out the map on the kitchen table, retracing their journey. He asked Walter to point out where they were, and the farmer obliged him in hopes of getting them out of the house. "My God," shouted Kohler, "we are at least 10 kilometers from our destination." He turned to Walter and asked the fastest way to Maurice's farm. Noting hesitation, he warned the farmer if they did not find the Staelens' home, they would return to take him and his family back to Brussels for interrogation. Walter did the only thing possible and pointed to the quickest route.

There was no apology; Kohler would not think of giving one, nor would Walter expect one. The soldiers piled into their trucks and, with Koehler's vehicle in the lead, took off for their rendezvous with the saboteurs. Ida and the children came downstairs. Walter kissed the bruise where Kohler had slapped her, and she made hot chocolate for the children. He propped the two broken doors up and would repair them in the morning. That night they all prayed that they would never see a German at their farm again. They also said a small prayer for the people Kohler was about to visit.

....

They walked single file through the fields, almost at a half-crouch. Sebastian and Max lead the way, their Sten guns slung over their shoulders; Eddie and Raymond behind them, each carrying the torches to light the landing path; Febe and Valentin bringing up the rear. It was a cold moonlit night, and walking through the fields made the going rough. The rains had made a mess of them, and the trip was taking longer than any of them had thought. Sebastian and Max were exchanging stories of their sexual exploits in these very fields. Each tale was more outlandish than the previous one. Max bragged, he had so many nights of ecstasy that he was unable to count all the times. Sebastian was suggesting that the count probably included a large number of sheep. Eddie, as usual, was complaining; this time about having to trudge through the muddy fields.

Valentin reminded them to keep their voices down, as sound traveled in the countryside. No one seemed to give him any mind until they heard an engine in the distance. Maybe a truck, perhaps a car. It stopped on the outer edge of the field. The group dropped to the ground, weapons at the ready. Someone staggered out of the vehicle and moved to the side of the road to relieve himself. A voice from inside the truck yelled something in German to the person taking a piss. The soldier nodded and buttoned up his trousers. Returning to the Kubelwagen, he fetched a search light and checked the field. Finding nothing, they went on their way. The group lay on the ground long after the truck pulled away and the sound of the engine disappeared. When they did get up, their clothes were damp and muddy, and a light breeze made it feel even colder. No one said a word. They moved forward, now aware of the rustling of leaves or a dog barking. The six of them arrived at the landing site, covered with mud and freezing. They had a half-hour before touch down.

....

Kohler could see how the mistake could have happened. In the dark, it was impossible to get the right bearing on location. Everything looked the same in the country. In the dark, they were searching for a farmhouse back from the road and an old barn adjacent. All the same, like the populace; the Führer should just flatten the Belgians, lay the low country even lower. But Kohler had no intention of absolving Sergeant Kriel. He would deal with that fool after the mission. No, with the disaster at the tailor shop, he was not going to be blamed for this should they fail.

At the farm, Kohler positioned his men for the assault. "Remember," he firmly told his sergeants, "I want them all alive; I will tolerate no failures." As before, one group moved to the barn, with the others entering the house from front and back. The first floor was dark and empty of people when Sergeant Kriel and his squad searched. They moved toward the stairway, where they met the Staelens' dog, Flea. The animal growled and showed them his teeth. Kriel gave him a hard knock with the butt of his rifle and would have shot him if Maurice had not appeared at the top of the stairs to call Flea back.

"What is the meaning of this?" Staelens demanded to know, but he knew the day he feared had finally arrived.

Maurice and his wife were escorted downstairs, pushed along by rifle barrels in their backs. Maurice kept a tight rein on Flea. Kohler was waiting for them. "Are you Maurice Staelens?" he asked, receiving a nod from both of them. "The saboteurs, where did they go? When did they leave?"

Maurice gave a quizzical look and replied, "Sir, there must be some mistake. There are no saboteurs here."

Kohler drew his weapon and walked towards him. Without warning, he shot Flea in the head. The explosion startled everyone, and all eyes were on Kohler. "Let me be clear on this. I will ask you one more time, and if you do not answer me truthfully, I will put a bullet in your wife's left kneecap. If I ask again and you do not answer, I will put a bullet in the other kneecap. Then I will leave her here while my men set fire to this house. You can listen to the screams before we take you to Brussels and let the Gestapo chat with you. You'll talk then, and your wife would have been tortured and killed for nothing. Are those murderers worth your wife's life? So, Herr Staelens, the saboteurs?"

....

As soon as the group arrived at the landing site, Valentin and the two young men surveyed the field to make sure there were no obstacles for the plane. It was uneven ground at a slight incline, but Desmit had told him they had used it before for a landing. Valentin thought it rough, but had to believe that the British knew what they were doing. From what he could see in the moonlight, it looked like it would be a bumpy landing and takeoff. Sebastian and Max set up the torches at the four corners of the field. They were to light them when they heard the aircraft engine. Once it had departed, they were to make their way back to their parents' farms and await further orders.

Valentin walked to a clump of dead trees where Febe and the DeBaets were waiting. Febe was listening for the sound of a plane; the brothers looked anxious. The two sat together. Eddie went to light a cigarette, but Raymond knocked the match out of his hands. "You want the German army to know where we are? Just sit there. We'll be out of here soon."

....

It took no time for Kohler to get the information he needed from the Staelens. While he would have liked to shoot both, there was still information he could coerce from them. Amateurs play a good game until they face the reality of a cold Luger next to their head. Maurice reluctantly went as their guide to the landing site, while his wife went on to Brussels.

Kohler now knew the location and time of the pickup. He planned to capture not only the saboteurs but their accomplices and the British aircrew all in one swoop. How he would enjoy surprising General Beck with the news. But not before he personally called the headquarters of General von Falkenhausen, the military governor of Belgium, to give him the report.

....

Febe and Valentin sat on the cold ground opposite the brothers. She watched as Eddie fidgeted, unable to relax. Raymond, on the other hand, sat very still, lost in his thoughts.

In the short time Febe had been with them, Raymond was the more thoughtful of the two, while Eddie would usually react violently at the slightest provocation. It was that reactivity, she guessed, that caused him to kill the German guard and make their mission a failure. Many in the Underground felt it was a mistake to send the brothers to England after their colossal screwup. But that was not for her to say.

"Are you alright?" Valentin whispered. She smiled back. "It won't be long now."

She hoped not. Her bones were feeling cold, and a light mist was settling upon them. Instinctively she huddled closer to Valentin, and in the moonlight, she saw a smile cross his face. She enjoyed working with him and appreciated that he had not treated her like the other men did. She was aware that the others didn't want to work with or put their lives in the hands of a woman, but not Valentin. Her feelings ran deep for him, but still, she thought, what kind of man risks his life for the cause but tolerates a wife who is a whore for the German General staff?

....

Two military trucks and a Kubelwagen with lights off slowly pulled up to a junction in the road. Maurice Staelens was in the back seat of the staff car, wedged between two soldiers. He felt helpless and disgusted with himself. He was about to betray his brothers in the Resistance, but he had no choice. If it were only him, it would have been a different matter, but not with Dora. He had no illusions of what awaited them in Brussels. But he could not let the Major shoot Dora and leave her to burn to death. He could not live with the screams. He bowed his head but would not let the Germans see him cry.

Kohler told the driver to stop and turning to Maurice, asked, "How far are we from the site?"

"No more than half a kilometer," Maurice replied, praying that maybe the plane had already picked up the boys and the rest had disappeared into the countryside.

Kohler would send Sergeant Kriel and a detachment of twelve men to circle to the rear of the field. Another group would approach from the front. When the plane was committed to landing, he would have the car speed to the field and block its takeoff path. He would have everyone in a tight net. Kohler looked at his men and reminded them, "I want to see live bodies brought back."

....

Max looked across the field and strained to make out Sebastian at the opposite end, a lonely silhouette in the moonlight. They had done this once before, setting directional fires for an RAF plane. To calm himself, he went through the steps, seeing it all in slow motion. The sound of an airplane in the distance. A quick run to ignite the torches. A plane is dropping out of the sky like a bag of rocks, making a bumpy landing. Picking up the passengers without coming to a complete stop. And finally, the whining of the engine and off into the night sky. He had mentioned how fast it all went to Sebastian once, and the only reply he received was, "Yes, almost as fast as you fuck." Smiling, he gripped his gun tighter and listened.

....

Sergeant Kriel moved his squad into position and waited. He knew that the enemy was out there, but in the slight moonlight, it was difficult to know where. The saboteurs would soon have to give themselves away when they signaled the plane. But how many were out here, and what kind of firepower did they have? The day was not going well. The raid of the tailor shop was a disaster. The driver should not have pulled up in front of the window, giving away the element of surprise. Then the wrong turn in the country and storming the wrong house. He knew that he was on Kohler's shit list, but what of it? It was still better than freezing to death on the Eastern Front or dying of some godforsaken disease with Rommel in North Africa.

....

Eddie sat restlessly with his back against a fallen tree, looking forward to escaping this hell. Once he arrived in Britain, he wanted a beer and a cigarette; oh, and one of the English birds that the Germans at the plant spoke about so much. Cold, like fish, that's how they described British women. Once he got to England, he would warm himself up a few. He wanted no more fighting, no more taking orders, and no more of the damn Underground. The members of the Resistance had made it clear to him that he had screwed up by killing the guard at the plant, but none of them were there. He had to act quickly. It was just bad luck, nothing more than that. Bad luck, the story of his life, but now England and a new life.

Raymond watched his brother fidgeting across from him. He hoped a new beginning would help them both out. To leave Belgium would be to let go of many memories. Working in their father's machine shop, the long hours, no pay, and no appreciation. It would mean forgetting the ordeal of the Congo with its heat and the constant threat of death. The nightmare of the German attack and the humiliation of being defeated in 18 days. Worst of all, the indignity of working for the Boche, their maltreatment, their superiority. But now a new life, a new beginning. Raymond was about to check his watch when he heard the distant sound of an engine.

....

Ten Kilometers out, Flight Lieutenant David Turner began to search for the landing zone. The trip across the

Channel in the de Havilland Puss Moth had been a bumpy one. It was tricky. The aircraft struggled, ascending and then descending rapidly. There was much turbulence, and it came without warning. It was nights like these that the Flight Lieutenant longed for something more powerful than his single-engine, with its 130 horsepower and four cylinders. He had been a spotter in Egypt for a year before being reassigned home, and his 3-passenger plane preferred the calm skies of the desert and more straightforward reconnaissance missions.

Turner found flying into the enemy country at night a different matter from the cloudless skies of Egypt and Libya. He had made this trip four times in the last month. The Lieutenant wouldn't say that it had become routine, negotiating the country and finding the target, but was becoming easier. Once over the Channel, he would hew to the countryside, staying clear of main cities; make a right turn at the quarry to the west of Brussels, and then follow the road until he saw the four lights designating the landing field. Landing in the dark, on uneven ground, not knowing if rocks or stumps would appear out of nowhere, was a leap of faith for Turner. But he loved it, telling his mates there was no thrill like it, swooping out of the sky in enemy territory, picking up an always grateful passenger and then returning him home. To celebrate--and they always wanted to celebrate-he kept his flask nearby.

In the distance, a flame was visible, and then another, until all four came into view. From an earlier mission, he knew the general layout of the field: uneven ground at a gentle slope. The signal fires designated the corners of the area, but where he landed was at his discretion. There was a tailwind while coming across the country. Now, he needed to overfly the field and turn back to land against the wind. Landing lights would be turned on at the very last moment to give him a chance with the ground.

....

Sebastian watched as the plane overflew the field and then banked around, coming in low. He wondered what took more guts: facing a Messerschmitt, or landing on this ground in the dark. Also, for a little engine, it made lots of noise out here in the middle of nowhere. Then to his surprise, he heard a vehicle coming down the road. Before he could react, there was a rustling in the bushes behind him. Turning, he thought it was Max but was greeted by a burst from an MP 40, its shells exploding into his heart.

Max unslung his Sten gun and headed toward the gunfire, stopping when he saw a group of soldiers approaching from the south. He let loose a burst and hit the ground. Light arms fire erupted from all over the field.

Valentin had his group keep low as the night lit up with muzzle flashes. Seeing the plane was still on a landing path, there was a chance the brothers could make it to the aircraft when it touched down. Turning to his group, he called out, "Let us move to the middle of the field, stay low, I don't want to draw their fire."

The first that Flight Lieutenant Turner realized there was trouble was when he saw the tracers from the automatic weapons. He had just touched down, but decided to abort the mission. Turner started down the field at full power, the de Havilland gathering speed, when a military staff car turned onto its path, throwing heavy automatic fire on to the craft. The plane began to lift as bullets ripped into the motor. It lost power, tilted toward the left, the wing kissing the ground, and then cartwheeled into a giant fireball. The flame from the plane lit up the field, silhouetting Max, who drew immediate fire. He tried to make a run for it, but it was too late. Death came quickly under a barrage of automatic weapons.

With the plane burning and tracers shooting across the field, Valentin and his group retreated to their earlier position. They would exploit the confusion to make their getaway. Beyond the woods was a small canal they could utilize to make their escape. They would run for it. Febe and Eddie were almost to the trees when Raymond yelled for help. A bullet had smashed into his shoulder. When they got to him, he was on the ground and bleeding profusely.

"Help me carry him," Febe commanded a dazed Eddie.

Each took an arm and started the slow journey to the tree line. With each step, Raymond let out a groan.

In the darkness, Kohler's nervous men were shooting wildly at anything that moved. Someone shot a flare off, lighting up the area, which brought some calm to the situation. Valentin, crawling while dodging lights and errant bullets contacted his group. Febe had Raymond's head cradled in her lap and was trying to stop his bleeding by wrapping the wound with Eddie's sweater. Within seconds the makeshift bandage was soaked with blood. Febe looked up at Valentin and calmly announced, "He's finished."

Before Valentin could say anything, Eddie snatched the pistol from Febe and put it next to her head. "We are not leaving my brother."

"I didn't say we were," answered Valentin. "We need to get to the canal; can you manage your brother?"

....

Major Kohler finally brought his men under control, *fools* he thought *I'm shocked they didn't kill each other.* He had them organized into a long line to do a sweep of the field.

"Two dead bodies, sir," Kriel reported.

"The saboteurs?"

"The men are bringing the bodies now."

When he saw the corpses and checked them against the photos, he exploded. "These two are not the DeBaets brothers. Expand the perimeter. We must find them before they get away." For good measure, he added, "Sergeant Kriel, once again your men opened up fire too soon. First the tailor shop, and now this. You better pray that the saboteurs are dead somewhere on this field."

In the chaos, the four slipped into the canal and made their way away from the scene. Valentin figured that it would be too dangerous to return to the safe house. They needed to find someplace to hide and to get word back to Brussels. He took stock of the night: two young boys probably captured or worse, a plane and pilot lost, Raymond severely wounded, the mission a failure.

CHAPTER 16

Valentin took the lead through the canal's shallow water, his Browning cocked and at the ready. In the darkness and confusion, no one had an idea of what had become of Sebastian and Max. Where they shot? Were they captured? Soon the countryside would be crawling with soldiers, and they could not afford the luxury of worrying about them now. They wanted to be as far away from the landing site as possible. There were four or five hours of darkness left, and Valentin intended to use them to his advantage.

The canal brought water to the fields during the summer and was left empty for winter. Enough rain had now collected in it to make the journey difficult. The water soaked through their shoes, chafing their feet with each step. Febe and Eddie were helping Raymond along, but every few meters, one of them would lose their footing and slip into the muck as Raymond gave a painful groan.

"How much longer do we need to stay in this mess?" asked Eddie. "We can make better time through the fields."

"We also have a better chance of being spotted," replied Valentin. "Just a little further, then we can make a break for it."

"To where? My brother needs help, and half the German army is looking for us."

"Do you want to leave him to the Germans?" There was no answer from Eddie.

Valentin knew they had to get out of sight before daylight, but where to go? It was too dangerous to return to the farmhouse. Whoever betrayed them would have also told the Germans of the Staelens. And what would become of those two defenseless people? A quick trip to the basement of Gestapo headquarters at 453 Avenue Louise? A few hours there and they would tell everything, and then what? Breendonk concentration camp? While neither Maurice nor his wife knew Valentin, they certainly now knew Febe and, of course, Pieter. He needed to return to Brussels as quickly as possible and warn Gie. But what to do about the brothers? There could be no way to transport them back to Brussels in Pieter's truck. If the Germans didn't catch them, then Raymond would surely bleed to death before reaching the city. But where to hide them until Valentin could return with help? The terrain consisted of open fields and an occasional farmhouse. There was no doubt the Germans would be searching each dwelling very carefully. Who would risk giving comfort to the DeBaets and incurring the wrath of the hunters?

....

Major Kohler had radioed back to the nearest base to send help for an extensive search of the province. There would be 100 men at his command soon. The land was mostly flat with little or no place to hide. He would find them. But who was them? He knew the DeBaets brothers, but who was assisting them? Surely those two dead boys weren't their handlers. No, there was someone else. Once he and Maurice Staelens were back at headquarters, he would find out whom. But now there was no time. He needed to find the fugitives. They had no more than a 15 minutes head start, and they were on foot. While firing flares for illumination, he positioned the newly arrived troops in a long line and had them sweep through the field.

It would be a calamity at the end of the day to return to headquarters and report that his mission netted an elderly couple and two dead boys. Again, a screwup; they were supposed to let the plane land before making their move. How things get out of hand. He had his driver bring him a map of the area to study. Less than a dozen farms were within a ten-kilometer radius. The search would begin as soon as the reinforcements completed the sweep of the crash site. He was still studying the map when one of his men called out.

Approaching, the Major found a corporal standing next to an irrigation canal, pointing his flashlight into the cut. "It is blood, sir, I'm sure of it."

"How can you be sure?"

"I tracked many a wounded partisan through the mud in Russia before my transfer, sir."

"Then we have them. Kriel, sent out every vehicle we have with a spotlight. Have a squad of men follow this ditch, and then have the rest fan out."

....

Febe struggled with the dead weight of Raymond. They needed to decide whether to find shelter or leave him. To leave him would mean they would have to shoot the brothers. Eddie would never leave Raymond, and she wasn't sure that Valentin could be that ruthless. But she knew, as they did, this course of action would only end with them in German hands or dead. The voices of the soldiers carried far into the country. They would be on them before long. It was at this moment that she realized there was a haven. What was it that Pieter told Sebastian? "Hide the weapons in the cellar of your uncle's barn." If the farm was close enough, they could hide there until Valentin could bring help.

"Stop!" Febe called out, then gently lowered Raymond to the ground. Valentin turned toward her. He was afraid she would argue for them to abandon their wounded comrade, or even worse. There was no time for a debate. Eddie, anticipating the same thing, let his free hand rest on the butt of the Browning he took from Febe. But Febe surprised them both when she described her plan.

"We don't know which farm it is," replied Valentin, " and even if we locate it, can we find the trap door to the cellar?"

"We know the farmhouse is south of the landing site, which is the direction we are heading. The road is to our left, and it can't be far off the path."

"That means we have to leave the canal and follow the road. There is only a slight berm to give us any kind of cover. It is risky."

It was Eddie who answered. "What choice do we have?"

"OK, we go," Valentin said decisively. He handed his pistol to Febe and shifted to help Eddie with Raymond. They moved quickly, not letting his feet touch the ground. The party had barely reached the road when they heard a vehicle approaching. A troop truck, its spotlight was sweeping from side to side, a machine gun attached above the cab. The group took cover behind one of the road berms and hugged the ground. The light shone just above their heads, but the truck made no effort to stop. They heard voices behind them and could see men with torches approaching. It was time to move. Getting to their feet, they could see the military truck dipping into a small valley. It stopped to investigate, the spotlight illuminating a small farmhouse and barn.

They could see soldiers opening the barn and entering. The occupants of the house came out to inquire about what was going on. Guards went inside to search the house while the leader interrogated the husband and wife. From his vantage point, Valentin could see a lot of hand waving and shaking of the head by the couple. The men who were searching the barn exited and moved toward the truck.

With soldiers closing in, Valentin wanted to use the darkness to move his people into the barn.

"Are you crazy?" asked Eddie. "They'll cut us to pieces."

"It is either that, or we shoot it out with them now."

"Fuck, that is a hell of a choice."

When the Germans finished with the barn, they left one of the doors open. It now obscured the truck's view of the entrance. The four quickly moved in, Valentin and Eddie carrying Raymond.

"Now what?" asked Eddie.

"Well, we know there must be a door to the cellar somewhere in here."

"We don't even know if we are at the right farm."

"It is the nearest farm to the landing field. It must be the correct one," whispered Febe.

"The trap door is covered with dirt or hay," answered Valentin. He looked around, light from the truck's spotlight filtering in through the cracks in the wooden wall. Febe stood guard at the entrance.

"It would probably be along one of the walls. Check the perimeter first."

"I can't find a fucking thing," complained Eddie.

"It is somewhere on the ground, wooden probably." Valentin kicked at the dirt floor to see if there was anything below. There were hay bales in the corner, but too many, and too heavy to move without causing a commotion.

Febe had Valentin replace her on sentry duty. She

walked to the middle of the barn and stood in the dim light. The barn was 7 meters by 10, with a large storage loft. In the center was an old tractor. There was a workbench over to the side, hay bales in the loft, wooden shelves stacked with pig feed against one of the walls, and tools scattered everywhere. She walked the circumference of the barn until she came upon a rake and pitchfork propped up against a wall.

She scratched the surface of the dirt floor with the pitchfork. She dragged it in different directions, hoping to hit wood. Instead, in the middle, next to the tractor, there was a screeching sound of metal upon metal. They swept the dirt away with their hands and found a small trap door. There was no handle, but they were able to find a screwdriver on the bench and pry the hatch open. Valentin held out his lighter and saw a wooden ladder disappearing into the dark. He climbed down and investigated. He had no doubts the pilot hid here. The room was small, a little under 3 meters by 4 meters, with earthen walls and a dirt floor. It was also damp and cold. A cot was against the wall with blankets folded on top. On the opposite corner was a small bench with a chair. On top of the small table sat a cup, a pitcher, and a basin. A small lantern swung from the ceiling, which he quickly lit. It barely illuminated the room. In the corner was a bucket, he assumed for relieving oneself. No place to live, but it would do for a day or two.

He asked Eddie to send Raymond down, who carefully guided his brother through the small opening. Valentin placed him on the cot.

"Now what?" asked Eddie.

"It is too dangerous for you to be on the road. Stay here while Febe and I go back to town and get help. We should be back by this evening, maybe tomorrow at the latest."

"With no food or water?"

"I'll get you water before we leave. You'll just have to hold on until we return."

"The woman stays with us."

"The plan was for her and me to return with Pieter to Brussels."

"I don't care about your damn plan; the woman stays with us, so I know you'll come back."

"That's crazy! Why wouldn't we come back?"

Eddie took the Browning from his waistband and looked at Valentin." You and your British masters would leave us to die in this hole, but with her here, I know you will come back."

Valentin looked at Febe, who nodded in agreement. He didn't like the idea of leaving her with Eddie but had no options now. Their conversation was interrupted by the Germans leaving the house. He sent both Eddie and Febe down into the cellar and quickly covered the hatch with dirt and hay. The only place to hide was the loft, his pistol at the ready. He relaxed on hearing the soldiers climb into their truck and drive off. They would be back, he was sure. He climbed down and pried the hatch open.

Febe passed a pitcher up for water. Valentin took it and carefully moved out of the barn to a horse trough next to the house. It had a manual pump that squeaked when he operated it. To his relief, no one from the house came out; or maybe they feared what they would find.

Valentin returned with the pitcher. Eddie took it and disappeared into the cellar to tend to his brother. He wanted to warn Eddie not to leave the basement, but knew he would pay him no attention. Valentin gave Febe his pistol and told her that if he wasn't back in a couple of days, they would have to make their way to safety.

"If I do not come back, it is because I am a prisoner or dead. You must separate from those two and save yourself, understood?" He would try to make it to the pickup spot and ride back with Pieter. She showed no fear and assured him that she could take care of herself, with the Germans and Eddie. He wanted to kiss her and take her in his arms. But all he had the courage for was to touch her face with his open palm. She climbed back down the ladder, pulling the trap door shut behind her. Valentin smoothed out the dirt and scattered hay until the area looked like the rest of the untidy barn.

Exiting, he could see lights approaching. His intent was to move fast, stay low, and make it to the bridge by the 6:30 AM pick up time. Sunrise, this time of year, did not occur until 8:30, so there was plenty of darkness to give him cover. His first inclination was to move away from the approaching troops, but that would take him in the wrong direction, and he was unsure if he could find his way back. The only choice was to return the way he came.

The lights were approaching fast; did they see him? It was a motorcycle with side car patrolling. Running to the middle of a field planted with broccoli, he lay face down. The cycle stopped; he could hear the boots coming as they trudged through the mud. They were almost on top of him, lights scanning the furrows. He held his breath; he could hear his own heart beating. Would there be a shot in the back? No, they would take him alive, and once they had him, they would eventually find out where Febe was hiding. One of the soldiers accused the other of imagining things. "It's too cold to trample through this godforsaken field for a ghost," he heard as they trudged back to the motorcycle. Should he wait to see what happened next? Would they return to the barn and conduct another search? *No, there's nothing to do now except get back to Brussels and find help.* He waited until he was sure no one else was coming his way and then slowly moved out.

It was much safer for one person to move through the countryside undetected than the four of them. Unfortunately, the fear didn't decrease by the same amount. A sound in the dark could be anything, and the consequence of guessing wrong would be a bullet. He reached the canal, following it to almost the exact spot they entered earlier. He could see the field; the plane had stopped burning, but now more trucks with troops had arrived. He stayed off the road but always kept it in sight as he made his way to the bridge. His journey was interrupted many times by motorcycles or trucks, some moving fast, others shining spotlights into the darkness. The good news was they were driving away from him.

Valentin arrived at the stone bridge nearly an hour early. He felt miserable; he had not eaten since yesterday morning and now felt weak. He got on his knees and cupped the running creek water. Each sip seemed to give him energy. He positioned himself under the bridge so as not to be seen and sat with the stones against his back. To keep his mind off his hunger, he started making a mental list for his return to Brussels. Number one was to see Gie; before he reached two, he was fast asleep.

His dream was so vivid, the colors so bright, the person so real. There he was on a small island in the Aegean, the water bluer than any blue he knew. A warm breeze, a soft sun, his easel set up overlooking the sea, a beautiful nude in front of him: Febe. She smiles at him, the kind of smile that could only mean mischief. He sets down his brush and moves to her, enjoying the contrast between her light skin and dark hair. He leans over and touches her lips with his--and then there was nothing. He looked out into the morning mist of grayness, the dampness reaching into his soul. Glancing at his watch, it was a quarter to seven. Was Pieter late? Had he come and, not seeing his passenger, left? Valentin didn't know how life could get much worse; all he wanted was to crawl back into his dream with Febe.

It was almost 7:00 AM when Valentin heard a vehicle approaching. He crept from his hiding place and snuck a peek. It was a truck, but there was still not enough light to determine whether it was friend or foe. He stepped back into his shelter and waited. He could hear the engine getting louder as it approached the bridge. Then the truck stopped, with a honk of the horn. Valentin swallowed hard and moved out, praying he was not moving into the sights of a Mauser.

Pieter sitting in his truck was surprised to see anyone come out from under the bridge. News had traveled fast through the village about what had happened. Valentin moved to his seat in the cab of the truck.

"I thought you might not come," Valentin softly spoke.

"I thought you might be dead."

Valentin described what had happened last night and how the other three had taken refuge in the barn.

"The roads and countryside are full of the Boche, and they would have run you all to ground in no time. It was smart to remember the cellar."

He only grunted when Valentin told him it was Febe's idea. Pieter confirmed that Maurice and his wife had been taken prisoner and were on their way to Army headquarters. There was no word on what had happened to Sebastian and Max. He had heard that there were two dead bodies, but did not feel that Valentin needed to know that with everything he had on his mind.

"I hope you did an excellent job of covering the trap door. The Germans are questioning Sebastian's family, and I am sure they are going over the farm very carefully, looking for weapons."

"What about you? Maurice knows your name, and will surely give you up when they start their dirty work."

"Like all of us, I knew this day would come. I say, come and get me."

The ride back to Brussels was long and stressful. They had farms to visit to collect their vegetables, and then the German patrols. Twice they were stopped. Papers were checked, the truck searched, and mini interrogations conducted. A particularly surly sergeant who was riding in a sidecar made them empty the lorry. Valentin expected the German looking at Pieter's papers to say, "Please come with us."

Their luck held. At the last stop, the sentries were more concerned about who was leaving Brussels than arriving. After a night traipsing through the muddy countryside, Valentin looked the part of a hired hand. Even worse, he smelled like a garbage heap. At the checkpoint, the officer called him a swine.

Pieter dropped Valentin off a few blocks away from his studio. One of Desmit's men appeared from nowhere. "I have been waiting for you, Monsieur. It is good to see you safe."

He could take no comfort in being safely back in Brussels. It had taken the whole morning to return to town. He worried about Febe and the brothers being without food and with almost no water. If he didn't return by tomorrow, they would need to venture out for food and water. Inevitably they would run into Germans. Turning to his contact, he said, "I need to see Gie immediately."

"Monsieur Desmit asked me to tell you that he is aware of the situation and that you should present yourself at the factory at two this afternoon." Valentin looked at his watch and was about to reply, but the man disappeared as quickly as he appeared.

Of course, Desmit was aware of the situation. Valentin hated the thought of waiting. He was tired, hungry, and in need of a bath. Covered with filth and smelling like a sty, he decided the wise course would be to clean up before heading to his rendezvous with Gie.

CHAPTER 17

Clarette was passing a slow morning at the studio, waiting for Valentin to arrive. He had left yesterday before noon, and she hadn't seen him since. It wasn't unusual for him to be gone a few days and then reappear as if nothing had happened. Her parents once told her not to inquire about his whereabouts. They were sure he was mixed up with the Underground and thought nothing good would come of her knowledge. But Clarette preferred to believe that his lost time was with his mistress. Someone beautiful, like the women who were in his paintings. Many mornings she witnessed as Elise slithered into the shop, her make-up smeared, looking disheveled. It would be poetic justice if he, too, were enjoying the delights of the night. Clarette had heard the stories about Madame de Vos and the German General and didn't much care for her, but then again, she didn't think Madame de Vos cared much for her either.

She sat at the counter and thumbed her way through a well-worn copy of a 1939 French Vogue, a hand me down from her mother when times were good, before the Germans. She had read every article and scrutinized every photo. Clarette loved to fantasize about what the life of a model would be. She could only imagine the beautiful clothes, the exotic places, and the charming men. As the war dragged on, she worried the Germans would never leave. The front door opened, jarring her away from the daydream. Valentin walked in, wearing old overalls and looking quite filthy. She wanted to ask what happened, but he lifted a finger to his mouth in a motion that told her *not now*.

Upstairs, Elise was still in bed, even thought it was noon. At least he thought she was still in bed. Her door was shut, which always meant do not disturb. He was relieved that it was closed. Maybe there could also be a chance that she might not even be there. He wanted no questioning from her, where he had been that night, or why he came in looking like a derelict. He stripped out of his clothes before wrapping them in a ball and throwing them in the trash. While shaving, he nicked himself a few times, then covered his face with little tears of toilet papers to stop the bleeding. His mind was on the events of last night, and not on the straight razor next to his throat. He was cold, colder than he should have been; the night chill had gone through his body, and he could not warm up. He looked forward to his bath to not only warm him but to offer a few minutes of peace. As the steam fogged up the mirror, Valentin sat on the edge of the tub and let his finger touch the hot water. Ah, hot water; yet another gift from her lover to her. He eased himself into the steaming water and took a scrubbing brush to himself. As much as he washed, he could not get the smell of the truck out of his nostrils or the thought that he had left Febe in danger out of his mind. He toweled himself off and opened the bathroom door, immediately coming face to face with Elise.

He stood holding the towel around his body while she sat at the kitchen table, looking haggard and disheveled. Her pink shawl pulled tight around her, she appeared almost demonic, with wild hair and black shadows around her eyes. Elise lit her first cigarette of the day, then nervously stood and poured a cup of coffee for herself before turning to Valentin. "You didn't return home last night." A hint of suspicion tinged her voice.

Any other time Valentin would have appreciated the irony in her question and might have used her favorite excuse,

"I was visiting my sister," but he had no time for little games this morning. "I was helping a friend with deliveries and could not return before curfew commenced."

She dismissed the explanation with a short laugh, replying, "There was trouble in the countryside last night, and two boys are dead." She watched him for any kind of emotion or acknowledgment. "You wouldn't know anything about that, would you?"

It pained him to hear the news about Max and Sebastian. More gossip she learned from her lover. It took all his control to coolly ask her why he would have any knowledge of the murders.

"They weren't murdered. The two were members of the Resistance, and they fired on German troops. It was self-defense."

Valentin just looked at her. Two boys, his responsibility, dead. "I need to go. I'm late for a meeting."

Elise crushed the butt of the cigarette into the ashtray, refilled her coffee cup, and retreated into her bedroom, slamming the door behind her.

Valentin dressed in a blue wool suit and white shirt, topping it off with his dark blue and silver tie. Overdressed to work in the studio, but certainly not to visit Monsieur Desmit at his offices to place an order for frames. Gie preferred not to meet at the factory; he trusted no one, and that included those who worked for him. But it was Desmit who had picked the meeting place, and Valentin was anxious to find out what he had planned.

He felt guilty, stopping in the kitchen to eat half a croissant and down a cup of coffee. He thought of Febe and the brothers in the cellar, with no food and very little water.

The sky was turning grey again as he left his studio, and the temperature dropping; more rain, he feared. He turned up the collar of his coat and ran to catch the number 4 bus that would take him to his meeting. The afternoon bus was a crush of people. With automobiles requisitioned and petrol rationed, buses, bicycles, or walking were the only modes of transportation for most people.

Mercifully the trip was quick, with Valentin standing the whole way. His stop was a popular one with connections to the outskirts of Brussels. Looking out the window, he saw long lines in front of every bus. Next to him, an old lady struggled with her groceries. The strap on her bag broke, and what few goods she had fell to the floor of the bus. Valentin quickly collected them and helped her down to the street. He was able to tie the broken strap, hoping it would last until she reached her home. A thin smile crossed her sad face as she thanked him. He tipped his hat and offered a smile back before heading down the street to the furniture factory.

When the first Gie Desmit opened his shop some hundred years ago, it was a one-room building where he did all his woodcraft. Now, after years of expansion, it was a large factory. It once employed over 300 people. The war robbed the company of many skilled workers, and business wasn't like it had been, but it was still open and happy to employ the people they could. Desmit's office was on the second floor, situated so he could look out of his glass wall and view his kingdom: the drying rooms, the cutting rooms, off to the left were the planking and drilling, in a closed area was the sanding room and in front of him was the assembly area--all the places where the craftsmen worked to make a Desmit original. It was not uncommon for Gie to look out, observe one of his craftsmen carving a piece of wood, and then be on the production floor in seconds, disagreeing or criticizing what the artisan was creating. He always told them any original that left this factory with his name on it had to be perfect. Of course, that was how he saw life: a struggle against imperfection.

As soon as Valentin entered the waiting room, the secretary showed him into Desmit's office. "The boss has been waiting for you," she whispered as he passed her. Valentin expected Gie probably knew more about the situation than he, and there would be little for him to say. Gie's office always looked more like it contained a typhoon than a successful businessman. One wall was filled with black filing cabinets; a long narrow table on the opposite one had dozens of folders; and in front of the glass wall was a beautifully crafted handmade desk, twice as big as most. Not one square centimeter of the surface was visible. The top was covered with files, books, catalogs, a humidor, and what must have been two dozen pens. One of Gie's passions and hobbies was the art of writing, and collecting beautiful instruments to do so.

When he entered, the boss was sitting with his back to him, staring out the large glass window the hustle of the factory below him. Valentin cleared his throat. Gie slowly turned, a sad look on his face. "Well, my friend, a not so successful evening?"

Valentin took the straight-backed chair across from the desk and reported the events of the last 24 hours, from the missed meeting with Michel Verhoeven to the moment he walked in the factory door. Gie sat listening, expressionless, occasionally asking a question. When Valentin finished, Desmit processed all that he heard and mentally matched it against his information from other sources. Slowly shaking his head in disbelief, and letting out a deep sigh, he sadly announced, "Once again, someone has betrayed us."

Gie confirmed that the two boys were dead. Their parents had been arrested, and in the case of Max's family, the grandmother was also in jail. Maurice and his wife were in the basement of Gestapo headquarters for interrogation. With regret in his voice, Gie acknowledged, "They knew so little, I fear they will suffer much. We will not see them again." Yes, they could identify Pieter; but Gie had sent him away, out to the coast to friends who would keep him hidden. But unfortunately, he had more bad news.

"Michel is dead, killed yesterday in a raid on the tailor shop." He let that sink in to Valentin's already fragile psyche. "The tailor was a prisoner, but our sources have told us he is now deceased, killed while trying to escape. My spy said he had nothing to give, so in a fit of anger, Kohler wrapped a metal pipe around his head. The wife seems to be the only one with any sense. She has disappeared." Valentin sat numbly in the chair, his eyes closed. "The only good news is General Beck is furious with Kohler for mucking up the capture of the brothers and is thinking of having him arrested for incompetence."

"What do we do now?"

The British said that our network is a sieve of informers and traitors, and they are going dark until we clear up the mess."

They both agreed that the first order of business was to retrieve the DeBaets and get them to a safe house. "We must involve Dr. Tillens," Gie said, "but no one else. There is a traitor out there, and I have a bullet for his sorry face. The girl, can she continue?" There was a simple nod from Valentin in reply.

Desmit lifted himself from his chair and walked to the wall where three portraits were hanging. Three generations of Desmits preserved in oil colors. He lifted the middle one, his grandfather looking stern, and revealed a safe. He retrieved a bundle of money and handed it to Valentin. "You may need this" They agreed once the brothers were in the safehouse, they would speak again. The factory had a delivery truck leaving. Valentin would stow away, and the driver would give him a ride to the bus stop. It would save time getting to Dr. Tillens home.

Valentin climbed up to the back of the covered lorry, taking a seat on a beautifully crafted couch. A high-ranking Nazi who had taken a house in the Woluwe Saint Pierre section of Brussels had purchased it. Fortunately, it was the same area where Dr. Tillens lived. Valentin loved that part of town, with its parks and beautiful homes. He used to go to the Parc de la Woluwe to paint or to visit the shops and restaurants.

When they arrived at the main square of Woluwe Saint Pierre, the truck stopped long enough for Valentin to slip out. He pounded on the side to let them know he was clear and then they were away. He caught a bus for the short ride to Overijse, where Dr. Tillens lived. Getting off at the Sint-Martinus church, he walked the four blocks to his destination. Doctor Rene Tillens was not only a sympathizer, but also one of the financial backers of the Belgian National Movement. His large but simple two-story house was painted white with a grey roof. In the spring, the planter boxes under the ground floor windows were ablaze with tulips, and in summer, his roses were the pride of the neighborhood.

Valentin approached cautiously, giving the area a going-over visually to make sure no one was watching. As was his custom, he walked along the side of the house and knocked on the back door. Dr. Tillens answered, and Valentin moved inside the home office. Tillens looked at him with his brown eyes that were still bright, despite their 75 years. He was a tall man with a trim physique. "It is in the genes," he would tell people when they questioned how he kept youthful and healthy. His carefully-trimmed beard was all grey, and his hair still had sprinkles of the chestnut brown of his youth. The doctor, dressed in a perfectly tailored brown tweed suit, exuded confidence. Valentin followed Tillens through an exam area and into an enormous salon. The aroma of sweet vanilla lingered from the doctor's pipe. They sat in wingback chairs, Valentin declined an offer of coffee but accepted a brandy from the good doctor.

Tillens asked about the mission that went awry. His guest recounted the events of the previous night, telling the horror of losing the aircraft and the two boys, describing Raymond's wound, and emphasizing the need to collect all of them as soon as possible. The whole time, the doctor puffed on his pipe and nodded his head. He asked but a few questions. How severe was the wound? Valentin was of no help, and could only confirm that he had lost much blood. Tillens' only other issue was, "Do all three need to be returned?" and Valentin answered in the affirmative.

"Let me collect my bag and a few other things, and we can leave immediately. We will need to be creative on this one trip if we are to bring them all back." Tillens left Valentin sitting, reappearing a few minutes later wearing his overcoat and carrying his doctor's bag in one hand and a picnic basket in the other. He smiled, "I'm sure they are hungry. It's not much, cold chicken and some potatoes, but a banquet for starving people."

They crossed the yard to the garage, a free-standing building next to the house. Tillens, throwing open the swinging doors, revealed a green 1936 Citroën Traction Avant, polished to perfection and shining even on this cloudy day. "Will you drive?" asked the doctor. "When we come to a checkpoint, I'll do the talking." The going was much faster than with Pieter and the delivery truck. The car handled well, and Valentin enjoyed driving something with that much power. He could imagine Tillens touring the seashore in this beauty on a splendid summer day.

The security stops were quick. Tillens being a doctor,

he had documentation that let him travel freely, even after curfew. A flash of the papers and a story, they were on an emergency call, and off they went. The only time Valentin was concerned was when they approached the station where Peiter had the run-in with the captain the previous day. Neither the officer nor the same guards were on duty this day. It was dark when they arrived at the farm, no sign of life anywhere, not even the pigs. Valentin parked the car in front of the barn and got out as Tillens searched the glovebox for a flashlight.

"Let me check the house first, Doctor." Valentin carefully approached the back steps and knocked on the door, the hardwood stinging his cold knuckles. No answer. He turned the handle, and finding it unlocked, pushed the door open. He gave a tentative "Hello," but the greeting went unanswered. Valentin walked into the living room. It was in a state of disarray; chairs turned over, cabinets open, drawers pulled out. Investigating the rest of the house, he found it in the same condition.

"The place is empty. Whoever searched it did an excellent job of ransacking the house," Valentin explained to the doctor outside.

Together they entered the barn. It also had been searched. Valentin's eyes went directly to the trap door. A large wagon used for transporting hay had been moved over it. Had Febe and her wards been discovered? Or was it moved when the Germans scoured the place? The two men cleared the opening and Valentin pounded on the cover, calling Febe's name. If they were alive, he didn't want to open the latch and be met by a hail of bullets. She called back to them. Valentin lifted the cover, flashing the light into the space. His nostrils were attacked by the foul air of the tight quarters.

"I brought a doctor," he called down to them.

Febe came up first, warning them that Raymond was not

doing well, exhibiting shallow breathing, fever, and dehydration. Tillens climbed down to attend to his patient.

"We could hear the Germans searching the barn," she said to Valentin. "Lots of noise. We were ready to end it right then. Thankfully they never found the door. Sometime this morning, we tried to get out to fetch more water, but the door wouldn't move."

"They had moved the wagon over it."

"After that, Eddie feared we would die in that trap, but I knew you would come back," she said in a soft voice touching his arm.

Valentin told her the sad news about Sebastian and Max as they walked to get more water.

"I had a feeling that something horrible happened to them. I'm sorry the mission was a failure." Valentin said nothing, only watched as Febe cupped her hands and drank, letting the water slide down her chin and on to her neck.

Tillens had Raymond lifted out of the cellar and onto the hay. His shirt was soaked with blood, as was the makeshift dressing. "A nasty wound your brother has, fetch me some water."

Raymond wandered from unconsciousness to consciousness and then back again. The doctor cleaned and dressed the wound the best he could under the circumstances and gave him something for the pain. Tillens brought the basket of food from the car, and within minutes Eddie and Febe had devoured the cold chicken and potatoes. Eddie wanted to know what they were going to do for Raymond. "You better have plan because we are not going back into that hellhole."

It was the doctor who answered. "We must get your brother back to town, but I will not lie, it is going to be a dangerous journey. If you all do as I say, we will be all right. My strategy is deception. I hope you are all up to it." Tillens had Eddie go back into the house and find a shirt that would fit his brother. He took a little time to clean up Raymond, removing the mud and dirt from his face and combing his hair. He then opened the trunk of his car and removed a stack of empty flour sacks and blankets, placing them on either side of the floorboard to be level with the driveshaft. They lowered Raymond onto the back-seat floor and covered him entirely with a blanket.

"I have given him something for the pain that will keep him out for some time, Believe me, he will be the most comfortable on this trip."

Turning to Eddie, "Your journey, sir, will not be as comfortable. It will be a very snug fit, but it's possible." The doctor was pointing to the back of the car.

"You are joking? Isn't that the first place they will search?"

"Leave that detail to me. Your job is to climb into the boot and stay quiet," the doctor responded, in a voice that would tolerate no objection.

Turning to Febe, "For you, my dear, the trip will be dreadful. I can only say what I will ask of you will be the difference between us being successful or ending up in the hands of the Gestapo."

"Whatever I must do, doctor."

He smiled and explained that it was vital that she not only acted ill but looked so bad that the soldiers would be hesitant to search. "First, we must make you look sick." Reaching into his bag and taking out a small bottle of alcohol he cleaned her face. He rubbed a mixture of brown sugar, butter, and grapeseed oil on her lips, which gave them the appearance of being swollen. Under her eyes, he rubbed a dab of coal dust to darken them. Taking out a little jar of red makeup, he smeared it on the end of her nose and at the corners of her eyes. He then pulled out a glass bottle that looked like a perfume atomizer, with a rubber bulb on the top which when squeezed produced a spray. "It is only water; however, along with the makeup, it will give the appearance of running a fever."

"This isn't so bad."

"Unfortunately, the worst is yet to come." He took out a thermos and poured the liquid into a cup. "This is warm water mixed with salt. You must drink it down, and in 20-30 minutes, it will induce vomiting. It won't kill you, but you'll wish you were dead." Walking to the well, he returned with a bucket. "For you."

"When should I drink this?"

"Now."

With one gulp, all the contents of the cup disappeared.

"Please, lie down in the back and cover yourself with the blanket," Tillens advised. "I would, of course, keep the bucket close by."

"You," pointing to Eddie, "will ride in the boot."

"And if I don't want to?"

"Then you can wait for our return in the barn," answered Valentin.

Eddie whispered something guttural under his breath but climbed in. It was very tight. He maneuvered the best he could to find a position that would be tolerable for the trip. Tillens closed the hatch carefully.

The movement of the car was enough to start Febe vomiting. She was still throwing up when they stopped for a security inspection. The doctor presented his papers and explained that he was rushing this woman who was deathly ill to the hospital in Brussels. When the guard pointed his flashlight into the back seat, Febe was once again using the bucket. The doctor cautioned him not to get too close in case she was infectious. The soldier gagged and quickly waved his hand to move them along.

"That was easy," Valentin observed.

"We still have at least two more checkpoints. Let's pray our luck holds."

Despite the chill outside, they had lowered the window to relieve the smell. Tillens would not let them empty the bucket as it was their best deterrent again snoopy police. By the time they had entered the outskirts of Brussels, Valentin was feeling queasy from the odor. It was well into the evening when they came upon the last checkpoint before entering Brussels. The sentry got a whiff of the inside as he approached the car and immediately stepped back, ordering Tillens out. The doctor explained the situation while showing his identity card and medical documents. The guard, not wanting to make the decision on his own, called for his sergeant.

The sergeant came out of the guard post, wiping grease from the chicken he had been eating off his fingers. Annoyed, he demanded to know what this was all about. Once more, Tillens explained the situation. The sergeant stepped to the back door and shined his flashlight into Febe's sweaty face. After 2 hours of riding in the car, smelling her vomit, she was indeed ill. The stench was the first thing to greet him; he looked down at the woman with blankets all around her. She seemed to be in total misery.

"Is she contagious?" he asked the Doctor.

Tillens lifted his shoulders, giving an expression of *I*

don't know.

"Proceed" was the response. The only thing the sergeant wanted to do was to breathe fresh air and to wash his hands.

Through it was past curfew, they were only bothered one more time, by two soldiers riding a motorcycle with sidecar. There was a sigh of relief from all as they arrived at the safe house. The home was built in the late 1800s and situated not too far from Valentin's shop. Once a stately mansion for an industrialist, now it was divided up into a dozen little flats. They pulled into the darkened courtyard and shut the gate behind them. Tillens escorted Febe to a first floor flat while Valentin released Eddie from the boot. Together they lifted Raymond from the car and brought him into the building. They were met in the vestibule by Madame Roels, the landlady. The doctor whispered that "she is one of us" and led them into the apartment. The flat was small, but clean and warm. It had a salon, kitchen, and bedroom; and was one of the few that also had a bathroom that wasn't shared.

They placed Raymond on the bed, where the Doctor once again examined him and changed his dressing. Madame Roels entered with a pot of water and a sponge to cool his fever.

"You need to observe him," the Doctor announced. "If the fever gets worse, you must contact me. I will be back tomorrow to check on him."

Febe, who was feeling better but still weak from all the vomiting, nodded her understanding while Eddie was looking through the cupboards for something to drink. Valentin wanted to stay but knew it wasn't possible. There was much for him to do. But looking at Febe, he felt guilty. She was pale and weak from the trip. "Will you be alright?" he asked.

"Yes, I just need to rest."

Eddie watched them leave and showed no interest when Febe suggested he bathe. He sat in an overstuffed chair, lit the cigarette he had bummed from Valentin, and sipped on the cheap brandy he found in the kitchen. Raymond always looked after him, kept him out of trouble, made the right decisions. Now his brother lay unconscious. What was he to do? He trusted no one. The Brits promised him a way out. If this group wouldn't help, maybe there was someone who could.

CHAPTER 18

The pain...Raymond's mind drifted from scene to scene, but always the pain was there. It made no sense to him, nor could he make it stop. One moment he was in an open field, an explosion and then a fiery ball, something struck him in the shoulder and then nothing, all his thoughts turning to black. One moment he had the chills, and then the stifling heat. The heat was the worst, his body covered in sweat; he could feel the drops falling off his skin...was he back in the Congo? Could it be malaria again? He would beg for something to drink, and then soft hands would cradle his head and give him fresh water, and then he would drift away. He thought he might have been in a cave, or perhaps making a trip by automobile? He could feel the warmth of someone wiping his forehead. Where was Eddie? He needs to find Eddie.

Eddie was of no use, pacing, worried, smoking cigarettes. Now and then, he would curse that they should take his brother to a hospital or fetch the doctor. He would then grab the bottle of brandy and retreat to the salon to brood.

A grey light started to spread itself across the eastern sky. While there would be no sun, there would also be no rain. Already city workers were sweeping down the street. A garbage truck was approaching with three workers collecting the bins and throwing their contents into the rear of the vehicle. In a few hours, the rest of the city would be up, passing the red banners with swastikas, catching buses to the offices or factories. None of this mattered to Febe; she had fallen into what she called her death sleep, darkness without dreams. She had curled up with a blanket next to Raymond's bed, a bowl of water on the nightstand and the Browning in her lap. Eddie was stretched out on the couch, having lost consciousness about an hour before.

There was a soft tapping on the door, which immediately brought Febe out of her sleep. Clutching the pistol, she threw off the blanket and moved swiftly into the salon, shaking Eddie on the way to the door. The younger brother was startled and, for a moment, had no idea where he was, but that passed quickly. He exhaled deeply, thinking to himself that he was still in the nightmare. Febe motioned for him to take up a position on one side of the door. His eyes were blurry, his head was pounding, and his mouth was dry. It took him a second to find his weapon before moving to the left side of the door. Febe disengaged the safety and moved to the opposite side of the door, the pistol held high.

In a firm voice, she asked: "Yes, who is it?"

"Tillens." The doctor entered, carrying a small valise and a baguette under his arm. He handed both to Febe. The loaf was still warm, and the aroma reminded her how hungry she was. "I brought you both some clothes in the suitcase. I thought you might want to change. My apologies, my dear, but my housekeeper picked yours, and they may be more suitable for a widowed grandmother."

He stepped to the bedroom to examine Raymond while Febe tore off a piece of bread. She offered the baguette to Eddie, but he told her that his stomach was in no shape to welcome any food. He sat there wishing he had a cigarette.

Dr. Tillens examined the wound, which was worse than it had been the day before. It was still bleeding. Raymond was also extremely dehydrated. "If he doesn't get proper care soon, he will die."

"I thought you were the proper care?" Eddie growled.

"He needs to be in a hospital."

"Where the Germans will find him?"

"I will take him to my clinic where we can stabilize the bleeding until the passage can be arranged for the two of you to leave,"

"And what if they can't arrange passage? What then?"

"One step at a time, my friend."

Eddie helped the doctor move Raymond out of the flat and maneuver him into the rear seat of the car. It still stank of vomit from the day before. He wanted to go along, but it would be too dangerous. He looked down at his brother and wondered if he would ever see him alive again. "Please don't let him die." Tillens had no reply, only a pat on the shoulder. The car slowly pulled out, as Eddie closed the courtyard gate and returned to the apartment.

Dr. Tillens drove through the nearly deserted streets, the only traffic being military vehicles and the cars of the Nazi collaborators--the Brussels elite that sympathized and, in return, received petrol and free passage throughout the city. Tillens would make a mental note if he saw an automobile and didn't know the owner. A day would come when all would be held accountable for their collaboration, and he didn't want to miss one of them. He drove to the clinic and pulled around the back to the courtyard. Stopping in front of a large cargo door, he gave a short honk of his horn and George, his longtime orderly, appeared. The orderly extracted Raymond from the car. A burly man in his 40's, unshaven and in a white lab coat, he had no problem lifting the patient out by himself.

Tillens tended to Raymond for almost an hour. He cleaned and bandaged the wound, but deemed him too weak to try to extract the bullet from his shoulder. Having done all that was possible, the doctor could now only hope for the best and try to keep the wound from getting infected. Considering all that Raymond had been through, the doctor thought that might be impossible. He washed up, and set out to visit Valentin's studio to fill him in.

....

"Will he live?" were the first words from Valentin, followed by, "Will he be discovered?"

"Two very different questions," replied the doctor. "He has lost much blood, and the chance for infection is high. The next day or two should tell the story. You must get to Desmit and say to him that I advise we contact the British and arrange another extraction. If we can't get him out quickly, then we will be burying him."

"Yes, but will the British agree to it?"

"We need to make them agree to it. The Germans smell blood and they will make life even more difficult for us until they find these brothers. They will indiscriminately start pulling people in who will tell them anything to escape interrogation. Talk to Gie. He'll know what to do."

....

Eddie paced the room like a caged animal. Raymond had always been there for him; had always been the one who made decisions. It was Raymond who wanted out of their father's business and who wanted to enlist in the Army. It was Raymond who wanted to go to the Congo. And it was Raymond who agreed to accept the British offer and set off the bomb in Köln. Each time Eddie had followed him, but now Raymond could not even help himself. Would Eddie ever see him again? The two had argued about trusting these people. He knew the members of the Resistance were a tight-knit group and were only out for themselves. No one cared about him or his brother. Everyone lied, the British and the Belgians, "We will get you out of the country," they told him, yet he was on the run, a hunted man. He didn't believe anything the doctor told him, and as far as he was concerned, the cold-hearted bitch sleeping in the next room was the worst. He could feel that she treated him with contempt. No, maybe there was a way out of this mess; he could save himself and his brother and still come out looking like a hero.

....

Valentin caught the tram from his apartment to the Central Station, and from there, he walked the short distance to the Cathedral of Saints Michel and Gudula. On Wednesdays, Gie Desmit always attended the mid-morning mass. Valentin made his way through the vestibule with its elegant stained-glass window and into the nave. There he could see Gie sitting toward the back, a lone figure dwarfed by the immensity of his surroundings. Valentin took the seat next to him and waited. He admired the massive columns that lined the center aisle and tried to name the twelve apostles attached to them. His mind drifted as the priest gave the sermon, and he followed Desmit's lead when he knelt. It was only then that Gie asked what the situation was. Valentin gave an abridged account of his conversation with the doctor.

Gie acknowledged that the brothers must be flown out, but was unsure if the British would accommodate. "Our comrades, *les goddams* as our French friends like to call them, aren't very friendly to us presently," he whispered. "They believe it is our two men's fault the mission failed, and now they have lost a plane and pilot. They point out the Germans seem to know more about the Underground than they do."

"Can we move them to the country?" Valentin pressed.

"We could, but I would imagine the good doctor will tell us that the wounded one would die without proper care. By now, the Germans must know that one of the brothers is hurt. They will start searching clinics soon, if they haven't already. The longer he stays at the clinic, the greater the danger for all of us. Let me work with the British. I may have a card up my sleeve." With that, they fell silent until they stood for the Lord's Prayer.

"Peace be with you, Valentin."

"And also with you, Gie."

....

Febe took advantage of the warm apartment and hot water to bathe. She couldn't scrub hard enough to rid herself of the last 48 hours, the gunfight, the cellar and the illness. Floating in the water, she enjoyed the comfort. It was peaceful and quiet, and her thoughts drifted to Valentin. How genuinely concerned he had been for her, the way he had touched her, and how she wanted to kiss him.

Eddie had worked his way through the bottle of cheap brandy long before Dr. Tillens arrived. Now he sat at the window starring out into the courtyard. A search through the apartment produced a couple of bottles of red table wine. He was deep into the last one, replaying over and over again the sequence of events that brought him to this moment, from meeting with Febe at the cathedral in Köln to his brother being taken to the clinic that morning. One big fuck up, he told himself over and over. Unless he did something, his brother would die, but what could he do?

He was in a stupor from too much wine and no food. While Febe was in the bathtub, the idea came to him. How do I save my brother and myself? How can we exit this nightmare? It was all there; he just needed to make it happen. The

Germans, of course, were his way out. They were the only ones who could make something happen. Yes, they wanted him and his brother, but they wanted the leaders of the Underground more. He drew up a list in his mind and checked it against what he had done and what he could trade. He had killed a German soldier and the conductor, but the tradeoff for them would be significant, plus he would be dealing with men to whom killing meant nothing. If they agreed to save Raymond and let both of them leave for Portugal, he would give them the whole group; the doctor, Valentin, Febe, the British major, the fool who drove the truck. The Germans would get a treasure chest of information from them. Of course, it would work, but how to go about it? How he wished he had a cigarette, he emptied the wine glass in one quick drink, feeling the fluid hitting the bottom of his empty stomach. When to move? He laid the automatic down that he was keeping on his lap and went in search of a smoke. Surely there must be one somewhere?

Febe toweled herself off and ran a brush through her hair. Wrapping a heavy black wool skirt around her and buttoning up a simple white blouse, she decided Tillens was right. The clothes did more justice to a spinster. She checked the Browning and then put it inside the waistband of the skirt, snug against the curve of her back. She put on an oversized black cardigan and looked in the mirror. She smiled, seeing that all she needed was her hair in a bun to complete the image of a widow. She chose not to button the sweater.

She went into the kitchen to make some tea. Eddie got up and leaned against the icebox, the sour smell of wine emanating from him. He was unshaven and still wearing the same dirty clothes from the barn. He said nothing, only stared.

"Maybe you should think about cleaning up," Febe suggested.

"Why, are we going somewhere?"

"You smell."

A thin smile crossed his lips. He moved closer. Grabbing her, he kissed her on the lips. She moved her head and tried to push him away, but he was too strong for that. Using all her might, she gave him a knee in the groin. He doubled up, gasping for air. "Bitch," he cried out.

"Try that again, and you'll wish you were never born," she coldly told him.

"What's the matter? I'm not good enough for you?"

"You need to clean up and focus. I'm sure there will be another attempt to get you and your brother to safety."

"It makes no difference to me. I know the game you and your friends are playing."

"And what game is that?"

"I see it. You all treat us like shit. We are nothing to you and the Underground. We are just two fools that will probably end up in a ditch with a bullet in our faces. The hell with you. I'm leaving."

"And going where?"

"To make a deal with the devil."

"You're drunk."

"Sure, I'm drunk, but we had a deal with the British and the Belgian National Movement, and what have we gotten? My brother is nearly dead, and I'm waiting to be arrested by the Gestapo. If I wait for those monsters to find me, I'm a dead man. But if I go to them, I can make a deal."

"A deal with the Germans? You *are* drunk."

"I have much to trade."

"You fool! You'll walk into their headquarters, and within minutes they'll wrap an electrical wire around your balls, and you'll be crying like a baby at the first jolt."

"Of course, that is what you would tell me," Eddie said as he lifted himself off the floor. He approached as though to retrieve the bottle of wine but swung quickly around, slapping Febe across the face. She stumbled backward. Eddie pushed her to the table, steering clear of her knees while pinning her arms behind her. She fought back, but he slapped her again, grabbing at her throat. With her free hand, she scratched the side of his face. He reacted by smacking her in the face. Slipping his fingers inside the collar of her blouse, he ripped the buttons apart, exposing a breast.

"I'll have a little of that before I leave."

Eddie had her bending backward over the table, trying to raise the heavy skirt. Freeing one of her arms and grabbing a bottle of wine, she smashed it against the side of his head. The bottle didn't break, but Eddie staggered back, blood pouring from his skull. In one motion, she retrieved her gun from her waist and pointed it at him. Eddie touched his head and looked at the blood on his hand. She thought he would charge her again. Instead, he spat in her face and headed for the door.

"Don't touch that door," she said slowly, each word a command.

Eddie gave no reaction. He unlocked the door and was turning the knob when Febe put three bullets in his back. She peered out the window. Some neighbors came out and looked around, then just as quickly went back inside.

She rolled Eddie over and placed her fingers against his throat, looking for a pulse. He was dead.

CHAPTER 19

Valentin had let Gie exit the cathedral. He sat in his pew, gazing at the stained glass of the Last Judgement and thinking about Gudula, one of the saints that the cathedral was named after. As the story went, she carried a lantern in her pre-dawn walks to the church when a demon extinguished the light. She appealed to God to relight it and relight it He did. Valentin, wondered what second chance, would God give them? Would they be able to spirit the brothers out of the country? And then what of Febe? He thought of her much the last few days. How he wanted her. He let himself daydream of slowly undressing her and making love to her. A large candleholder was knocked over at the back of the Cathedral by two workmen moving a table. The loud noise reverberated through the aisles and brought him to the sudden realization that he was sitting in church with these thoughts. It activated the deep Catholic roots of his childhood, when his mother would slap him for laughing with his friends during service. He could only imagine how many Hail Marys he would need to offer for his amorous musings. He checked his watch--over ten minutes had passed since Desmit had left. He stood and carefully looked around, collected his overcoat and then departed through the central aisle. On his way out, he deposited a few francs in the contribution plate to atone for his lustful thoughts of Febe and then moved out into the open air.

The day was still grey and cold, and he felt a pang of hunger, having skipped breakfast. He thought about going to The Egyptian, a small café not far from the cathedral. Its fare was limited these days, but there was always good lamb stew on the menu. The sheep were raised on a farm owned by the uncle of the owner. The Egyptian was one of the city's gems, at least until the Nazis came to town. You could always depend on three things at the Egyptian: excellent lamb, good coffee, and strong tobacco smoked in their hookah pipes. The conversation was either about politics or football, and the clientele came from all sections. The owners had returned to America before the invasion. They sold the place to a couple from the Congo who had come home to Belgium to live in peace. The war had made the coffee and tobacco scarce, and the Nazis had made the conversation impossible.

Valentin was hungry but had been away from his studio longer than usual. In the last few days, there was only Clarette to look after the business. He still had a shop to run; regrettably, he would save the lamb for another day. He chose to walk the distance from the cathedral back to the studio, wanting the time to think. He worried that Raymond was not up for the journey to England, and if Gie was correct, the Germans would be checking all the private clinics for anyone recently brought in. If Raymond and Tillens fell into the Gestapo's hands, how long would the rest of them have?

Then there was Eddie: how long could they hide him? How much longer could Febe be expected to look after him? Her holiday would soon be over, and she would have to return to work. Her return to the trains would diminish his opportunities to be with her. It was hopeless for him to worry; in the end, his fate and those of the brothers and Febe were in the hands of others and not his. He could only hope that the card that Gie told him he had to play would be a good one.

In the days when he and Elise would take a stroll, she always complained that he walked too fast. He enjoyed moving at a brisk pace, and today was no different. But, turning onto his street, he came to a sudden stop. In front of his place, there were two German staff cars parked. His heart sank. His first reaction was to walk the other way, but unfortunately he was already sighted by the soldiers looking after the vehicles.

Had his time finally come? A betrayal by some faceless informer? How he wished for a weapon. But then what? A shootout in the middle of Brussels with the German army? He calmed himself. *Stop thinking like a guilty man. Walk-in there and face them down*, he told himself. *Whatever happens, buy time so the others can escape.*

In the reception area of his shop were two privates with automatic weapons slung over their shoulders, flirting with Clarette. They turned as he entered; he nodded in their direction, and then made eye contact with Clarette. An upward motion of her head told him that whoever was there was waiting for him upstairs. At the top landing was another guard posted at the entrance to the apartment. He stepped in front of the door, barring Valentin's entry into his own home. The sentry knocked on the door, keeping an eye on Valentin. A few seconds passed before it opened. Entering the salon, he found General Beck sitting on the couch, sipping Champagne. Elise's lover was running his hand through his hair to smooth it out, smudged lipstick visible on his cheek.

"Ah de Vos, there you are, I came to inquire about my painting, and when I couldn't find you, your beautiful wife invited me up for a drink. Champagne?"

"Champagne?"

"Of course, my good man, I brought it with me, we have a perfect French wine merchant who seems to keep us always stocked with the best from France. I brought it as a gift for your beautiful wife." Hearing that, Elise made her grand entrance into the salon. Whatever she had on while entertaining Beck, she had now exchanged for a simple skirt and jacket. Her traveling suit, Valentin called it.

"My dear, bring a glass for your husband." He always seemed comfortable giving orders and particularly comfortable giving them to Elise, who duly obeyed. She placed Valentin's flute on a side table across from Beck and then sat in the overstuffed seat between the two men. Valentin slowly sipped the Champagne, on an empty stomach, he feared he might get dizzy, and his lips become loose. He thought it surreal, all three smiling, no one speaking. He had disturbed their plans by coming home?

"de Vos, tell me, how goes the painting? When do you leave for Morocco? Your travel papers are waiting for you at my office."

"I have some work to complete before I can depart."

Elise jumped in sarcastically, "He has been so busy lately."

The General looked uncomfortable; again, a tight smile at Elise. "Yes, of course, but how much longer once you have your colors?"

Valentin looked around the room; next to the chairs by the dining table was Elise's suitcase. Obviously she was planning a little getaway with her lover. She caught his eyes and followed them to the valise, then picked up her glass and sipped her Champagne, looking neither at him nor Beck.

"General, I am working on a masterpiece; it is a painstakingly slow process to recreate something as famous and recognizable. You certainly would not want me to give you something that is a cheap imitation, would you?"

"No, no, I wouldn't. But you know Major Kohler believes your trip is unnecessary. He said that he has consulted with experts, and they believe the colors could be obtained here in Brussels."

"General, I would be happy to give up my commission if there is someone you feel is more qualified to finished the work."

The General began to fidget with his sleeves and then tried to loosen the tight collar around his ever-expanding neck. "No, the Major is no art expert, and to tell the truth I don't take his advice on military matters, why should I on art?" There was a nervous laugh from Beck. Valentin could tell that he was anxious to leave. He wondered how the General was going to accomplish this and take Elise with him. "Just remember, I want that painting by the first of February."

Silence filled the room before he decided to push the General's patience. "Thank you, I appreciate your confidence in me, sir. Now you must come down to the studio and see the progress I have made on the painting."

"That is not necessary, de Vos."

"General, I insist."

"Do not insist with me, de Vos." With that he stood up, looking at Elise and then back to Valentin. In a friendlier voice, he continued, "I would like to be surprised when I see your finished product. Now I must leave." But he made no effort to move towards the door, the three of them standing there.

"General," Elise blurted out, "I am off to visit my sister and was wondering if you would drop me off. It is on your way back to headquarters."

Looking relieved, Beck nodded, "It would be my pleasure, Madame de Vos."

"Could you have your man collect my bag?" Turning to Valentin, she said, "I won't be back in time before the curfew and will spend the night with the family." He smiled.

The General summoned the guard outside the door, and with a snap of his fingers, he pointed at the valise and commanded him to bring it along. "Good evening, de Vos, I look forward to seeing a finished painting soon."

"When I return from Spain, it shouldn't be much longer. I will come by your office tomorrow, sir, for the travel documents."

"Yes, the papers are waiting for you."

As they left the apartment, Elise turned to Beck and asked disingenuously, "General, how long will this dreadful curfew be in place?"

"Sorry, madam, a necessary inconvenience. If all the residents of Brussels were as charming as you, it would not be necessary." With that, they were out the door and quickly down the stairs. From the window, Valentin could see Beck, his arm around Elise helping her to the car. She stopped, throwing back her head and laughing, He gave one last look at the shop before moving into the vehicle.

....

Before the war, Valentin had kept his shop open in the evenings. While he would not see a steady stream of customers, enough would drop in to engage having a painting restored or a reproduction produced. Occasionally someone would wander in to inquire about one of his portraits that hung in the lobby. A coffee or perhaps a glass of wine would be offered, and their conversations could last well into the night. On those rare occasions when someone would buy one of his paintings, he would lie awake wondering what would have happened if he had only continued with his art. If he had remained in the Aegean and painted and never returned. But then morning would come, and life would resume again. Even his beloved islands now had the red swastika flying over them.

Unfortunately, with the curfew, when sundown came, and it came early in winter, the city's streets were vacant. The only footsteps he would hear would be the nightly patrols. Still, he enjoyed working in the evenings, mainly when he was restoring an old painting. It was time-consuming, and he had to focus on the job at hand and not worry about the happenings around him. There would be nothing he could do about the DeBaets or Febe until morning.

After Elise left, he opened the doors to the apartment, put a jazz record on his Victrola, and turned up the sound to let the music drift down to the studio. While he appreciated the local groups that performed in Brussels and Paris, his heart was with American jazz. His favorite was Duke Ellington. With the melody of "Sophisticated Lady" in the background, he set his mind to the task at hand.

The portrait in front of him was from the mid-1800s. A stiff and stern-looking face of a woman, somewhere in her 60's, glared back at him. It was brought to him by a well-dressed man who turned out to be a banker with the Belgian National Bank, which now could be considered the Deutsche National Bank.

"It is a portrait of my wife's great grandmother. Her parents are coming for Christmas, and we want to show it off to them."

Valentin estimated that one of the many artists of the era who lived in Brussels was responsible for the painting. The colors were dark and cold, and after a hundred years of candles and oil lighting film, it was in dire need of restoration. The muted colors would not let the transformation look so dramatic, but he assured the man it would look much better.

The actual cleaning was a slow process, and he would only work on it in short bursts. Tonight, he was to work in the area around the mouth. As he looked at the woman in the painting, he wondered if a kind word ever crossed those tight lips; was there ever a night of real passion? He took a soft shaving brush and rubbed it over the canvas to remove the dirt. While others used chemicals, he preferred the tried-and-true method of lemon juice and warm water. Dampening a cotton ball with the liquid, he gently caressed the painting until the area around the mouth was damp. He took a moistened sponge and gently wiped off the solution. He would let it dry before starting the next step of cleaning with sodium carbonate and warm water.

Valentin turned off the lights in the studio and pushed the back door open. The cold air felt good after the intensity of effort and the heat from the lamp he used to light the painting. He loosened his tie and lit one of his Gauloises taking long drags into his lungs, thinking how nice a cup of coffee would taste about now when he heard a noise at the end of the alley. Nothing good came from anyone who was out after curfew. He was about to shut the door when he heard a soft voice call out, "Valentin."

He stepped into the alley. Through the darkness appeared a silhouette that he was very familiar with: Febe. His surprise quickly gave way to fear. He motioned for her to come inside, securing the door after her.

"What are you doing here? Is something wrong? Where is Eddie?"

She calmly took the cigarette out of his mouth, inhaling a few drags before returning it, and asked if she could have some water. Shaking his head apologetically for forgetting his manners, he disappeared up the stairs and brought back a tray with a glass of water and two brandy snifters. From a drawer in the small studio table, he produced a bottle of French cognac-- a gift from Gie Desmit that he rationed judiciously. He filled the two glasses and motioned for Febe to sit next to him. Taking a cigarette from his pack, he lit one and placed it between her lips. A smile crept across her face.

A sip of the cognac and she began to tell him what happened with Eddie. He could feel the anger rising when she spoke of him striking her and tearing her blouse. She told him of shooting Eddie and then dragging him back into the apartment. "He was drunk and crazy, and on his way to make a deal with the Boche. I had no other option." Valentin wanted to console her, but shooting Eddie was not what upset her; putting the mission in jeopardy did.

Valentin cursed the Germans for making war, he cursed the British for coming up with this mission, and he cursed the brothers for being so incompetent. "This mission has been a disaster from the start; we should never have picked those two."

She emptied her glass, savoring the last drop. "Now we have one wounded and one dead, can it get much worse?"

"It can; I have more bad news. We have heard from our informants that the Germans know that one of the brothers has been wounded and they will start searching hospitals and clinics in the morning. We must get Raymond out of Tillens' clinic."

Febe hung her head, fearing that her actions had now complicated everything. "No Febe, don't blame yourself. There are many to share the blame for this mission's failure, but you aren't one of them." He picked up the bottle and refilled her glass. "I will contact the boss in the morning and see what he has to say. Right now, it is too dangerous for you to leave."

Febe's eyes lifted toward the open door, and upwards. She was starting to shake her head no, when Valentin told her that his wife was not home. "There is a bed in the cellar that I will make up for you." She drained her second glass of cognac and picked up his still untouched drink before following him down the stairs to the basement. He struck a match and found his way to an old lantern. Its dim glow was like not having a light at all. The room was medium-size and cluttered with old canvases and boxes. Damp, cold, dreary; but she liked it better than the safe house. In the corner sat a narrow bed and a small table. He placed the candle on the table while Febe tested the mattress. She expected it to be much harder.

"You must be hungry? Let me bring you something?"

Febe looked up, finishing the cognac. Then she reached up, grabbed Valentin's tie, and pulled him down to her.

CHAPTER 20

Even before Valentin left the arms of Morpheus, he knew this vision was no dream. Throughout the night, from sleep to twilight, to sleep again, he replayed being with Febe. The way she reacted to his touch, the smoothness of her skin, the natural motion of their lovemaking. She lay there in his arms, her warm body next to his; the room didn't feel as cold, his life didn't seem as bleak, and the war didn't look as close. He forced himself to get out of bed, admiring her naked body before covering her again. He could see his breath in the cold basement air as he quietly moved toward the stairs and into the apartment. The warmth of the apartment felt good as he dressed, then went to the kitchen to make a pot of coffee and find some rolls and jam. A quick look out the window, even in the early morning light, told him all he needed to know about this day: cold and overcast. Placing the coffee and rolls on a tray, he returned to the basement.

"I thought you had deserted me." Febe had found his shirt and put it on, leaving enough buttons undone to make her breasts inviting. He wanted to devour her then and there but controlled himself, instead pouring the coffee. She sat on the bed, her knees up to her chest, holding the cup firmly against the body to warm herself. A sip of the drink and a surprised look came to her face as she realized it was real coffee she was tasting, not the brown water that wartime Brussels tried to convince you was palatable. Valentin hoped that she wouldn't ask where he had procured such a treat. He didn't want to admit it came from his wife's German master. They sat there on the bed huddled next to each other, enjoying the coffee and each other's warmth.

Finally, she asked, "What is our plan?" --praying that he had one.

How unfair life was. How often had Valentin thought of her, and now wanting nothing more than to spend the day making love, they must leave. He forced himself to turn his thoughts to what needed to be accomplished. "I must contact Gie and explain what has happened with Eddie. He can arrange the disposing of the body. We must also move Raymond. The sanatorium can no longer be safe for him or the doctor."

She pulled the blanket around her for warmth. "I have been wearing those old lady clothes too long. I want to go home and change."

He took her hand; it was freezing. "We need to get you warm. Come with me upstairs."

Febe raised her head towards the apartment. Valentin could sense the hesitation and wanted to reassure her. "Don't worry; we are alone."

Febe collected her clothes and followed up the stairs. The first thing she noticed entering the salon was how comfortably warm it was. The second thing was the pictures of Elise placed everywhere, showing her in all her beauty. On a cupboard were snapshots of Valentin and Elise in Paris, in Istanbul, on a Greek island. It was strange to see pictures of the man with whom she had spent the night making love holding another woman so close and looking so happy with her. Above the fireplace was a painting that she assumed Valentin did of Elise when she was younger, her long hair falling over shoulders, the sun on her body, a defiant look in her eyes. Febe tried to reconcile the pictures of Elise with the collaborator she knew her to be.

Valentin could see the expression on Febe's face as she looked at the pictures. Before she could ask any questions, he said in an almost whisper, "That was a long time ago. That world and woman no longer exist."

"Why do you stay with her?"

"It serves my purpose, Febe, but don't mistake it for love."

She gathered her clothes and went to the bathroom to dress. When she came out, Valentin smiled, "I see what you mean about the outfit."

She touched the side of his face. "I haven't been to my flat for days and I would like to get a change of clothes that fit me." They agreed to meet at the transit station later that morning. They walked downstairs, through the studio and to the back door. Valentin forced the door open and a gust of cold air greeted him, along with a sunless sky. With a kiss, she disappeared into the colorless morning. He returned to the apartment to wash and dress. It was still too early for Desmit to be at the office. Usually, he wouldn't think of contacting him at his home, but this couldn't wait.

He kept an eye out for anyone following him. At this time of the morning, the streets were still empty and anyone suspicious stood out. Valentin hopped the trolley a block from his shop, and with almost no traffic to slow them down, it was a quick 15-minute ride. Concerned about being tailed, he exited two stops from his destination and then worked his way through the neighborhoods until he reached Gie's. He lived on a short road with three large mansions on each side of the street. It was difficult to see the houses from the curb with their high walls and giant pin oaks that obscured the view.

Desmit had a large white three-story villa, which sat in the middle of the block. This section of town housed the well-heeled of Brussels. There were no sidewalks, and it was the kind of neighborhood where the owners kept their cars in the garage, not parked on the street. It was for that reason that a black Mercedes positioned across from Gie's house was enough to catch his attention. Valentin veered off to the side and watched. Even from this distance, he could see there were occupants in the car, at least two men. He could not make out who they were, but the man on the driver's side was using field glasses to observe the house.

The Germans liked to keep tabs on the successful and wealthy. But this was new, and Valentin thought the coincidence was too strong. Could they suspect Gie? Or had they learned of his involvement? Maybe the Gestapo had already arrested him, and set a trap for whoever tries to make contact. If this had been an ordinary meeting, Valentin would have waited and met him at the factory, or rendezvoused at a café. But this discussion could not wait, and walking up to the front gate and ringing the bell was not advisable. He moved away from the street and circled to the back of the villa. The wall in back was 3 meters high and covered with ivy, and it was guarded by overgrown shrubbery, making it challenging to get close. In the corner was a Judas gate wrapped with vines. He hated using this entrance. If seen, it would be hard to explain why he was there. But there was no other way.

He unlatched the gate, fought with the vines, and made his way onto the estate. Gie took great pride in his garden, where in happier times there had been great parties. Valentin remembered those nights. The prize roses would be in bloom, lights strung, tables set, and a small band playing. Today it was colorless in the winter grey. The flower beds were covered in mulch to protect them from the cold and offer them the opportunity of rebirth in the spring. The garden centerpiece was a round pond, a fountain of sculpted dolphins rising from the center. The fountain lay quiet, and the pool was dry; dead leaves covered the bottom.

He followed the path to the main house. Off to the side were a bank of floor-to-ceiling windows, their shutters open. A warm yellow glow came from the room. Valentin was looking into Gie's study, where he worked in the early morning. He approached and could see the boss having coffee at his desk and reading. He stepped up to the glass door and gave a light rap. Gie moved his hand to the desk's middle drawer, where Valentin knew he kept his pistol. Looking up, Gie recognized Valentin and shoved the drawer closed again. He moved to the door and invited him in. Ever the gentleman, he guided his guest over to the fireplace, which had a roaring fire going, to warm himself. Coffee was offered and declined.

"Then maybe a little of this to warm you on a cold morning," Gie suggested, picking up a brandy snifter from a side table. "I always have a little bracer before I leave in the morning. To protect me against the cold."

Valentin long ago stopped trying to guess how Desmit came across his fine French cognac. It was enough for him that his host was always willing to share. They sat on the sofa in front of the fire; the brandy indeed was warming him up. Gie opened up his arms in the *what gives?* gesture.

Where to start? First, Valentin warned him of the black Mercedes parked in front, but of course, Gie was already aware. "Whenever the Germans are at a loss for clues, they put a tail on everyone. They can never decide whether I am worth watching or not, but it is good that you saw them and came in a back way."

Another sip of the brandy and Valentin filled him on what had happened between Febe and Eddie. Gie sat there not saying anything. Then he walked over to his humidor and took his time choosing a cigar, or maybe he was just thinking. A man lost in thought. He clipped the end of the cigar and lit it. He stood at his desk, his head engulfed in a cloud of smoke, then coolly addressed Valentin. "Monsieur DeBaets' death solves half our problem. Do nothing with the body. Someone will collect it, but we must find a safe house for the other one. Tillens will know where to take him. Also, it is time for the girl to go back to work. She has taken too many risks, and the odds always catch up with you. It is better if she stays inactive for a while."

Valentin acknowledged with a nod. He didn't want to send Febe back to the trains and out of his life, but he knew better than to argue with Gie.

"Move the wounded man, then go back to your studio. I will contact you later tonight." Valentin finished the last of the brandy and departed using the same path that had brought him to the boss.

....

Febe arrived at the transit station early and found a seat on a bench that sheltered her from the elements. She was happy to be wearing clothes that fit and not looking like a matron. Even though her bath had been in cold water, she was relieved to wash away the events of the recent days. She thought happily of the moments she had with Valentin; in the uncertainty of her life, even a single moment of pleasure was to be cherished.

Sitting on the bench, wedged between two rather large ladies, Febe found the arrangement uncomfortable after 15 minutes. It was almost time for Valentin to arrive; just a few more minutes. She stood to see if she could make him out in the crowd. To her left she heard a commotion. Turning around, she saw members of the Flemish National Union, the fascist political party and collaborators, checking papers. From where did they come? The VNV were the lapdogs of the Germans: pro-Nazi Belgians, obeying their masters and betraying their friends and neighbors. They were to Belgium what the stormtrooper was to Germany. No more than hooligans, she thought, shakedown artists who would confiscate anything they felt they could eat or sell for money to curry favors from the Germans. She looked around to see if there was a way out, but leaving now would only call attention to herself. She cursed herself for daydreaming about Valentin and not paying attention to what was happening around her. Pulling papers from her purse, she waited for them to approach. She again had automatic tucked in her waistband, snug against her back. There were four of them, and it appeared they all had been drinking before they decided to do their morning shopping.

They were getting impatient as there was little to take. An old lady had a bag of vegetables, and they were able to lift a little tobacco and a few bottles of wine, but this was turning into a waste of time for them and tempers were getting short. Two of them had had enough and boarded one of the buses to see who they might roust, but the two remaining still hadn't finished. They approached the bench where she was sitting, both men extremely thin and drawn. One had sandy-colored hair and the other's was black with much gray running through it. Unshaven, with soiled uniforms, Febe could only imagine what the real police force thought of these thugs. The sandy-haired one looked at the old lady sitting next to her. Before he could ask for papers the lady jumped up and started yelling that she had nothing for them to take. People scattered. Febe, seeing an opportunity, stood to leave, but the one with black hair stood in her way. "Not so fast."

His partner grabbed the old lady's hands and lifted her arms above her head. In mock admiration, he said, "Well then maybe we'll take you with us, a little time with the boys will put a smile on your face." The women started wailing. He slapped her across the face. "Shut up, whore. None of us are drunk enough to want to see you naked."

Febe pulled the woman away from them. "Leave her alone," she admonished.

The dark-hair one moved in close to her, putting his face within inches of hers. She could smell a mixture of wine, cigarettes, and body odor; she almost gagged. "Watch your mouth, my little cabbage."

"What kind of man strikes an old woman? You should be ashamed of yourself."

"Open your mouth again, and I'll show you what kind of man I am. Your papers!"

As the sandy-haired one examined her papers, the other stood behind her and amused himself by blowing his cigarette smoke in her direction. She turned around and shot him a glace. He only smiled through his broken teeth.

"What do you think, Deni?" the sandy-haired one asked. "Should we take her back to the station for further questioning?"

"A good idea, Lucas, maybe for a body search." He leaned in closer and whispered in her ear, "A little time on your knees, back at the station, will put a smile on that face of yours." He then pushed her into Lucas, whose hands quickly slipped inside her jacket and moved directly to her breasts. She pushed him away and spat in his face. He slapped her hard, knocking her to the ground. Then they stood her up, one under each arm. "Striking an officer is a capital crime," Deni observed. "Let's take her back to the station and see how she likes the inside of a cell."

Febe tried to break away but was grabbed and thrown again to the pavement. Lucas straddled her body, gripped her collar with his left hand to lift her head off the ground, and then struck her three quick times with his right. She could taste blood trickling from her nose to her mouth. The two thugs were yelling at her, but everything was just a blur; she couldn't move. Lucas went to strike her again, and this time, she brought her knee up between his legs. As he rolled over in pain, Febe went for her gun. She wanted to kill both of them, but her reflexes were dulled by the blows to her head. Deni kicked the weapon out of her hand. Lucas leaned down and struck her again.

"The little bitch has a gun," Deni shouted, as he leaned over to pick up the automatic.

"Well, well, well, how did you get a gun, kitty cat?"

The blood was now streaming from Febe's nose. Her left eye had a nasty welt and was beginning to blacken.

"I smell money here, Deni. I'm sure our friends will pay handsomely for the opportunity to find out where she got this heater."

Valentin had arrived just before the two VNV men started to harass Febe. His heart sank as he witnessed the scene from afar. His instincts were to step in and rescue her, but he knew that would be hopeless and would only get him killed. *My God, every time he thinks it can't get worse, it does.* Desmit would tell him that she had compromised herself by carrying a gun and then losing her temper with her tormentors. Valentin watched as they stood her up. The dilemma was, did he follow them, or proceed to Tillens' clinic? His heart begged to follow Febe, but his brain knew his responsibility was Raymond. That was his mission. Valentin watched as they hauled her away, one of them on each side of her holding her up, her face bloodied. *Someone will pay for this*, he said to himself.

CHAPTER 21

Valentin waited to the last moment to board his bus, jumping on just before the door closed. Content that no one had followed, he took a seat close to the back. His mind was on Febe, both for her safety and the potential damage to the cell. He was sure the two thugs that took her had no idea who they had. For them it was just a frisk that had gone bad. The problem was the gun. Having a firearm marked a person as a criminal or a member of the Resistance. They would eventually turn her over to the Germans, if for no other reason than to collect a reward--their pieces of gold for arresting one of their countrymen. The Gestapo, however was another matter. Once they knew she had been on the train with the DeBaets, it would only be a short time before they would connect the dots. How much time did they have before the professionals went to work on her?

The bus approached the Avenue de Daim. Valentin sat casually in his seat, making no effort to leave. At the stop, he watched the people exiting, scanning their faces. The door wes half-closed when Valentin made his getaway. The bus was moving before anyone realized he had gotten off; a look over his shoulder told him that no one else had exited.

Valentin forced himself to stay focused: not to think of Febe, not to trip himself up, not to put Tillens or Raymond in danger. He was sauntering down the street, occasionally stopping to look into a shop window, while paying attention to the reflection in the glass. A woman with too many children and not enough hands caught his eye. He tipped his hat, opening the door to the building, and helped put the children and a small bag of groceries into the empty lobby before moving on again.

Valentin walked another block and turned down a narrow street toward an old three-story building, painted white with a placard on the mahogany door identifying it as The Sunrise Clinic. He knew this to be a place where the very rich of the city would come to sober up or recover from a nervous breakdown. Valentin walked past the street entrance to the main entrance, where an ambulance and cars were parked. He recognized one of the vehicles. It was Dr. Tillens', the one used to drive Febe back to Brussels. He moved to the loading dock, and then through the back door attended by an orderly. The attendant was a large black man behind a standing desk, wearing a freshly laundered lab coat. He was making his way through two lists of inventories, trying to reconcile them. Valentin waited for the man to acknowledge him but finally had to clear his throat to get his attention. Slowly, the orderly put his pencil down and took off his reading glasses to give them a cleaning before addressing Valentin. "Yes?"

"Please advise the doctor that Monsieur Joseph has arrived," he replied, using the code name that he and Tillens had agreed on.

With the experience of a man paid to see nothing and to say even less, the orderly picked up the phone and informed the doctor. In a voice revealing his Congo roots, he instructed Valentin to follow the hallway to the stairs. The doctor's office could be found on the first floor, third on the left.

At the top of the stairs, Valentin was met by a nurse who directed him to Tillens' office and assured him the doctor would be along presently. The doctor's office was a small, cramped affair with a desk, two chairs, and walls covered with bookcases that were overflowing with books. Behind his desk was a window onto the main entrance. The building had once been a hotel. In 1914, the Germans commandeered it when they came through Belgium the first time. When they departed in 1918, the building was left in a state of disrepair. Sometime in the early 20s, Tillens and two partners purchased it and turned it into a sanatorium for the wealthy. Since June 1940, it had been used predominately by the occupation to handle family members of administrators or high-ranking military and occupation officials. The doctor noted with the conflict going on in Russia, more and more military men had checked themselves into the clinic.

Valentin stood by the window, looking down into the entrance. Its circular driveway, with a fountain in the middle, stopped where was once the reception salon of the hotel. Like most fountains in Brussels, the water feature no longer worked, and the driveway was missing enough brick pavers to make one cautious when parking. The joke at the clinic was, the bricks only mattered if you could afford to have a car.

Valentin had been here once before and knew the ground floor was for storage and therapy. The first was for offices, and the top two levels were for patients. He could only assume Raymond was being kept there under an assumed name. It had to be a concern to keep DeBaets at a clinic that had so many German patients. Men with gunshot wounds would not come to this clinic. A simple slip of the lip by one of the employees, and it would be all over.

No matter how many times he admonished himself to stay focused, his mind wandered to Febe. His thoughts were interrupted by Dr. Tillens entering the room. He gestured for Valentin to sit, taking his seat behind the desk and looking to him to give a reason for this visit. All the events that had transpired since they last met poured out of Valentin: the shooting of Eddie, the meeting with Gie, and now Febe's capture. He warned that keeping Raymond here put everyone at risk, and it was Desmit's order to move him in anticipation of having him flown out of the country. Nodding, Tillens pulled out his pipe and loaded its bowl, using the time to think. He explained his dilemma: "Moving this boy could kill him, but having him discovered would be his death warrant and probably ours too."

Valentin's nervous energy was getting the better of him. He stood, then leaned over the desk and spoke, "Desmit's network reported that the police have started to check hospitals and will soon start looking at private clinics. Someone will say something, whether by accident or on purpose. We need to get him out of here and then out of the country."

The scent of sweet vanilla tobacco filled the room as Tillens acknowledged the inevitable; it was indeed too dangerous with Raymond at the clinic. Valentin asked him what their options were.

Tillens took his pipe out of his mouth and, using a small penknife fiddled with the bowl before relighting it. "We can't keep him here, and we can't move him back to the safe house. There is only one place we can take him temporarily. My home until we can get him out of the country."

"Which means we need to transport him once more, and the dangers that entails."

"It is either that, or we leave him here."

"We take him and pray that Gie can get him out of the country."

The doctor buzzed for Mrs. Jacobs, his head nurse. When she arrived, he asked her to prepare the patient in 334. "We are transferring him to another facility."

She looked at him curiously. "Does the doctor believe it is advisable to move this patient?"

"Yes, the doctor does believe it is advisable to move this patient," he snapped back.

"Very well, sir, how will he be transported?"

"Bring him to the lift, and Lewis will handle it from there."

On the third floor, the nurse carefully moved Raymond from the bed to a gurney. Mrs. Jacobs had worked for Tillens for many years. She knew that many wealthy and influential people came through the clinic, and the key to her continued employment was never to ask questions. Her conversations with the patients were always about the weather or how well they were doing. If by chance she met any of them outside the clinic, she would never acknowledge meeting them before. She gave care to all, regardless of their condition or belief, but Mrs. Jacobs was relieved to see the departure of the young man in room 334. His case was not one of alcoholism or losing touch with reality. She recognized the wounds and what caused them. She knew only trouble followed him, and maybe even death.

She whispered into Raymond's ear that they were moving him, but he was unconscious. She pushed the gurney to the only lift in the building and pressed the button to summon it to the third floor. It seemed to take an eternity to arrive, but eventually, the door opened and Lewis, the orderly, exited. He took the gurney from her and rolled it carefully into the lift, turning to indicate there was no need for her to assist. He secured the door closed, and the long creaky ride to the ground floor started.

Valentin and Tillens met the lift and walked with Lewis through the hallway to the back entrance. Stopping at the door, the orderly opened it and scanned the entrance. He gave a nod that it was all clear, and the three of them moved the gurney to the car. "I need to monitor him. Put him in the back seat." The orderly obeyed the doctor's request, picking up Raymond as if he were a doll and laying him down gently in back.

"Help me with this blanket," Tillens instructed Valentin.

"What if the police stop us?"

"Pray that they don't."

The doctor eased himself behind the steering wheel and started the car. There was no traffic as they pulled out of the clinic. Valentin hoped that the absence of vehicles on the road would not draw attention to them. Even with a medical doctor emblem on the car, he was concerned. What usually would be a short 15-minute drive to the doctor's office seemed like an eternity now. He continuously kept looking out the back window, then at the patient. Raymond's breathing was shallow, and twice Valentin leaned over the front seat to check his pulse.

It was dark by the time they arrived at the doctor's house. He pulled up close to the side entrance and turned off the engine. Together they moved Raymond inside, an occasional moan coming from him. They set him up on the examination table, and the doctor went to work checking his vitals. They were interrupted by a knock at the door that separated the house from the examination area. Tillens motioned for Valentin to stay in the examination room with Raymond and then moved through his office to answer the door. Valentin could hear voices but not the conversation. Within a few minutes, Tillens returned to inform him that Desmit had sent a message.

"He asks for us to wait for him here."

Another groan came from Raymond, and the doctor

went to him. "Whatever we are to do, we must do it fast. He has a fever that is the result of the wound. He needs medical care that only a hospital can give." Valentin sat in the straight-backed chair next to the table and waited for Gie to arrive.

The wait was not long. He came in a few minutes later via the side door. Gie followed the doctor through the reception area into the examination room. Looking at Raymond on the table and then at Valentin sitting, he wasn't sure he could help either man.

"The city is on full alert. You two were fortunate to have arrived here without being stopped. The Germans know this man is here in the city."

Fear flushed through Valentin that Febe had already been broken and had given up the whole operation. He rose to warn Desmit.

"Valentin, before you say anything, I know about Febe. She was taken to the police station and then turned over to General Beck's headquarters."

"Has she talked?"

"Not yet, but she will eventually tell them all they want to know. The man who will interrogate her most certainly will be Beck's henchman, Major Kohler. He is ruthless and thorough. We are all in danger if she talks."

Valentin wanted to know, 'If she hasn't told the Germans about Raymond, then who has?"

"Once again, we have been betrayed by a friend. For some time, we have employed the wine merchant Alain Legrand. Because of his contacts, he was able to travel easily between France, Belgium, and Germany. Unfortunately, he receives money from both sides. Somehow he found out where we were hiding the DeBaets."

"Will he be able to identify Febe?"

"Only as a person he knows from his train travels. They have had no other contact, nor would they have known that they were both working for the cause. I will deal with him later. Right now, we need to get this poor man out of the country, and Febe out of jail."

"Will the British help?"

"I think so. We can sweeten the pot by also offering the Brits one of their flyers shot down over Belgium. We are in the process of contacting them now."

"And Legrand?"

"A bullet to the face for Monsieur Legrand."

"I think not, Gie. I have a better idea that may help us rid ourselves of him and free Febe."

When Valentin finished explaining, the three men parted: Desmit to contact the British, Tillens to look after Raymond, and Valentin to start to put his strategy in motion.

CHAPTER 22

Lucas and Deni hauled Febe into the police station with one man under each of her arms, dragging her, hardly letting her feet touch the ground. Deni took pleasure in putting an occasional elbow into her ribs whenever she lagged or showed any kind of resistance. Febe knew that the mistake was all hers; she should never have been so stupid as to let these two morons get the better of her. Her face hurt from the blows and felt puffy. At least her nose had stopped bleeding. Had Valentin seen what transpired? It made no difference now. Gie preached the rule constantly: hold out for 24 hours to give your comrades time to get away. She was sure her current jailers would not be a big problem. They were bullies, yes, always happy to slap a woman around; but she had a weapon, and that would mean a bounty from the Germans for turning her over to them. She also knew the Gestapo would be a different matter.

The police station was overflowing with people who all seemed to have an expression of fear on their faces. There were too few chairs and even fewer police officers. A sheet of paper on a desk at the entrance served as a waiting list. Occasionally an officer would walk over, scan the list, and call a name. Men stood in small groups smoking and speaking in hushed voices, while what few chairs existed were occupied by the elderly. The massive double doors that led into the station were open to allow the cigarette smoke to escape. Unfortunately, the cold air came rushing in. There was no relief from the chill. People hunched inside their coats, stamping their feet to keep warm.

Febe was taken up a set of wooden stairs to the second floor, where there were several holding cells all in a line. It was impossible to see the occupants, but she certainly could hear the moaning coming from them.

Deni nodded to his partner in the direction of the interrogation room. "Put her in the sweatbox. Let's see if we can get any information to help our cause. Then we can call Major Kohler's office."

Lucas pushed her into a dingy, airless little room that smelled of cigarettes and vomit. Its four blank walls were dirty, with brown paint peeling off in large swatches. A water leak from the roof caused a stain on one of them that ran from the ceiling to the floor. A small wooden table was in the middle of the room. The light in the room had an ugly glare from four bright blubs that heated up the small area.

"I think we should make sure she has no other weapon," a leering Lucas proclaimed.

Deni pulled off Febe's coat and held her straight up as Lucas searched her. Not content with a pat-down, his hands moved across her body. He pulled up her sweater, slipping his hands under her bra, making sure to pinch each nipple. In one motion, he lifted her dress and pulled her panties down. Febe kicked out at him but received another blow on her swollen face. She then stood passively as he ran his hand across her. Remembering stories of women dealing with interrogators who started to get sexual, it occurred to her to try to put them off by urinating. Deni quickly let go and moved away from her.

Lucas gave her another slap across the face. Then he pushed her down into one of the chairs and picked up her purse, which had fallen on the floor. He emptied the contents on the table, scrutinizing her identity card before moving on to her work permit. Finding her change purse, he pocketed the few francs he found. All the while, Deni sat across the table, exhaling smoke into her face. She tried to look through rather than at him. Lucas satisfied that there was nothing of value to be found in the purse, sat down, lit a cigarette, and started the interrogation.

....

After a stroll through the neighborhood to put off any tails from the doctor's house, Desmit and Valentin arrived at the car. Gie settled in behind the wheel of his Citroën Traction Avant. It had been his gift to himself on a trip to Paris in 1939. Now, he thought about selling it, as he had heard it was becoming the favorite car of the Gestapo in Paris. He loved the way it drove and had had it painted a rich burgundy color at no small expense to himself. He would drop Valentin off at the tram stop and then head back to his office. Valentin sat next to him, silent, lost in thought. He had broken one of Desmit's golden rules: "Never become emotionally involved with your fellow resistance members. Not personally, not romantically, and certainly not sexually." Valentin was letting his emotions get the better of him, thinking like a Frenchman, not a Belgian.

There was a group of people waiting for the bus as the car approached the stop. Valentin nodded his farewell and exited the Citroën, quickly disappearing into the crowd. The car sped away down the boulevard. Desmit knew there was no easy way to contact the British. After the last attempt to rescue the DeBaets had failed, they wanted nothing to do with him or his band of brothers. They had become suspicious of the informants, traitors, and political infighting of the Underground in Belgium. While he had come to recognize that each man had his motives for turning on his fellow countrymen, he could never accept any of their reasons. To him, a traitor was a traitor. He tired of hearing from those that he caught, begging for forgiveness. He had heard it all. "The Germans threatened my family," "We were starving," "They tortured me," "Why fight the Nazis? They are never going to leave." It was slow going, but he was uncovering the scum and sending them to hell one by one with his trademark bullet to the face.

His British contact in Brussels was Major Griffin, the same officer who had started this mission. Of course, now that the operation was falling apart, Griffin had gone into hiding. He had little use for Desmit, and the feeling was mutual. Gie blamed the Major for this whole debacle. It was he who had picked the brothers without consulting him, and then continued the operation even after Gie advised that the two were not reliable yet the British laid the failure entirely on Gie's organization. He shook his head. *The price of doing business with the devil*, he whispered to himself.

Time was running short. If Gie played it safe and tried to contact Major Griffin through the usual messenger system, it could take days. With the city-wide search going on, any use of the short-wave radio would bring immediate German response as he and Griffin had no code between them. He had no option but to contact the Major directly. It would undoubtedly infuriate the Brit, but no matter; he could think of nothing else. The British may have thought Gie and his group incompetent, but they were not so clumsy that they couldn't discover where Griffin was hiding.

A few days before Griffin, and another man had taken up residence in a secluded farmhouse outside the village of Daens in the Aalst region, northwest of Brussels. A group of boys on their way to fish stopped at the house to investigate the new arrivals. They were shooed away by a man, and later they laughed about how poorly he spoke Flemish. One of the boys related the incident to his father, Karel Van Hoebeek, a member of the Resistance. The father investigated and sent a full report to Desmit, who immediately recognized the description as Griffin's. That thought Gie, *is the difference between life and death, small mistakes and chance encounters.* The Brit was very lucky that it was Gie and not the Germans who received the report. He turned his car on to the Hausman Boulevard and headed towards Aalst. A black sedan following at a discreet distance did the same. The plainclothes occupants were two members of the German military police under the command of Major Kohler.

....

After Tillens let Gie and Valentin out the back door, he watched them disappear into the row of houses. They took a roundabout way through the neighborhood before returning to the car. As an added precaution, they drove past his house. If Tillens saw a tail, he would leave a coded message at the factory for the boss. From the salon window, staying behind the curtains, he saw Gie's Citroën pass and then waited long enough to see a black Mercedes take off after them. His heart raced, but he knew that Desmit had experience handling curious Germans. All the same, it was a cause for concern. He called the factory, leaving the coded message.

Tillens worried they had overextended themselves on this mission and would now all pay dearly. He filled with a sense of dread that the Hun would never go. They were ruthless, and able to spend on informers. On the other hand, their small group was a coalition of the willing that always seemed to put one foot forward before taking two steps backward.

After making the warning call, Tillens climbed the stairs to his second-floor bedroom. There was stiffness in his back with each step. It had bothered him for years; "the gift of aging," he would tell his patients. The cold and stress seemed to aggravate it more, and in this dark winter of Nazi occupation, it seemed to be always hurting. He reached under his bed and retrieved a gripsack he kept there in case he needed

THE KÖLN EPISODE

to make a fast escape. From the wall, he took down a picture that was hanging over a chest of drawers. The grainy black and white photograph was of his parents, a scratch line running just over his father's head. They sat for this portrait, stiff and upright, long before the Germans came the first time. How very long ago that seemed now. Turning over the frame, he took off the back. Behind the picture was a Spanish passport, a gift from Desmit. From the top shelf of his wardrobe, he retrieved a .32 caliber Barretta, a box of shells, and an envelope containing a few thousand francs. Although he had not fired the pistol in some time, he remembered the way it fit in his hand. Tillens checked the clip, put a round in the chamber, and slipped on the safety. He slid the money and gun into his grip and replaced it under the bed.

The doctor was startled by a loud cry from downstairs, more primal than identifiable. The morphine must have worn off. He hurried to check on his patient, the pain in his back even worse on the trip down. Raymond lay there in a pool of sweat, with a weak pulse, shallow breathing, skin a pallid yellow, and now a running fever. The doctor fetched water from the kitchen tap and sponged his patient's face. He was mumbling incoherently, making it difficult for Tillens to understand what he was saying. Looking down at the man, he feared that Raymond might not make it through the night, let alone survive the flight to England. There was not much more he could do for him. Raymond fell back into unconsciousness. Tillens checked his pulse one more time before going to made himself a pot of tea, then returned and sat next to the poor man to pray for the impossible.

....

The two soldiers in the black Mercedes kept their distance from the burgundy Citroën. The driver, Hans Klein, had followed this man before and thought him predictable. He was explaining this to his young partner, Otto Zimmermann, a draftee who had just arrived in Brussels. Otto seemed indifferent, only concerned with how much longer they would be working. Being part of a police detail was not his idea; he had hoped for guard duty at the railroad yards. The word was, the work was smooth, and if you had quick wits, there was money to be made with the black market. It was not unusual for shipments to be lost, or on occasion, added to, and all for a price. But even with corruption, the German army had a seniority system. He had to wait, even bribe the duty sergeant. In the meantime, he sat with this Hans and his constant chatter.

"My time has taught me the furniture maker makes stops for wine and women. And I can tell you he likes his wine old and his women young." Hans loved laughing at his own jokes. "Major Kohler has me follow Desmit every so often. He employs many young women at his factory, and I am guessing he is giving them all the Schwanz."

What he didn't tell Otto, nor Major Kohler, is that Monsieur Desmit was a difficult man to follow. On more than one occasion, Desmit was able to shake him. The only way to pick him up again was to return to the furniture factory, where he always accommodated Hans by showing up. However, Hans decided long ago that it would be unwise to include these episodes in his report. The Major took a dim view of anyone losing a tail. He remembered the ugly incidents when his comrades reported back that their suspects gave them the slip. There were recriminations, canceled leaves, and, even worse, transfers to work details. No, he liked the sheltered life in Belgium and would keep that information to himself. Hans preferred getting fat in Brussels to freezing in Stalingrad. He had had enough of Russia, having been severely wounded on the first day of Operation Barbarossa. A veteran of the Polish and French campaigns, he thought that when they invaded the Soviet Union that September, the Reds would give up by Christmas. While Goebbels and his crew were touting victories, friends who made it back told a different story. The Russians weren't the weak animals they were led to believe, but fearsome fighters who made you pay dearly for every centimeter of ground. There were tales of Russian soldiers overrunning German field hospitals and decapitating all the patients. Then there was the Russian winter; to live and fight in those inhuman conditions. Hans shook his head; no, he was happy to be posted where he was. In Belgium, his biggest worry was that he had a partner who was young and more interested in booze and dames than the two men they were following.

Desmit eventually let his passenger out at the bus stop. The man disappeared into the crowd, and neither Hans nor his partner was able to get a good description of him. Hans decided they would stay with the Citroën. If Otto weren't so young and inexperienced, Hans would have had him follow the stranger. But he feared that Otto would not only lose his target but probably get lost himself. And then who would be to blame?

Instead of taking the route to his factory, Desmit detoured, taking the road leading out of town.

"Hello, this is new." Hans was irritated that the nightly routine had changed. "I hope he's not planning a drive into the country."

"It's past curfew. Can't we pull him over?"

"Not an option. Major Kohler has given him a pass to move around past curfew."

"Why?"

"In hopes he will lead us to something useful. I'm not sure, the Major doesn't confide in me, but I don't think he trusts the cabinet maker."

Otto was hoping this would not mean they would be

working late. After all, they weren't the fucking Gestapo. Hans had assured him Desmit's nightly activity was that he stopped by the factory by eight and was home for dinner by nine. He had been looking forward to joining his friends for a few beers and then hopefully taking full advantage of the young girls who gave themselves up for favors.

Instead, he heard, "Stay alert, Otto. We need to keep our distance; we don't want to be spotted."

....

The wine merchant slept peacefully in his large bed, with its soft mattress, in the best hotel in Brussels. The outside world was locked out, and only the comfort and luxury of the Hotel Metropole were engulfing him. These days, getting accommodations in the Hotel was nearly impossible. Rooms were either taken by the Nazis for residences, or reserved for guests of the Reich. Alain Legrand was in a deep sleep of satisfaction with his connections and money from his German masters.

The day had been successful for him, selling Champagne to the bars whose clients were prominent Nazis. It was better dealing with the bars that catered to the Germans than selling to them directly. It was a hard-learned lesson: the Boche either forced him to take a deep discount or would not pay at all. He also had a quiet meeting with the Resistance. He learned nothing new to report back to Kohler, but felt something big was coming his way. And that too would yield him money in the long run.

Alain Legrand never heard the door open, or the footsteps come across the room. Jolted out of his deep sleep by the sudden glare of his table lamp, he tried to rise, but an arm came out of the darkness and pushed him back down. "Look up at the ceiling and don't move" was all the wine merchant heard. What he felt was the cold muzzle of a pistol in his ear.

"Please, if it is money you want, my wallet is on the cabinet."

"Alain Legrand?"

Fearing his next words would be his last, he nervously answered, "Yes."

"Do not worry." The voice sounded more mocking than reassuring. Legrand struggled to make out the shadow, but it was hopeless. What little he could see was in silhouette, and the stranger appeared to be wearing a mask. "I have been sent by your friends, the Belgian National Movement."

Had the moment he always feared finally come? Had the betrayer been betrayed? He waited for the bullet to the face.

"Don't look so scared, you are going to wet the bed." Sweat poured off his head despite the coolness of the room. "We need your assistance."

Legrand exhaled, "Surely this is not necessary?" He attempted to point to the gun, but the intruder slapped his hand away.

"I trust no one, Monsieur Legrand."

"What is it you want of me?" He could hardly get his words out. "May I have a glass of water?"

"Listen to me. We have a critical mission for you."

"What can that possibly be? I am only a wine merchant."

"Ah, but one with powerful friends. We need a messenger to travel to Switzerland tomorrow night."

"Are you crazy?" Legrand blurted out. "Tomorrow? That is impossible..."

"This is not a request." The voice hardened, and the

muzzle pushed further into his ear canal. "It is an order."

"But why me?"

"Because of your profession, you have reason to travel, plus we believe we can trust you, yes?"

"You know my loyalty is with the cause," Legrand swiftly responded.

"And of course, the Germans trust you," delivered with a hint of sarcasm.

"What is it that I am to do? Relaying gossip is one thing, but I have no training for clandestine activity."

"You will deliver a package to friends in Geneva."

"What is in the package? Are you aware that I will need a special pass to proceed to Switzerland?"

"What you will be delivering is not your concern. You are merely to carry and deliver. Later today, someone will contact you. You'll receive money, your travel papers, and tickets, along with the briefcase you will be delivering. You will board the 7:20 PM to Munich, then transfer there for the Geneva train."

"And to whom will I hand over the package?"

"They'll find you."

There was nothing about this that Legrand liked. The time had come to disappear. But it was as if the tormenter could read his thoughts.

"Monsieur Legrand, in case you are worried about your safety, we will have people following you until you are on the train, and even beyond. Do not leave this room until you are to depart for the station. The hotel has excellent food service." Legrand thought his heart would leap out of his chest. "'This is all for your protection, of course."

"If I am to be out of town, there is much I must do tomorrow."

With another poke of his automatic, his visitor spat out the words, "The Germans can wait a week to get their wine. Be at the station at 7:00 PM. Understood?"

Legrand nodded his head. His tormenter switched off the light and moved across the room quietly. Legrand looked over when the door closed but the stranger had already slipped out into the hallway.

In the darkened hallway Valentin removed the ski mask and proceeded to the back staircase. He was met inside the door by Rene, a member of the Underground and the Hotel's night porter. Valentin exchanged the mask and pistol for his scarf and overcoat.

"Keep an eye on him, Rene, although I don't think he will be any trouble. He is scared enough that he won't even leave his bed to pee."

"Not to worry. We have someone coming to make sure our friend won't get into any mischief."

The two men shook hands and then Valentin was off, casually moving down the stairway and then exiting the hotel. He stayed in the shadows of the building, deciding what would be the best route back to his flat. With the curfew, it would take some time to weave his way home. And once there, he had much to do before his day would be over.

Legrand lay in his bed, unable to move, trying to get his breathing under control. He feared that he might have a heart attack. The wine merchant poured himself a glass of water from the pitcher and tried to process what had happened. In the past, the Resistance had used him for small assignments.

He regularly collected gossip that he gleaned from his clients and reported back. Would this be a new phase? Were the MBN now taking him into their confidence? Should he go through with this mission? Or once on the train and away from his minders should he open the documents, get off at the first available stop and return to Brussels? He could deliver them to Kohler for a price, and if this was as important as his night intruder had mentioned, it could mean enough gold to get him out of Europe and start a new life. Away from the Resistance and the Germans, maybe Argentina. But if he went through with the assignment, would the Underground not be indebted to him? He stared at the ceiling and tried to decide: which would be the better deal for Alain Legrand?

....

Gie approached the checkpoint leading out of Brussels. In his headlights he could see both guards scrambling out of their little hut. They were young, and neither appeared to be expecting any night visitors. One was buttoning his tunic while the other was wiping the sleep from his eyes. His unexpected intrusion on their rest probably explained their gruff attitude as they approached the car. They ordered him out of the vehicle, one keeping his rifle at the ready, the other demanding his papers. Recognizing that he was not an officer, they assumed it was another drunk breaking curfew. They were relieved that he had the proper documents, figuring that he must be a VIP to have a night pass. They were particularly amused when they asked him to state what business brought him out at this time of night, and he suggested he was off on a romantic adventure. "Even in these desperate times, an old man must have his needs met, and there is a little miss in Daens who knows why we have tongues." The bored soldiers happily accepted his offer of French cigarettes and cheered him as the car pulled away.   They were surprised when a minute later, the black Mercedes pulled up. They explained their interaction with the driver of the Citroën, Hans felt his intuition confirmed when they told him the gentleman was off to visit one of the local girls.

He turned to his dozing partner. "Forget your beer and dame, Otto. We have a long evening ahead of us."

Desmit always knew when Kohler's men were following him. Unlike the Gestapo, the military police had no training in the art of tracking someone while being invisible. He believed that when the Major had nothing else for his agents to do, he would assign them to follow him. They were easy to identify, prompting him to adhere to a regular schedule, keeping his activities as predictable as possible. He had discovered that when he needed privacy, it was never too hard to lose them. Tonight, with only two cars on a country road, it was impossible to tail a person discreetly. He feared that they were so far behind that they would get lost, which was something he did not want to happen. Gie figured that the sentries would relay his final destination to his pursuers. He would deal with them in his own good time.

He arrived in Daens, one of the many villages that made up the Aalst region in Flemish East Flanders. He drove to the village square, an 18th-century church its centerpiece, one of the many named Cathedral of Our Lady. He parked in a prominent place right in front of the church, making it hard for anyone following him to miss. He ran across the square, then down an ally to a wooden staircase in the back of a two-story building. Gie arrived at the home of Karel Van Hoebeek, a Dutchman who had lived in Belgium since before the first war. He was a blacksmith, with a wife, six children, and a mistress. With matinee idol good looks, he always found a way to land himself in trouble with the local mademoiselles. His days were long and hard, but he profited from being the only blacksmith in the area. He was known to tell friends that the only thing he hated more than the forge was the Germans. He had joined the Resistance immediately after the invasion. But with so many children, Gie was always hesitant to give him an assignment that would put him in harm's way. Unfortunately, tonight that would have to change.

Climbing up the wooden stairway to Karel's home, every step creaking, Gie was sure that not only Van Hoebeek knew he was coming but so did the town. He gave a gentle rap at the entrance and a lone figure in a nightshirt, holding a candle, opened the door slightly. It took Van Hoebeek a moment to recognize Desmit.

"Oh, my lord, Monsieur Desmit. Please come in." He extended his hand, which felt like a vice to Gie.

As he entered, Van Hoebeek's wife appeared in her dressing robe, looking both irritated and scared. In the low light, Gie could see the children's faces peering from a dark hallway.

"Madame Van Hoebeek, I am sorry for this late-night intrusion, but I must speak with your husband. It is of utmost importance."

Before she had a chance to reply, her husband told her to get the children back in their rooms, and he would join her shortly. Karel invited Desmit into their small kitchen and offered to make coffee. When Gie declined, his host offered, "Maybe a shot of homemade Jenever?"

"No, thank you, my friend." He moved closer to Karel and lowered his voice so as not to be heard by the wife. "I need your help."

"You need only to command."

"You will also need some help. Are there any men you can trust?"

Without hesitation, he answered that he knew at least one or two that could be trusted. "We have waited a long time to be of service."

Gie walked over to the window and peeked out. He saw the black Mercedes parked across from his car.

"Karel, do you still have your motor scooter?"

"I do."

Gie motioned for him to sit, and he outlined his plan. They would have to move fast. To Karel, the hardest part was not the Germans but explaining to his wife that he was leaving in the middle of the night. She had always hoped that the war would not reach their little town. That there would be no house to house searches, there would be no recriminations, and they would be left alone. She pointed out the consequences if he went out this night. But he feared them if he did not. He would do anything to eliminate the Nazis from his world.

Van Hoebeek parked his pride and joy at the base of the steps, a 1932 Sarolea. Initially bought by one of the farmers in the next village, it came Karel's way when its former owner plowed it into the side of a truck, killing himself and almost destroying the bike. The wreck was retrieved from the widow and painstakingly restored. Staying in the shadows, they pushed the machine until they were out of earshot of the Mercedes' occupants. Van Hoebeek kick-started it, and they were off. The journey was enough to give Gie an ulcer, riding in the dark, at high speed, on a dirt country road that when it wasn't going up and down, took extreme turns. He kept his nerve, and they soon arrived at their destination—the hideout of Major Hugh Griffin. Gie saw no reason not to drive directly to the farmhouse, fearing a quiet approach might be more dangerous. Once there, the two men embraced, then Van Hoebeek was on his way back to town to begin his mission.

....

Major Griffin found sleep impossible. One of the few pieces of furniture left in the old house was an overstuffed chair, and no matter how he turned, he was prodded by one of its many worn springs. His hideaway had been empty for years and showed all the neglects of a vacant house. There was no water, no indoor plumbing, and worse, no heat. He was unwilling to start a fire, fearing it would attract attention. But, this was the only place they could find on such short notice. One by one, their hiding places had been compromised. Griffin was lucky on many occasions to get out alive. He loved Belgium, but had come to distrust many of its people. Informers lurked everywhere.

His Belgium posting had been a series of failed missions, political infighting, and betrayal. The Köln bombing mission should have gone like clockwork if not for the hot-headed brother killing the German guard. Then there was the fiasco of the rescue mission to get the brothers out of the country. His first instinct was to leave the whole lot to the Germans. They were useless to him. As far as he was concerned, the Underground couldn't kill the informants fast enough. He had done what he could, but all the same, London was giving him the blame. Since the failed attempt in Köln, the Boche had offered a reward for any information concerning the mission. Griffin had to move twice, once just ahead of the Gestapo, before settling on this farmhouse. He wasn't sure how long he could stay.

He made numerous appeals to Headquarters for his withdrawal, but they denied each request. Griffin also had to worry about a missing British airman who had crashed during a reconnaissance flight. His masters in London were very eager to get the pilot back and keep his knowledge away from the enemy. They would not discuss reassignment until Griffin was able to deliver the airman. How could he accomplish that? His only help was Emile Gillet, a corporal from the Belgian army who was at the house with him. Gillet had made it out at Dunkirk and volunteered to return to work with the Resistance. There were days Griffin wasn't sure that he could even trust him.

In the quiet of the country, Griffin could hear the motorcycle approach before he saw it. Grabbing his Browning 45, he snuffed the candle and moved to the window. He pulled aside the heavy drapes, which stirred up enough dust to make him cough. In the partial moonlight, the Major could make out one man, and then another. He cocked his gun. Two men just don't wander out in the middle of the night, in this country, with German patrols everywhere. He whispered up to Gillet, who was tracking them from the second story window with his Bren gun locked and loaded.

"Do you see any movement other than those two jokers?"

"Negative."

One of the men dismounted, while the other on the motorcycle left in the direction he came. A figure approached the farmhouse with his hands up in the air. Whoever it was, he knew they were in the house. Griffin thought whether friend or foe, this was not good.

Desmit stood in front of the old oak door. Before he could knock, it opened, and Griffin grabbed him by the lapels, pulled into the house, and pinned him against the wall, a pistol to the side of his head. In less than perfect French, Griffin spat out, "Who the holy hell are you?"

"I had hoped for a more cordial welcome, Major," came the reply.

Griffin pulled his lighter from his pocket and lit it in front of the man's face. "Desmit, how did you find me? Christ, if you know, the fucking German army probably knows."

"Not the case, my friend."

"Get this through your bloody head. I am not your friend."

Undeterred, Gie continued, "I have come in hopes that you and I can help each other, and with any luck, resolve our problems."

"At this time of night? Your help has nearly gotten us killed."

"Let's not fight the same battle over and over. I know that there are traitors in my organization. But I also warned you those two brothers were inexperienced. Now we have both paid for our mistakes. Let us settle the bill."

"What are you suggesting?"

"First, you might put that gun down."

Griffin lowered his weapon and motioned for Gie to take a seat on the couch. As he sat, his body sank so far into the cushions, he feared he would fall through to the floor.

"We have your man, the pilot Group Captain Anthony Dankworth-Murray. He is safe and well." *Finally, some good news,* thought Griffin. Desmit continued, "We are ready to help you with his escape. But there is a condition."

Griffin swallowed hard. "Your price?"

"You must also take Raymond DeBaets and a female agent of ours with him."

"And the other brother?"

"Unfortunately, he has been killed."

"By you, or the Germans?"

Gie chose to ignore the question. "During the previous

attempt to rescue him, Raymond suffered a serious wound in the firefight. Without proper medical help, he does not have long to live. Help that we cannot provide for him here. We need to get him to an English hospital tomorrow night."

Startled and annoyed, Griffin shot back, "There is no way we can arrange a pick-up that fast."

"If you want your pilot and all the information he possesses back, then it must be tomorrow night, or the Group Captain will be our guest indefinitely. Hopefully, we can keep him safe. Although from what my men tell me, he is more interested in the local beer and female companionship than returning to England."

"It is too dangerous to make radio contact."

"It is a chance we must take. There has not been military activity in this area, nor is it patrolled vigorously. There have been no sightings of tracking trucks."

"There will be, if we start broadcasting."

"They will be out of the country before the Germans can get a fix on us."

"They won't use the same landing site from the last time."

"No need to worry, I have a new area in mind."

It was a gamble, but Griffin saw no other way out. Getting the pilot back to England would finally be a victory that would catch his superiors' attention. And maybe, just maybe, this could also be his ticket out of the country.

"Follow me, Emile, keep a watch." Griffin grabbed the candle holder and led the way up the stairs. Each one creaked, and Gie prayed they weren't in the same condition as the couch. From the second-floor landing, they climbed up a ladder to the attic. In the corner was the radio setup, a wire antenna snaking up the wall and then through the roof. A single window at the end of the room let in what little moonlight there was. Griffin, with Gie's help, quickly composed a note, checking his map to make sure that he had the coordinates for the landing site correct. He switched on the set, the tubes adding light to the room, and started keying his message.

....

  Without Gie's weight, Karel was able to return to town in half the time. His only scare was a tree limb that had fallen across the road, which he barely avoided. His heart was racing, but he kept on at high speed just the same. Approaching the village, he switched off the engine and coasted to the bridge, the entryway to the square. To avoid the black Mercedes, he moved off the road and across a stream that ran through the north side of town. While the water was not deep, it was certainly cold, soaking him up to the shin. He pushed his bike up a small hill and came to the back side of the Inn Foret, the town's only hotel. Collecting some small stones, he threw them at one of the second-story windows. He misjudged the size of one of them and nearly broke the pane, but it was enough of a commotion to bring the Inn's proprietor to investigate.

  Arno Lejeune had run the Inn with his son since his wife died ten years ago. During the summer months, they used to have many guests who came to escape Brussels and fish in the streams around the village. Since the occupation, there had been few visitors, and he and his son Nick had taken on odd jobs to survive. It was particularly hard on Nick, who had suffered a broken leg as a youth, which never had healed properly. The only good that came from the injury was that he was passed over by the Belgium army during the invasion and now was no use to the Germans for labor.

Arno was also a member of the Resistance. In the two years since the Germans arrived, his only assignment had been to hide a British airman. Recognizing Karel as soon as he opened the window, he hurried his large frame downstairs to let him in. A visit at this time of night scared him. Could there be an emergency with the children? He was relieved to hear everyone was safe, but his adrenaline started pumping when told of the mission. He woke his son, who dressed and came downstairs while Arno visited the cellar.

Karel sat in the large reception area, lit by a small lamp in the corner. A large fireplace took up one wall, and holiday decorations hung across the room. He had forgotten it was almost Christmas. In happier days, the two families would sit in front of a roaring fire, drinking punch and singing carols. Now they plotted to kill Germans.

Nick joined him in the room, acknowledging Karel with a salute then pulling up a chair next to him. Soon Arno returned, having retrieved a Browning FN pistol and Mauser model 1889 rifle that he kept in the cellar. The only thing that looked older than the gun was the rifle. He laid the two weapons and boxes of cartridges on the table. Karel put his hunting knife beside the small arsenal and thought that it was not much to fight a war. They huddled together as he went over the mission.

....

It had been nearly two hours since Hans and Otto had taken up their station in the square. Otto, who was like a bored child, kept asking how much longer they needed to wait. Hans would nip at the bottle of schnapps that he had under the seat. They were cold and stiff, Hans refusing to run the car heater for fear they would draw attention to themselves.

"We are the only black Mercedes in the Square. I think we have already drawn attention to ourselves," an exasperated Otto complained.

Hans ignored him.

"Do you think I will draw too much attention to us if I go take a piss next to
that tree?"

Again, no answer. Looking over, he saw that Hans was fast asleep. Pulling himself out of the car, Otto heard the snoring start. Happy to be out of the Mercedes and standing, he stomped his feet hard on the ground to get some warmth and rubbed his hands together in an attempt to get the blood flowing in his fingers. Hungry, cold, with a snoring partner who had been passing gas all evening--Otto thought, it just couldn't get worse. He walked over to a giant beech tree to the left of the church to do his business. The tree looked like a surreal creature coming out of the night, lifting its naked arms, ready to pounce.

Karel and his group had moved into position some five meters behind the car. The intent was to surprise the occupants before they could respond. They decided to change tactics when one on the passengers left the vehicle to walk across the square. Karel motioned that he and Nick would follow the one walking, while Arno would handle the driver.

Arno kept low as he approached the car, moving to position himself by the driver's door. He thought his mission blown when he stumbled over a rock, sending it clattering across the cobblestones, but was happy to hear snoring still coming from the inside of the car. Arno approached the driver's side, grabbed the handle of the door, and swung it open. Before the surprised German could react, Arno silenced him with the butt of the rifle. He then dragged him out of the car, relieving the German of his pistol. It was only then he checked to make sure his prisoner was still breathing. The order was to take them alive, but no one had said they couldn't rough them up a little. He rolled his man over, gagged him, and tied his hands behind his back before slipping a flour sack over his head.

Otto leaned against the tree with one arm while using the other to help himself pee. He could feel his lungs filling up with the frigid air, God, how he needed a cigarette! When buttoning his fly, Otto heard footsteps. As he turned someone put a pistol to his head. In broken German, a voice told him to do as they say. His hands were tied and a sack put over his head. Any hope that Hans would come to his rescue disappeared when he heard his comrade moaning on the ground.

They all piled into the Mercedes. To disorient the Germans, they drove the country roads for nearly an hour before bringing them back to the Inn. Karel took the car to hide it in the woods while the other two took Hans and Otto down to the cellar. They bound them like pigs for slaughter. Both Belgians ignored their captives' complaints that the ropes were being tied too tight and they needed to use the toilet.

....

Desmit was hopeful that he would reach Brussels before daylight. The evening had been a success. The British had agreed to his terms to evacuate the flyer and his people, the two Germans soldiers were prisoners, and with a little bit of luck, this whole unfortunate Köln episode would be behind him. The Major gave him a lift back to the village, a trip as harrowing as the one on the motorcycle. Now, his last obstacle for the night would be the checkpoint going into Brussels. He had taken off his tie, mussed his hair, and taken a generous drink of cognac in hopes that he would resemble a man who just had a roll in the hay, rather than one contributing to the downfall of the Reich. He was lucky. The same two young men he had spoken with earlier were still on guard duty. Getting out of his car, Gie greeted them like old friends. He gave each a slap on the back, pulled out cigars and put one in each of their mouths, and finally offered them a drink of cognac from his flask. He only smiled when they asked how the night went. The sentries sent him on his way, laughing as he sang a heavily accented English version of "Don't Sit Under the Apple Tree."

CHAPTER 23

It was still dark when they came to take Febe away. She had no idea how long her interrogation by the two thugs had lasted; they were drunk and incompetent and took turns passing out. The two were getting nowhere with the inquiry, causing frustration for them and more pain for her. Deni and Lucas had no experience interrogating people. The best they could come up with was, "Who gave you the gun?" which they kept repeating no matter how many times she retold her story. She had found the gun in the restroom, on the train, and decided to keep it for her protection rather than turning it in. Looking at her interrogators, she pointedly said she wasn't wrong about needing it.

Inpatient and expecting a bounty from the Germans, the two finally gave up and put her back in the holding cell. It was a free-standing wire cage with a metal bed, a pot to relieve oneself in, and a light so bright it made it difficult to sleep if that was even possible. As they walked away after securing the cell gate with a lock and chain, she could hear one of them say, laughing, "Believe me, little girl, five minutes with the Gestapo and you'll be missing us."

She couldn't remember closing her eyes or being asleep, but she was startled out of a twilight unconsciousness as someone was rattling the lock. Looking up, she saw two brutes in ill-fitting suits unlocking the chains. With brisk efficiency, they ignored all questions, searched her, put on handcuffs, and marched her down to the street where a third man was waiting in a car to take her away.

Expecting to be pushed into the seat, she was surprised when they helped her in, making sure she didn't strike her head on the door frame. They then took positions on either side of her and, without a word spoken the driver accelerated. The car glided through the empty streets at high speed. Through her swollen eyes, everything was in a haze, but occasionally she would look up and recognize a landmark. Febe exhaled a breath of relief when they passed Avenue Louise, where Gestapo headquarters was housed, and didn't stop. Within a few minutes, she recognized the old Electrobel Mansion that the Wehrmacht now used as their headquarters in Brussels. The car pulled on to the stately grounds and then drove to the back of the building. The two guards once again helped her exit. They marched her past the sentries into a maze of hallways, took a lift up to the third floor, and showed her into a small waiting room.

A young corporal sat behind an oak desk, even at this early hour; he looked fresh, wearing a crisp uniform and with hair slicked back. She could see him wince as he looked up and saw her. He picked up one of the two phones on his desk and, without dialing, announced that they had arrived. The corporal returned to his work, saying not a word to either the guards or her.

Febe's face hurt. She had a massive headache, and her ears were ringing. She had had nothing to eat or drink since noon the previous day, and as she stood there, she felt life was leaving her body. Feeling faint, she tried to grab hold of the guard but collapsed. They placed her on a chair. The corporal helped her with a glass of water since her guards refused to take the handcuffs off. It was at this time that Major Kohler entered the room. His two men snapped to attention, one of them producing Febe's papers, which they had received at the police station. The Major methodically looked over her identity papers and then her work permit. She tried to focus her eyes on him. It was impossible to keep her head up as she slumped back into the chair.

The Major turned his attention to Febe. He wanted to make sure she understood what he was about to say. He nodded to one of the guards, who grabbed her hair from behind and forced her head to raise. Looking into her bloodshot eyes, Kohler showed no emotion when he spoke.

"You have been arrested for carrying a weapon, which is strictly prohibited. You are not part of the German military, so I must assume you are an enemy combatant. Since you are not in uniform, you must be a spy. I have the authority to shot you outright or to turn you over to the Gestapo. I will soon be asking you questions, and I do not have time to play little games. No matter what your fellow terrorists say, it is a mistake to resist. Eventually, you will tell us what we want to know and will welcome death when it comes. On the other hand, if you cooperate, you will be considered a friend of the Reich and rewarded. The choice is yours. We will give you a little time to think over your decision. Make a wise choice. There will be no second chances. Do you understand what I am saying?"

Febe was unsure whether she nodded her head in agreement, or the guard who had hold of her hair did, but it was enough to satisfy the Major. He turned without saying another word and reentered his office. She was taken downstairs by her escorts, allowed a toilet break with one of the guards keeping watch, and then deposited in a claustrophobic little room that resembled a closet more than a cell. A single wooden chair was its only furniture. The overhead light was large and bright and warmed the room to an uncomfortable temperature. The top part of the door had a mirror, which she assumed was for viewing from the other side. Febe looked at her reflection and could barely recognize herself. Both her eyes were black and swollen, her top lip cracked and looking like a tennis ball. Her face was puffy, dirty, and grotesque. She wanted to cry, but would not give anyone observing her the satisfaction of believing she was weakening. She tried sitting in the stiff chair but could not get comfortable. Breathing was difficult; it felt like one of her ribs might be broken. Alone in her misery, she wondered what lay ahead at the hands of her enemy.

....

Valentin had worked all night on his plan to rescue Febe. Sitting in his studio, surrounded by his work and fueled by coffee and cigarettes, he went over maps of the possible landing sites. Hopefully, Desmit had secure the information that would be needed to complete the plan. A few hours before, one of Gie's men reported the police transferred Febe to the military headquarters. The new information added to his anxiety. He was determined to get her out of there before they started working on her. Valentin was putting the final touches to the document he had been forging when there was a knock at the back door. Startled, he looked for his pistol, but realizing the Germans would never bother to knock, he laid the weapon down and pushed the heavy door open, letting Gie in.

The two men huddled around the small wood stove in the corner of the room as Gie brought Valentin up to date on his meeting with Griffin. He went over the evacuation plans and where the pick-up would take place, and informed him that they now had two German hostages in Daens. They both agreed the prisoners could only help as a bargaining tool. Valentin told him of the meeting with the wine merchant and showed him the document that he was finishing. Gie scrutinized the papers, holding then up to the light. "Perfect forgeries. Even the watermarks-nice touch."

Valentin laid out a map of the Daens area. Gie remarked that in a short time, they had accomplished much, but there was still much to do. They both stood there, realizing the enormity of what they were hoping to achieve.

"So much to coordinate. One mistake and the whole escape falls apart." Valentin was looking deflated and speaking more to himself than Desmit.

"Have you ever played pool?" Valentin shook his head no. "This is like hitting the eight ball and sinking all nine balls at once," said a smiling Gie. "Difficult, but I've seen it done."

....

Kohler sat in his office, peering out the window into the dark morning. He had been able to sleep a few hours before returning to headquarters. The Major shaved and put on a clean uniform, then got back to his desk. Through his network of informers, he learned that the saboteurs from the Köln bombing were here in the city. They would be his prize. He assigned every available man on the case, and now he had heard that two of his agents had not reported in from the night before. Could they be on to something? Or had they just fallen asleep on duty? It wasn't as if that had never happened before. Kohler had felt for a long time that the men doing garrison duty in Belgium were becoming complacent and soft. These two had been following the cabinet maker, Desmit. But he was too smart a man to let those fools get the better of him. It was a waste of time and resources to go looking for them.

Since his dragnet began, the police had detained dozens of suspects, but no one could offer up any new information. Kohler did not expect that the woman in custody would be any different. He knew that a little time with the boys downstairs would confirm if she were lying. It had been his experience that most people start talking before the interrogation begins. A short time in the cell and then the long walk to the interview room gets them thinking. Once the door opens and they have a taste of the chamber, you can't stop them talking.

If she had nothing to offer, then to the Gestapo she'd go. They enjoyed working people over whether they had information or not.

He checked his watch; it was nearly seven in the morning, almost time for his rendezvous. Every day, once in the morning and then again late evening, he would visit the small café across from headquarters.

"You know, Major," his adjutant once noted, "If anyone wants to assassinate you, all they would have to do is wait for you at the café." Kohler prayed that he would be out of Brussels before that came to pass.

What the adjutant didn't know was these daily visits were vital to Kohler's existence and future. He had built up his private network of informers. If they had to make contact, the café was where they would signal him. Kohler had an arrangement with the owner. For his help as a middle-man, the Major would make sure that the supplies he needed were always available. And if that wasn't encouragement enough, he assured the proprietor that any hesitance on his part and he would put a bullet in his head. This group's information allowed the Major to stay a step ahead of the Resistance and, in turn, make a name for himself. He had spent two long years in Brussels under the command of that idiot Beck. He knew promotion and glory would only come once he was away from this city and commander.

Kohler left his office. The sky for once was not showing clouds, and there was a promise of a weak sun on the horizon. He crossed the boulevard, staying alert, and entered the café precisely at seven. He acknowledged the proprietor and then made his way to his corner table. Before he seated himself, the waiter had brought the usual: coffee with milk, black bread, and cheese.

The proprietor walked by, laying that day's copy of *Völkischer Beobachter* on the table. If any of his spies had information and needed a meeting, he would find a note in that day's newspaper. Kohler casually sipped his coffee and sliced off a piece of cheese before picking up the paper. He long ago stopped reading what he called Goebbels's fantasy rag, but preferred to use it as a prop because it made him look like a loyal party member. As he turned the page, he was careful to check for a note and then plucked it from the paper's crease. The small sheet of paper was placed on his lap and discreetly unfolded.

It was from the wine merchant, Legrand. *Have vital information, must see you today. 1100 hours, Usual place, 1000 franc, Swiss.* Kohler despised dealing with that man. The Major wouldn't be surprised if Legrand also sold information to the Resistance. Although, he was correct about the printing press, and the saboteurs. A thousand Francs? More than had been asked before. Kohler could only trust that the information would be worth the asking price. If not, he would dispose of Legrand forever. Kohler called to the waiter to bring him a cognac, which he drank and then left. As was the custom, the Major never asked for the bill, nor was one offered.

....

The public office for the German High Command opened at 8:00 that morning, and Valentin was determined to be there on the dot. There was much to do this day, but the travel documents were an integral part of his plan. Even before approaching the old mansion, he encountered the first ring of defense surrounding the headquarters. There were roving command cars and dour-looking sentries with automatic weapons. A line was already forming, but the guards refused to acknowledge anyone until the appointed hour. Falling in line, Valentin lit a cigarette and looked up at the old mansion.

He knew that Febe was somewhere in there. He prayed that she was alright and that she could hold on until tonight. If his scheme worked, she would be safely on her way to England. If not, they would all be dead.

Even though he was the fifth person in line, it took nearly a half-hour to pass through the examination of papers, the questioning of reasons for being there, and the search for weapons. In Valentin's case, the guards were skeptical that the General would be offering him anything. There were a few back-and-forths with Beck's office before he was admitted.

At the main entrance to the building, the guards insisted that he go through the same routine again. Valentin explained that he had been through all this at the first checkpoint, but his complaints were ignored. More phone calls went to Beck's office before finally he was allowed in, this time accompanied by a guard.

They entered one of the lifts, its operator looking suspiciously at Valentin. The guard barked which floor they wanted, and they were moving. Valentin glanced over at his chaperone. He looked like a man who just wanted the littlest of excuses to pull his weapon and shoot him dead. Valentin avoided eye contact as the elevator slowly made its way to the fourth floor.

Exiting, they walked down a long hallway until they came to the General's suite. There was another sentry at the entrance who motioned for them to wait while he went inside to announce them. Finally, Valentin was in the outer office of the high command. The room was occupied by secretaries and support staff. Standing in the middle, Valentin contemplated where to go until one of the clerks waved him over, a Belgian man in his 50s, with a bald head and sour disposition. The travel documents were ready; all that was needed was to verify his identity and sign a receipt. Valentin checked his watch.

He needed to move on to his next appointment.

....

Febe sat in the small room. Somewhere on the floor, she could hear an interrogation going on. It was hard to judge how close or far they were, but the victim was a woman. She could barely make out the interrogator's questions, and the woman's answers not at all. After a few minutes, the screaming started, chilling Febe to the bone. The poor woman begged for them to stop, she knew nothing. Febe heard a thud as some object struck flesh, and then there was only silence. She feared that they had killed the woman, but after a few minutes, the questioning started again. At some point, the interrogator said something to the women about the basement. The interviewee pleaded that she would tell them all they wanted to know if they would not take her below again.

It was disconcerting to Febe. She knew it would not be long now before they would come for her. She knew the rumor that members of the Resistance carried cyanide capsules in case of capture, and she wished that she had one now. Her body was aching, her head throbbing. She did not fear for her safety, but rather what she might reveal under torture. She also knew that when they finished working her over, if she was still alive, she would be sent to Residence Belvedere-Gestapo Headquarters. There they would either shoot her or send her to a concentration camp. Her anxiety was rising to the point that she felt nauseated.

The overhead light heating the small room, coupled with her exhaustion, made her feel drowsy and she involuntarily closed her eyes. Within seconds, someone struck her across the legs. Surprised, she peered through the fog that engulfed her mind to see a horrid-looking woman with a riding crop, admonishing her for sleeping. The women's crooked nose, streaks of grey hair, and high-pitched voice reminded

Febe of childhood witch stories her friends would tell to scare her. Uncontrollably, she started laughing. The woman raised the stick to strike Febe but stopped when a voice from the doorway ordered her to leave. The matron looked at Febe, spat in her face, and left.

The voice came from a large man; his white shirt opened at the collar with his sleeves rolled up. He was reading a document from a folder of papers, moving to position himself in front of Febe. He was a menacing sight, over one hundred eighty-eight centimeters tall, with a shaved head and large ears. But what caught her attention was his hands, his fist was the size of her face.

He seemed in no particular hurry, stepping out of the room to fetch something to sit on and then returning. He rested one foot on the chair, looking upon her as one would do when deciding which meat to select. Laying the file down, he withdrew a cigarette from the case he had in his back pocket and lit it with a stick match, taking his time to watch the flame inch close to his finger before extinguishing it. After a few puffs, he casually sat with his hands resting on the back of the chair. She strained to listen as he spoke to her in heavily accented French.

"You are Febe Janssen? You are an employee of the railroad?" She nodded her head. "I am Oberleutnant Karlmann, and Major Kohler has asked me to speak with you." The friendly voice turned harder.

"The charge against you is carrying a weapon and attempted murder of two policemen," he said, pausing to flick ashes from his sleeve. "I do not care about the two who arrested you. It would not have been a loss if you had killed them. No, but I will tell you what I do care about."

He moved closer, putting his hands on either side of her face and lifting her head to look into her eyes. "I have looked at all the information we have on you. I don't consider it a coincidence that you were in Köln on the day saboteurs attempted to blow up a fuel dump and murdered a German soldier. I don't consider it a coincidence that you were on the same train they used to escape and kill a conductor. What I do believe is you abetted these murderers and know their whereabouts. These walls are thin, and I am sure you heard the discussion we had with a woman earlier this morning? She, too, wanted to tell us she knew nothing. We know you are a member of one of the criminal organizations. You may save yourself much pain if you speak clearly and truthfully now."

They were bluffing, not about the pain, but knowing she was a member of MBN. She just needed to hold out a few more hours. *Give us 24 hours and then save yourself*--isn't that what Gie always told his people? "I am not a member of the Underground. I found..." She never got a chance to finish her answer.

He grabbed her by the arm and jerked her up, her handcuffs pinching her wrists. "I was hoping it would not come to this. Just remember this is what you chose."

She felt like a rag doll as Karlmann pulled her down a back staircase. They descended until there were no more stairs, and an iron door greeted them. He unlocked it with a key from a large ring of keys he carried. They entered the machine room of the mansion, the sound deafening. On one end, the machinery and pulleys that worked the elevators clicked on and off. At the other were four large boilers that heated the building and sounding, like they would explode, were hissing steam. They negotiated a narrow corridor between the giant machines.

At the end of the pathway, there was another door that opened up onto a much smaller room. Inside, two men were smoking and enjoying a cup of coffee as if they were delivery men on break. On the table lay a clear bottle of something;

she assumed it was alcohol as it disappeared when they saw the Oberleutnant's disapproving look. White tiles covered the room from floor to ceiling. While there were many ominous-looking devices littered through the area, the piece that caught her attention was a large bathtub in the middle.

Karlmann handed her over to the two men. The handcuffs were taken off, and she was stripped naked. Febe grimaced as they pulled her sweater over her head, rubbing against her swollen face. Nude, she could see that her body was a quilt work of ugly blue bruises. The left side of her rib cage was tender to the touch.

They each took a leg and arm and carried her over to the tub filled with freezing water. Chipped ice floated on the top, and a metal bar was at one end. They dropped her into the water. Her whole body felt like exploding; she could feel her heart rate accelerate, and she started gasping for air. They tied her legs to the bar across the tub. She was already numb all over and could feel nothing.

Oberleutnant Karlmann leaned over her. "We will start. When you tell us the truth we will stop."

One of the men pulled the bar upward, which dragged her under the water. The quick motion took her by surprise. Within a second, she was swallowing water; her lungs were about to explode. When they brought her back up, she coughed and then threw up. Febe had no time to catch her breath before they pulled her under again, this time for a longer time. They repeated this over and over, each time asking her if she had anything to say, and each time she shook her head. They were wearing her down; in desperation, she tried to drown herself. It did not work, for these men were experts in inflicting pain, and still keeping their victim alive.

CHAPTER 24

Major Kohler had just finished knotting his tie when his assistant buzzed to let him know the driver was waiting. He had changed into a dull grey suit for the meeting with Alain Legrand. Showing up in uniform at the warehouse by the docks would only bring unwanted attention. The wine merchant was a fanatic about secrecy and would not show if he thought the appointment would be compromised. For once, Kohler had a high expectation of going into a meeting with Legrand. The wine merchant would never have the guts to ask for so much money if the information he could offer wasn't vital.

On his side wall behind a mirror was a safe. He opened it, pulling out a Walther P38, checking the clip, and then putting it in the waistband of his pants. Also lying there, nicely stacked and tied together with twine, were bundles of bills: Reich marks, French, Swiss, and Belgian francs, pounds sterling, and American dollars. 'Gifts' from his captives who hoped it would buy their freedom. It never did. He took a bundle of Swiss francs and counted out a thousand, then slipped it into an envelope and put it in his inside coat pocket. He replaced the mirror, taking one last look; a wisp of hair had fallen out of place. Smoothing it back, he grabbed his overcoat and hat and headed downstairs.

At the entrance, his driver waited in Kohler's automobile. The Major had seen the car, a 1935 DeSoto Airflow painted royal blue, when he first arrived in Brussels. He loved American cars and hoped that this would be his first of many.

Of course, its former owner, a Jewish merchant, had not been keen to part ways with this gem. But he soon found out about life under Nazi administration. The merchant was one of the first to be picked up and shipped to the Neuengamme camps. Kohler's assistant was retrieving the keys from the man as they hauled him away.

He took the seat next to the driver, a sergeant from his staff who was also wearing a suit. Though he had been chauffeured by this man many times, he had never bothered to learn his name. His only greeting was to bark out, "To the docks!" without giving an exact address.

The driver put the car into gear, leaving the well-groomed grounds of the mansion behind and soon turning left on the Avenue des Arts. They skirted the Parc de Bruxelles and were moving through the center of the city. The sergeant had come from a large industrial town in Germany and found Brussels enchanting and beautiful; preferable to the steel mills of Dortmund. He enjoyed the food, and the women, although many young girls were now refusing to become involved with Germans for fear of reprisals from the Resistance. The result was the prostitutes were charging double their prices to capitalize on the women shortage. He looked over at Kohler, figuring that this man would not be interested in discussing the cost of whores. Men like him never paid for a woman; they either charmed them or threatened them. Knowing Kohler, he figured he employed the latter.

The sergeant thought the charade of not wearing uniforms or driving military cars senseless. Back in the barrack; he and his comrades would joke about the officers who believed they were stealthy by wearing civilian clothes and driving private cars. The English and the Russians knew how to blend in. The German army might as well put a siren on the vehicle. Better to be like the Gestapo, dress in black, and drive their big cars. It scared the shit out of everyone, even him. But he had learned from experience the less said, the better life would be with the Major. He kept his eyes on the road and his opinions to himself.

They were approaching the docks when Kohler instructed the sergeant to change course and drive down to a row of warehouses a couple of blocks away. A few of the buildings had men loading boxes on to lorries, while others were boarded up and deserted. Kohler looked at his watch. He was almost an hour early. Surveying the area, other than the workers, he could see a few drunks asleep in doorways bundled up with whatever they could find, hoping to catch a little sun should it come out.

Kohler ordered the sergeant to move the car out of sight. Once the Major was satisfied that the automobile was safely parked, something he never worried about with a staff car, they walked back to the buildings. Across the street, a couple of lorries waited their turn to unload. The major positioned himself behind one of them and scanned the vicinity, focusing on an alley that ran between two sets of buildings. He offered not a word of explanation of what he was expecting. There was still some time before Legrand would show, but Kohler always preferred to be the first one at the rendezvous point in case his contact thought about being creative. Feeling bogged down by his heavy coat, he handed it and his hat to the sergeant and issued one last order.

"Keep an eye on the entrance to the alley. If someone comes out before me, arrest him. If I do not come out in half an hour, come looking for me. Understood?"

The sergeant acknowledged with "Jawohl."

Kohler touched his breast pocket to reassure himself that the money was still there, then withdrew the Walther, cocked it, and held it close against his right leg as he came out from behind the truck. A blast of cold air greeted the Major as he crossed the street and immediately regretting that he gave up his greatcoat. He soon disappeared into the alley. Kohler did not like this place to meet. There was only one way in, and the area was perfect for an ambush. But Legrand would meet at no other location. As long as the information was useful, he would make this accommodation.

In daylight, without the rain, the alley was much different than the last time he was there. Now, not only could you smell the garbage but could see it scattered throughout. Kohler had to pick a path through the trash. There were a few spaces where indigents had taken shelter: a lean-to, torn blankets, a cold fire pit; but no one there at this time of day. A military truck had been abandoned in the middle of the alley, stripped to the frame. The Major negotiated his way around it, careful not to step in any excrement, either animal or human. There was a stifling stench close by. Convinced it was a body, and worrying that it might be Legrand, he investigated. The smell was coming from under a tarp, which he cautiously lifted. It was the remains of a dog, its head staring back at him. He doubted in this alley that the beast died from natural causes, but instead rather someone's dinner.

Kohler took up position in the doorway at the end of the alley; its lock still was broken from his last visit. The truck obstructed his view but he decided to stay where he was, listening for any sound. The Major was starting to feel the cold and could see his breath. There was a sudden noise near the truck; he tightened his grip on the Walther and waited. A man stumbled around the bumper. Was he one of the derelicts that lived in the area? Kohler was distracted for just a second, but that was enough time for the door to open behind him. Someone put a vice-like grip on his shoulder to keep him from spinning around. A pistol was placed against his head. Feeling the cold steel, he stood motionless.

"Drop the gun, Major."

Kohler stood still, assessing what his options might be.

"I will not ask you again."

Kohler let the weapon fall from his hand. "I wish I could say I am surprised by this. The possibility of a trap had occurred to me, and I have men waiting for me. Whatever your plan is, you will never get out of here alive if anything happens to me."

"I know where your man is, and I want you to walk out of here as much as you do."

The intruder swiftly jerked the Major's jacket from his shoulders to midway down his arms, then pulled him into the building and pinned his face against the wall. The only light squeezed through the boarded-up windows.

The Major noted the man spoke German, but with a Flemish accent. There was something about his tone that was familiar. "What have you done with the person I was to meet?" Kohler demanded to know.

"I will ask the questions, but I will tell you that Monsieur Legrand is no longer your concern. I asked you here not to kill you, but to make you a proposition."

"Then there is no need for a gun. I will pay you what I was to pay the wine merchant for his information."

"I'm not here to collaborate. I'm here to make a deal with you."

"A deal? Why would I make a deal with you?"

"Let's just say it would be in the best interest."

Defiantly Kohler spat out, "What could we possibly have in common? And if I say no, are you going to shoot me?"

"Will you hear me out?"

"Do I have a choice?"

"Probably none that will make you happy. You have a woman in custody, Febe Janssen. I want her back."

"That's it? A woman? Shoot me now, and let's end this calamity. Do you have any idea what danger you are causing yourself for a woman?"

"At this very moment, she is being interrogated. She's a minor figure in our organization who can tell you nothing, Major."

"As always, I am at a loss how you know what goes on inside the German headquarters. If this woman is nothing, then why do you hold a gun on a German officer? I am sure she has a story to tell."

"Let's say the information I can give you would be more valuable than anything she could offer."

"For all I know, she may have already given my men the information you offer, and maybe even your name."

"I think not. Let us say the quality of this information would certainly mean recognition and promotion for you."

"And why the interest in my career?"

"You have torn the city upside town looking for two people that you believed killed a German soldier. I can give you one of the fugitives. Plus, I can give you information that would cause much embarrassment and possibly even arrest for your General Beck."

"There are two saboteurs."

"One is all I can offer up."

"Please excuse me if I find this all hard to believe. Are you willing to give up one of your own for the woman? And then you tell me she is an insignificant piece in this puzzle you have outlined?"

"It is as simple as this; we both have something the other wants. Do you believe the information the woman can give would be worth more than the information I have described?"

"And what if this is just a trick to release the woman, and your information turns out to be worthless?"

"There will be ample opportunity for you to decide if the information I will give you is worth the price of your prisoner."

"I do not trust you."

"And I do not trust you. But, surely, what I have offered is worth the risk. To show my good faith, you have two missing men. They are free and will contact you."

"You would have done me a great service if you had shot them," Kohler replied, shaking his head. The risk and the opportunities ran through his mind. The capture of one of the saboteurs would make amends for the previous failures, and yes, bring him to notice by the high command. But to rid himself of Beck, to send him off humiliated, would be worth quite a gamble. Only yesterday, the General in one of his dressings-down suggested that the Major might better serve the Reich fighting with the heroic troops on the Eastern Front. There would be ample opportunity to recapture the woman and personally deal with this stranger who spoke so strongly while holding a gun to his head.

At length, Kohler said, "Agreed. But I will not be alone when we make the exchange. I will bring my adjutant, and rest assured if there is anything that resembles treachery, I will have the woman killed without hesitation." There was a long silence. "That is my condition. If not agreeable, then shoot me now."

"And you remember, Major, if anything happens to your prisoner, I will hold you accountable. You will be contacted this afternoon and given directions on where to meet."

With that, the intruder pushed the Major into the alley. He stumbled, as his arms were still locked down by his coat. He righted himself, straightened his jacket, and retrieved his dropped Walther. For a moment he considered charging back into the building, but thought better of it. No, he would see how this played out.

Valentin watched him sprint away, and then moved through the abandoned building to an exit on the other side out of view. One of the delivery trucks was waiting to drop him off at Gie's factory. As he made his way through the city, he asked himself, *Was I convincing? Or have I signed Febe's death warrant?*

CHAPTER 25

It was early morning and quitting time for Stefano Pagnotto. As was his custom, he limped out of the German headquarters as fast as his wooden leg would take him. He would submit to the daily search of the guards, and in his friendly Italian way, would offer to take off his wooden leg to have it examined. The guards tended to pass him through quickly, as they complained that he smelled of a combination of lye soap and body odor. Amongst the guards, they called it the "curse of Pagnotto" if trapped in a conversation with him. He loved to tell and retell the story of how he once saved Mussolini's life. More than one person pointed out that the tale got longer with each telling. Stefano worked as a janitor at the German high command in Brussels. As an Italian Fascist in good standing, he had the sensitive duty of cleaning the office of General Beck.

In reality, Stefano Pagnotto was Santino Tocci, a small-time burglar and safecracker from Palermo. He left Italy under cloudy circumstances, migrating to Belgium, and soon found himself in a Brussels jail cell. It was there that he came to Gie Desmit's attention. A few strings pulled, a little money paid, and Signore Tocci was in the employment of Desmit. It was Gie who thought up the idea of placing him in the military offices and provided him with all the documentation to prove Santino was a card-carrying fascist. He had started working at the Electrobel Mansion shortly after the Germans moved in. One of his first assignments was to crack the General's safe and photograph documents. This was made easy since the guard who was supposed to be watching him spent more time on the balcony smoking. What Monsieur Desmit asked of him this time was less stressful, but more dangerous. Inside the safe was the monthly report that General Beck sent to his superiors. In the past, Tocci would photograph and then would bring the film to his masters. This time his orders were to steal the report. In a few seconds, he had the safe open, and the report secured in his false leg.

On the way home, Santino stopped at the local bar, which stayed opened for those who had finished the night shift and needed a drink to calm their nerves. They did a brisk business, and the place was full when he entered. The bartender placed a glass of grappa in front of Santino. After taking a sip, the Italian pushed through the crowd to use the water closet. Once there, he relieved his bladder and removed the document from his leg. Wrapping the report in his jacket, he pulled the chain to flush the toilet and ventured out.

He took his usual seat at the far end of the bar and downed the drink, then waved his empty glass and called for another one. The bartender kept the bottle under the bar, as the Italian was the only one who drank it; most of the Belgians preferred beer. He filled up Santino's glass, but before he turned away, the Italian blurted out, "I can't move here. Put my coat behind the bar, will you?" He handed it over and then leaned up against the bar to sip his grappa. He eyed the room-a nod to a regular, a joke with the man standing next to him, a flirtatious back and forth with the young girl who cleaned tables; then finished his grappa. He looked at his glass, thought better of ordering another, put some coins on the bar, and called for his jacket. He bundled up, gave a wave to all, and was on his way home. The report was on its way to Gie Desmit.

....

Gie sat at his desk, the smoke from his cigar hanging like

a giant cloud around his head. The blinds to the window that overlooked the factory were closed to exclude any curious eyes. He had already read the report from Santino Tocci and was now going through his checklist. All morning there had been runners sent with messages to finalize the night's plan. There was so much to concern him this day: getting the British airman to the pick-up point, getting Legrand on the train without panicking him, releasing the two soldiers who were prisoners, planting disinformation among the Germans, moving Raymond, and of course setting up the exchange for the girl. Febe, she would be the trickiest and the most dangerous. In his heart, he felt there was no chance Kohler would live up to any bargain. He feared the outcome would be that not only the girl would be lost, but also Valentin.

Gie looked at his pocket watch: Valentin should be there at any time. A successful outcome from the meeting with the Major was critical for the whole venture to work. He prayed that if the meeting turned sour that Valentin would not be taken alive. Desmit knew what the Gestapo was capable of, and in the end, they would force him to betray the organization. The anxiety, coupled with no sleep and many cups of coffee, gnawed at him. At one point, his breathing became shallow, and his chest hurt. He thought he might be having a heart attack. He poured himself a drink, which calmed his nerves.

He was relieved when there was a knock at the door and Valentin entered. He accepted Gie's offer of a Brandy, draining the glass in one swallow and then shaking it for a refill.

"You know my friend, that is a 50-year-old cognac. You might think of savoring it."

Sipping the second glass, he asked if there was any news about Febe. Gie had received word earlier from his network inside the mansion that Kohler's men started interrogating

Febe. Knowing what that meant, he chose not to share this with Valentin. The man was near exhaustion, and he needed his focus on the mission.

The two of them sat at the large desk and brought each other up to date on what had transpired since they last met. Both were encouraged how in such a short time, so much was accomplished. A desk lamp illuminated the map on the table. Valentin hunched over it as Gie pointed out the area they chose for the exchange of Febe, and then the route to the landing zone. They fine-tuned the timeline for the mission and synchronized their watches.

They both were sure there would be some sort of betrayal from Kohler. The best they could do was try to anticipate it. Desmit knew that for Valentin, this was about rescuing Febe. But for him, it was about keeping the organization together, and the British as support. Neither the Major, nor Febe, could be allowed to jeopardize this mission or the organization. He relit his cigar which had gone out, and once again filled both their glasses.

In a clear voice that offered no interest in a debate, he advised Valentin, "The plane will arrive at the landing zone at ten. It will land, take on its passengers, and leave. There will be no waiting. If you do not have the girl there it will leave without her. You must remember if the Major springs a trap and there is no escape, I expect you not to become a prisoner. Understood?"

....

Major Kohler had barely stepped into his office before he started giving orders to his adjutant. He wanted all phone calls to him put through immediately, and traced regardless who the caller claimed to be. The Major wanted all his agents assembled and awaiting orders from him. Two squads of men were to be put on alert and ready to move at a moment's notice. It was an afterthought that he inquired about his missing agents. Did the Underground have them? He wasn't going to waste his time looking for those two fools. He would wait and see if they would be released, but if they were alive, by the time he was through with them, they would wish they were dead.

Sitting down at his desk, he picked up one of his two phones and called down to the basement to see if there were any revelations from the interrogation of the woman. The answer was negative. They had stopped after she had passed out, fearing she might die; but she was coming around, and they would begin again shortly. He ordered that they put her in a cell and do nothing until they heard back from him.

Kohler ordered coffee and sat back in his chair to analyze the situation. The woman was the key. What did she know that was so important they would give up one of their members? He thought it amusing they insisted on the exchange for that night, or the deal was off. There was not enough time to break her, or to set a trap.

But what would be the complication of putting the screws to her and forgetting the deal? Kohler knew the woman had something to tell him. But, if it was legitimate, then arresting one of the saboteurs was inviting and certainly would do much for him. If it were a trap only to free the woman, then he would make sure she would never see freedom. The truly intriguing part of this drama was the promise of incriminating evidence against General Beck. Oh, how he would love to send that sorry excuse for a man packing back to Germany in disgrace. He would wait for their phone call before deciding his next move.

....

Hans Klein and Otto Zimmermann prayed to a merciful God that they would live to see another day. Thrown into a dungeon, they felt helpless and vulnerable, lying on the dirt floor. They had been stripped naked, their arms tied behind them, their legs strapped together, and then a rope through both the bindings that pulled their arms and legs back. The ground was cold against their skin, and the old onion sacks over their heads had an overpowering stench. The fear was paralyzing. They had both heard stories of soldiers that fell into the hands of the Resistance—the torture, mutilation, and then death.

When they first arrived, Hans attempted to speak, to brashly tell them they were making a big mistake, that others would be coming for them. Instead of an answer, he received a blow to the side of his head, enough to make him lightheaded. All his bravado had left him. He knew there would be no rescue. No one in Brussels was aware they had ventured out of the city to follow Desmit. Major Kohler would not bring Gie Desmit in for questioning; it would mean admitting they were following him. And even if they did question him, what would he tell them? That he went to Daens to see a woman? They could be anywhere now; how long did they drive them last night? It was all a blur. No, the Major would sacrifice them to haul in a bigger fish. The more Hans thought, the more he became depressed. It was a nightmare.

Upstairs, Karel had just returned from securing a hay wagon from one of the farmers. Since they were a common sight in the area, he thought it a less conspicuous way to move the Germans out of town. He joined Arno, who was finishing a breakfast of hard bread, cheese, and wine. Karel laid out a hand-drawn map of the area, going over the plan one more time, determined that if the mission fell apart, it would not be because of him or his men. Downstairs it was Nick's turn to guard the prisoners, taking great pleasure in feeding their fear. He only wished that he was allowed to inflict real pain upon them, but alas, they were needed alive. That didn't stop him from introducing the butt of his Mauser to one of their heads.

The door to the cellar creaked open, and Nick watched his father climb down, each step groaning as a foot touched it. Arno looked at the hostages and then his son and mouthed, "It's time."

Without another word, they grabbed Otto by the arms and legs and picked him up. The German thought that his arms would be pulled out of their sockets by way the way they carried him. He let out a scream, "You fuckers!"

His complaint was met by Nick, who let go of the prisoner's legs and let them crash to the ground. Arno watched as his son punched the man's kidneys and then told him, "Shut up, or I will give you something to moan about, any more crying, and you'll find your balls in your mouth." He could feel Otto's body start to shake.

They took him out the back door of the Inn and threw him onto the waiting hay wagon. Hans was a little more challenging to maneuver. His extra girth made it difficult to get him up the stars. Nick, with his bad leg, struggled, losing his hold a couple of times, which caused Hans' knees to hit the stairs. After hearing the threat to Otto, Hans was anxious to keep his private parts attached to himself and made no sound. Eventually, they were able to shove him into the wagon. They laid hay over the two Germans, and with Arno taking the reins ventured off to meet with Karel.

The two soldiers on the wagon were nearly suffocating from the hay that was piled on them. At some point, they took them off the wagon and threw both onto the back seat of the Mercedes, one on top of the other, still naked. The only complaint was Hans cursing Otto for having his cock too close to his ass. Hans gave a nudge, and Otto slid off the seat and fell on the raised part that housed the car's axle. Bound and sightless, they had no idea how much time had passed. Hans thought it an hour, but Otto thought longer. At some point, the car stopped, and they were deposit into a ditch. They both thought the next sound would be their execution. Instead, the rope binding their legs together was cut, and then the car along with its occupants was gone. It took them a while, but they were successful in getting the sacks off their heads. But not so in undoing the knots that held their arms behind their backs. Hans recognized the area and knew there was an Army post less than a kilometer away. So they walked naked, hands tied behind their backs, down the road, working on the story they would tell to Major Kohler to hopefully save their necks.

....

"I expect you not to become a prisoner." Desmit's last words were still ringing in Valentin's ears as he made his way to the loading dock, avoiding the main floor and any curious workers. Taking the back stairway, he stopped in the employees' room to change into a pair of grey overalls. At the dock, the large cargo doors were open, and Raphael Dufour, one of the factory's drivers, was loading a secretary desk to the flatbed of a 1934 Volvo LV 75. Valentin helped to secure the piece and then stepped up to the large double cab and hauled himself up.

Dufour would take them to the site chosen to meet with Major Kohler. Of course, there was the matter of getting out of the city safely with their cargo. Their pretense was they were headed out to the country to pick up lumber for the factory. With the war, wood had become more and more challenging to obtain. The company's truck was a familiar sight on the country roads. They had one important stop to make before they would head out of town.

Valentin liked Dufour, a short, stocky man with close-cut gray hair, a constant two-day stubble, and always a cigarette in his mouth. He was one of Gie's most competent operatives, and the best sniper he had ever met. It was a skill that he put to good use in the first war and was always happy to exercise now. Valentin looked behind his seat, where there was a toolbox. Hidden in the long box, under the false bottom, was Dufour's Gewehr 98. Valentin felt confident knowing Dufour would be his back up. There was hardly a word said between them as they drove through the city, the roaring of the truck engine making conversation almost impossible.

The Volvo pulled up to the doctor's house, two delivery men dropping off a secretary's desk. They went through the motions of knocking at the door, speaking to the occupant, and then pulling around back to unload, out of view of any peering eyes. Tillens held the door as they carried the desk into the house, depositing it in the foyer. They followed him into the examination room. His patient lay motionless on the table, Valentin feared that they had arrived too late. He could see that Raymond was conscious and bathed in a pool of sweat.

"Raymond, we are going to get you to safety, stay strong."

His voice was hardly a whisper. He used what strength he had to lift his head a little. Valentin leaned over to hear. "My brother?"

There was nothing to be gained by telling him about Eddie. Once recovered and healthy, he would have to deal with it. "We are here to help you."

"Will he be on the plane?"

"I don't know, save your strength."

Dufour stood over Raymond, ash from his cigarette floating down. He touched the poor man's head, and it felt like it was on fire. From the water bowl on the table, he took the wet towel and wiped the man's head. Dufour lit a cigarette and put it in Raymond's open lips. He took two deep drags, coughed, and closed his eyes.

Tillens motioned for them to join him in the next room. They followed him into the den where a fire was blazing. The room was cold, and you needed to stand within a few feet of the blaze to feel any warmth. "I know I am only here to assist," offered Dufour, "but this man is in no shape to travel. It will kill him."

The doctor walked over to a large cabinet and selected a bottle of sherry and three glasses. "We have no choice, he will certainly die here, at least he will have a chance if we can get him out of the country." They stood silent as he poured a drink for each of them. "The English have drugs that can control the infection."

Valentin followed Dufour out to the truck. The Volvo had a large double cab with front and back seats and an open truck bed. Behind the back seat was a sizeable wooden box that ran the width of the cab. Dufour used it to store tools as the truck had no enclosure to secure equipment safely. The woodworkers at the factory had cleverly fitted the box with a false bottom. A person or contraband could fit under it with tools placed on top. Lifting the panel out was a two-person operation, as it was heavy with woodworking tools. Dufour had already put his rifle there, in its leather case, next to a green duffel bag. He moved them to the side and laid a blanket across the floor.

The doctor had just administered a shot of morphine as they re-entered Raymond's room. "This should hold him until he reaches his destination. He is running a fever, and you will, from time to time, need to give him water." Valentin spoke softly to Raymond to explain where they were going, and what the plan was. He blinked in acknowledgment and then drifted off into unconsciousness. They wrapped him in a blanket and carried him to the truck. There was a moan when they placed him in the hidden compartment. With the rifle and duffel bag, it was a tight fit. Valentin leaned over, putting a hand on Raymond's warm head, and whispered, "Stay with us. We'll get you out." They placed the false bottom over him and secured it. Dufour started the engine and waited for Valentin, who had gone back to bid the doctor farewell.

Tillens was already cleaning the exam room, determined to eliminate any evidence that he was a party to illegal activities. Valentin extended his hand to him. "If our plan works, then I won't be seeing you for some time, Doctor. Gie is sending me off to one of the provinces until everything dies down."

Tillens smiled back, grasping Valentin's hand in both of his, "And if it doesn't work, then I won't be seeing you until the Germans leave. I think it wise that I stay out of sight for a while. Long ago, I found a safe house for just this event." They embraced, and then he escorted Valentin to the truck, watching as they pulled away.

The doctor wrote a note for his housekeeper, explaining that he would be away for a few days, and then made a call to the Clinic, giving them the same information. Retrieving his bag from the bedroom, Dr. Tillens locked the house and walked in the direction of the bus stop.

....

Alain Legrand sat on top of his unmade bed, an ashtray overflowing with cigarette butts next to him, trying to decide which was more dangerous: betraying the MBN or the Germans. After his initial enthusiasm wore off, he started to worry about the whole affair. If he brought Kohler the documents and doubled-crossed the Resistance, he would be marked a traitor and hunted down. But a long journey to Switzerland had a high probability of failure. He could be tripped up at any of the numerous checkpoints and become a ward of the Gestapo. Whatever those documents contained, he was sure they were trouble for him if captured. Kohler would probably deny knowing him. Either way, he would be a dead man. When it came to revenge, the Germans and Belgians were very much alike. Retribution was swift and extremely final. Up until now, he had successfully blurred the line between patriot and traitor, an act which made him rich and a friend to both groups. To actively participate in a mission that could get him tortured and shot by his German masters was unnerving. On the other hand, to refuse the Resistance would cut him off from any future useful information, which would leave him worthless to the Germans and probably get him a bullet in the head for all his troubles.

Not even in his darkest thoughts had he imagine there would come a day when he would have to make himself scarce, to become invisible. Panicking, he could see no right way out, except to disappear. He couldn't go back home to France; it would be too easy to be found. He had money safely hidden away, and his work papers let him travel. A train to Lisbon, a flight to Istanbul, and he could melt into a population that had so many anonymous faces. He knew people in Turkey who could help him buy a new identity, and from there, he could secure passage to one of the French Caribbean islands, or maybe even South America. He was a smart man, and he could start a new life. But he would have to move fast.

Unfortunately for Legrand, his dream disappeared when he realized that his magnificent room in Hotel Metropole had turned into a prison. He picked up the phone to inquire about train schedules, but no one at the switchboard would answer. He dressed to go downstairs to use the lobby phone. He cracked the door enough to scan the corridor, and it was empty. Legrand had just stepped out into the hallway, keys in hand, when a person emerged from the exit. He was a giant of a man in a black overcoat that went almost to the floor, his hat brim pulled down tightly to his eyebrows. The man looked like death himself. Legrand stopped in his tracks. The creature didn't say a word, only shook his head No, and gave the wine merchant a glare that had him retreating into his room.

Legrand passed the rest of the day sitting in an oversized chair, looking out the window and fretting. The room smelled stale with cigarette smoke. His only interruption was when the maid brought dinner, a meal that he had not ordered. He placed it on a side table where it stayed uneaten. He opened a bottle of wine from his samples and took a long drink. Not even what he liked to call the nectar of the gods could calm his nerves.

Precisely at six, there was a knock. Like a dead man he approached and opened the door. A figure pushed past so fast that Legrand stumbled backward a bit before catching himself. The man was short, 152 centimeters at most; his bulky overcoat made it difficult to tell whether he was stout or slim. The contact sported a neatly trimmed beard and wore round glasses that magnified his blue eyes. He was clutching a briefcase to his chest.

They stood in the middle of the room, staring at each other, neither willing to say a word. The man reached into his coat pocket and produced a thick envelope and handed it to Legrand. Opening it, he found a letter of introduction, travel document, and rail tickets. The travel document was impressive, signed by General Beck. He thumbed through the other papers and money and then turned to the little man. "What is my reason for traveling to Switzerland?"

"You're a wine merchant, you fool, why do you think?" came the dismissive reply. "You should not need to speak much and, if challenged, tell them that General Beck asked you to take on this mission to bring back Swiss wine."

The man spoke heavily-accented French. Legrand thought him to be Polish or Hungarian.

"I am traveling at great risk to myself. What sort of protection will I have?"

"We are all at great risk," the contact replied as he handed the wine merchant the briefcase. "This should never leave your sight. It is the sole reason for your existence."

Legrand examined the leather case and tried opening it. It was locked. "What is inside?"

"I have no idea what you are carrying, and, if you like breathing, then I suggest you curb your curiosity and leave it be."

"And my contact?"

At this, the little man pulled out a lapel pin of a trumpet. "Clip this on your coat. When you arrive in Geneva, wait under the main clock in the terminal. Someone will approach you and point to the pin. They will inquire if you play in an orchestra. Your reply will be, yes, I play the saxophone. Instructions will follow."

"And what if no one shows?"

"Then we are all fucked, aren't we? Your train leaves at seven-twenty tonight. Be in your seat no later than seven. Do not worry, we will have people close by to help should something go wrong." With that, the man turned to leave, then stopped. Glancing over his shoulder and wrinkling his nose for effect, he gave a last piece of advice: "I would shave and shower before you leave." He then exited the room as quickly as he had entered it.

....

Febe felt the searing pain as her whole body shook from the cold. Slowly opening her swollen eyes, she found herself back in a cell. Focusing, the silhouette of one of her tormenters came into view. He was standing over her metal bed, nudging her awake. She was surprised and scared at still being alive. One of her last memories was water filling her lungs and everything going black. As she slipped away, there was a comfort that it would all be over, but now the lousy dream continued. She didn't know how much more she could take. She tried to lift herself from the bed, but she was unable to move. The guard jerked her up, and she immediately felt the blood rushing from her head and vomited. He took a step back, cursing her, then threw a grey medical gown on the bed and barked that she should put it on. She thought it strange that she was thirsty, considering how much water had filled her lungs. But her throat was dry, and she couldn't even produce saliva. No part of her body wanted to work. It was a struggle to put on the wrap they had given her.

Febe had no idea how long she sat there, back against the wall, going in and out of consciousness. She had only been able to dress partially; just to get that far had exhausted her. Propped up against the wall, the left side of her body exposed, she felt like a scarecrow with all its stuffing pulled out. It startled her when the cell door opened again and the two goons who enjoyed trying to drown her entered. Both had the same expression that she would remember forever, those sick smiles that she saw when they dragged her under the water, enjoying their job. One of the guards pulled her up and placed her left arm through the remaining sleeve, then handcuffed her.

When the guard released Febe from his grip, she collapsed. They dragged her away, letting her feet scrape along the cement floor, the back of her gown flapping open. She lifted her head and could see they were heading towards the elevator, *thank God they aren't going to haul me down those stairs.* The doors opened, and the cab operator looked startled. Considering how small the lift was, he moved as far away from her as he could. Arriving at their floor, she was relieved not to be back in the basement but at the entrance. The daylight came in through tall windows. The brightness was already hurting her sensitive eyes. A woman carrying a stack of documents approached but on seeing the prisoner and guards, stepped around the group. It was as if she had found some dog dropping and didn't want any on her shoes.

It was difficult for Febe to stand, becoming dead weight for her two guards. They pulled a chair over and let her fall into it. Exhausted, it took her a minute to compose herself. When she looked up, Karlmann was standing in front of her. In a voice that was barely audible, she asked: "Where am I going?"

....

Group Captain Anthony Dankworth-Murray stood by the kitchen window, sipping tea and processing what he just been told by his cheerful host and member of the Resistance, Jarno.

"You're going home, old chap," said Jarno, mocking his guest's favorite expression. "They're flying you out tonight. You should get your gear together. We will be leaving soon."

Murray had mixed feelings about going home. He was, of course, happy to be returning to England and away from the daily stress of worrying about capture. In the last three weeks, there had been seven moves for security reasons. The Group Captain felt guilty about the danger he posed to Jarno and the selfless Belgians who had helped him. At extreme jeopardy to themselves, they had protected and sheltered him. No, it was the reception in London that concerned him. He knew that his superiors were desperately trying to secure his return. Not so much for their personal feelings towards him, but for the knowledge he possessed. There would be a severe dressing-down and reprimand for sure; and possibly even a court-martial.

The Group Captain, a veteran of the Battle of Britain, was on the Air Vice-Marshall's staff for strategic bombing. Unhappy with the squadron's bombing results and lacking hard intelligence for sites, he decided to take matters into his own hands. Commandeering a Hawker Hurricane, Murray would zip across the channel to personally check out targets and their defenses. He had successfully done this twice in France, but on the third try his plane was intercepted by three Messerschmitts in Belgium and crashed. It was by luck, and the grace of God, that a farmer found him and hid him until he was collected by the Underground.

Dankworth-Murray knew that if he fell into the enemy's hands, they would have hit the jackpot with the information he possessed. His knowledge of not only British but now American squadron strength and target priorities would put the allied bombing effort back months and could affect the outcome of the war. He also reckoned that if British intelligence couldn't get him out soon, then they would have him eliminated rather than let him fall into the hands of the Gestapo. Would it be his friend Jarno, or someone else that would pull the trigger? After he lost his weapon, he noted no one would give him one, even after repeated requests. It was a discomfiting thought as he returned to his room to collect his gear. Into his kit, he packed the maps which he had annotated with information while with the Resistance, his first aid kit which thankfully he didn't need to use, and his RAF cap.

The Group Captain had assembled a farmer's wardrobe traveling from farm to farm. Dressed in oversized old brown corduroy work pants with the belt pulled tight, a green sweater with worn elbows over a flannel shirt, a burlap coat, heavy boots, and scraggly beard, which to his surprise was all grey, he resembled one of the locals. Unfortunately, if caught and out of uniform, carrying information about the enemy, he also resembled a spy. On a side table next to his cot lay a small wooden cross given to him by the wife of the farmer who first rescued him. Picking it up, he dropped it into his coat pocket. He would need all the help he could get.

Dankworth-Murray went looking for Jarno and found him standing by the water trough. To the Group Captain's delight, he was holding the reins of a draft horse. Eyeing the poor tired animal, he inquired:

"Our transportation?"

"You told me you are horseman?"

"I'm not sure we would call this beast a horse in England, mate."

"The pick-up point is not far away. I know a short cut through the woods that will keep us out of the sight of any patrols. It will be much quicker and safer this way."

It had been a while since Murray had ridden a horse, and even longer since he had ridden bareback. He watched as Jarno, with one smooth motion, took hold of the reins and threw his leg over the horse. Sitting up straight, he offered his hand to the Captain, who suffered through the indignity of multiple attempts before finally mounting the horse. With a nudge from Jarno, their steed moved on at a slow, steady pace.

....

When the phone call came through, Major Kohler hoped to keep the caller on the line as long as possible. He took his time getting to the phone and then tried to stall, wanting assurances that the caller was legitimate. But the person was having none of it. The directions to the rendezvous point were given succinctly, and the Major was told to be there exactly at

4:30 PM. Once there, he would receive further instructions--and then the line went dead. Kohler immediately called down to the switchboard to see if the trace was successful. The best the technician could determine was the call came from within the building. *Damn the Belgians*. He asked himself, *how many spies do they have in this building?*

Kohler spread out a map of the exchange area. The meeting point was a weigh station located outside of Daens. It had been built by the government in the 1930s to help with taxing produce going to market. At the time, there was an outcry by the farm owners. The process affected their livelihood, as they made a profit by not declaring all their goods. The government gave up, and the station was abandoned. Kohler could see it stood on top of a hill. Anyone at the station could see a vehicle approaching for miles. *A smart place for a meeting,* he thought.

A second call came through to Major Kohler not long after the first. It was from an officer who commanded a checkpoint outside the city. Two men, naked and with their hands tied behind their backs, had shown up at his post. They claimed they were on the Major's staff and needed to speak to him immediately.

"Let me speak to the sergeant," growled Kohler.

Hans Klein stared at the receiver when it was handed to him, slowly reaching out to take it. He took a deep breath, going over one last time what he planned to tell Kohler.

Hans felt the chill from Kohler as soon as he started his report. The Major cared not a bit that he and Otto were safe. The sergeant explained how they had followed Gie Desmit, sure that something was not right. While on a stakeout, they were overpowered by a dozen hooligans and then tortured, but eventually were able to escape. To Kohler, these two were wasting his time. He should have them shot immediately for incompetence, or put them on the next train for the Russian front. Fearing that he was not convincing his boss, Hans played the only card they had. During the ride in the car, they had overheard one of the men start to tell the other about a pick up near the Alyssum field before being told to shut up. Kohler's ears immediately perked up. He had seen intelligence reports that there was a strong Resistance presence in that area. The field was not far from the station and could easily accommodate the landing of a small plane. Yes, that made sense, they would take the woman and evacuate her out of the country.

Kohler called to the corporal outside his office to have his car brought around. He then alerted his police team to be ready to move on a moment's notice, and, he put two squads of soldiers on alert. Everything was fluid now. It all depended on execution; if done correctly, the Major expected to roll up the gang of saboteurs. Checking his watch, he needed to move if he was to be at the meeting point on time.

CHAPTER 26

The beautiful ornate door of the elevator opened, and Major Kohler emerged, buttoning his greatcoat. He scanned the crowded hall, and it was easy to spot his group. They were like a leper colony seated in the corner. All the passersby had given them considerable space. With Febe's swollen body propped up on a chair, guarded by the demons of death, no one was anxious to get close to them. Kohler moved toward his party as a path cleared; neither soldier nor citizen wanted to have any interaction with the Major. Febe's head was down, and she appeared to be unconscious. Kohler nodded toward one of the guards, who got her attention with an elbow to her bruised shoulder. The pain went through her body like an electric shock, her eyes immediately opening. The Major was glaring down at her. She wanted to stand and spit in his face, but her body would not respond.

"Oberleutnant." Karlmann snapped to attention. "You are coming with me. Collect your weapon and have the men put the prisoner in my car." His men leaped into action.

Kohler strolled out the door, putting on his gloves while ignoring the two sentries saluting him. At the car, he dismissed his driver, who beat a hasty line back into the warm building. The guards brought Febe and sat her in the back. She asked if they would unhandcuff her, but she might as well have been invisible as they closed the door and walked away. Feeling weak and dizzy, she rolled over on her side in the hope that she wouldn't throw up. It was impossible to find a position of comfort. There was no place on her body that didn't hurt. She had no idea where they were taking her. Gestapo headquarters? To be shot? None of it made sense as the cold now started to invade her bones. Time in the ice water had taken its toll on her. She was sure her lips had turned blue. She was barefoot and had no coat, still wearing only a hospital gown that was thin and opened in the back. There on the seat, she shivered and waited to find out her fate.

The Major walked to the rear of the car and opened the trunk. Inside was a new Luftwaffe short-wave radio, and the MP 40 machine pistol he requested. Kohler tested the communication by calling his two captains who were on alert for this mission. Satisfied that all was working correctly and that his men were ready, he switched off the unit. He checked the MP 40's clip and secured it under the driver's seat. Oberleutnant Karlmann, who had just exited the building, joined him as he spread out the map on the hood of the car and went over his plan.

Pleased that he had taken all the precautions possible, Kohler placed himself behind the DeSoto's steering wheel and invited Karlmann to take the seat next to him. The car fishtailed as it accelerated. The Major enjoyed the powerful American engine as he went screaming through the streets, ignoring stoplights and narrowly missing cars and bicyclists.

....

Raphael Dufour had driven the country roads for years working for the furniture factory and was familiar with the area. It was he who suggested to Gie where the exchange should take place, and had found the site for the landing. It brought a sense of relief to him and Valentin that the trip had been uneventful, with even the stops and searches routine. A quick check to see if photos on identity cards matched faces, a glance in the toolbox, and they were on their way. They were able to stop a couple of times to attend to Raymond, who continued to run a fever. During the drive, Valentin could not help but look back at the toolbox and pray that DeBaets would hold on until they could get him to England. Raphael told him that it would not be long now, and soon after that, they came up over the hill and could see the valley stretched out before them. Even though they were far away, Valentin could see the weigh station.

Three men with weapons emerged from the building as the truck neared. Valentin, not recognizing them, was alarmed. Raphael reached across the seat and put his hand on his chest to calm him.

"Friends, not to be afraid."

They jumped out of the cab, and Raphael introduced Valentin to Karel Van Hoebeek, Arno Lejeune, and his son Nick. Karel and Arno were to take Raymond on to the landing site. Nick would stay behind and guide them to the site after they had finished with the Major.

Valentin asked if they had brought the body.

"It is inside the building," replied Karel, "delivered this afternoon by a man who was very happy to give him to us."

The building sat on top of a hill, the road crossing in front. At one time, to the side of the station were scales to weigh the trucks. They had been gone for many years now. The building was in disrepair, with the doors and windows missing. A fire a few years back destroyed half of the station and all of the roof. Valentin could see why Raphael chose it. It had a commanding view of the valley, with only one road that passed through the valley and then on to Brussels. Less than a kilometer behind the structure was a large creek that emptied into a lake. That area was rugged and made the approach almost impossible for vehicles.

The room with its charred walls was empty, illuminated only with the dull light coming through the roofless top. In the corner was the body of Eddie DeBaets, brought from the safehouse, a blanket wrapped around him. Valentin was uneasy giving the dead brother to the Germans. Even though it was his idea to use him as bait, he felt guilty. Earlier, when he mentioned it to Desmit, the boss' absolution was instantaneous.

"Valentin, I am the only one who must answer to God for this, and believe me, someday in a free Belgium, I will be happy to take whatever punishment the good Lord gives me."

Arno climbed up to the cab and helped Raphael remove the toolbox. Seeing Raymond, he wondered if the man was still alive.

"He is," replied Raphael, and then looking straight into Arno's eyes said, "and it is your job to keep him that way."

"He is safe with us."

Raphael lifted his gun case and then the green duffel from the box and placed them both on the ground. Reaching into the bag, he pulled out three British Sten guns and ammunition, which he distributed to the group.

" A gift to you from the MBN," he called, as he passed the weapons to their new owners.

All three men accepted the machine guns like children receiving gifts at Christmas time. Nick was the only one who had familiarity with the weapon, and quickly gave the older men a lesson on how the gun fired. Raphael searched the bag for one last gift, a Browning 45 automatic, which he handed to Valentin with the reassuring words, "Just in case."

Valentin checked the magazine, and slipped it in his waistband. Turning to the men, he took one last opportunity to make sure everyone knew what to do. The group shook hands, with the new men nervously wishing each other success. It was Raphael who sensed their fear. "Follow the plan, and you will all be fine."

Valentin watched as the truck with Raymond drove away. Nick was left behind to assist with the escape. Picking up his new Sten gun, he walked towards the creek to await the action. Raphael had already moved to find a spot, rifle in hand, and was halfway to a clump of trees when Valentin spotted him. There was nothing left to do but wait. Valentin knew he should stay inside, out of view, but sitting there looking at Eddie's corpse was more than he could handle. He pulled his coat tighter around him for warmth and sat down outside, his back up against the building.

Raphael had scanned the area looking for a vantage point so he could cover Valentin, and hopefully Febe. He discounted hiding in the station as it did not give him a clear view of all the participants, plus he would have to reveal himself should he need to take a shot. The closest cover he could see was a group of trees a short distance away. Counting his steps, it was just over 50 meters from the trees to the weigh station. It was the right spot that gave cover and an escape route through the woods to the stream. Kneeling, he pulled his Gewehr 98 out the case, attaching its Zeiss telescopic sight. He took a prone position next to a tree that gave him a full vista of the field. He zeroed in the scope as best he could, then cradled the rifle next to him to wait for the drama to unfold.

....

Major Kohler was still a few kilometers away from the meeting point when he slowed and drove the DeSoto off to the side of the road. He didn't want to arrive early, and, still had some last-minute details to finalize. He did not believe this would be a simple exchange and had prepared for whatever might happen. There would be no repeat of the last debacle. Before leaving Brussels, he ordered a squad of men to follow him, to be close by should the meeting turn out to be an ambush. Whatever happened, once they concluded their business, the Major would have the troops move on the weigh station. He also prepared for the possibility that he would indeed receive hard information, so he had Captain Geisler, of his military police, stand by in Brussels to make arrests.

It was nearly 10 minutes' wait before a staff car and troop truck pulled up next to the DeSoto. The Kubelwagen, which was painted in a bluish-grey camouflage, blended into the countryside. Captain Ulmer, commander of the group and no admirer of the Major, saluted. Kohler immediately got down to business, and his orders were simple. They were to wait at their present location. He would send up a flare when they were needed.

"Once you see that signal, Ulmer, I will be counting the seconds until you are there. Do not make me count for long."

Understanding the implications of the threat, he replied, "You may count on me, Major."

Oberleutnant Karlmann retrieved the MP 40 from under the seat and a flare gun from the truck.

Kohler wanted to make sure Karlmann understood his assignment. "Should I be shot or captured, shoot the woman first and then fire the signal."

There was a nod of acknowledgment. "Yes, Major."

"Good, let's finish this business."

When the car stopped, Febe expended what energy she had to sit up. She was surprised to find herself in the middle of the country. A few minutes later, when a truck with soldiers arrived, it alarmed her—working over in her mind what could be happening. Why did they stop her interrogation? Why bring her here? A sickening knot developed in her stomach. She was being used as bait.

Febe could see Kohler snapping at his officers and giving orders, but could not hear what he was saying. She watched as Karlmann approached the car. He pulled her out of the back, stones digging into her bare feet as they hit the ground, and pushed her into the front seat. The Oberleutnant sat directly behind her. She could hear him cock his pistol and then nudge her behind the ear. The Major, having finished with Captain Ulmer, returned. He looked approvingly at the current seating arrangement and smiled when he saw the Luger next to her head.

....

The roar of the engine traveled across the valley like thunder, shaking Valentin from his thoughts. Stretching to shake the cold from his bones, he could see a royal blue car bouncing along the dirt road. He took refuge in the weigh station, positioning himself next to one of the windows. He expected Kohler to try something and would not have been surprised if half the German army was coming over the hill.

The DeSoto slowed as it approached the structure, parking about 10 meters from the building door. From his vantage point, Raphael could see two people in the front seat, less clear was someone sitting in the back. He tracked as the driver's side door opened, and Kohler exited. The Major enjoyed making a show of taking off his overcoat and draping it over the hood of the car. Then he withdrew his pistol from its holster, holding it up for anyone to see, and placed it on top of the coat. He walked halfway between the building and the car; there, he stopped and spread his arms out. *What a cocky bastard* thought Raphael, as he placed his crosshairs directly on the German's head.

Febe watched as Kohler seemed to be waiting for someone to appear. He withdrew his cigarette case, casually taking one out and lighting it, illuminating his face in the dying light. A figure appeared in the doorway of the building. As the person came closer, he came into focus. It was Valentin. For a millisecond, her heart soared at seeing him, but then she realized what this was all about. There was going to be an exchange: her for someone or something. But Valentin didn't know there was a company of German infantry just over the hill waiting for orders. "No, no, no," was all she could voice. Karlmann nudged the pistol into her neck.

It was hard to tell if Kohler was astonished or disgusted, "You? The painter?" The Major had never trusted him or the wife. What a fool the General had been, but he would deal with him later.

Valentin looked past the Major to the car. He could make out two silhouettes. He zeroed in on the dark figure in the back; there was a clear outline of a pistol against Febe's head. Kohler followed Valentin's eyes to the car.

"Yes, she's there, and any departure from our agreement will mean her death."

"Just to be clear, Major, there is a man with a high-powered rifle aimed at your head. If there is any betrayal, you will be the first one to die."

The German scanned the horizon to see if he could see where the sniper might be hiding. "I am anxious to conclude this little episode. You promised the saboteur."

"He's inside."

Looking towards the building, the Major didn't want to be out of view of Karlmann. "Have him brought out here in the open."

Valentin gave him an *as you wish* expression and disappeared into the station. Returning, he was dragging something wrapped in a blanket. Stopping in front of the Major, he let go of the quilt, which opened enough to expose a dead body.

"What's this?"

"The man you have been looking for."

"I expected him to be alive."

"I didn't promise him alive, Major."

Kohler pulled the blanket open to fully expose the body. No stranger to a corpse, he could tell that this one had been dead a few days. "How do I know this is one of the DeBaets brothers and not some bum you picked up?"

"His identity and work papers are in his coat pocket."

The Major reached into the pocket, retrieving the papers, and checked the photograph against the face in front of him. It was not difficult to confirm the man's identity, even though rigor mortis had set in and there was some blistering of the face, and the body was starting to bloat. In the end, he decided there was enough of a resemblance to claim him as Edward DeBaets. "And the other brother?"

"That was not in our agreement."

"Nor was a corpse."

Valentin said nothing.

Finally, it was Kohler who spoke. "And the matter of the General?"

"There is a person about to depart on the 19:20 for Munich. In his briefcase, you will find evidence that the General is collaborating with the enemy."

The Major checked his watch. "I am to believe that?"

Valentin withdrew a sheet of paper from his jacket and handed it to Kohler. "Do you recognize this?"

He was holding a page of General Beck's monthly report to Berlin. The full document contained troop strengths and their placement, airfields, storage units, and anything else that affected the Wehrmacht in Belgium. It was an 'eyes only' document that Kohler did not have clearance to read. "How did you come by this?"

"The man sitting in car 12, compartment 3, seat 6, is carrying a briefcase with the full report and a letter from the General to the British Intelligence."

"You as a concerned citizen of the Reich are afraid this information will fall into the hands of the enemies?" Kohler replied sarcastically.

"We both have our reasons for seeing the General out of Belgium. In this case, why would I lie? You have the evidence there in your hand, and if you don't use it, I'm sure someone else will. What would be my motivation for lying?"

"The girl."

"You have your suspect on the train. I'm sure you can come up with a story that makes you look good on how you captured him. The General is the icing on the cake for both of us."

"This man on the train, you will give him up freely for the girl?"

"Let us say that his usefulness to us is over. It's either offer him to you, or a bullet to the face."

The Major took stock of the situation. One of the saboteurs was in custody. Dead, but he would spin a story to make himself the hero. The man on the train was problematic, but Valentin had much reason to resent the General, so he could be telling the truth. Plus, once Kohler was out of the sniper's crosshairs, his men would be able to move in and capture the woman and de Vos.

"How do I know you won't shoot me once you get the girl?"

"I shoot you, your man shoots me."

Kohler wrapped the blanket around Eddie, then pulled him up and threw him over his shoulder, and returned to the car. Opening the trunk, he dumped the body in the back. Now was the moment of truth: releasing the girl. If anything were to happen, now would be the time. He walked around the passenger's side. "Karlmann, be ready." He glanced over to a group of trees, a perfect hiding place for a sniper. Opening the passenger door, he motioned for Febe. Gathering all her strength, she slowly moved away from the car, Karlmann keeping his MP 40 on her. Kohler slipped into the seat and then across to the driver's side.

"Do I shoot, Major?"

Kohler looked up. If there was a sniper in the trees, he had a clear shot. "No, but don't take your eyes off of them." He started the car, wanting to get out of the sights of the sniper.

Valentin was appalled as Febe stepped away from the DeSoto, wearing only the hospital gown and a hideously swollen face. He rushed to her, putting his coat around her shoulders. Sweeping her up in his arms, he carried her back to the building. Raphael was zeroing in on the man behind the driver's seat. He was hoping that Valentin could make it to the building before the car left, his finger lightly touching the trigger.

The car pulled away with a jerk, spinning around 180

degrees to head out in the direction it came. It fishtailed on the dirt road, sending the coat and pistol flying off the hood. Valentin was almost to the building when the machine gun came out the window, Karlmann didn't get a shot off as Raphael sent a bullet slamming into the side of the door. The vehicle was accelerating as the second shot came in through the back, smashing through the window and into the Oberleutnant's shoulder. He let out a howl. Kohler screamed at him as another shot hit the car. "The flare, you fool, the flare!" But Karlmann was prone on the back seat, trying to stop the blood pumping from his shoulder. The car had gone half a kilometer before it dipped into a ravine. The Major applied the brake and started to skid over the loose gravel. The vehicle veered to the left and went over a large rock, landing with a loud thud. The hard impact caused a bolt of pain to shoot through Karlmann's body, and the trunk of the car to pop open. The Major reached in back for the flare gun and fired it in the air to alert his troops.

Valentin followed the arc of the flare and figured that he had ten minutes at the most before the area would be crawling with Germans. Raphael returned, and with Valentin cradling Febe, they moved off to the south of the station, down an embankment and across a field that was intersected by a large stream. At the edge of the water, Nick Lejeune was waiting with a raft that would transport them downstream. Their destination was Lake Angeline, and the waterway would take them close. They would have to transverse the last half-kilometer to the landing site by foot.

The RAF planes in the past had not made amphibious landings, and the assumption was no one would be expecting this one. It would be dangerous to attempt a night landing on a lake, but the British had confidence their man could accomplish it. Hoping to confuse the enemy, Desmit had planted misinformation too. His informants had purposely let the fake landing site be known to the two German prisoners before they were released.

There was a tinge of disappointment in Captain Ulmer when he saw the signal. He had hoped that the MBN would do everyone a big favor by shooting the Major. He ordered his men who had been huddled together by the side of the road back into the vehicles. The staff car was taking the lead, and the two trucks followed. It didn't take long before they found Kohler taking refuge behind the DeSoto and shouting into his short-wave radio. He was giving orders to his man in Brussels to proceed to the station and arrest the man on the train. He could hear Kohler screaming into the microphone. "No, I don't have a name or description! He is car 12, compartment 3, seat 6, and carrying a briefcase. Arrest and hold him for me."

Approaching the car, Captain Ulmer could see the shot-out window and an arm protruding out of the boot. On closer inspection, he found the Oberleutnant wounded on the back seat. The captain called to have first aid administered. Looking into the car, Kohler was more upset that the man had bled all over the back seat than concern for his well-being. He turned to Ulmer and ordered the men to disperse in a full arc and move toward the weigh station.

"This is the only way out," the Major shouted. "There is at least one person with the woman, maybe two." He didn't mention that the second person was a sniper.

The Major retrieved a pair of binoculars and watched as the men approached the weigh station. He could see a group of soldiers inching their way toward the building and then cautiously entering, then one of them standing in the doorway and shaking his head to indicate that it was vacant. Darkness had now set in, making it impossible to continue the search. Kohler ordered the Captain and his men to proceed to the assumed landing site. Eddie DeBaets' dead body was still in the trunk and Oberleutnant Karlmann in the back seat. The Major had one last order to the Captain before he would speed off for the return trip to Brussels.

"Ulmer, whatever you have to do. I want them all taken alive."

CHAPTER 27

The creek was running fast due to the rains over the last few weeks, and Valentin thought the raft carrying the four of them a little too flimsy as it crashed through the water. Their transport consisted of a few logs lashed together, with the three of them huddled in the center and Nick Lejeune using an oar to steer. Despite the concerns, the young man navigated the rocks and darkness effortlessly, and soon they came to a spot where it was too narrow to proceed any further. "Not far now," Nick explained, "but we must walk the rest of the way." Valentin carried Febe as Lejeune led them towards the lake. There was a thin moon above that gave off the slightest of illumination.

Every move by Valentin caused Febe pain; even breathing was an effort. She had never felt so tired in her life and decided that she had reached her limit to go on. "Leave me," she mouthed to Valentin.

"We are flying you to England," whispered Valentin. Through the dim light, he could see the confusion on her face.

"England? Me?"

"You are in too much danger here."

"We are all in danger. Are you coming with me?"

Valentin shook his head, "No, there is only room in the plane for three, and we are also flying out Raymond and a British flier."

"I don't care; I can't go on. Leave me here with a gun. I'm only going to slow you down."

"Stop it. The worst is over, and we don't have much farther to go. Once in England, friends will take care of you and nurse you back to good health. Our struggle is a long one. Trust me, it is safer for all of us if you leave."

She had no more strength to argue and fell quiet.

....

Alain Legrand checked his watch as he took his seat; it was precisely 7:00 PM. Leaving the hotel, the menacing man in black followed him to the station. The train's destination was Munich, and most of the passages were Germans heading home for the holidays. Legrand hoped to get lost in the crowd. But his minder stood nearly a foot taller than the other travelers, and every time Legrand turned to look, he could see the man glaring back at him.

Once on the train, Legrand felt thankful to be away from the omnipresent eye of his shadower. He even had a quick thought that he might exit the train from another car. Before there was any serious consideration of the idea, someone put a hand on his back to gently push him along. Standing behind him was a man in his mid 60's with salt and pepper hair and carrying a cane. Legrand tried to step aside to let him through, but the man nudged him toward the compartment. Standing at the compartment door, the man motioned for Legrand to enter. The wine merchant threw his suitcase in the overhead rack and then sat huddled in the corner, clutching the briefcase. He waited for the stranger to speak, but the man said nothing. He sat there in a perfectly-tailored grey suit, reading a letter he retrieved from his coat pocket. Looking out the window, Legrand could see the black-clad man standing at the newspaper kiosk staring straight at him. How many people were watching him, and why? There could be no escape.

Departure time came and went, but the train showed no hurry to leave the station. The man sitting opposite stood and cracked open the compartment window for fresh air. Legrand went to stub out his cigarette, but the small ashtray next to his seat was full. One of the passengers inquired about the delay. The explanation was, they were uncoupling cars, but there was no motion to indicate that was happening. Legrand looked across to the man. There was a serene look on his face as he read his letter, while the wine merchant sat there sweating.

Legrand looked again toward the newspaper kiosk for his minder, but he was gone. Looking further up the platform, he saw a group of soldiers gathering. A captain joined them, gave them orders, and then they split up. He could feel the sweat soaking his shirt; he took out his handkerchief to wipe his brow.

The soldiers approached from both ends of the car, converging on Legrand's compartment. One of them carrying a machine pistol slid open the door, and an officer stepped in. The other passenger already had his papers out, presenting them without being asked. The captain examined the identity card, holding it up to the light to see if he could detect a forgery. When asked his reason for traveling, Legrand was surprised to learn the man was a German citizen returning home to Munich. His papers were carefully refolded and returned.

The wine merchant sat in a state of shock as the officer stood in front of him, his outstretched hand waiting for documents. When the officer finally spoke, it was an order rather than a request. "Papers." Legrand said nothing, his mouth too dry to speak. One of the soldiers started to approach, his right hand already forming a fist. Finally, Legrand reached into his suit pocket and brought out his papers. "And your ticket."

Legrand fumbled through his pocket to find the ticket and handed it to the Captain. The German double-checked the compartment and seat number against what Major Kohler had given him. Satisfied he had his man, there was a simple "stand up." As soon as he stood, one of the soldiers relieved him of the briefcase and placed him in handcuffs.

Legrand summoned what courage he had left. "What is the meaning of this? My papers are in order, and I have travel documents signed by General Beck. The General..." He never got a chance to finish. The captain ordered him removed.

Looking over his shoulder to the officer, Legrand tried a desperate plea, "I insist that I speak with Major Kohler."

Laughing, the captain assured him, "Oh, the Major is most anxious to speak with you too."

....

It was slow going, and the ride uncomfortable, but Group Captain Anthony Dankworth-Murray was enjoying his journey on top of the old horse. His guide Jarno was an expert with the reins as they moved through the countryside, and he offered commentary on where he hunted or property he wanted to buy. "I think I could farm this land," he commented as they passed over a rocky patch of dirt. "It just needs work. I have made an offer, but the owner thinks it is worth more."

"Is farming difficult with the Jerrys around?"

"The Germans, the French, the English, the Italians, it makes no difference to me. My family has lived in this region for hundreds of years. Belgium has seen wars, has had monarchies and republics, foreigners and opportunists. Yet, our house still stands, we hunt in the same woods, fish in the same streams. Like all the rest, the Boche will someday leave."

The Group Captain marveled at how Jarno considered the war as just another inconvenience in life. He was about to ask him about his family when they came to a crest, and Arno held up his hand for quiet. "The lake is down there." Murray could see the outline of the shore. They dismounted.

The two were about 20 meters from the edge of the lake when they were met by Major Griffin, carrying a Sten gun. He ignored Jarno. "Group Captain Dankworth-Murray?"

"The same." He extended his hand. "You are?"

"Major Griffin. Captain, it is good to meet you finally."

"Well, I am sure there are a few Jerrys who would like to say the same thing. Do you have a smoke, old chap? I am dying for one."

"We can't afford to give away our position, just in case, but this may help." He pulled out a flask from his back pocket and handed it to the Group Captain.

"Bless you" He took a long swig, then passed it to Jarno, who had an even longer one. Griffin gave a disapproving glare at the Belgian and wiped the spout before also taking a drink.

The group made their way back to where Karel Van Hoebeek and Arno Lejeune were waiting with Raymond. Dankworth-Murray looked at the man propped up next to a log. "What is wrong with this person?" Moving next to him, he put his hand to the man's forehead. "He's burning up." To the distress of Griffin, he pulled out his lighter and observed Raymond. "This man will die if we don't bring this fever down." With that, the Group Captain moved into action. He instructed Jarno to bring water from the lake, and then from his flight bag pulled out his first aid kit.

With nothing else to carry water, Jarno used his hat, losing most of the liquid before returning. But it was enough that Murray was able to dip his hanky and bathe Raymond's head. Opening the blood-soaked shirt, he was able to clean the wound and apply sulfa from his first aid kit. Wrapping the shoulder with a clean bandage, the airman administered a syrette of morphine. Taking off his jacket, he wrapped it around his patient. "We'll get you out of here, mate." Raymond attempted to say something, but the drug went to work, and he drifted off.

Jarno spoke with Karel and then took the reins of his horse and approached the Group Captain. "I must leave and get back to my farm. These are good men. They will take care of you."

"I can't thank you enough, mate."

Murray extended his hand, but Jarno embraced him and whispered into his ear. "I am glad I didn't have to shoot you, my friend." Even in the darkness, he could see the Englander smiling.

....

Major Kohler returned to Brussels in record time, running the DeSoto at full throttle, passing the hospital, and going directly to military headquarters. At the entrance, his adjutant informed him the suspect from the train was in the conference room.

"The body of one of the saboteurs is in the trunk. There was no choice but to shoot him," Kohler told his aid. He would work on his story later, but this would be his kill. "Have him held at the morgue. Also, Karlmann is wounded, he's in the car."

The adjutant rushed out to find Karlmann unconscious in the back seat. Kohler left to interrogate his prisoner. Legrand was being held in the old mansion's conference room down the hall from the Major's office. The captain who arrested Legrand was waiting for Kohler as he exited the elevator with his report. The Major listened to the officer describe the arrest and then hand over the prisoner's identity papers and the contents of the briefcase.

"I glanced at the documents, Major, but once I realized they were classified, I returned them to the briefcase."

Sitting behind his desk, Kohler didn't hear nor did he care if the captain had read anything. He was looking at another surprise: Legrand's identity card. He asked himself, *why did the Resistance give up the wine merchant? What game were they playing?* He leafed through the report, and all the pages were there save the one Valentin had showed him. He marveled at how they could have come into de Vos' hands. He gathered up all the papers and went to speak with the prisoner.

The conference room was used for executive meetings when the mansion belonged to the electric company. It was a magnificent place with paneled walls and a high ceiling, topped off by a chandelier that was a gift from the King when the building opened. In the center of the room was a long mahogany table with fourteen high-backed chairs surrounding it. On the table in front of each seat was a desk blotter and bankers' lamp. At the end of the table sat Alain Legrand, visible by a single light, no longer a friend of the Reich but its prisoner. Legrand stood as Kohler entered, hoping to approach him, but was pushed back down by his guard. The Major dismissed the sentry and then took a seat next to Legrand, who tried to speak but was silenced by a wave of his captor's hand.

The Major neatly positioned the papers in front of him and then leaned back and lit a cigarette. Legrand with dry throat was too scared to even pour a glass of water from the pitcher on the table. Kohler sat just outside the reach of the lamp that illuminated Legrand. Through the darkness, his voice felt like it was coming out of hell.

The Major was formal in his delivery. "You have in your possession, forged travel papers, a letter which implicates you committing treason against the Reich, and highly classified documents that you were trying to deliver to the enemy."

"Herr Major, please believe me. I was forced by the Belgium National Movement to carry out this mission. They had me under surveillance, and I could not refuse or contact you. Please, I had no idea what I was carrying. I was going to escape and notify you. You must believe me. I can still be of use to you. We can say that my cover story held up, and I was released. You can follow me and arrest my contact in Geneva." Before he could continue, the Major cut him off.

"Do you know how we found you? Your friends in the Resistance told me where you would be. They are on to you, and for them to give you up, you must have nothing to offer. The only thing waiting for you in Geneva is a bullet."

"Then you must know this is a setup, a folly."

"That could be true, but I have a man in custody who was on his way to Switzerland with highly classified documents. A person who was planning to cooperate with the enemy. With that evidence, I am sure they will give you a fair trial before they hang you."

"Please, Major, you know that is not the case."

Kohler sipped on the glass of water and then lit another cigarette before continuing. "These are the three options for you, Monsieur Legrand. First, I can release you, in which case you would probably be dead in the morning, courtesy of your friends in the Resistance. Second, I can turn you over to the Gestapo, who would probably spend the evening doing unpleasant things to you, and then hang you. Or I could shoot you and claim you were trying to escape."

"Please, no."

"Or there is a fourth option."

"What do you want of me?"

"To confess to the charges against you and implicate the General."

"But they are not true. I would be signing my death warrant."

"We are not speaking of the truth here, Legrand. We are speaking of saving your miserable life."

"It would be my word against the General's no one would believe me."

"You forget, I would believe you. When you finish telling your story, the Gestapo will think it is true. You have the forged papers, the documents, and I will provide you the story."

"Then I am shot for treason."

"Not necessary. You need only be around for the accusation. The military will want nothing to do with a trial of a general. They will quietly turn him over to the Gestapo and he will probably find himself hanging at the end of a wire by nightfall. If you cooperated, I could say you were working for me. My police will detain you, and then when everything quiets down, I can arrange for an exit visa. One to Spain or Portugal, and from there, then you would be free to go wherever you want."

Alain Legrand sat in the high-backed chair, going through the first three options. He could see how each would end up with his death. The only one which could give him time was the fourth. "I accept your offer, Major."

Kohler nodded and retrieved writing paper and a pen from the lacquered cabinet that stood at the far end of the room. He placed it in front of Legrand. Then he started dictating the wine merchant's confession.

....

Valentin prayed that their good luck would hold until he was able to get Febe and Raymond out of the country. So far, so good, but he remembered the previous extraction went awry at the last moment, and he would not relax until she was safely in England. He was also thankful for Nick Lejeune leading them through the darkness to the rendezvous site. His thoughts were disturbed when they heard someone approaching. Laying Febe to the ground, the men crouched low and readied their weapons. Just out of their sight, a voice called out in uneven French, "de Vos? Don't shoot, it's Major Griffin." A figure emerged from the trees, all three men still at the ready. They were uneasy with the man claiming to be the Major, but were reassured when Nick saw his father Arno trailing the officer. There were quick introductions and an even faster hike to the camp.

They placed the shivering Febe next to Raymond, who was being attended to by Group Captain Dankworth-Murray. "Has she been wounded?" he asked, kneeling next to her.

"She was the guest of the Germans," replied Raphael.

Murray didn't have to ask if she was in pain, as he could see it on her beaten face. "Any broken bones?"

"My rib, I think."

"I broke my ribs once Luv, in a plane crash. Hurt like hell." Laying his hand on her forehead, he was satisfied that she had no fever. "I think we can make you a little more comfortable." He reached into his satchel and pulled out a pair of heavy work socks. "I won't be needing these," he said, rolling the socks onto her feet. Valentin felt a pang of jealousy watching the gentleness of the Englishman as he touched Febe. Next, he pulled out his syrette of morphine, "I'm going to give you this shot, Luv. It should ease the pain."

"No, I want to be alert should anything happen. I don't want to be taken alive."

Valentin took her hand. "No one is going to harm you, I promise. Let the Captain give you the shot." The injection had an immediate effect on her, the pain eased, and within a few minutes, she was asleep.

Major Griffin gathered everyone together for a briefing. "Right, we shan't have long to wait. When we hear the plane, the lads here will light the three smudge pots they have put in the lake. They will then take a position and give cover fire should we have any last-minute party crashers. I'll signal the plane over to us. It won't be able to come to shore, so de Vos and I will take the canoe and ferry the evacuees out." Turning to Raphael, "Monsieur Dufour?" He received a nod of acknowledgment from the Belgian. "Monsieur Desmit requests you to return to Brussels with the truck." He paused knowing the request would not be well received. "Immediately."

Raphael would have disobeyed the order if it was anyone other than Gie Desmit. He understood that the boss was always looking at the big picture and did not want him or the factory to be an accomplice should anything go wrong. He felt like a coward leaving, but he kept that to himself.

Valentin took his hand. "Thank you, Raphael; there is nothing more for you to do here. I will see you back in Brussels someday."

Karel Van Hoebeek led him back to where they had parked the truck. "On Monsieur Desmit's orders, we managed to locate some wood to take back to the factory. It appears our friend never lets an opportunity to mix business and business pass by." Karel helped him stow his rifle and then watched as the truck faded out of sight.

....

Kohler was unsympathetic to the plight of his two hapless agents, Hans Klein and Otto Zimmermann. When he finally spoke with them, he ordered that they resume following Gie Desmit. He did not care to hear about their captivity, hunger, or loss of sleep.

He did offer, "If you lose him again, you should pack enough warm clothes for Russia." He had given Desmit a lot of latitude, but now it was time to show the cabinet maker a room at the mansion and sweat him. But that would have to wait until he dealt with the General.

His corporal brought in the freshly-signed confession of Alain Legrand. Now the tricky part would begin. Kohler personally could not arrest a general without permission from General Falkenhausen's headquarters. The General, the Commander of Belgium and Northern France would surely take over the investigation. Once Beck was disposed of, Kohler knew there would be recriminations against him if it was known he had betrayed a fellow officer. There was only one unit that could arrest the General and not be accountable to the German High Command.

He placed a call to Kriminalkommissar Pfeiffer of the Gestapo. In a room of nasty men, you could depend on him to be the dirtiest. A devout Nazi, he joined the movement after the failed Munich putsch and was rewarded with a position when they came to power. He had a strong dislike of Jews, Communists, and the military, and had a reputation for sending them all to the camps. The Major was able to track Pfeiffer down at a little cabaret that catered to the Gestapo. The Club

Himmel on Avenue Louise was not far from Gestapo headquarters. The owner, a German and brother-in-law to the head of Gestapo in Brussels, had taken it over after the previous owner met with an unfortunate accident. The joint was famous for plying its customers with German liquor, songs, and women. Pfeiffer tersely received Kohler's call, and after a little give and take reluctantly agreed to come to his office.

With Pfeiffer now sitting in the outer office, Kohler was ready to put his scheme into action. He opened the door to the reception area, his eyes first focusing on the corporal sitting at his desk. The young man was visibly uncomfortable with a glaring Pfeiffer sitting across from him. The Kriminalkommissar looked like he could use both exercise and sun. His Hitler mustache and steel grey eyes made him look like his hero, Heinrich Himmler. He seemed to be in his 50s and of medium height, but Kohler knew him to be much younger. Spotting the Major, Pfeiffer didn't allow for pleasantries, he stood and walked into Kohler's office, and then admonished him.

"Kohler, I do not appreciate being summoned at this hour."

The Major offered him a seat at his desk. He placed the Beck letter, Legrand's confession, and the classified report in front of him. "Look at these, and if you think I have wasted your time, then I am to blame."

The Kriminalkommissar was not a man who rushed; he slowly examined each pile before reaching into his jacket to pull out his glasses. He meticulously extracted his bifocals, cleaning them with his handkerchief. He picked up the letter the General had written; his lips moved as he read it. He placed the document back on the desk and was about to pick up the confession, but as if realizing what he had just read, he picked up Beck's letter again.

"Can this be authenticated?" he asked, not believing

what he was reading.

"It can. Please read on." The Major pointed at the second document.

Kohler watched him closely as he studied Legrand's confession. Pfeiffer read through it once, and then again. Then he turned his attention to the Monthly Status Report, which he immediately recognized as a confidential document requiring a high-security clearance to read.

"Who has access to this document?"

"In Brussels? SS Gruppenführer Reeder, head of Civil Administration, your boss, and General Beck. It is the General's responsibility to forward it to General Falkenhausen."

Pfeiffer pushed the chair away from the desk and, stretching his arms wide, he asked, "You believe all this to be true?"

"I do. I also have independent confirmation that his mistress is married to one of the leading members of the Underground."

"Do you have this man Legrand in custody?"

"He is under arrest and being held in this building."

"You will, of course, turn him over to me."

"I trust you understand the precarious position I occupy?"

"That being?"

"General Beck is a fellow officer, my commander. If my superiors discover that I went outside formal channels without first informing them, my career is over. And possibly my life."

"I do not care about the military chain of command.

This man is a traitor."

"I believe you will bring him to justice. But I must not be involved."

"And these documents?"

"All yours."

"Will this French wine merchant cooperate?"

"I am sure he will support anything you request of him."

The Kriminalkommissar stood over the desk, looking at the papers and calculating whether to believe the Major. After what seemed like an eternity to Kohler, he asked, "And the General?"

"He is at his residence, not far from here."

Kohler scribbled the address and passed it to Pfeiffer, who picked up the phone and called Gestapo headquarters. He ordered his men to meet him at the address given, then scooped up the piles of documents put them under his arm, and walked out. Before reaching the outer door, he turned and called back, "I'll send someone later to collect the Frenchman."

"As you wish."

"And if this is a hoax, I'll send someone to collect you."

CHAPTER 28

Captain Ulmer had just finished inspecting the area where his superior believed the British would land. While it was a large field, it was apparent to him that Major Kohler had not surveyed the ground himself. Walking the area, he tripped over a fallen tree, and on closer examination, realized the field was full of stumps. There were also rocks, though not boulders, they were big enough to disrupt any landing. The Captain sent the staff car out to see what other sites could accommodate an airplane. This field was not the landing site. He tried to get through to headquarters for instructions, only to hear that the Major wasn't available.

Ulmer spread out a map on the ground and, using his flashlight, started searching section by section for an area suitable for a landing. He was pondering his next step when the scout car returned. They reported that they had done a 10-kilometer search and could find no area that would easily handle an airplane.

"Everything is up and down around here, Captain," reported his sergeant. "It was almost impossible to drive the car, let alone land a plane."

"Any activity? People?"

"Nothing, sir." We came across a truck heading back to Brussels, but that was all."

The Captain's ears perked up. "What kind of truck?"

"It was hauling wood; the driver was taking it to a furniture factory for processing in Brussels."

"This late in the evening? He would return after curfew. Do you remember which company?"

"It is the one where all the big shots buy their furniture."

"The factory owned by Gie Desmit?"

"I believe that is the company, sir."

"Did you search the truck?"

"We did, and found nothing. The driver's papers and cargo checked out, and he had permission to be out of Brussels."

Captain Ulmer was not a man who believed in coincidences. It was interesting to come across a truck belonging to Gie Desmit, the same man Major Kohler suspected of illegal activity, the same man who two agents disappeared while following. Ulmer asked where the squad had stopped the vehicle. The sergeant pointed out the area on the map. The countryside was uneven land and a lake on its edge. If there were to be an extraction tonight, Ulmer believed it would not be at their current spot. Playing on intuition, the captain decided to take a gamble and move his men closer to where they stopped Desmit's truck.

....

Kohler was freezing as he followed the Kriminalkommissar's Mercedes 260 through the streets of Brussels. He had had to roll down the windows of the DeSoto. His beautiful car stank of the dried blood of the wounded Karlmann. There was no traffic on Avenue de Tervueren, and they were traveling at full throttle on the vast park-lined street. It did not take long before they came to the well-to-do area of Woluwe-Saint-Pierre and the General's residence.

While he could not be part of the arresting party, the Major certainly wanted to see the General brought out in handcuffs. He parked across from the stately home built in the 1800s that Beck had commandeered when first posted to Brussels. The house was surrounded by a fence about 3 meters tall, consisting of a low brick wall and two meters of iron grate on top. It allowed for an unobstructed view of the home. At the entrance to the driveway stood a guard post, with a bored sentry inside trying to stay warm.

The guard reluctantly left the warmth of his little shed and moved toward the black Mercedes that had pulled up. He snapped to attention when the Kriminalkommissar flashed his credentials. Kohler watched as the gate opened, and the two cars pulled onto the estate. Four men emerged from the second car, all in their grey Gestapo uniforms. They conferred for a moment, and then Pfeiffer knocked on the door.

The Kriminalkommissar had to knock a few more times before someone finally appeared. An elderly gentleman, half asleep with his trousers pulled over his nightshirt, stood in shock as he looked at the five men. They pushed their way past him, and found themselves in the foyer of the home, a grand staircase in front of them.

"We are here to see the General," Pfeiffer spat out. The butler, looking like he was about to collapse at any moment, offered to announce the party. "That won't be necessary," was the reply.

"But he has company, mein Herr."

"His room?"

The man pointed up the stairs.

The group softly walked up the marble staircase to the second floor. There were five closed doors. One of the agents put his ear to the first door but could hear nothing. He slowly opened it, finding only a dark room. They were about to try the second door when from the end of a hall, they heard a woman laughing. The five converged towards the bedroom. They pushed the door open, and with guns drawn entered.

The five men stood there flabbergasted. In front of them spread-eagled across the bed, hands tied to the bedpost, was a naked General Beck. Hunched over him, with her head bobbing up and down, was Elise de Vos.

Madame de Vos jumped off the bed, wrapping herself with a sheet that had fallen to the floor. She was about to scream as the agents moved close, but thought better of it and backed herself into the corner. The General, bound to the bed, was only able to raise his head and shout, "How dare you? What is the meaning of this?"

The Kriminalkommissar flashed his silver-colored warrant disc, the swastika reflecting in the light.

"Do you know who I am?" roared the General

"A sad excuse for a German officer, Generalleutnant Gottfried Beck. You are under arrest."

"You have no authority over an officer of the Wehrmacht."

"We shall see about that. The charges against you are treason, spying, and consorting with the enemy."

"You are mad, untie me!" Pfeiffer nodded to his men, who untied the General and then handcuffed him. "This is absurd. I demand to speak with General Falkenhausen."

"Take them both down to my car and then search this room and his office," commanded Pfeiffer. "I will return to headquarters."

Two bright lights that illumined the house entrance allowed Kohler a perfect view of the prisoners. The front door opened, and the General and his mistress were pushed out. Both were in handcuffs. They also appeared to have no clothes on, using bedsheets as wraps. Beck was still protesting when one of the agents stepped on his sheet, which fell to the ground exposing his naked body. Wholly humiliated, they pushed him into the back seat and the wrapping in after him.

The whole scene brought great pleasure for Major Kohler. So far, it has been a good night: a saboteur killed, a traitor exposed, the General off to an uncertain future. He felt confident that Ulmer and his men would recapture Valentin and Febe. But his night was not over yet. He had one more arrest to make, and he would do that himself.

....

Captain Ulmer sat in his staff car, unsure of what to do next. If there was to be a landing tonight, he had no idea where it would happen. It was apparent that the field the Major had ordered watched was not suitable for an airplane. Ulmer also knew that if there was a successful escape tonight, he would be held responsible. Standing up in the field car, he thought he heard something. It was the sound of a distant engine. Looking up to the sky to identify the aircraft, the moon offered just enough light to make out a small airplane. His heartbeat quickened. But where would it land? He grabbed his binoculars; it had momentarily flown behind a cloud, then it reappeared. He studied the silhouette. The plane had pontoons.

"Of course, how stupid could I be?" Turning to his sergeant, he blurted, "The lake, they are going to land on the lake. Take three men and the staff car and approach the from the far side. I will take the rest of the men and attack from this side. Quickly! We don't have much time."

....

It was late. At the little bar in the Les Marolles district, there were only two customers left, and the bartender wanted them to go. He knew that many of his customers collaborated, but he took issue with these two, how they kissed the asses of the Germans, and sold out their countrymen. When he walked over to their table to throw them out, the sandy-haired one brandished a gun and demanded more shots of Jenever. The bartender stayed at the end of the bar waiting for them to pass out, and then he would deal with them.

Deni and Lucas sat at the table in the corner, drinking their gin and complaining about their lot in life.

"Nothing, Deni, nothing. That's what they gave us."

Lucas barely coherently replied, "We gave them that bitch and our reward? A couple of coins. Fuck them, fuck them all."

When Kohler's men had come for Febe, they handed Lucas an envelope with a few francs inside. He counted it and immediately told the guards that they expected more for the woman.

"You did?" asked the German, plucking the envelope out of Lucas' hand. He opened it and took two of the four bills out, and then gave it back. "Open your mouth again, and you'll be sharing a cell with the women."

What money they had received was gone already on booze.

"Hell, they even took her pistol, more money lost," added Deni, but Lucas didn't hear. He had slumped down on the table and was fast asleep.

Neither of them saw Santino Tocci enter the bar for a

bracer before he went off to his cleaning job at the military headquarters. He ordered a beer. As the bartender placed the glass in front of him, he whispered for him to go in the back room and stay. The man looked bewildered, but Tocci moved his head in the direction of the two in the corner. Whatever was about to happen, he wanted none of it and walked into the storage room.

Tocci took a sip of his beer, withdrew his 38 Smith and Wesson with a silencer, and, holding it close to his leg, approached the table. Deni was oblivious that anyone was standing in front of them until Tocci kicked the chair to get his attention. Looking up, Deni slurred, "Fuck off."

Tocci lifted the pistol and shot Deni between the eyes. He fell backward out of the chair, his foot coming up and striking the table enough to knock over the glasses. Lucas lifted his head to see what the commotion was all about and was staring at the 38's muzzle. He started to open his mouth, maybe to shout, perhaps to plead for his life, but it didn't matter: Tocci put a bullet through the man's left eye. He put another bullet in each of the men, walked over to the bar counter, and left money for the drink. He headed off to work, whistling an aria from the Marriage of Figaro.

....

Kohler's men followed Gie Desmit to the L'Escargot, one of the city's crème de la crème restaurants. Before the war, it had enjoyed a clientele that included the wealthiest of politicians and business people in Brussels. They dined on the French cuisine, watched a floor show that starred some of the most beautiful women in Europe, and for a select few, there was gambling in the private smoking room. The rumor was that in 1937, Guy de Rothschild lost 50,000 francs in an hour at the roulette table, trying to impress his mistress. There was still a scattering of locals dining, but the restaurant had been taken over by the privileged members of the occupation force and the nouveau riche, the black marketeers.

Major Kohler collected his two agents, Hans and Otto. One had been covering the front entrance and the other the delivery door in back. Kohler breezed by an objecting maître d' as they entered the restaurant. In front of them was the main room, and even at this late hour, it was packed. At the far end of the room was a raised stage with a small band playing American dance music, and a few couples dancing. To the left was the bar, where a group of young officers waited who had neither clout nor money for an immediate table. On one of the walls was a balcony that accommodated those who preferred to be away from the crowd. It was there that Kohler spotted Gie Desmit sitting with another man. The Major with his little entourage approached. Hans could feel the eyes staring at them; he felt like an old black crow in a field of swans in his ill-fitting suit.

The major approached the table as Desmit and his guest had just finished a bottle of Champagne. Gie's guest was ordering another bottle. Kohler did not know who the other man was, but could hear that he spoke perfect German.

Gie looked up, "Oh, Major Kohler, what a pleasant surprise."

Kohler clicked his boots and then in his most formal voice, announced, "Herr Desmit, I must ask you to accompany me."

"Surely, this can wait until morning?"

"I'm afraid not."

"But the night is early, and I have my guest."

"Herr Desmit, I must insist, I would hate to have my men escort you out and cause a scene."

"I think not," came the words from the other man sitting at the table. Kohler looked down at the gentleman, who casually put an American Camel cigarette into his holder and lit it with a gold lighter. He wore black formal evening wear, with his bow tie perfectly tied. He looked fit, with a receding hairline.

Irritated by the audacity of the man, Kohler was about to arrest both. "And you are?"

From out of nowhere, two SS bodyguards appeared, the man raised his hand to call them off.

"Major Kohler," said Gie with a smile. "Allow me to introduce Herr Albert Göring, connoisseur of beautiful furniture, a friend, and the brother of the Reichsmarschall."

"Excuse me, sir. It is an honor, Herr Göring," Kohler said, at full attention now, "but this man is not who he appears to be. I have strong evidence that he is fully involved with the Resistance."

"Major, I have known Herr Desmit for years. There is no one less political than him. I will be touring his factory tomorrow. He has designed and is building a piece of furniture at the Reichsmarschall's request. I believe it will be a gift for the Führer. I can vouch for Herr Desmit's character," he paused, "and my brother can vouch for mine." Turning to Gie, he said, "Look here, the Champagne has arrived."

Kohler did not move, until Göring curtly dismissed him while refilling the two Champagne flutes. Albert Göring had been Gie's insurance policy: a man who did not share his brother's values or beliefs. On many occasions, he had helped to smuggle Jews out of the country or encourage anti-Nazi activity. He was only too happy to come to Gie's aid.

The Major, being a realist, counted his victories for the night and determined to get Desmit another time. Kohler clicked his heels and saluted, then walk briskly out of the building, leaving his two men to scamper after him.

....

It was young Nick Lejeune who first heard the distant engine, alerting the others to spring into action. With a word from Major Griffin, he pushed off and was paddling the old canoe they had brought to the lake. Nick quickly lit the three signals they placed to guide the plane. Karel and Arno took positions behind a group of rocks, their Sten guns at the ready.

Flight Lieutenant Reggie Linton was no stranger to extractions behind enemy lines, but this was a first for him, an amphibious landing. Though he had made water landings, it had been a while, and not in these conditions. There was no real visibility. His reckoning and map reading told him he was in the vicinity, but short of someone shooting off a flare, he would need to circle to search for the three flames that would guide him in. He was lucky; banking to the left he could see a fire, then a second. He leveled out and could barely make out the outline of the lake. If not for the three torches, he would be flying into a black hole. He positioned himself at the far end, lined up in the middle of the lake, and eased the Bellanca CH-300 Pacemaker down. He hit hard, sending water across the windscreen and bouncing the plane back in the air. He settled it down and taxied toward the lantern on the shore.

Captain Ulmer could not see the plane, but looking down from the hill, he could see the smudge pots that illuminated sections of the lake. He fanned out his two squads and led them toward the sound of the whining engine.

Lieutenant Litton slowly closed in on the light until he

was given the sign not to come any closer, due to debris floating close to shore. He swung the Bellanca around and waited for his passengers. Litton was acquainted with the last attempt to spirit the saboteurs out of the country. He was a close friend to Flight Lieutenant David Turner, who had lost his life. Litton anticipated a quick takeoff.

The moment of truth arrived. They boarded the canoe, with Dankworth-Murray looking after Raymond. Valentin waded into the water, placing the unconscious Febe near the front then grabbed an oar and took the spot just in front of her. With all aboard, Major Griffin pushed off and climbed into the rear. They headed toward the aircraft as fast as they could paddle.

The flame from the three pots gave more illumination to the shoreline than the lake, and the light allowed Nick Lejeune to see the Germans before they saw him. He popped out from behind a boulder and let loose a burst from his Sten gun. It caught Captain Ulmer square in the chest, sending him back a few feet. Karel and Arno joined in, and a firefight ensued. In the low light, everyone was firing wildly and into the unknown. The best anyone could do was to aim at the muzzle flashes.

Major Griffin wanted to get everyone out before the Germans started firing on the plane. They approached the starboard side pontoon as Litton swung open the hatch. Valentin was surprised to see that the craft would seat six. Litton gave the group captain a quick salute and then helped him with Raymond.

Onshore, the Germans recovered from losing their Captain; a corporal took control, rallying the men. He ordered those clinging to the ground to put maximum fire on the muzzle blasts. He split the squad, sending one group along the shore and another around in hopes of outflanking them. The three Belgians had used most of their ammunition, and now were looking for an escape.

Litton helped Valentin with Febe, laying her across the middle seat. "Take care of her, Lieutenant," he said, but as he turned around to leave, Griffin was standing on the pontoon, blocking the hatch.

"I'm afraid your orders are to accompany the group."

"What?"

Griffin handed Valentin an envelope. "These are Desmit's instructions to you. He told me to tell you that it was best for the organization for you to leave. He also said not to worry, he would take care of your studio and employee." The shooting onshore intensified. "Gie told me to threaten you if you refused, but that won't be necessary, will it?"

Valentin shook his head, stunned. He also felt something else: guilt. Not because he was leaving, but because he wanted to go.

Litton let Griffin get clear of the plane before winding up the engine. The sound drew the notice of the Germans, and they moved to the shore to open fire. Griffin was almost back to shore when he took the flare gun out of his pack and shot it in the direction of the soldiers. There was an eerie silence as it arced through the sky and exploded, turning the whole picture into daylight. As the flare parachuted to the ground, from the opposite shore Corporal Gillet, opened fire with a Bren light machine gun. Germans fell as the tracer bullets came towards them.

Litton used the diversion and light to his advantage, gunning the engine and starting the run down the middle of the lake. The plane bounced once, twice, and then was off the water and heading into the Belgium night. From the back, Murray shouted above the sound of the engine.

"Jolly good takeoff, Lieutenant."

"Thank you, sir."

"Think we'll see much action on the way home?"

"I hope not. As we get closer to the channel, there is cloud cover."

....

Major Griffin made it back to shore in time to intercept three Germans trying to flank the group. A burst from his Sten gun put all three on the ground. The remaining troops saw the plane lift off but could do nothing, as they were still taking fire from the opposite shore. The signal fires were barely visible, and the flare had extinguished entirely. Griffin called for his men to fall back. They moved up the bank on the south side of the lake. The remaining troops took cover and directed their fire toward the machine gun emplacement.

The Mercedes taken from the Germans was waiting for them. Griffin herded the group into the car and then drove down the road and picked up Corporal Gillet. They were speeding off to a safe house that Gie Desmit was providing. Coming from the opposite direction was the military staff car carrying the sergeant and his men that Ulmer had ordered to attack the lake from this side. When they were close enough, Gillet poked the Bren gun out the window and opened fire. The car veered off into a ditch and overturned in flames.

....

Valentin cradled Febe in his lap as the plane moved through the darkness. He wanted to read the letter, but the pilot told him it was too dangerous to shine a light. Valentin was sure what it said. The authorities knew who he was, and it would eat up too much time and resources to keep him hidden. Valentin had knowledge that would be disastrous if he fell into the enemy's hands. The war would go on, and there would be much for him to do before he would see the end of the Nazis. His main concern now was to get Febe healthy.

In the distance, Litton could see two Messerschmitt night fighters streaking to the south. He thought it best to keep that sighting to himself. There must be an RAF bombing raid tonight, and those blokes have more important fish to fry than us.

Raymond asked for some water. The pilot passed the canteen to the Group Captain, who thought his patient was showing some improvement. "You looking better, mate. I think you're going to make it."

"My brother?" DeBaets whispered, "my brother?"

"Your brother? Don't know anything about him, but I'm sure they'll sort it out in London."

Litton pulled a flask out of his flight jacket and offered it to the group. Valentin took a long swallow before passing it on to Murray, who was happy for the drink. Somewhere over the channel, they ran into rough weather, the plane pitching up and down. It was enough to wake Febe. Opening her eyes, she thought she was dreaming when she saw Valentin holding her.

"Where are we?" she asked.

"Free."

Made in the USA
Monee, IL
21 March 2025